DRAGONSWORD
Return of the Dragonriders
Book Three
by Raina Nightingale

AREAER NOVELS

Return of the Dragonriders
DragonBirth
DragonWing
DragonSword

Legend of the Singer
Children of the Dryads
Sorceress of the Dryads

Dragon-Mage
Heart of Fire
Scars of Fire
Healing of Fire*

Novellas and Standalones
The Gifts of Faeri
Kindred of the Sea
Gryphon's Escape
Promise of Fire

KAARATHLON NOVELS

EPOCH OF THE PROMISE: Dawn Unseen
EPOCH OF THE PROMISE: Vision's Light
EPOCH OF THE PROMISE: Wings of Healing
EPOCH OF THE PROMISE: Darkness Bright*

Other Novels

Kingdom of Light

*Not yet available

This is a work of fiction. All characters, places, and events are products of the author's imagination.
DRAGONSWORD
Written by Raina Nightingale

Paperback ISBN: 978-1-952176-05-0
Ebook ISBN: 978-1-952176-10-4

Cover art by MidnightRose.
Cover design by Raina Nightingale.
Maps by Raina Nightingale.
Interior Design by Raina Nightingale.
Illustrations by Raina Nightingale.

Published by Raina Nightingale
www.enthralledbylove.com

Author's Note

Hello again!

This is the conclusion of the *Return of the Dragonriders* series, and I think I will assume if you're reading this, then you've read the author's notes for the others (and you probably have them on hand if you haven't).

DragonSword is by far the most epic and the least cozy/slice-of-life of these stories, and it's also the one with the most romantic involvement (though it's still very much a subplot) as Noren and Silmavalien are reunited. I hope, however, that I kept the closeness to the people living their lives, suffering and enjoying and triumphing and enduring!

Fundamentally, that's still what this is about, and if you're going to be disappointed if I tell you even now Silmavalien and Noren aren't going to change the world and the way dragons are treated, that by the end of *DragonSword*, we won't have a world all neat and perfect, where people accept dragons as the wonders they are – then you're going to be disappointed. Because I never set out to create one of those endings that often bother me, as if it's all over and done – even if a new villain pops up in the next series.

This is still the story of Noren and Silmavalien, and how they see the world – for better or for worse.

But the dragons *do* fly again!
-Raina Nightingale

Table of Contents

Map of Aneri

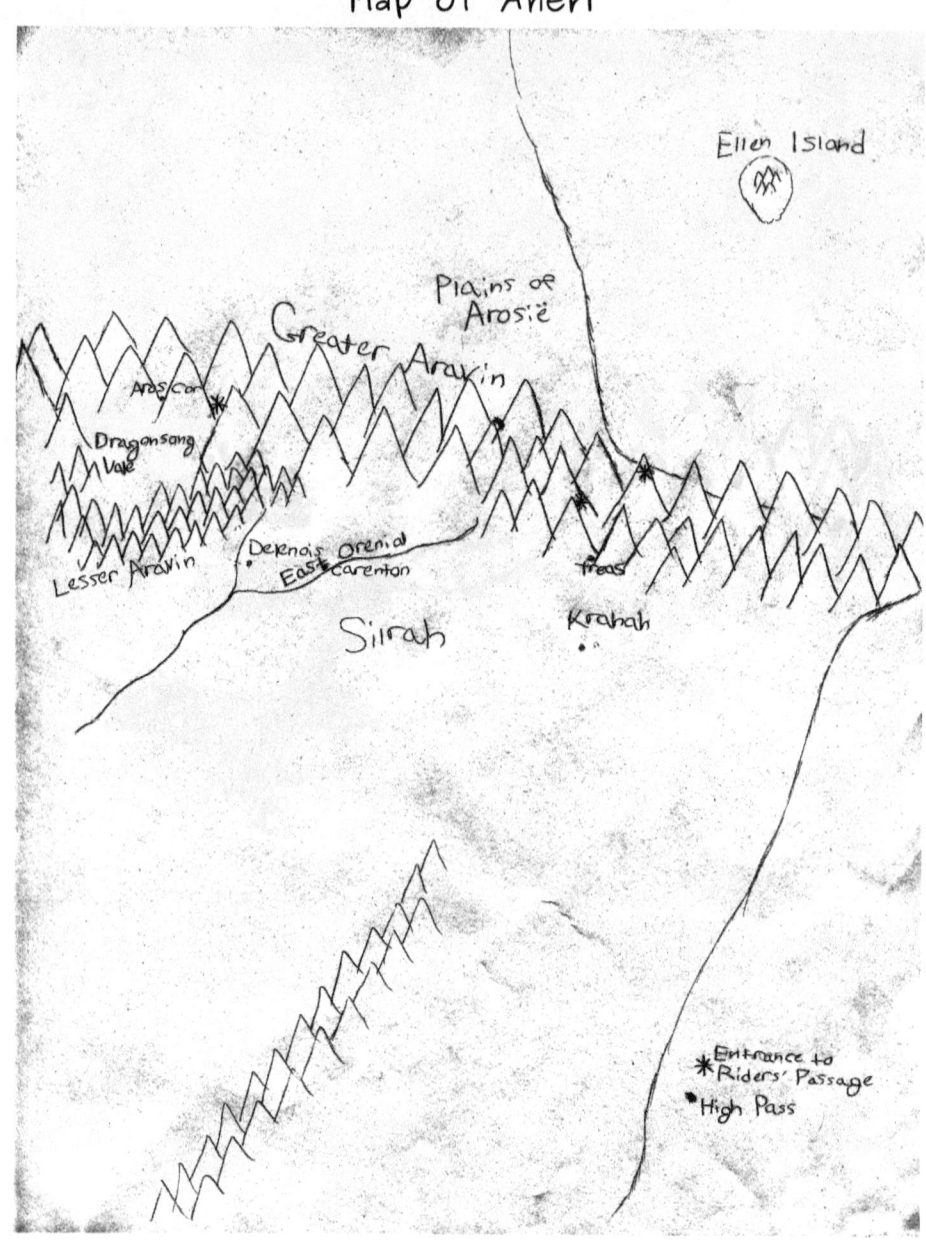

1

An Awkward Rescue

A beam of light fell from Silmavalien's upraised hand and surrounded Noren, and then another beam surrounded Elninya. The light was solid to the executioners, and they could not step into it.

The crowd of people that had come to watch him die turned to stare in utter shock at the thirteen dragons descending from the sky, almost diving, towards them. Bowmen on the walls tried to shoot Noren, but their arrows stopped dead and dropped to the ground where they hit the light.

It took a moment before Noren was half-aware of what was happening. People were screaming and running towards the city. Arrows fell from the light. He began to realize he might not be about to die. A grim smile turned his lips at the behavior of the people. Neither he nor Silmavalien were witches! They were not about to face the fate to which they had condemned him and would have condemned her.

Elninya roared in jubilation and breathed out fire. Starting to her feet, she realized the light had dissolved her bonds. They fell from her and broke as she stretched.

Noren tested his bonds also, but the ropes held fast.

In a few moments, Minth landed, and Silmavalien leapt down from the white dragon. With a quick, muttered thanks to the Lord of Light for guiding her, she drew her hunting knife and quickly cut the ropes binding Noren to the stake. Then, she stepped back.

At his first glance, Noren did not recognize her. Dressed in a silver deerhide vest, with a brown bearskin cloak falling from her shoulders, and a skirt made of feathers that fell half-way down her calf and had slits down the sides to accommodate both running and riding, she looked to him, in his half-dazed state, almost like a goddess. She was taller and more filled-out than she had been, too.

"Who – what are you?" he asked.

"I'm Silmavalien," she answered, smiling a smile he had never seen before. She was thinking of what she had done, how she had deceived him, and flinching as she thought about how he must feel about it. Looking upon him, she could see that he had not been treated well. He was thin, obviously half-starved, and bruised, but that did not hide the changes in him. He had grown and filled-out since she had last seen him, and thin as he was, she saw the broadness in his shoulders and the power in his build.

Elninya raised her wings, and became painfully aware of her own weakness. She, too, had been half-starved, and kept in conditions even worse for her health than Noren's conditions had been for his. Constantly netted, she had been hardly able to move, let alone spread her wings.

"I'm going to change the saddle. I don't know if Minth can carry both of us very well," said Silmavalien.

"No," said Noren, finally getting his voice again. "They have some kind of witch-craft, with which they can catch dragons. Unless you know how to counteract all kinds of witch-craft, we have to go now."

All right, Minth.

To Noren, Silmavalien said, "All right. You climb on Minth and get into the saddle. I will ride Airrock."

Noren stepped away from the stake, stumbling over the wood. As he approached the white dragon, he saw another woman, taller than Silmavalien and dressed like her, but without the cape, climbing back onto the blue dragon. *Her* dragon, no doubt. He would have liked to ride Elninya, and she would have liked that, too, but she was too weak.

It would be all she could do to fly.

A minute later, they were in the air again, and for once, Minth was not the weakest. Elninya struggled far more than he did, her wing-beats chaotic. But they still pushed as they could, or rather as she could. Everyone was in one accord in wanting to be as far away as possible, lest they be found and caught in the nets or some other witch-craft.

Shortly after nightfall, they landed in a field next to a large copse. Noren sat against a tree and ate what Silmavalien gave him with great pleasure. He had not had so good food or so much of it in months! He had not *tasted* meat in months. The dried fruit was exceptionally good, too!

Next to him, Elninya made quick work of the meat Silmavalien gave her, telling her it was all they had right now. A few minutes later, they were both fast asleep.

Meanwhile, Silmavalien and Keya discussed how Noren and Elninya had been captured, and Coroneth took it upon himself to organize the dragons into a watch, with two of them always watching, and at least one of them always circling in the sky.

With that in Coroneth's capable and proud talons, Silmavalien felt the need to be alone, and she could not sleep yet. She stepped away from the others, and stood, looking up at the stars twinkling in the sky from beyond the eaves of the little copse. She thought of Malchoris. She thought of Noren. She thought about the fact that she had no idea how she stood with him, or what he thought of her. She would understand it if he were flaming mad at her. He had been about to be burned alive – with Elninya! She had contributed to the situation, by not being willing to risk – if there was any risk at all – what he would think or say. If she had only told him, they would have been able to run away together.

It would have been hurtful enough to him for her to run away from him like that because she did not trust him, even if no danger had come to him or to his beloved dragon on account of it. Now, she had no idea how to approach him or relate to him.

She knelt down and took the ring of light from her finger to place it in her palm. She spoke to the Lord of the Light, thanking him for bringing her and Noren together and that she had been in time to save Noren and Elninya's lives. Then she asked him to show her how to relate to Noren.

Finally, Silmavalien went and lay down under Minth's wing.

ℵ

Noren woke early in the morning, before it was light. He stirred, wondering if he should get up and get everyone else up to flee again, and sat up. Just then he heard Silmavalien's light footsteps as she approached him, carrying a jar.

"Why don't we spread this oil on Elninya?" she asked without greeting. "She's so uncomfortable, and I'm sure it will make her skin feel much better."

Of course, she had noticed the state of Elninya's skin, not only cracked and bleeding from being unoiled and dry for so long, but cut by the net.

"That's a stupid idea," he scoffed, pushing himself to his feet. "We want to be away from here as fast as possible. Besides, it's much more important for her to eat. Let's go."

Silmavalien nodded and turned back, and a few minutes later they were in the air again. But the day was not half-gone when Elninya's strength completely gave out, and they had to find a place to land as quickly as possible. The best they were able to find was the far end of an orchard, where they hoped they would be far enough no one would come across them, and that they had not been seen. The silver dragon launched herself into the sky again almost as soon as they landed, and Elninya told him she was going to hunt whatever small game she could find for Elninya and her rider. Airrock said she and the other dragons were not too hungry yet.

Then she drooped down, looking as flat as a dragon could look, and too exhausted even to think, leaving Noren to decide how to approach Silmavalien on his own. He *was* upset at her, but he was also struck anew by her beauty and he was still interested in her. He hated that she had not trusted him, and he did not see how she could possible trust *him* now. Yet he was angry at her for lying to him, both because he wanted that relationship of trust, and because if she had not lied to him, he and Elninya would not have suffered what they had, and they would not have almost been burned alive.

To complicate matters further, he really did not want to tell her about the girl he had murdered, but he knew that if they were to be close, he had to tell her.

Now would be a fine time to oil Elninya's skin. He rose to ask Silmavalien.

Just as he stood, he saw her walking towards him, her eyes downcast. She looked so timid to him, and he supposed she must feel as insecure about their relationship as he did. Beside her walked the other woman, carrying the oil jar and radiating confidence and security. "With three of us, this should not take long," she was saying to Silmavalien.

His love nodded and then raised her eyes to look at him. He saw her blush. She was still in love with him. She thought he was handsome, even in his present poor condition.

"Shall we oil Elninya now?" she asked.

"Yes," said Noren.

Silmavalien paused, nervous and uncertain. Then, she said, "Noren, I'm really sorry. I'm really sorry I didn't trust you. None of this would have happened, if I had." Her eyes filled with tears and her voice quivered and almost failed.

Noren nodded. "That's true. This would not have happened if you had." He did not know how to respond to her admission of guilt. He felt bad responding to her obvious pain and grief in that way, but what else could he say? He couldn't say that it was okay. He couldn't say he forgave her, either. What did that even mean?

Silmavalien's friend interrupted the awkward moment by pulling the stopper from the oil jar, but Noren still found it unendurable working beside Silmavalien to oil Elninya's skin. She wept, and he gathered from Elninya why she was cried. It was only in part because of the way he had responded to her, though that had not helped. Seeing the damage on Elninya horrified her, and that more than anything else made her cry.

He wanted to comfort her. He always had wanted to comfort and protect her.

How *could* she have so distrusted him, when all he wanted was to comfort and protect her, to make her happy and safe? Of course, he would have trusted her over any crazy story that he knew from the outset could not be true!

S

Noren touched her arm. "Stop for a moment."

Silmavalien turned, clutching the oil-soaked cloth in her hand. What could he be trying to tell her right now? Elninya would tell her directly if she was not being gentle enough or she wanted something Silmavalien could do for her.

"Fear has made me do worse things," he said, softly and severely.

Of all the things he could have said! Silmavalien turned back to Elninya. She could not think about this right now. She had no idea what she could say to him, how she could respond in a way that wasn't a lie and would hurt him. And Elninya ...

Arrows of Light, the poor dragon! The conditions she had been kept under, netted under the ground, hardly fed, her pain ... none of it mattered any less because Elninya was not bonded to *her.*

"Look at me," Noren demanded.

She pulled up, just as she was about to dab Elninya's skin, and cast a glance towards the dragon's head.

It's okay? Listen to him? It's really okay.

All right. I'll do it.

She turned back to Noren, giving him her full attention. "What?"

N

Noren found he did not know what to say. So he said something. "You were too scared. You could not have helped it."

"Someone who can do a bad thing because she's scared is a bad person!" she retorted, suddenly angry. "And I thought you might be a bad person because I might have been a bad person and acted in the bad way I feared if I had been in your place!"

Noren fought the anger rising in his chest. He wanted to do something to her to make her accept his comfort! Yell at her, maybe! He recognized – perhaps it was Elninya's thought – that this behavior would not have the result he wanted, in fact, quite the opposite.

Clamping his lips shut, Noren turned away. He would work on a different part of his dragon's body.

S

Why did I say that *of all the things I might have said?* Silmavalien wondered, as she watched him walk down Elninya's wing, and then reapplied herself to carefully oiled the dragon. *He just told me he did a very bad thing. Now, I don't know what it was, but of course what I said made him mad. He thinks I was implying, in an underhand way, that he is a bad person, and it is all his fault for having been a bad person in the first place, long ago, in Treas!*

Elninya, can you tell him that's not what I meant? Not what I meant at all! I wasn't even thinking of that! I said what I meant, not what I didn't mean – but that will upset him, too, because he'll think he was a bad person and that I will think he was a bad person, instead of excusing his wrong with fear. But, I don't know very much at all! I don't even know what he did, still less what I'll think.

Elninya replied that she did not think her rider thought Silmavalien meant that at all, but if she noticed him thinking that she did mean that, she would definitely tell him it was not true.

She was very thankful that Silmavalien was trying to take care of her skin. She was so gentle!

2

Would You Hate Yourself?

Noren lamented to Elninya that his struggle with anger had come back. He was getting angry with Silmavalien for not being as comforted by his attempts to comfort as he wanted! What was wrong with him?

"You told her things you know aren't true," said his dragon friend.

What do you mean by that? I didn't say anything I know isn't true.

"You didn't?" queried Elninya. Had he not made fear of death out to be an excuse for doing bad things that could not be helped, rather than a way of thinking that was at the root of the problem and must be helped?

Noren gently swept the cloth over her skin, and realized that he had noticed her growing happier, even as they waited for death, as she realized that they were drawing closer together, nearer to the point where they could think with each other and help each other and point each other to good. And she was right now. When he thought about what he had said, it was obvious that his attempts to comfort Silmavalien, to make her feel like she had done no wrong and was not to blame, had been mixed up with excuses he no longer believed or wanted to believed.

If he had not meant it, he had still said it.

Noren felt warm happiness from Elninya. She was glad they were together, now. The shadow between them was gone. But she was tired. She would move, so they could get to other parts of her body to oil them, and she would sleep while they finished. She was going to stay awake to eat what Airrock hunted, but she was so tired she could not even eat right now.

Noren continued to slowly think while she dozed, and about half an hour later, he approached Silmavalien. Quietly, so as not to disturb Elninya, he said, "I didn't speak very well. How much of what I said earlier is or isn't true, I don't know. But I want you to know that I don't blame you. I don't hold myself better than you, and I won't condemn you."

"Okay," said Silmavalien, slowly. After a short pause, she said, "That wasn't how you spoke several minutes earlier. 'That's true. This would not have happened if you had,'" she quoted, imitating his tone, which had been anything but sympathetic. "I don't understand you, Noren."

S

"Does it help any that I don't understand you, Silmavalien?" he said, smiling at her.

He was so infuriating and endearing, and she realized she was about to slap him only when her hand was half-away up. She dropped it back to her side. Relating like this was not going to help them clear anything up, and Elninya still needed her wing oiled.

A few feet away, Noren followed her example and went back to oiling his dragon. She wished he could have moved a little farther away, to oil some other part of Elninya, *especially* after the interaction they had just had.

And especially because she wanted to talk to Keya, but she would not with him so close, even if they would be speaking a language he could not know.

All right, Veine. I'll just do what I'm thinking.

You're stupid. How can you feel hurt I want to talk things over with Keya, too? You all think with me, and you probably influence my thinking more than any of us know. At any rate, I'm always taking into account and considering your thoughts. The fact that I don't have to deliberately do this does not mean I do it any less, or that you should feel jealous of those whose thoughts I have to deliberately look for.

Silmavalien carefully did not take her hands or eyes from Elninya's hide, as she spoke. "Noren, what you said was probably true. I probably was so scared I couldn't help it. I've been so scared I couldn't anything at all. But that doesn't mean it was okay to be scared. It certainly doesn't mean it was good. And, if I was bad and could not help being bad, the being unable to help being bad didn't make me less bad."

"I guess that might make sense," said Noren, after a long moment. There was another longer pause, and when she did not expect him to continue, he went on. "But if you could help being bad or doing a wrong, and you chose to be or do wrong even though you could help it, that would make you more bad. At any rate, I should think you were more bad. If you had the wrong in you and could not help it, but tried to be good, I would be able to like you. If you had the wrong in you and could help it, but gave in when you did not have to, or, still worse, tried to be worse, I think I would hate you. Unless you were Elninya, of course, but she can't try to be bad. I don't think she ever gives into wrong when she can help it, though I don't know for sure. I doubt you are any different, but I think I might love you still even if you were. Most people I would hate."

As he spoke, Silmavalien thought that she was not at all certain that she had never given into wrong when she could have helped it. The thought was huge, and she was not sure. Could she have been less scared? Thoughts had occurred to her, which might have helped her if she had followed them, thoughts that might have encouraged her and Minth to fear less. What about obeying and surrendering to the Lord of the Light? Certainly, then, she had given into evil which she could have helped! Then a new thought had thrust itself up in her head. Her dragons were almost never any use at keeping her mind on a particular thought, unless for some reason one of them was especially interested at the moment and decided to have a conversation about it. They were more likely to be distracted.

So, as soon as Noren finished, Silmavalien said, "Does it then follow that if you were not yourself then you would hate yourself?" It suddenly seemed so wrong to her to hate some people for wrongs for which one would not hate someone one really loved or knew. Someone was not less of a person because she did not happen to be bonded to one! For example, Tanz, Elninya, and Naklath were all just as much dragons as Minth, or Airrock, or Lighter, or Songeth, or any other of hers.

ℵ

Silmavalien spoke so quickly, and it took him a moment to realize what she had said. "Why would I hate myself?" he asked, more pointedly than he needed to, but trying to keep his tone softer. There was an accusation he did not quite follow in her tone.

"Well, because you told me that you did a worse thing than what I did," she said. "And you said anyone who did a worse thing you would hate unless they were Elninya, or possibly me – or, I guess, yourself."

Noren was taken aback. "That wasn't exactly what I meant by 'worse', there," he said. "I meant it was a worse thing to other people. Not a worse thing in myself." He realized that he had meant both. The two meanings had been confused in his head, in his feelings, in his thoughts, and in his words. It had not till now occurred to him that they were not the same meaning.

"Oh," said Silmavalien, and to his great relief, she did not ask what he had done. "Well," she continued with her previous question, "would you or would you not hate yourself if you had done a wrong when you could have not done a wrong?"

He considered that for a short moment and then said, "I am too hungry to eat and do this job at the same time."

S

"All right," said Silmavalien. That made sense to her. She was hungry herself, and he must be far hungrier, since she had been eating reasonably well, while he had been kept in a cell and fed almost nothing. At least, he looked like he had been fed almost nothing, and that stirred her anger when she thought about it.

She felt like crying. He was *Noren!* She *loved* him. It was not okay that anyone had done that to him!

But then the conversation they had been having distracted her. She had never thought much before about the distinction between doing a wrong because one could not help it and giving into a wrong one could help, and it puzzled her. When she thought about her life, about how and why and where she had done wrong, about specific wrongs, she felt that, in most cases, the distinction was meaningless. So much of what she had done seemed to fall either into neither category or into both categories. Sometimes, she thought all three of Noren's categories had no distinctions between them. One instance in which this seemed to be the case was when she had explicitly disobeyed the command of the Lord of All Light to 'go down' to the plains. But she was not sure, and she did not like Noren's categories. It felt wrong, either that or it was very hard, or both, to put any instance of wrong-doing into any of them.

N

Meanwhile, Noren also found himself thinking about their conversation. He did not relish talking to her about 'the wrong' he had done. Silmavalien's question about whether or not he would hate himself did not much interest him. He would not say that he hated himself or ever had, but some of his memories and thoughts suggested that he had done something very much like hating himself about it. Somehow, he did not feel any hatred towards himself or about it now.

He thought the change in his outlook towards death was the cause of this, but he did not really know why. Nonetheless, he felt like he could not at once think like he now did about death and also have hate himself the way he had. He also could not think like he now did about death and do what he had done – or he did not think he could. It seemed strange to him that his new outlook should make an evil deed more impossible, and also make him feel less hatred and agony over having done it.

Now that he was thinking and talking, he could not even pin down the change in his outlook about life and death. He definitely could not say, or even think, what *was* his view of death, and this troubled him.

It was only the fact that he shared it with Elninya, and that both he and Elninya knew that each knew something of what the other knew, that convinced him that he actually knew something, that his outlook had changed and was definitely different from what it had been before. That there was any truth at all to this thing which seemed extremely solid and well-defined as long as one did not think about it, but turned vague and evasive the moment one thought about it.

Otherwise, he would have thought that the whole thing was a trick of his nerves, if it was anything at all.

3
A Real Meal

"What do you think?" Silmavalien asked Keya.

"About what?" replied Keya.

"Lots of things," said Silmavalien. "Noren's categories, about doing bad because you can't help it, or giving into bad you can help, or deliberately doing bad."

"I don't know anything *to* think about them," said Keya. "If you try to do bad for the purpose of doing bad, you must be very bad indeed. I guess some creatures might be that bad, but I can't imagine it."

"So, that's what Noren meant by that last one?" asked Silmavalien. "I thought it was something else, like doing bad that you could help doing and did not have to struggle very hard to help doing – so hard, you feel like you can't keep on struggling. Well, that makes a lot more sense!"

"I don't know for sure," said Keya. "I can't understand most of the words. Sometimes, I can make out what you or he might be saying."

"It's a bummer you can't be part of our conversations," said Silmavalien.

"Would I want to be?" asked Keya, mostly in fun.

"But," continued Silmavalien, "about the other two. Is there a difference? Does the difference matter? Songeth and Linol both tell me something I can't say, or even think of trying to say. Minth tells me he would say the same."

Keya stopped her work to look Silmavalien straight in the eye. "If there were a difference, I suppose it *would* matter, for it is a rather big difference. But, I suppose your question is rather: does the difference matter to me? Does it matter to me in determining my dealings and thoughts about myself or about other people?"

"Yeah, I suppose," said Silmavalien.

Yes, Airrock, I think you might be right. 'Is there a difference?' and 'Does the difference matter?' may well have been my way of asking the same thing I couldn't quite say in two different ways, to point out that I'm asking something I can't quite ask.

Then tell Keya that? I don't think so. I think it will be too confusing. I'd rather hear what she has to say about this.

"I've never thought about the question before," said Keya. "I don't know."

"All right," said Silmavalien. *I can definitely understand why Noren doesn't feel well. I'm beginning to feel like passing out myself.* After a few moments, she pulled her thoughts together, and said, "I'm still afraid, I think. I can't imagine being anything other than completely terrified were I placed now in a similar situation to when Minth hatched."

Keya replied, "I can understand that, but sometimes I think your imagination is rather lacking. You can only imagine one side of something at a time! Remember when you were telling me that, if you thought about Noren, just Noren and no one and nothing else, you could only imagine him behaving in one way, but if you thought about the situation you could only imagine him behaving in a different way?

"Try remembering, when you imagine, what you know and have experienced about the Lord of All Light and Love now, that you hadn't then." Keya's voice rang with delight.

"That's just the thing," said Silmavalien. "I'm not so sure that I didn't know it all, then. I already knew half of that song I sang to you a bit of, about being together, and I already knew my and Minth's impression song. So, if I didn't know, was it because I didn't want to – but of course I wanted to! Anyone would want to know this. But I still don't know about death. I still don't know why Love allows death. He told me he would tell me about death, but I'm still waiting. So there's that."

"Well," said Keya, "my advice, for all it's worth, is, don't worry too much about it."

𝒩

Noren found himself listening to the voices of the two women, conversing in a language he did not know. It was intriguing. Some of the words sounded very like words he knew, but he was too tired to try to figure out what they were saying. Silmavalien's voice was so beautiful, though. Between her voice and his own weariness, he was thoroughly distracted from his thoughts. For a brief moment, he thought that he had not yet learned so much as the name of her friend.

He reached the edge of the wing span he was oiling and saw that the two woman were working on a part of Elninya's body, which was all that was left that anyone could get to. There was not much space for him, there. With a sigh of relief he sat down and dozed.

A few minutes later, wing-beats roused him. He looked up to see the silver dragon, Airrock, flying in. She dropped rapidly and flared her wings as she landed. Her bearing communicated her pride in how she had managed to keep multiple kills at once, as she dropped two birds and a rabbit on the ground in front of Elninya. Noren smiled, as she woke up enough to gobble the food right up, in a few huge gulps, and then dropped right back to sleep.

He lay down and went to sleep, too.

ℕ

The next evening, they were able to make it to a wilder place, at the foothills of the mountains. Most of Silmavalien's dragons left to hunt, along with the blue one. Tanz. Elninya told him they were going to bring something back for the Dragonriders to cook, and then they would bring back food for her and Minth, and then they would gorge themselves.

He felt a flicker of laughter in her thoughts, and then the image. Her attempts to cook. He smiled as she realized she was explaining what she had done to the dragons. It almost seemed as if she were feeling better already, or maybe the anticipation of a real meal made her feel better.

Suddenly, he heard Silmavalien laugh, and then she turned to her friend and explained something in the language he did not know. As tired as he was, something about the interaction interested him, and then that reminded him that he wanted to ask how it was that she was attended by a bunch of dragons, many of whom seemed to be bonded to her. She certainly talked as if they were.

He called to her. She turned to face him, and he asked her about it.

S

Silmavalien was about to respond, when Keya looked at her in a way that reminded her that it was now her turn to translate – only, this time, she would really be translating, instead of only re-stating or re-phrasing, which was mostly what Keya had done. It took her only a moment to find the words, and then she turned back to Noren and said, "It's always been like this. They call me – Keya, and the people on the northern side of the mountains – a dragon-speaker or a dragon-keeper. A long time ago, before Minth hatched, someone spoke to me, out of a black rock, I think. I'm thinking that someone was a dragon. So many things I've learned and heard since then make me almost sure of it, though I didn't think it at the time."

Again, Keya looked at her, and then explained. "I understand some of what you say, but by no means all of it, and it's very hard to follow. I am trying to learn it, but we're all tired and hungry right now. It will be easier if you just tell me what you said."

This time, it took her a little longer to find the words, since it was more complicated. She turned back to tell Noren what was going on, but he already looked asleep.

That might be a good idea and she suggested it to Keya. The dragons would wake them up when the food was ready for them to take their part in preparing it.

ℵ

So that is her name, Noren noted when Silmavalien mentioned Keya, but then, as interesting as what she said sounded, he just could not keep his focus. She turned then, and began in the language he did not even know, and in a few moments her beautiful voice lulled him into sleep.

He woke to the smell of the cooking meat. As hungry as he was, and most of his sleepiness coming from hunger, he did not want to go to sleep again once he smelled the food. Elninya was slowly eating her way through a deer. *You're feeling better already,* he commented to her.

Elninya responded that she had been feeling better since she smelled the fresh air, and especially since that horrible net fell off.

Ah, yes, said Noren. *I wonder,* not really asking her, *will death be kind of like that?* At the next moment, he thought that he did not want to talk or think about death or anything related to it for a long time.

Excitement soon turned into frustration, since it took a very long time to cook enough of the meat to satisfy everyone, and Noren could feel the two women's irritation, even though both of them tried to hide it. When the first bits were done, Silmavalien and Keya offered him the largest share, but then he glanced at Elninya, who was not devouring her deer wholesale the way she had done with the tidbits Airrock had brought earlier, but making her way through it rather slowly.

"Do you remember how long I took eating my last meal?" he said. "I'd devour it, feel half-full and half-hungry, and half an hour later, ask for more. I can't eat that much that quickly like this. I haven't had any kind of meal in more than a day; I haven't had something since that morning. It'll be better for me eating it in little bits."

They tried to include him in their conversation after that, as if they had not really noticed he was awake before, but the conversation was stilted at best. It was constantly interrupted by someone checking on the meat, flipping it, or preparing a new slice, he was not the only person who lost the thread of what he was trying to say, sometimes mid-sentence, and to further complicate matters, Silmavalien had to translate everything either.

The good thing about that was hearing her voice so much.

N

The next day, they flew farther into the mountains. In several more days, they found a nice vale, where they decided to settle down so that he and Elninya could spend a few months healing and otherwise recovering, always provided that they did not have to move for some reason. That was when Noren finally thought about the fact he had lost his bow and his sword, something he had not previously noticed. His sword would be much harder to replace, but right now he cared about the loss of his bow and arrows much more. But since he knew how to make them, he asked Silmavalien if he could borrow her hunting knife, and set about doing so with whatever strength and energy he had, grumbling to himself about being limited in his choice of woods to use by the lack of an axe.

He did not want to break Silmavalien's hunting knife. That would be very inconvenient, and it would be rude. But even apart from that, if he broke it, he would not be able to use it anymore.

4

What Makes Sense and Doesn't

Silmavalien sat on the grass, staring at the green of the oaks, which grew bluer as the year wore on and made a harmonious color against the brilliant blue of the sky. It was beautiful! The colors fit together so nicely.

She had forgotten how much she liked this side of the Aravin Mountains.

She remembered what Aelaza had told her about Malchoris and about death. Something about passing from one world or state into another further into the heart of Shallim-Araldor, who she was pretty sure was the same as the Lord of All Light and as Love. Even if there was a difference between these, she decided it did not matter. If he or they cared, he or they could easily let her know and correct her and, as far as she could see, it did not make a difference in how she thought or lived or related to him or them whether they were all the same person or not. So, she would just think and speak as if they were all one, unless they revealed otherwise to her.

It made sense, enough, Silmavalien thought. Maybe death was such a door or gateway closer to Love. Maybe the world she had sung of in songs was the world into which death was the way. However, that could not be all there was to it. The Lord of the Light had told her that death was the perversion of the law of the universe. Death was pretty perverted. She knew that was true. But what was the law of the universe of which death was the perversion? She had not yet been told that. A door, a passing from one world into another, hardly sounded like the law of the universe to Silmavalien. The Lord of the Light had said 'the law' too, not 'a law', and she was sure there was a meaning to that.

Thinking again, Silmavalien thought that what Aelaza had said about death did not really make sense. It might be true of the 'burning out' of a star. If so, the 'burning out' of a star was nothing like the death of a human or a dragon or an animal. Aelaza must have been mistaken about that. Death, such as that of human or dragon or animal was a perversion far too horrible to be a fitting or sensible passage into a world closer to the heart of Love. It did not make sense at all.

But Veine was not so sure that there had to be a division between the law of the universe and a passage into a world closer to Love.

A thought occurred to Silmavalien! It made so much sense. She stood and went to find Noren, sitting on the ground and working with his materials for a bow. "Hi, Noren!" she said.

He looked up at her. Silmavalien thought he was so different from what he had been when she had left Treas.

"I just thought of something," she said, then paused, gathering her thoughts to put them into words. He kept on looking at her.

"It doesn't really matter," she said, speaking excitedly, "whether we're responsible in any exact sense for the wrongs we do, whether at the moment of doing the wrong we could have done otherwise. Whether, if there were an assembly to try us for whether or not we're guilty for the wrong we've done, we'd be found guilty or acquitted. What matters is becoming the kind of person who can't do the wrong at all!"

"I see," said Noren.

Silmavalien could tell that he did not see. He was hardly listening! Meanwhile, she was almost jumping up and down in her elation at having finally found what she thought and figured out how to say it. She *was* bouncing on her toes a little.

"No, you don't. You didn't even listen," she said, exasperation coming through in her voice.

Noren's eyes focused into hers a little. "It's the kind of thing I might be able to see," he said. "It sounds like there's something to see."

"But you don't, yet!" she said.

"I don't know about that," said Noren. He paused for a moment, and Silmavalien thought he might be thinking about what she had said.

The moment dragged on. She wondered if he was discussing something with Elninya. She did not ask, though.

Noren looked at her again. "How do you become the kind of person who can't do wrong at all?"

"Well," said Silmavalien, "I don't really know how. I know how so little I haven't thought about it at all. I couldn't, even. What I do know is that Love is a person and that Love is more powerful than anything and victorious over everything. I also know that the best thing for anyone and for everyone is for us to be the kind of things that can't do wrong. So, that means Love wants that for us. So, I asked Love to make me the kind of person who can't be bad. I am certain that Love will do it, for the reasons I've already explained."

Now Noren looked at her with light, with interest and thought, in his eyes. Silmavalien knew he had understood something, though she did not know if it was something she had said.

"That's right," he said. "That's really right. At least, that makes sense. That explains so much. I never saw it before, but it must be something like that. Love is the power in control."

"What does that explain?" asked Silmavalien almost breathlessly, in her turn interested almost beyond endurance.

Noren looked at her with something in his eyes that was somewhat intimate, yet which she could not name or pin down. "Why I and Elninya were captured and made certain we were going to be killed. Death. What I've come to learn, or maybe only to un-learn, about death, since being made to look at it, instead of always avoiding looking at it."

"What is that?" asked Silmavalien. She was still interested. This might touch on her questions about death!

"I – I can't say," said Noren.

For his part, he was intensely interested by what she had said. Hazalel had told him he must get to know the Lord of All Light. Silmavalien spoke about Love that was a person or a person that was Love. Once he put that together with his experience with death so much of Elninya's thoughts and understanding was suddenly clear to him. Perhaps not clear, but present, tangible. He had wondered about the nature of the Lord of the Light. Was he the Love Silmavalien spoke about?

Noren asked her.

"I'm not exactly certain that the Lord of the Light is Love, and not the highest servant of Love, closest to Love, with whom I've been in contact. I think he is Love, though," said Silmavalien. "At least, I can't think anything else. I don't know if I think that. But I found that I had long addressed him as if he were Love. Why? Do you know him too? Do you think the same?"

"Do either of us think anything yet?" asked Noren, looking up at her with a smile.

"Us?" asked Silmavalien. "Us? Is it then going to be us?"

Suddenly, Noren turned somewhat grim. "Maybe. I hope so. Not yet. I don't know," he said.

Silmavalien stood for a moment, watching him. Then she said, "Goodbye, for the moment."

"Goodbye," he said, clearly in a somewhat unhappy mood.

Silmavalien went to find Keya, who she found preparing oil. "Thank you!" she said. "I know it's not Tanz who needs it."

"Of course, Silmavalien," said Keya. "The dragons are all your friends, and also Tanz's friends, so that makes them my friends, too.

Anyway, I know this isn't why you came to me right now."

"What I want to know," said Silmavalien, "is whether what I said to Noren made sense. Most of the dragons like what I meant, but they can't judge whether I used words well. Noren understood something, eventually, but I don't think he really ever got what I meant to say."

"All right," said Keya. "Tell me it. I might not be able to tell you if you said it well, especially since this is a different language, but tell me anyways. I want to hear what you have to say."

Silmavalien started to speak, but Keya interrupted her right away. "Wait," she said. "I'm sick of not knowing the language you and Noren use. I want to be able to understand and talk. So, why don't you tell me what you and he said, in as near the words you used in the language you spoke as you can remember, in addition to telling me in the language I know? I think I will learn much faster that way! In fact, why don't we, whenever we talk, you tell me everything in that language too?"

"It'll take a lot longer," said Silmavalien.

"That's okay. I want to be able to speak," said Keya.

When Silmavalien was done narrating the conversation, Keya said, "So, first, I can't think of a better way to put the part about it not mattering whether you'd be guilty or not, but what kind of person you are. I assume that was what you meant, when you asked if you said something okay?"

Silmavalien nodded.

"Also, why don't you sing Noren that song you and Songeth sang, that you couldn't stand? I think he might understand it."

"I don't want to," said Silmavalien. "Besides, I'd need Songeth to help me."

This last part did not need to be said. Even while she spoke, Songeth told her that while he would not be ready to do that particular song at just any time, he'd be quite willing to sing it again sometime.

"Songeth'll do it," said Keya. "*He* didn't hate it." Laughter shimmered in her voice and in her eyes.

"What made you think Noren will understand it?" Silmavalien asked.

"I didn't say *will*. I said *might*," replied Keya. "With that, you can guess it easily."

"Now," said Keya, after a pause, "tell me the conversation we just had, both what you said and what I did, in your language. Let me guess who said what."

5

A Village in Ashes

The next day Noren asked Silmavalien where she had been living this whole time, and how she found him and Elninya. When she told him about the pass over the mountains, he asked, "Can we cross the mountains right now?"

"No," said Silmavalien. "The high pass is far too high for Elninya to make in her current condition. Most dragons can't even fly at that height at all. They walk it. As for the Riders' Passage, I get the idea that it was once possible for dragons to go through, but the end has shifted, and there's no way for a grown dragon to fit in this end. I also don't know how long it would take –"

"That's enough," said Noren. "You've answered my question. We can't cross yet."

"Also," said Silmavalien, "I don't know why you would want to. The other side is just as dangerous."

"Oh yes," said Noren, "those nightmare creatures."

He was aware of the tension in his relationship with Silmavalien. He suspected she had realized this before he did, but he constantly began to relate and respond to her in ways that were not conducive to their current situation. Talking to her, teasing her, and otherwise feeling about her like she was his about-to-be-wife would not help them sort through the changes in their lives and their relationship at all. It would not bring them closer to marriage.

But the days went on without them really resolving anything, though he and Elninya grew rapidly fatter and stronger. Some of the ropes had cut into Elninya badly, leaving inflamed and very irritating wounds, but it became clear that while some of these would scar, for the most part she was healing quite nicely. Silmavalien told him that she thought the oil she had received from Aelaza – who was the Ellena who seemed to speak to her as Hazalel spoke to him – not only protected the dragons' skin from the sun to some degree, but had healing properties.

Then one night, they heard a bow of the Ellenari sing three times.

For some reason, the next morning, they decided to pack everything up, and go to look at Treas. They had no plans of setting down, but Keya was willing to go along with them, and Noren and Silmavalien both wanted to see the place where they had lived and grown up.

That is, where they had grown up half-way. Much growing up had happened since they left Treas.

It was several days before they reached Treas. The Dragonriders communicated their thoughts through the dragons, and at first Noren and Silmavalien were certain they had found the wrong place. They circled high in the sky, and all the land marks looked like they expected the land marks around Treas to look from above, but the land just looked burnt and charred. There were no orchards or houses.

Then someone thought that the burn looked recent. It was certainly more recent than the last visit Noren had made to Treas.

What if ... what if the village had been burned? Completely razed to the ground until only ashes were left?

Dreading what they might find, they circled lower and lower. The certainty of Silmavalien and Noren that it was indeed Treas, or rather the burnt remains of Treas, grew as they descended. Soon they were low enough to see what now looked like the scattered remain of buildings, burned and crumpled, and the layout resembled Treas more and more.

They landed, and the few remaining trees now looked unmistakably like ones he and Silmavalien recognized from their childhood. Their branches were burned and their bark was blackened, but they were definitely the same trees.

When Noren slipped off Elninya, who had insisted on carrying him today. His feet touched the charred earth and ash and he bent down to touch it. "How did this happen?" he asked, already wondering if the fire demons who had almost destroyed him might have attacked Treas. But why? Then again, why had they attacked him?

Next to him, Silmavalien dismounted on of the smaller white dragons – Daurth. "What happened to the people?" she asked, looking around, her tone almost frantic.

"Oh my! What is this?" Keya gasped.

A moment later, the dragons alerted them to the presence of a very angry human nearby.

Noren felt a wave of terror and reached for his bow. Then he stopped himself. What was this? One lone human was not a threat to them, unless that human were a witch and had the help of demons – in which case, what use was his bow? Why did he get ready to kill before he thought? Was all that he had thought about death, all that change in his outlook, something that lasted only so long as he was powerless to fight against impending death? Had nothing in or about him really changed? *NO!* He would rather die than be that kind of creature again.

For the first time in his life, he tried to cry to the Lord of the Light. He did not know if he would be heard, if it was the right way to call on the Lord of All Light, or even what he felt about this Lord of Light, but anything was better than being that kind of creature. *Please don't let me go back to that! Lord of All Light, Love, whoever you are, make me what I had a glimpse of being.*

Out of the woods and into full view stepped one of the older men of Treas. Noren and Silmavalien wondered why he was not afraid of so many dragons and three Dragonriders. "Go!" he yelled, anger in his voice. "Go to your fate! You have betrayed us. You have brought upon us the demons and doom! You have cursed us! Go and be cursed yourself. May the High One curse you! May Queen Valiena never look upon you in favor!" He continued his rant, naming other gods and goddesses, heroes and heroines, of his religion, names known both to anyone who had grown up in Treas.

Airrock shook herself and breathed out little spurts of fire. Several other dragons, among them Lighter, did the same. Elninya relayed Lighter's apology. He really should not be laughing at the poor, confused man!

Then Silmavalien repeated it. "Lighter says he's sorry for laughing at your ranting!" she yelled.

The man looked at her and said, "How did you do this to us? The demons came and burned us to the ground. Most of us have died or fled, but I could not leave, not yet. Why? Why did you join the demons?"

"I didn't," said Silmavalien. "I fight them. It is not my fault they hate us."

"And Noren," he said, as if he did not hear her, and spat.

"Well, I shall go now," he said. "If you have come to finish the desecration of my home, there is nothing more left for me here. May the gods fight you and avenge us all." He turned, walked right through the dragons settled among the ruined houses, and continued south. He vanished like a ghost strayed out of the night, a dream strayed into the waking world, gone as suddenly as it had come, as if it had never left the concealing darkness.

"I feel so sorry for them," said Silmavalien.

"I do, too," said Keya. "He was yelling, and I could not get most of the words, but I think I mostly understood what was going on."

"Probably," agreed Silmavalien.

Noren kicked up some of the ashes into the air. "No one will listen. I tried to get people to think about whether they actually knew what they had heard. About dragons and riders, and about numerous other things. No one listened. Most of them acted as if they thought I was joking. Elninya wasn't with me, so I don't know if they really thought I was joking, or only pretended."

"When was this?" asked Silmavalien.

"When I was a low-priority courier," said Noren.

"What?!" she exclaimed.

"When I was low-priority courier," repeated Noren, and then told her about his scheme for looking for her.

Silmavalien collapsed on the ground in a fit of laughter.

Noren turned towards Keya and asked her, "Do you know what this is about?"

"No," said Keya. "At least, not mostly. She was on the other side of the mountains, so there was no way you could find her on this side. That's all I know. Maybe that she would never come up with the idea of living in cities like that? So, even if she was on this side, you were doomed to fail?"

Watching Silmavalien laugh, Noren felt laughter growing in himself. "When I was a low-priority courier," he repeated to himself under his breath, noting how funny it sounded.

"Should we leave now?" asked Keya. "This hardly seems like a good place to stay, especially if demons did it."

"No, not quite yet," returned Silmavalien, stifling her laughter and sitting up. She stood, desolate and relaxed. "I wish something could be done for the people," she muttered.

Noren did not hear her words, but even without Elninya he would have had no difficulty guessing at the thought and feeling behind them. He gave her a moment for her sorrow, then said, "We don't have to stay in the village, but I want to see if the horses are around and well."

In particular, he wanted to know if Evena was fine and if she had a foal which might be Victor's. He missed Victor and was very glad indeed that the boy had him. He would not have wanted him to belong to someone who did not care about him or did not get along with him. He also would have liked to show him to Silmavalien, he thought. It would be nice to teach her to ride a horse, too, like he had taught her to shoot so long ago. Teaching her to ride a horse would be so much better than teaching her to shoot had been.

6

Out of the Ashes

"I don't want to leave just yet," Silmavalien said to Noren and Keya. "I never told you, I think, about the obsidian rock, but before Minth hatched I found a black rock which spoke to me and told me it was the Avenger of the Dragons. It also told me that it was not the right time for it yet. But what if it is now? I mean to look for it. I think it's a black dragon."

"All right," said Keya. "We can do that."

Several minutes later, they found the obsidian rock under some burned bushes beside the stream that flowed by Treas. A hard tapping sound led them to the place where it was hidden. The burn was still recent enough for there to be hot, or even burning, spots left, so Noren carefully lifted it out of the crisped, blackened branches.

It was just as Silmavalien remembered it: shiny, jet black, roughly oval and slightly irregular in shape, with bumps and dimples. He laid it on the ground, a few paces away from the bushes, and Silmavalien knelt down beside him to watch it hatch.

Slowly, a crack opened in it. This egg was hard as rock and the line was sharp. The egg wobbled, shock, and rolled as its inhabitant struggled to make its way out.

"Should we help him?" Noren asked into the air.

"I know no reason to do so," said Silmavalien.

"Does that mean we should not help him?" asked Noren.

"I wouldn't," said Silmavalien.

The crack became jagged, running through the irregularities of the rock-like egg. The cracks divided and ran in different directions. One triangular piece had one tip pushed out, but remained attached to the larger portion of the egg.

The egg rolled down towards the stream and what remained of the bushes. Noren darted after it and brought it back to where he and Silmavalien were watching it.

The cracks had widened while he carried the egg. In a few moments it began to split. Silmavalien got her first glimpse of black scales.

A few moments later a dragon emerged, far more proportionate than any of the other dragons had been, though the creature did not look flight-worthy. The webbing of the dragon's wings was brown. From the dragon's nose down to the tail ran a patch of brown scales. The patch grew wider or thinner more or less proportionately to the thickness of the dragon's body. His eyes looked like red jewels, dark but bright, and glittered.

Silmavalien expected him to turn and eat his egg, like all the other dragons had. Then she remembered that he could not. His egg was as hard as a rock.

"Silmavalien, you asked me before to come with you and protect you. I told you then that it was not the time. My time is now beginning.

"My name is Onyxalis."

She stretched out her hand, palm up and out. The dragon stretched out his neck and touched her palm.

The connection had never felt like this before, which made sense. This was an obsidian dragon, a creature very different from other dragons, even if he was descended from them. She felt like liquid fire flowed between them. Her palm and the dragon's snout grew warm, even hot. A spark flashed. She felt like she was immersed in the heat of a volcano, swimming in the midst of that acrid, maddening smell.

Simultaneously, both she and the dragon pulled back.

Next, Onyxalis turned to Noren. *"I have come for you too, Noren,"* he said.

Noren acknowledged Onyxalis with a nod. Tentatively at first, then more confidently, Noren extended his palm towards the black dragon.

Silmavalien watched, not thinking anything at all, but perceiving the overflow of excitement and happiness from Noren and the dragon.

This was different from anything she had imagined before. Then again, she had always known the Obsidian Guardian was something else entirely. He had never been like the other dragons.

She did not know what the connection between Noren and Onyxalis was like, but she doubted very much that it was anything more like his connection with Elninya than her connection with Onyxalis was like her connections with the other dragons. It was a completely different thing.

When Noren and the dragon withdrew from each other, he looked towards her and their eyes met in a shared expression of something more or less like, "What?! That?!"

It seemed almost as if, for perhaps once in their lives, Noren was more shocked, more surprised, more taken off-guard than herself. He may have made fewer assumptions about the world than she had, believed far less that was false, and so never have had her experience of realizing nothing was the way she had thought it. However she had more experiences which might have prepared her for Onyxalis. Meeting Onyxalis was new and strange for Noren in a way in which it was not for her.

"I am hungry," said Onyxalis. *"If I am to grow, I must eat."*

Silmavalien looked behind them, and saw Keya standing a little ways away, watching. Their eyes met. Keya smiled a smile like water under a blue sky with the sun in it.

Silmavalien stood and walked towards her.

"Tanz told me," said Keya, "but I heard that. He is really different, isn't he?"

"Yes," said Silmavalien. "But I told you once about the Obsidian Guardian."

"Well, even if the way the nightmare creatures do things is different from any way I understand," said Keya, "I still don't want to stay in this burned-out village overnight, and I doubt you or Noren want to stay here anymore." She considered something, paused, then turned to Onyxalis. "It is late enough in the day that I would like it if we can look for another place to stay now. Perhaps, while some of us do that, you could ask another dragon to hunt for you?"

"Yes, Keya, that will do nicely.

"You do not have to speak out loud to me. If you think to me, I will hear you. I am a dragon."

"Silmavalien and Noren won't, though, so if I want to include them I must still speak out loud. But will you hear me if I think to you however far away we are, like the dragons hear each other?"

"I will hear Silmavalien and Noren, and they will hear me, wherever we are. I do not know about you, Keya," answered Onyxalis.

Coroneth and Wydth suggested a ridge overlooking Treas and several hundred feet higher for them to stay that night. Silmavalien rode Daurth again, and Onyxalis asked to go with Noren on Dance, and they flew to the ridge. By the time that everything was set up, and Onyxalis was working away at the meat Veine had brought, Noren said that it was definitely too late to look for the horses. "I want to talk to you about something," he said, motioning to Silmavalien.

She followed him and they walked along the ridge. Keya came with them.

Noren took them to a high spot, from which they could look down either direction into the valley. They stood for a few minutes, admiring the view which was splendid, especially as the blue of the oaks showed beautifully against the blue of the sky, and then Noren spoke. "I can feel power from or around Onyxalis."

Silmavalien and Keya both looked at him. He was going to say more.

"I and Elninya were captured by a bewitched net. I don't think that net would have been stronger than Onyxalis. Do you remember when I said that we needed to get away as quickly as possible unless you knew how to counteract witch-craft? I think Onyxalis can."

"He told me years ago that he would be the avenger of the dragons," said Silmavalien.

She remembered something he had said to her then. *"If you kill us we will still burn you."* "Do you think – do you think it's possible that the people of Treas killed a dragon, and that Onyxalis was the cause of their destruction?"

"Why?" asked Keya.

Silmavalien repeated what Onyxalis had told her.

"I don't know," said Noren. "How could they have? Someone else would have had to find a dragon egg – which *is* possible, I suppose."

Keya turned to Silmavalien. "Would Onyxalis know if he did?"

"I don't know," said Silmavalien.

"I would rather we not ask him," said Noren.

"I'd like to know, though," said Silmavalien. Her eyes settled on the distant black spot that had been Treas. Without turning to Noren, she said, "Don't worry. I won't ask him. I don't know what you feel or think, but I think my inclinations are in the same direction."

"I won't, either," said Keya.

"Though," said Silmavalien, "I think you might be right about the power and the witch-craft. It makes sense."

They watched the sun set behind the mountains. The cloudless evening air, and the dark silhouettes of trees and ground against it, had a heavenly feel, as if they were a faint vision showing through, a flat shadow, the transparent shape or bleached-out colors, of something behind, beyond, within them, something out of which they came, beautiful and real, from beyond the world and truer than the world.

It made Silmavalien's blood hum. Softly she sang something like her and Minth's impression song:

> Before the worlds were born
> This was and is a world of its own;
> Only those to love forsworn
> Know this world to which no eagle has flown.
>
> Now see and behold, lo!
> This world more deep than eyes may see.
> Come and find what no mind may know
> Where all may dwell and as one be.

She jumped a few verses, and sang again, barely audible:

> This is where your heart can learn to fly;
> These are the lands of true flight
> Where there is no end or limit of beauty and sky
> And you can race flame, soar on light.

Then she sang, more loudly and confidently, from the old song that had come to her when she found Minth's egg, which she always thought of as her introduction to Love and the Lord of the Light, her first glimpse of him. It was the song she thought of as her Dragon Song:

> Sweet, sweet heart of mine
> Together, away we shall fly
> To lands more fair and fine
> Than any we have yet come by
> Amidst the beauty and wonder of that sky.

She finished and Noren exclaimed, startling her. She had almost forgotten he was there, listening. "I know that song! I remember one time it was sung, around the fire, perhaps by a bard, one winter-time. How old was I? Five? Six? I always ... well, I can't say, but now I think I have an idea what it means."

They walked back to their camp.

7

Horses

The next morning, Noren said to Silmavalien, "If you can remember the verses, can you sing the rest of that song I knew?"

"Sure," said Silmavalien. "Between me and Songeth, we can do it."

The dragon walked over, and she stood next to his shoulder and placed for hand on his shoulder. He opened his mouth, and a moment later their two voices joined in song.

When they finished, Noren said, "I don't recognize some of those verses."

Silmavalien shrugged.

"It's beautiful," said Keya. "I like hearing the whole thing."

There was not really anymore to be said, and they left Onyxalis – who already looked bigger to Silmavalien, and Noren and Keya both agreed with her – with a couple of dragons, and then the rest of them went to look for the horses.

Don't eat any of them, Silmavalien said to the dragons. *We're not looking for food. We're looking for ... well, animals.*

The dragons all assured her that they would not think of eating the horses. They were her – or Noren's – friends – the two were much the same. They were not food. The dragons' humans loved them.

Aren't all the animals animals? thought Silmavalien, feeling disturbed. *The fact that they're not my friends doesn't mean they're nothing, that they aren't, or couldn't be, or wouldn't be, somebody's pet or work creature, or friend, or whatever. Somebody could love them. Maybe somebody does. Probably they love each other.*

Distressed, she thought, *Love, Lord of the Light, why do you allow the world to be such that we have to kill and eat animals to live, instead of loving them all and being friends with them? How is it good? How is it love, loving, lovable? How is it possible? How is it for the best?*

He spoke to her again much as he had spoken to her years ago. Or at least she remembered what he had said as if he said it to her again ... now.

"Please show me that of which this death and eating is the perversion! It is so perverted and horrible, how can you let it be? You

are Love! Love is powerful over everything. Love can do what love wishes. Love must be able to do whatever is loving. HOW IS THIS LOVING?"

At that moment, she realized that she said and believed that Love had more power than anything else, or even than everything else altogether, but what she really meant and believed was even more than that: that Love had power over everything. Nothing had any power against or over Love.

But was it true? That would mean that Love was much more powerful than the greatest gods of lore, for all of them had enemies who could keep them from doing what they wanted.

Yes, it was true. She had always known that Love was greater than all the gods. It was in the nature of Love to have this power.

"I have told you before that I will show you when the time is ripe. I will keep my promise. I will show you as soon as it is best to show you."

I wish you would show me now! thought Silmavalien.

"You're not ready yet. First you must become willing and able to see what I have shown you. If I were to show you more now, it would not be showing you, for you are not able to see it. I have shown you, but you cannot see it yet."

Well, help me to be able to see! Help me to be willing to see! Show me where I'm not. Show me how to be, she prayed.

A few minutes later, Linol found horses grazing in a meadow. Tanz, Minth, and Elninya joined him, though most of the dragons stayed a little further away, so as to scare the horses less easily. They found a place they could land that was enough away not to alert the horses, but close enough for the humans to easily find the meadow.

Then they hiked in.

𝒩

Noren lead the way eagerly. It was simple enough to walk the right direction and find a large meadow. It was not as if the whole lay of the land did not tell him where it was likely to, so it did not take much attention. A screen of trees and bushes partially blocked the visibility, but with the first glimpses of a horse's rump, Noren almost broke into a jog. This was not hunting. The horses would be at least more or less tame, and they would not bolt simply because they scented or heard a human.

He found a thinner patch in the bushes and pushed his way through, followed by the women. His eyes roved over the herd, leisurely grazing or standing in the sun or the shade. A few of them were even lying down. Almost at once, before he had even picked out Evena from the herd, he recognized one that bore a marked resemblance to Victor.

She did not look like Victor. Noren had seen many horses who looked far more like Victor than this mare did, but none of the horses anyone had in Treas looked nearly as much like Victor. A moment later, she noticed him. She tossed her head in the air and stood with her head up and her ears forward, watching him finish pushing his way through the bushes.

Next to her was a younger horse, apparently her colt, who also had some of Victor's features, though fewer than she did. Skies above, she was beautiful. Evena's star-stripe glowed on her face, and her coat was the same golden brown as Victor's.

Noren stepped out from under the bushes, straightened, and took a few steps aside for Silmavalien and Keya to come through. He searched the small herd over for Evena, and it was not long before he found her. Silmavalien stood next to him, and he pointed out the horses to her.

"Victor must have been the most beautiful horse!" she said.

"He really is," said Noren. He had told her about him and about the boy to whom he had given him.

Keya stood, admiring the animals. "I've never seen such creatures before," she said, in an awed and quiet voice. "They're – they're not like deer, not really, but kind of … They're beautiful!"

Noren stepped forward into the grass, and explained to Silmavalien and Keya he was going to try to catch Evena's foal. She had evidently been tamed, as had her colt, and she was shier than he was. The two women spread out a little as if to help, as he walked around a little.

He kept an eye on Silmavalien – and on Keya, who might know nothing at all about how to approach the creatures. He saw Silmavalien meander to a halt and then stand still. She did not look unhappy, but she looked uncertain, and then he noticed the colt starting to approach her. He stopped to watch.

Silmavalien stood, not too tense, not really moving, but not truly still either. Slowly, the colt wandered closer under the watchful eye of his mother, until he was close enough to touch. Silmavalien raised her hand to touch his twitching, beautiful muzzle, at which he shied back, but then he approached her again.

Noren watched, fascinated by her approach to it. She reached out her hand again, but not as far, and after a while the colt came closer again. He reached out his neck, blew on her hand and nuzzled it, then retreated a step and repeated the process. Again. Again. Again. After several minutes, he came closer still, until he blew right into her face.

Only then did Silmavalien reach out a hand to touch his neck. He startled again, but this time he came right back.

Noren waited a minute or two for them to get more comfortable together, and then he approached them. Silmavalien turned to look at him, and he laughed. "It looks like he likes you," he said.

"I'm sure he likes you just as much," she said a little shyly, and stepped back to let Noren and the horse meet each other.

𝓢

They spent the rest of the day in the meadow. She and Keya spent most of the time getting to know the horses, with Noren occasionally giving them instructions and advice. He corrected Keya much more often, since Silmavalien had some experience with the horses from Treas, but Keya had never seen a horse until that morning.

Sometime in the afternoon, they were standing on the edge of the meadow, with a few of the mares nuzzling them, when Noren wandered by from where he had been with his favorite horses, Victor's off-spring. Silmavalien turned to look at him at the sound of his tread. It was heavy and careless, and that meant he was not happy.

"If only I had my bridle!" he said, when she met his gaze. "I wouldn't even need the saddle. I'm sure I could ride that mare."

He paused for a moment, and when he continued he sounded a little less upset,

though still angry. "At least it wasn't those witches who stole my bridle and saddle like they did my bow and sword. At least, I don't think they did. Victor's boy probably got his bridle and saddle. If somehow I'd kept them, he wouldn't have them for him, so that's fine, I guess."

A bit later they were all standing together, Keya untangling the mare's mane, while Silmavalien helped him with her tail. "You do know we can't stay here with the horses, right?" she asked.

"Why not?" he said, kneeling on the ground while he carefully worked out a knot without tugging on her hairs. "It's as good as any place, and if it isn't for some reason, we can take the horses where it's better. Since you've told me the other side of the mountains is just as dangerous there's no reason to go there."

"But there is," said Silmavalien. "We have to go to Ellen Island. Onyxalis has to go to Ellen Island. I'd know it even if Aelaza had not told me I would have to bring the obsidian dragon there, since Onyxalis himself knows. At least, he knows he has to find the volcano. He was telling me that last night."

Besides, she thought, they could not stay with the horses anyways. If they did not know they had to go somewhere else soon, they might be able to stay here for a while, like she had stayed with Keya's family, or at times on the Steep Descent. But they had to be always ready to obey the Lord of Light and go where he wanted to go, and given what Onyxalis had told her and Noren when he hatched, she was rather certain that they had something to do sooner rather than later. And now that Onyxalis was bonded to Noren, she was almost certain that he would be the warrior-champion of the Dragonriders to whom she must give the Dragon-sword, and then he would destroy the Fire-Shadow in the abyss beside the Riders' Passage.

If only Noren would marry her! Then everything would be perfect, at least with regard to that portion of her life, of the world. But she was quite certain that she and Noren had something to do with whatever Onyxalis had to do, and that sounded big and scary.

But she did not mention any of this. The immediate reason they could not stay with the horses was because they had to take Onyxalis to Ellen Island.

Well, she had to take Onyxalis to Ellen Island. She supposed Noren did not have to come, though she felt like he should, and not just because she wanted him around her. In fact, she would have welcomed some relief from his constant presence. Their relationship was too confusing. Sometimes it was almost like they were husband and wife, but they were not. Sooner or later, something had to be done about it. Her idea was for them to get married, like they had been going to, but if Noren was not ready for that, or not right for that, then they should not do it. Certainly, if the Lord of the Light did not want them to marry, they should not marry.

"Okay," said Noren, "but I will come back to them if I can. I want them to know me."

Minth touched her mind. He really liked the horses. She smiled, both at the happiness in his thoughts and at the image he sent her, of himself standing next to a horse, with his wing over the creature, still smaller than him but much nearer to him in size than she was. He had his neck bent back, and they were touching noses.

I can really see why you like the horses, she said. *I am really liking them myself.*

Yes, that is a bummer. I don't know how you could be friends with a horse. You'd have to convince him you didn't want to eat him.

Maybe we can stay here another day and you can see if you can figure out how to do that. You might ask Tiela for ideas, since she has done it with smaller animals. Or Songeth. He makes friends with birds so easily!

8

Call of Vengeance

A week and a half later, they decided to temporarily settle in another valley, higher up and closer to the high pass. Onyxalis was growing extremely rapidly. He could not yet fly, but he was too big for any the dragons to carry far in their mouths or claws, and even Lighter was not comfortable carrying him on his shoulders for long.

Besides, whatever the flying dragons thought about it, he found being carried distasteful for some reason Silmavalien did not understand.

"How can he grow that fast?!" she asked Noren and Keya.

"There's powerful magic in him," said Noren.

Keya nodded vigorously. "There is," she stated.

S

The oil Aelaza had given Silmavalien was starting to run low, and during the time they stayed in the valley, she, Noren, and Keya asked the dragons to bring them many of their kills. Noren spent many hours alongside the others working on getting the fat out of the animals and turning it into the grease they smeared on their skins.

One day when all three of them were working on slicing up the fattiest portions of a deer, Silmavalien asked him and Keya, "What my question is, is this: why does it have to be this way? Why must some die for others to live? It's wrong!"

"There's the possibility that the world is not ruled by Love?" suggested Noren.

"Well, I don't believe that, and I don't think you do either," said Silmavalien.

Keya said, "I certainly believe the world is ruled by Love – or something like that."

"The world *has* to be ruled by Love. It has to have a purpose. There *is* purpose, and Love is that purpose," said Silmavalien.

Noren did not respond. She did not think he believed the world might not be ruled by Love? It was not meant as an insult, and it did not bother him. It was something for him to consider, and he did not know what he believed exactly. He knew there was something real – in the words of Silmavalien's song, a 'world more deep than eyes may see'. His experience with death had left him knowing that much. Beyond that, he did not know what it meant, or at least not much.

Finally, he said, "I don't know if I think that or not. You say there has to be a purpose and that purpose has to be Love. I think I agree with that. There is something, and we might call it Love, that is not ended by death, or that death leads to. I don't know very much, so don't take anything I say too seriously. I might have said it all wrong. I just mean that there is *something*, that I know there is something, but I hardly know what it is at all. I don't know if I do know what it is. I certainly can't say it. Even I and Elninya can't talk about it, though she says that's got nothing to do with either of us not knowing it, in the way she means know. Or maybe she says that's got nothing to do with it not being. I can't say what she says, except that everything I say is wrong and everything I don't say is wrong, and it's wrong not because something else I could say is true, but because my thoughts to begin with aren't right."

Silmavalien laughed lightly. "That's what dragons' thoughts are like. Anyway, I heard Elninya."

"But I didn't," said Keya. "I need one of you or Tanz to tell me what she says."

"Well," said Noren, "and remember, I'm just making a suggestion, and Elninya says it's all stupid nonsense, one way or the other, true or false. At least, that's the closest I can get to what she says, which really does sound like nonsense in this language. Love might not rule all things. Love might be the purpose. Love might one day rule everything that wants to be ruled by Love – or maybe even everything. But Love might not rule the whole world, now. This world might even have come into existence out of another world we might call Love – that's what your song sounded like, Silmavalien – yet not be ruled by Love. It could be anything. There's certainly hatred – a kind of rebellion against the law of Love, if you will."

"I don't know," said Silmavalien. "Some of what you just said really does sound like stupid nonsense."

"But not all of it?" asked Noren with a twinkle in his eye.

"You were right that the song sounded like its saying this world came into existence out of a world of Love. At least, a world that's open only to Love and full of Love, where there is nothing contrary to Love. I think that's much the same thing," said Silmavalien.

"Anyway," she continued, "I hate this."

Both Noren and Keya agreed with her about that.

"We will take revenge on all evil and punish it. We will avenge what has been lost," said Onyxalis. *"I will fight beside the King of Dragons and you will be with me, and we will shed the blood of all that is evil and take our vengeance, avenging the blood of more than just the dragons and the Dragonriders, but all that have been killed because of the rebellion of the Nightmare Lord."*

That doesn't answer me, replied Silmavalien. *It's not the solution to my problem. I don't want to shed blood. I don't want to take vengeance on whatever has made this horrible situation. I want this horrible situation not to be! I don't want to have to kill animals. The horses reminded me. I hadn't thought of it so much, since I haven't been hunting, but that reminded me. It's horrible! I don't understand why the Lord of Light permits it. It's wrong. I – I want to love everything.*

She felt many of the dragons agree with her. She wanted to love everything. That was right. So did they.

Yet hunting when they or their friends were hungry did not bother them, and she did not understand how this was. Minth, Veine, Songeth, and Linol all felt so strongly the same desire she did, to love everyone and everything. She knew it. Yet, somehow, their minds seemed not to notice the horror of having to eat other lives in the way she did. They hunted, they ate, they forgot about it, they grew hungry, they hunted again.

And they were not haunted by the horror every time they killed, though she could not believe they cared any less than she did.

There had to be so much to be known that she did not know. And they could not tell her. When she asked them, they only answered that was the way it was, the way they were, and there was nothing to be said about it. She thought they could not even understand or hear her question. It was as incomprehensible to them as some of their thoughts were to her. They did not doubt there was sense in it, but it was nonsense as far as they were concerned.

But Onyxalis bothered her. Why was he so interested in vengeance? As if the slaughter of the beloved could be righted by killing the slayer? As if the killing of the slayer would somehow resurrect the beloved and make it as if the beloved had never been slain?

No, Onyxalis had never said, or even implied, that. He seemed to think slaughter corrected slaughter, not that slaughter undid slaughter, an idea which she found nonsensical – and not in the sense that she did not understand it at all, but that she understood it to be nonsense.

Unless she misunderstood the idea? Unless it meant something other than what she understood it to mean? What if she misunderstood Onyxalis, too?

Onyxalis and Jareth seemed similar and yet when she thought about it, they did not seem similar at all. Did Onyxalis and Jareth have a similar problem, or were Jareth's problem and whatever was going on in or with Onyxalis only similar in a superficial way? Perhaps, she misunderstood Onyxalis, because she interpreted him through her experience with Jareth's bitterness and cruelty.

She hoped Jareth would not likewise misunderstand Onyxalis and become worse!

Her thoughts returned to the dragons' hunting. She thought again about what Noren had said, as if some people he should really love, and others he did not have to love. It almost seemed similar to the way the dragons were, but she was not confused even for a moment. Minth most certainly did not have this idea, and neither did Songeth or Linol, or many others. To some of them, like Airrock and Veine, it was so strange and alien she could not understand how they related to it, but she knew they completely agreed with her that they should love everyone, that some people or other creatures should not be excluded from love. Yet they could hunt some and not others, and this did not bother them? Why? How?

𝒩

Noren was also bothered by Onyxalis' speech. As he worked, he considered. Onyxalis felt angry and hateful. He did not seem as possessed by anger and bitterness as Noren had felt himself before the end, for so it seemed to him. He had been certain that he was going to die, that he was come to his death, the end of his life in this world at least, when he had found himself free from hatred and bitterness. Thus, that imprisonment still seemed to him to be 'the end'.

It seemed to Noren that Onyxalis was on the same path that he had been. There might be occasions for hating, Noren thought, but the way Onyxalis hated, the way his desire for revenge seemed to be the main thing to him, felt like the way that led to being destroyed by hatred, all the love sucked out of oneself as bitterness ate one's soul.

Yet, Noren considered, Onyxalis believed he was chosen for this revenge. Who was this King of Dragons? Who had chosen Onyxalis?

Had Onyxalis been chosen, and so been granted his magical powers, or chosen because of his magical powers, or did he think he had been chosen because of his magical power when he had not been chosen at all? Or, at least, not chosen for the revenge for which he thought he was chosen?

Was revenge okay for some and not for others?

Noren certainly did not want to slip back into the torment and slavery of bitterness and hate. He could not help but think that Onyxalis was, in some way, bound by the same thing. It was so freeing not being forced to be bitter and hateful! He no longer wanted to take vengeance. He had not been thinking, bound to that stake, about how coming back from the world beyond death to visit vengeance upon his persecutors. How could it be good or right to think in such a way? How could it be happy? How could it help anyone? Protecting those you loved against those who threatened their well-being, when it was possible to do so, was a good thing. But vengeance after the fact? What good did that do? What love?

A thrill of joy from Elninya swept through him. He felt her happiness that he shared her thoughts, that she understood him and he understood her. They were one again, and even when their thoughts were not the same, they were close enough to think together, to discuss and be in union!

Could it be in accord with Silmavalien's Love who was supposed to be the Lord of the Light of whom Hazalel had told him?

Perhaps, he could ask. If he met Hazalel again, and if Hazalel let him, he would ask Hazalel about this.

He might also ask Silmavalien what she thought. He could ask Keya what she thought, too. He would not think something because they thought it, however certain they were, but he would think about what they thought. It might help him understand what he already knew.

As for Elninya, she thought nothing at all, and could think nothing at all, about Onyxalis and his vengeance.

Noren hoped Onyxalis was wrong. He did not want to be with Onyxalis in executing vengeance, and he was sure Silmavalien wanted it far less than he did.

9

Love!

Several days later, Noren woke in the morning to the scuffle of Veine playing with several of the male dragons. They were teasing and harassing each other, biting at one another's tails and wings and necks and growling at each other in a way he had not seen yet.

Elninya answered his curiosity by telling him that Veine was ready to mate.

Later in the morning, once he actually got up, he found Silmavalien and Keya talking about the dragons' behavior. "This has happened several times before," Silmavalien was explaining, "and she hasn't mated. I don't know why. Maybe none of the male dragons suit her? Maybe she doesn't suit any of them? Dragons don't do this much like humans do, but they aren't like any of the animals I know, either. Even if this was a first time or so, and she and one of the males seemed to like each other, I wouldn't know. I was almost certain Tiela and Wydth were going to mate, but no. It was Songeth Tiela mated."

The thought of the dragons, even if they weren't going to mate, turned Noren's mind to himself and Silmavalien, something he had managed to push out of his thoughts for a few days. He wanted to marry her, but he was sure they could not pursue that again until he told her what he had done, and he was worried she would be angry with him. Things would probably never again be the same between them. Also, he was embarrassed to tell her. It did not fit his idea of the relationship he wanted to have with her.

S

Veine jumped off the ridge, spreading her wings and rising, white and purple, against the evening sky.

Silmavalien put down the herbs she was wrapping to keep them potent, as Lighter roared and breathed out a stream of fire. A moment later she saw his golden scales and white wings flash above the ridge line, as he flung himself up from his lower perch.

She turned a radiant look on both Keya and Noren. She did not know if Tanz and Elninya knew what she knew, but she could hardly have helped saying it anyways. "Lighter and Veine are mating!"

A moment later, a tendril of worry and unhappiness broke through the excitement and joy. What if Veine's eggs were defective, too? What if some of them *died*? Silmavalien knew there must be something wrong with the dragons that she did not know about, and she had no reason to think it had been fixed since Tiela mated and laid her egg.

If she saw Aelaza or another of the Ellenari, she would ask! It had to be fixed. She did not know if it would affect, or how much it would affect, Veine's eggs if it were to be fixed after she mated but before she laid her eggs. But it had to be fixed. As soon as possible.

Of course, Aelaza might not know. Oaeiae might not know. Others might not know. All of them might not know. But she had to ask, since any of them might.

She also wanted to correct the relationship between herself and Noren. She wanted to discuss marriage with him again. She knew so little. She knew, from the dragons, that he had done something that embarrassed him, that worried him, that he absolutely abhorred, that he thought that he had to tell her if they were to marry, and that he desperately did not want her – or anyone, for that matter, but her more than others – to know.

She had no idea what to do about it. She could hardly tell him she would feel the same about him no matter what it was. She did not know what it was. Even if she could know that, no matter what it was, she would still see and feel about him the same, she could not expect him to know or believe that. She could not even be hurt by him not knowing or believing that. It would not mean he did not trust her as a person.

Silmavalien decided to ask the Lord of the Light to help her to figure out and fix whatever was wrong with the dragons, so their eggs would not be killed or hurt. She added, "I don't need to figure it out and fix it. I just would like you to have it fixed. Can you please heal the dragons? I don't particularly care how you do it."

Another thought occurred to her. It was so obvious! "Can you please fix and heal what's wrong with the whole world? I'm not quite sure if you can in one way, but I'm absolutely certain that you can in another way. Can you please do it? I'm sure it's good! I'm sure it's good for everything to be ruled by Love, for everyone to love everyone else, for everything and everyone to live and exist together in a relationship of love. Can you please do that?"

A few days later, Onyxalis took his first flight. Even Airrock had not learned to fly like he did, almost as if he already knew how to fly, and even his muscles already knew how to fly, and he just had to wait until his wings were grown. But, watching him fly, Silmavalien had no doubt that Airrock was, and always would be, the better flier. There was just something about her relationship with the wind.

That evening, a few hours after Onyxalis came down, Silmavalien felt the presence of evil descend and darken the stars and moon. Almost before she realized what she was feeling, Onyxalis said, *"The demons come. We shall fight them. Our vengeance is about to begin."*

She wondered then whether he was really ready to fight the nightmare. She knew he had power none of them had, and power of which she had never dreamed. But he did not seem ready. How would he fare against the fear, the hatred, the raw evil? How would he fare against the pride? She had not forgotten her encounter with the medusa, and she could help but feel it was to the medusa's temptation, or to something much like it, that Onyxalis was most vulnerable. He seemed to have it in himself, and even his words right now rang with a proud hatred. She could so easily see him relishing the image of himself as final King, Avenger, and Judge.

She could see him giving in without even fighting. Would he not look on the one who offered that image to him as a benefactor, a friend, showing him what and who he really was and how to grow into his full potential?

She became afraid and addressed the Lord of Light. *Please, do not let Onyxalis join the nightmares!"* she pleaded. *"Do not let him – or any of us – become demons. Teach us Love.*

She dragged her saddle out of the bags and Airrock lay down to make it easier for her to throw it over her shoulders, while she glimpsed a creature who somehow moved in a way that reminded her of Aelaza. Noren moved towards him, as he stepped out of the forest and held up his saddle. "I know you have questions, Noren, but there is no time. I bring you and Elninya a saddle, without which it will be hard for you to survive the flight you must make."

"Flight? No. We will not fly. I was born for this battle," said Onyxalis.

Airrock heaved herself to her feet so Silmavalien could get the strap under her belly. Out of the corner of her eyes, she glimpsed the Ellenar helping Noren put his new saddle on Elninya.

"You might have been born to fight evil," she heard the Ellenar – Hazalel, that was his name, Noren had told – telling Onyxalis, "but it was not all for which you were born. You are not ready yet."

"Perhaps," said Onyxalis. *"I must fly to Ellen Island and the volcano. When I have emerged from the volcano, then I will have the power to defeat all the dragons' foes."*

Fumbling, she finished clasping the saddle straps. Aelaza appeared out of the forest now, flashing like a small star as she confronted the arrogant obsidian dragon. "Onyxalis," she said, "you are in danger of becoming a demon until you forget your own greatness!" she said. "While all you think about is the fact that you were born to be the great avenger and protector of the dragons, you cannot do so."

Silmavalien's whole body tingled with fear. She did not know Hazalel. She knew there was too much danger and they were in too much of a hurry for her to look at him. However she knew that two Ellenari shared her concern. If Onyxalis were to meet something like a medusa in his present state, what might he become? The thought terrified her. He would be so horrible, and so powerful, and bonded to her! He would be, too, a dragon. Her thoughts stopped short in horrible fear.

"Love," Silmavalien whispered to herself, both pleading, and reminding herself that Love was real and must be finally triumphant.

Onyxalis, love*!* she said.

The gust from Elninya's wings as she flung herself into the sky tossed her hair and almost knocked her back. She grabbed the bags as quickly as she could and tied them around Lighter's neck, while Dance, Veine, and Coroneth followed Elninya. Tanz and Keya a moment later. She dashed back to Airrock and jumped into the saddle, while right in front of her Aelaza and Hazalel both stood in front of the black dragon. "Onyxalis, fly!" they said.

Silmavalien felt that Airrock wanted to fight herself. She realized, then, of all the dragons she knew, Airrock might be most like Onyxalis. Jareth was nothing like him.

Not yet, she told Airrock, and the silver dragon acknowledged her. She knew that. However, she would be glad of the day when the time finally came to fight the demons!

Then she launched herself into the sky, and in a few moments was flying level with Tanz, then with Veine. The rest of the dragons followed.

"Onyxalis, you can't fight. Not now. You will only be defeated and corrupted!" Silmavalien heard Aelaza say.

ℵ

The wind whistled in his ears as Elninya carried him into the sky, and Noren wondered if Onyxalis had any happiness or peace, any security, from his wrath and bent on vengeance. However he saw clearly that Onyxalis' bent on vengeance was not like his anger had been. It was primarily upon the nightmare monsters that Onyxalis burned to take vengeance. Perhaps the fear of death and other evils that had been behind Noren's anger was also present, but the dominant element was wholly different.

He looked down over Elninya's shoulder and saw Onyxalis reluctantly fly after them, taking off just behind the last white dragons.

S

As the dragons flew, Silmavalien felt the moment when Jareth changed and saw. Her heart beat with exhilaration and hope, not fear, as she felt things fall into place for him. He turned from the abyss of bitterness that infected every thought and feeling, he turned from meanness and hatred. What happened inside him was beyond her comprehension, but she knew that it had something to do with Onyxalis, with Onyxalis' thoughts, with Onyxalis' view of the world and especially with his understanding of how to respond to evil.

Then Veine explained to her that she had understood wrong. To think of her own understanding, whether of the lack of it, or of the presence of it, was to understand imperfectly. Understanding was a nonsense-idea, a non-idea. She might understand something perfectly if she would only cease to think about understanding; to behold the thing, not think about whether she understood it or how well she understood it.

10

The Rock in the Sky

Once again, the sky around them was full of storm. The dragons found themselves on a wild wind that threw them up into the mountains. It was all they could do to stay in the air, to stay away from the ground, to avoid being dashed or hurtled into the ridges and cliffs of the mountains. Except for Airrock. She did not exactly find flying in the storm *easy,* but she did not find it dangerous or frightening or even hard. Instead, she found it exhilarating. A few of the others, such as Dance, did not find it dangerously difficult either, and among them – surprisingly enough – was Jareth. He almost seemed to having fun, almost like Airrock.

"I shouldn't be having to do this," Onyxalis complained. *"I am made to fight, to roar and to breathe fire. I am not made to fight the wind! I am a dragon of the earth and fire more than of the skies."*

Silmavalien thought, reading his tone of voice and emotions, that he must be inherently unused to having to struggle and to feeling overpowered. The wind certainly was overpowering, and as hard as it was to survive, she knew it was carrying them away from the battalion of demons much faster than they could have done unassisted by it. They were not fighting the wind. They were fighting *with* the wind.

He resisted it when she told him this. He hated being in the grip of the wind! It was stronger than he was, and he felt like everything in his being protested against this – against being controlled or outmatched, unable to *fight.*

Somehow, his protest was funny, though she tried to keep the thought from him, knowing he would not like it. They flew through the night, until finally the wind slackened. The eastern sky was tinged with dawn when the weary dragons descended on a rocky summit, polished by the winds, and touched with the first light of morning. They glided to it wearily, though there was no way to descend safely for any creature that was not either a rock-climber or a flier.

Minth and Elninya dropped down heavily, as if they did not feel like they *could* fly any farther, while Airrock circled behind. Onyxalis complained that he was exhausted too, and she scolded him. He had never flown before that day, and he had managed quite nicely. What on earth could he mean that he was more of earth and fire than of the skies compared to other dragons?

Maybe he *was* more of earth and fire, but he was not less of the skies! Even Airrock had taken weeks to fly that, she told him.

Then Airrock landed, exhausted herself, and even more exhausted than Onyxalis Silmavalien thought. She was surprised at the obsidian dragon's hardiness, as she slid off Airrock and then crawled across the rock to where Minth had landed. Half the dragons were already asleep.

"You all probably should wake up now. The sun is rising high into the sky. You should find a better place to sleep. Otherwise, you'll sunburn."

Keya's voice broke in on Silmavalien and the dragons' sleep.

They were all so tired. They were so sore. Even the thought of flying made them feel faint. They just wanted to go on sleeping.

She crept out from under Minth's wing. A moment later, she saw Noren appear from behind one of Elninya's wings. Keya stood on a hump of rock onto which she had somehow climbed. Her dark hair streamed from her face, blowing in the wind.

"If they won't wake up, we should at least oil them," she said.

"We're almost out of the Ellenari oil," said Silmavalien.

"No, we aren't," said Keya. "Look." She pointed. "There's more."

Silmavalien and Noren both followed her finger. "A lot more!" said Silmavalien.

"The Lord of the Light must have known we needed it," said Keya.

ℵ

Noren watched with intense interest as Keya came down from the rock. She and Silmavalien stood together, and Silmavalien took the ring off of her finger. She and Keya both placed hands around it, and began to speak to the Lord of the Light, thanking him for their safety – somehow, this included thanking him for the storm – for making Jareth happier, and for the oil. They also asked him to continue protecting them.

Noren was at once interested and wondered if he should do much the same, but he found the idea uncomfortable. He had never believed in, never prayed to, gods, and while the Lord of All Light was certainly not any god such as those he had heard others speaking of, yet this practice of prayer reminded him of Kriela. Either that, or a meaningless ritual, such as when he had spoken of Vorli, simply because it was the way others talked about rain. Sometimes he had thought that many people did not really believe, at least not most of what they said they believed. They did not talk like it.

Besides, he was not certain of the Lord of the Light, at least not in a way for him to speak to him in this way.

But Silmavalien's ring interested him, and when the two women separated, he came closer. "Can I see that?" he asked.

"Sure," said Silmavalien. She held it out on her palm for him to examine.

Noren bent closer. It had such interesting, delicate engraving. No one could engrave like that. The dragon, the tree, and the stream were so artfully done, in such tiny detail, among a great many other details. In all his travels, he had never seen anything like it.

"Where did you get this? Why do you pray with it?" he asked.

"Lexamarian gave it to me. She was a Dragonrider, but she's dead now, and her dragon died long before I met her," said Silmavalien. "As for why do I pray with it? The Lord of the Light often uses it to communicate with me and to work his power. Numerous times while looking at it I have been guided, and never falsely. It tends to be the source of the light through which he protects me from nightmare monsters. Sometimes he uses it just to give me light to see by."

"Oh," said Noren. He shuddered when Silmavalien said 'and her dragon died long before I met her', but as she went on to speak about the ring, an idea occurred to him. "So, that light that protected me and Elninya for the little time between when you appeared and when you freed me? Did that come from the ring?"

"Yes," said Silmavalien.

Suddenly, her practice made sense, and he decided that he should give thanks to the Lord of the Light, too. It seemed natural now to thank whoever protected him and Elninya through the ring, but he would not do it publicly. That felt wrong.

"Let's take care of the dragons," he said. Taking quick, determined strides towards the jars of oil, he said, "We won't need to ask them to roll over, since this is mostly to protect them from the sun, but I think we should put extra on them, unless anyone thinks otherwise"

"First," said Silmavalien, "we should put a little on all of them."

"I agree with that," said Noren. "And we should put it first on the sides that get the most sun."

"That's a good idea," said Keya.

When everyone was confident they had a thick enough layer of oil, they went back to sleep. Noren decided he was only less tired than the dragons were.

S

Silmavalien was wakened from a light sleep by Elninya. *"Do you remember when you were thinking about death and whether or not it might be a gateway to the world of Love?"*

Yes. What about it?

"I thought of something. What if death is like hatching? Your song reminded me of hatching and of how I feel. Someday we will hatch into a yet wider, brighter world. What if death is what that looks like from this side? What if death is release into the real sky – to be made free of the whole world? We hatch – or for you, are born – into a world wider and brighter than the one before. I don't know that death is the last 'hatching' so to speak, but I'm sure it is one of the ways through which we are made free of more of the world, more of light. And this seems to me just like what you were saying about a gate into another world or state nearer to the heart of Love."

Silmavalien was distinctly aware that Elninya had tried to share this with her rider years ago.

Death is disgusting. Death is horrible. And it comes in such horrendous ways! ... But I do see what you mean. At least a little. I think, replied Silmavalien.

Thank you, Elninya.

She stood and walked out on the rock to marvel at the view. The summit on which they stood dropped away first in sheer cliffs and then in slopes and valleys of forest-clad earth and rock, down to valleys low and blue with mist and distance. They seemed to be in the middle of the sky. Above them reached up slopes and peaks far higher than they were, their upper slopes covered with dazzling snow that never melted.

She wondered if the view had reminded Elninya of something she had thought of saying much earlier.

She was supported by the mountain and lifted by it into the sky, and lifted the higher into the sky that the higher peaks rose so high above her! Looking around her, up into the sky and to the snowy peaks she could never reach, down into the valleys full of trees and meadows and running streams and mist, across the wide spaces, she felt the sense of a space so wide that it suffocated her, a freedom so great that it was an imprisonment.

It was not the sort of feeling she would have usually called delight or pleasant, but it could not have been farther from being an unhappy sort of feeling.

Elninya told her that she had something of the same experience.

The dragon added that she was also still very tired and sore and wanted to go to sleep again. She did not really want to leave the rock in the sky either. However, maybe they could find a better place to sleep?

When the others started to wake up, they decided to move to a part of the rock spire that was overhung and shaded from the western sun. It was not too far for the tired dragons to fly, and there they spent the afternoon.

11

Snow and Flame

They were in the region of the snows that never melted, making their way up towards the high pass. Somehow or other several of the dragons, including Songeth, convinced Silmavalien to sing with them the song that she hated.

When she first began to sing it, she wondered what in it she could have hated as much as she remembered hating it. Then, as she continued singing, a sense of horror fell upon her and slowly grew. She felt like it was about to materialize before her eyes – or before her thoughts. She shrank from the growing sense of something horrible foreboded in the song. When she ended, she still could not shake it, but felt as if a horror beyond anything she had imagined, beyond anything even her current foreboding suggested, was about to be revealed to her.

She looked at her audience. Keya's eyes sparkled much as they had when she had first sung it. On Noren's face was a look of concentration, and perhaps something like understanding, but she did not understand anymore than she often understood the light in Keya's eyes.

"I think I understand something of it," he said, "or something in it. I like it, I think, though I might dislike it."

Silmavalien and Keya both waited. Silmavalien got the impression that Keya was much more eager than she was to hear what Noren would say.

She remembered how Keya had told her she thought Noren might understand it.

"It's like – a little like," began Noren. He stopped, then said, "No, I won't say it. It's too much unlike for my saying it to do any more than confuse, except perhaps to Elninya."

The sense of horror coalesced into something solid in Silmavalien's mind. It all fit together. 'Bright the blackest flame, a scorching death to higher life.' Again, 'Is the smoth'ring flame and hotter dark the open door.' Noren's imprisonment! How she had found him!

Gasping, almost breathless, in utter horror, Silmavalien panted, "You don't – you don't mean that it means you'll have to – have to be burned alive!"

N

Noren looked up at Silmavalien from where he had been sitting to listen to her sing. Had she said what he thought he'd heard? *"Yes,"* said Elninya.

"Why should that be a problem?" he asked, though he had never thought that. The song reminded him of the release he had experienced through his imprisonment, and he guessed he had told Silmavalien enough about his experience – and perhaps Elninya had spoken to her also – that she at once guessed what he had been about to say. Probably her bond with dragons who also sensed his thoughts had contributed. He had to remember that she was bonded to twelve dragons!

"Because – because," said Silmavalien, "because it's so horrible! It's obvious why! I mean, you!"

"You've not been there," said Noren. "What do you know about it?"

"It's torture. It's horror. It's!" said Silmavalien. "You've not been burned alive either."

"That's irrelevant," replied Noren. "We are all going to die. What is this about?"

"It's a most horrible way to die!" said Silmavalien. She burst into tears. "Why can't you understand?"

"I think I do understand," said Noren. "I think I used to feel and think much as you are doing right now. But being certain that I was going to be killed – I'm not sure how much the 'burned alive' part mattered – and being unable to do anything cured me of it. I was forced to stop doing the things I did to avoid looking at reality, at what I really did and didn't know, and to really face death. I've told you some of this before."

"But it's so horrible!" said Silmavalien. "It's a horrible, torturous, horrendous way to die – t-t-to be-be k-k-killed!"

Confusingly, Noren found that, for some reason, in the face of Silmavalien's incomprehension, he was fully aware of what he had been then. He felt almost as he had then, certain he was about to die. He had been beginning to fear that he was falling back into the old way of thinking and feeling about death, but for some reason he did not know, confronted with his beloved feeling the old way about death, suddenly there was no trace of the old way in him!

"We are all going to die, Silmavalien," he said. "One way or another, at one time or another time, we are all going to die. I don't see that it matters in the way you are making it matter."

He could see the fury on her face as he spoke. He was *happy* she loved him this way, and the look on her face, as if she wanted to kick some sense into him, was almost endearing, as was the way she moved as she yelled, "Yes, it does matter!"

"Not to me. Not like that," he replied.

"Well, I love you! You're stupid, too. What if when you really are dy-dy-dying, b-b-being b-b-burned, you don't think or feel that way!"

"That's irrelevant," said Noren. Before the words had finished coming out of his mouth, he corrected himself. "I don't mean the fact you love me. I mean the stuff about what I feel. That kind of thing is just plain nonsense. It's stupid."

Silmavalien stamped her foot on the snow. Then she put her hands over her face and cried.

"Look here," said Noren, desperate to explain to her whatever he could. "I don't want you to feel this way, and I can't show you. But I'm going to die. Okay? It doesn't matter what it's like. If the song doesn't tell you why it doesn't matter what it's like, if it's not obvious to you, I don't see how I can, either. Death is death. But does that tell you anything? No –"

Silmavalien interrupted him again, shouting, "But what if this was the other way around! What if it was me we're talking about, not you." The pain in her voice was obvious, as if she felt like he was being purposefully cruel.

"Well, then it might as well be," said Noren softly, trying to correct things. He stared at his hands clenching and unclenching the material of his pants almost as if they had a will of their own, as he spoke. "If that song says anything about how one person is going to be burned alive, it might as well say it about how another person is going to be burned alive, or even about how all persons are going to be burned alive. I agree with you that it's horrible, too. But that's not what matters. Not to us."

"Seriously?" asked Silmavalien. "Seriously? If it was you considering me, not me considering you?" He had got her attention, and she was talking now, not feeling like he was trying to be hurtful.

"I don't know if I *should* be considering you," he said. "It would be really stupid to do so. Certainly, if someone were going to kill you, I'd do everything to protect you. I'd die for you. A thousand times over if need be. Gladly. So, I don't want you to be worried about that. I love you, too. But I think what you're doing right now is really stupid. It's not happening. What should I feel if it were happening – to you? I don't know. It's not happening. I didn't know beforehand how I should feel waiting to die! Besides, how I feel is just not the point. I don't think that how you feel is the point either, not to hurt your feelings or suggest I don't care about you. But that's one of the things I learned. Real is real. That's what matters. Stop asking yourself what do you feel, and look for what is real, what is the thing."

Noren paused for a moment and looked up. Silmavalien was too upset to say anything, and he continued, hoping he could somehow say this in a way that she'd understand. "I don't think you *can* feel right, until you stop making what you feel the important thing. You'll just be feeling about your feelings, not feeling about reality, and since the feelings about which you are feeling aren't even feelings about reality, you'll be feeling about nothing, or even a lie."

S

Airrock touched her mind, trying to show her, and Silmavalien half-snapped, even though she knew the dragon was only trying to be kind. *I know you think I'm being stupid, but I don't see what you see. I know you think the same as Elninya about fire, Airrock. I don't!*

She could not think of anything to say to Noren. Words all died on her tongue, if they did not die in her mind first.

"Look," said Noren, "I don't want you to be angry at me, and I'm not angry at you, but if I know anything, then this is it. A long time ago Hazalel, an Ellen, told me that if I wouldn't face reality, who I was, what I was, what was real, and if I wouldn't meet the Lord of the Light, disaster would befall me.

"Well, disaster did befall me. I can't say I liked it or am glad of it. Yet I am. It wasn't an arbitrary punishment. One disaster or another had to befall me, until I learned to see reality. If I don't face reality, I will perceive it as disaster. So I'm glad the disaster befell me which made me surrender to reality. It's the best thing that ever happened to me.

"What if dying turns out to be an even better thing than thinking I am going to die? Even the torture, Silmavalien – if sitting in a dungeon could make me see something, make me start to change out of a bad thing, or view of things, into a better one, could free me from a slavery worse and more complete than chains, why not that?"

"It's just wrong. Horrible. Evil," said Silmavalien. It was unendurable to listen to him, sitting there, talking like *this*. Sternly she warned Onyxalis. *Do not speak to me about revenge. It is beside the point. DO NOT.*

"*Seriously,*" said Elninya, "*remember the song about the freer, wider, more beautiful world of Love? Remember how the song that started this whole thing is all about release, freedom? Remember whatever that was about Malchoris and a gate or path into the heart of Love? This all makes sense. It all goes together. Remember what I told you about hatching?*"

It's horrible! It's disgusting. HORRIBLE! responded Silmavalien.

12

Changed

Noren sat, shoulders slumped, even his hands still. He did not want to make Silmavalien angry or sad, but he was completely failing to express what he saw, and he wanted to comfort. But he had no idea how. At the same time, he was unhappy, in a way her unhappiness could not taint, however much he wanted to do something it. *I'm sorry about this,* he told Elninya. *But I'm so glad we're together. Isn't it so wonderful we're together, seeing the same beauty, the same world, flying together?*

It *did* feel like soaring.

When I said it was the best thing that ever happened to me, I didn't mean you weren't, aren't, the best thing that ever happened to me.

Elninya knew that.

I can't blame her for not seeing. I understand. And she is right, as far as she goes. I didn't see for so long. How can she even see yet? But I do wish she could!

After a few minutes, he rose and approached Keya. "I'm sorry we do this," he said. "Do you understand what's going on?"

Keya examined him for a few moments. "Plainly, I don't understand all of it. I won't judge what you've said, either. As far as I can understand it, it makes sense to me."

"The understanding is nonsense, the being is what matters? Something like that?" asked Noren. "At least, Elninya told me something like that. I can't say it exactly."

"Probably," said Keya. Then she asked him, "So you really know the Lord of the Light?"

"I'm not sure I know what *that* means," said Noren. "I wish this didn't upset Silmavalien so much," he continued, "but then again, Elninya used to upset me like this."

How would Silmavalien react to knowing what he had done?

"Keya, will you promise not to tell Silmavalien what I want to tell you?" he asked.

"I can't say I promise. I don't know what it is yet," said Keya.

"What if I tell you it's something in my past, and I promise you that if I ask her to marry me, I will tell her first?" said Noren.

"Then I can say I'm almost certain I won't have to tell her. I can't see any reason why I would, but it's so hard to be certain about these things, since I don't know ahead of time what you're going to tell me."

"All right. If you feel she must know right away, will you tell me, so I can choose if I want to tell her, or to let you tell her?"

"Yes," said Keya. "I'm pretty sure I can do that."

Elninya and Tanz took them a short distance away, so that it was less likely Silmavalien's dragons would hear what he was going to say. Then he told Keya about how he had come back to Elninya one early morning to find a human in the thicket, and of how in his fear he had shot her before realizing she was just a girl out looking for eggs, and of his shame and anger at what he had done.

Keya nodded, listening. "Why are you telling me this?" she asked.

"Doesn't Tanz feel enough?" asked Noren.

"I want to hear you tell me. Tanz only gets some of it."

"All right. I *can't* tell Silmavalien. And I can't even think about marrying her until I tell her. Even if I knew how she would react, I couldn't tell her. But I don't know how she will react. Tonight reminded me of that. What do you think about how she'll react or what I should do?" explained Noren.

For a long time Keya said nothing, and Noren sat still and quiet.

Finally she spoke slowly. "I don't know why you ask me how she will react. You know better than I what she knew of you and what your relationship was like before … all this happened. You know better than I, probably, what your relationship is now. That affects this so much.

"As for what you should do? That depends very much on what you want. If you want to marry her, I definitely think you should tell her yourself. If you don't want to marry her … well, what you do is really up to you. Either way, really, what you two do is up to you and her … and, I guess, the dragons bonded to you. It's not my business, really, either way, whatever the two of you decide to do about your relationship."

"Do you have any idea how she will respond?" asked Noren.

Keya was silent for a long time. Then she said, "I'm kind of uncomfortable responding to this. It is such a big thing. Even if I knew exactly how Silmavalien would respond, I'm sure I couldn't tell you. What can I say?" She threw up her hands, then continued, "I think she will continue to love you. You've changed, right?"

"I determined never to do anything like that again as soon as it happened," said Noren miserably, "but the potential to do it remained in me. I don't know if I *could* do such a thing now, or not. I pray I won't.

I've asked the Lord of All Light to make sure of that. In my imprisonment, my view of life and death changed, so I've cast off not only the deed, but the view of life and death which made it … not appealing, I guess, but which made it … which made protecting my life no matter the cost necessary." *Is that something of what Silmavalien means by loving each and every creature, no matter if it's you or someone close to you? Isn't that what you've been trying to tell me all along, Elninya? It seems so absurd! Not this, though sure enough when I had that other view of life this would have seemed absurd, though I don't think it could ever have seemed as absurd as the idea of only oneself and the few one knows being important seems now. Even then I understood from you the idea of all mattering and mourned killing of any sort, even thieves, since they too were persons who had lives!*

"It … seems ridiculous, absurd, I know," he said to Keya.

"That's hardly what I was thinking," said Keya. She raised her head and looked him straight in the eyes with her interesting blue ones. "What I was thinking was: you could tell her that, too. Really, this is up to you. How will she respond? I believe she will still love you, and I don't mean just as another creature, another person. Will something change between you? Of course it will! Things are always changing between all of us. It would be absurd for you to try and go back to have the relationship you had when you were, what, sixteen or something, and she was thirteen or so, before you were Dragonriders, or met Love as you have now. Things will keep on changing between you all your lives, if you live your lives together."

"She did not understand what I was saying this evening. Will she understand my change?"

"Some of it, I think she will," said Keya. She got to her feet. "But who am I to know everything Silmavalien will or won't understand? I don't even know everything Tanz will or won't understand!"

"Silmavalien is a human," said Noren with a smile. "Tanz is a dragon."

"So, though being bonded to Tanz, I know her in ways I know no other, there still might be ways I know Silmavalien better? Yes, but that's beside the point," said Keya. "I've said all there is to say. Besides, Silmavalien has gone through major changes, too. I think she understands things you don't, too." She threw up her hands again. "We all understand things none of the others do! I think we all know that, too. But I've nothing more to say. I'm going back."

S

Silmavalien was still awake, sitting close to the dying fire when Tanz landed, and Keya slid off Tanz's. From the way she walked towards her, Silmavalien sensed Keya had something to say. "What is it?" she asked.

"You know you don't know everything and there's a lot you don't yet see, and you should try to remember that, act like it, and think like it," said Keya.

"I know that," said Silmavalien smiling wanly. "Dragons have been talking to me."

Keya smiled a little in return. She sat down near to Silmavalien.

"I and Noren act so weird," said Silmavalien. She felt prompted to say it by something coming from Keya.

"You do," agreed Keya. "Sometimes, you talk as if you think you're husband and wife. You were doing that earlier. The way you were yelling about how you loved each other, and then he said, 'So you don't need to worry about that' and that he'd die for you. Yet you don't act like married people either. Both of you seem to half-think and half-feel that you're married to each other, and the other half-think and half-feel that you aren't. Actually, I don't know if you feel like you aren't married, but you don't look to me like either of you fully feels you are married."

"Well," said Silmavalien, "we were literally about to be married, and we still love each other."

"Then …" said Keya.

"But we've changed so much and so much has happened. Were we ever meant to be married? Were we ever right to be married? Are we now? We – I mean, look at this thing that just happened."

"I think you're both tense because you feel like you're married, but you aren't, so your relationship is crazy," said Keya. "As for all the things you don't see in common – from all I've learned, it can hardly be less than what you didn't have in common, what, six years ago? You both need to learn from what the other knows."

"Yes," said Silmavalien, "I think the same things. But there are obstacles. I think it might still be a problem that I broke trust and ran away from him. If we're to be married, we have to really trust each other. And I don't know anything about marriage. I don't know if Noren does either. And so much has changed, I don't even know if either of us knows the other one anymore."

"I don't have anything to say," said Keya.

13

The Voice

Silmavalien was so distressed and so afraid that Noren was destined to be burned alive that she could not sleep and did not want to. After Keya left and – presumably – went to sleep under Tanz's wing - she spent the whole night laying in the snow begging the Lord of the Light to neither make nor let Noren suffer such a death, such a horror. She told him she would do anything he required for this. The very thought of Noren dying that death was almost an impossibility to her mind and heart, and it made her feel sick and faint and horrible.

At one point, she thought of something, and added to her plea, "Anything, O Lord of All Light, only don't make something horrible happen to someone else instead of to Noren, even if it isn't a someone else who belongs to me. Please, just don't make or let anything horrible happen at all!"

She remembered at once both what Noren had said about the best thing that happened to him and also her request to Love to make her good, not simply to make her circumstances such that she would not do evil, but to make herself the kind of person who could not do evil. What if – o horrible, horrible thought! – she was right now engaged in asking for Noren to *not* have the best, to not be fully loved, to be kept an imperfect creature, the kind of person who could be bad?

The thought did not make her feel better at all. Silmavalien could not want anyone to remain bad or possibly bad. However it was an unthinkably horrible idea that horrible things might be required to make someone good! She begged the Lord of the Light to make it so that people could be made good without having to go through horrible things. If he could. Because maybe that was not possible.

She remembered when the Lord of the Light had told her that things horrified her because she did not see the Meaning and that she had to go through the surface, and that he was and would help her to do so. She remembered, too, one sunset when it had looked as if the sky would fall and its fall be, not the end, but the beginning of the world. That thought seemed so much like what Elninya said about hatching and death.

But it did not satisfy her. The thought, *But if only good comes from it in the end, is it really so horrible?* arose in her mind.

"How else would you have me turn evil into good? How *would* you have me mend all the wrong in the world?" the Voice asked her.

To that Silmavalien had no answer. *I would have evil have never been, never be,* she thought.

"You do not yet know what things are. You have asked me before to keep you from deceiving yourself and to help you to see. Stop thinking you know what you do not know, and judging it as if the surface as you see it is all there is. Do you *want* to see the Meaning, the reality, or not, Silmavalien?"

ℵ

Noren still sat on the stump where he had talked to Keya. The stars burned bright and cold far above him in the black sky. A bitterly cold wind swept down from the peaks and chilled his face and hands. His fingers and feet burned with a cold pain that somehow seemed like the stars above.

What if Silmavalien is right? he wondered. *After all, I have not known. I have only hoped. I have only learned that I did not know what seemed. I have never really experienced this thing for which I hope. I have only experienced the hope of it. I have neither experienced the world beyond death nor died. What if this hope isn't?*

There was no concern in his mind that Silmavalien *knew* the way she talked and felt about death was the right way. But in this moment, he could not shake the fear that maybe he was not as certain as he would like to be, either. Did he really know a truth which contradicted it, or did he only imagine himself to know?

Noren felt Elninya watching him and his thoughts carefully, but she did not tell him anything. It was not the time. She could not have thought anything that would help him here. But he did not sense that she was disturbed.

His mind continued to spin in circles and find nothing solid upon which to rest. He could not imagine that the hope that had come to him was based on nothing real. He could not un-think the change in his thinking. When he really considered it, he knew that he could not throw away the things he had tried to tell Silmavalien. At the same time, he could not know that he knew them. He did not know. He only hoped. How could he know?

How can *I know? How can I know anything?*

Out of the black and the white, the blackness of the sky above, the whiteness of the stars shining in it, the blackness of the deep shadows, the whiteness of the snow in the starlight, out of the empty space that seemed to have no borders, infinite and cold, he heard a Voice speak.

"You can know me, Noren."

Who are you? How can I know you?

"I am the Lord of the Light – and of the Dark. (Light has the power of the Dark and over Dark; Dark has no power of or over Light.) I am Love. I will teach you what is life and what is death. I will be to you the Meaning of life and of death," replied the Voice.

"How can I know you, though?" asked Noren. Somehow it felt more respectful to speak out loud. "I don't mean to be rude or disrespectful. There's nothing I mean less. But I don't see how I can really know anything. Even the stars overhead. How do I *know* there is something there, and it is not my imagination? How do I know *anything?* I mean that literally. I can think there's something, or that something is. I can bet on it. But how do I *know?*"

"You can keep on thinking about yourself and about whether you know or not and what you know. You can keep on worrying about whether you know that you know and trying to come up with a way to prove knowledge to yourself. But there is no real knowledge if you go that way – it is a dead end of thinking you know nothing. Or you can surrender to reality. You can stop thinking about whether or not *you know,* and instead you can begin to know. You can stop thinking about yourself altogether. Do you want to know me?" asked the Voice.

"Do you want goodness? You have asked me to make sure you do not fall back into your old way of thinking that made you evil. Do you still want that?"

Noren stood. He could stay seated no longer. "Yes, I want that. Please."

"Then know me. Be willing to know me. I will show you goodness and will make you good. It is what I have been doing since you were born," the Voice assured him.

"What you know matters like what you feel matters. If you think about whether you know something and try to know about your own knowledge you will end by knowing nothing, or an illusion, much like you told Silmavalien about feeling."

That makes sense, thought Noren. Out loud he said, "Thank you." A moment later, he added, "And thank you for hearing me. Thank you for having listened to my plea."

Though he did not hear the Voice again, he knew that he was heard.

"What do you want now?" Elninya asked him. He felt from her a quiet relief and a thought he could not quite get.

Why don't we go back to our camp and sleep there? I wouldn't mind sleeping out here, just with you, though.

Well then, why not sleep out here, if he'd like it?

We're probably more vulnerable to the nightmare monsters if we're separated or by ourselves, responded Noren.

"They're here!" said Elninya. Simultaneously he noticed the presence of fear and hatred and realized he had felt it for a few moments.

How many? Noren asked. Already he knew the answer. Five orcs and a fire imp.

They'll follow us to the camp and tell the whole big army where we are if we don't kill them, won't they? he asked Elninya, striding through the snow to where she lay.

"Maybe."

Noren stopped to string his bow.

"Get on my back!"

Through Elninya, Noren felt the presence of one of them several feet behind him. His bow in his hand, he ran to her and was barely seated on her shoulders – he had taken no saddle out with him – when she jumped into the air. He had never felt her take off quite like that before.

It must be horrible for her to feel them, all that evil, the way she does, he thought.

He realized that one of her paws had been scratched by the orc's blade. At the same moment she responded to his thought. It really was not like that. She did not feel them like *that.*

He gripped her back between his legs as tightly as he could, while grabbing an arrow from his quiver and bringing his bow to bear on the orc who had been about to kill him and had just scratched his dragon.

His arrow went through the orc's shoulder.

"Great. He won't be able to shoot me," thought Elninya. *"Hold tight!"*

She swerved to avoid another arrow and a ball of flame from the imp. Noren barely held onto his bow while clinging to her.

He did not think his arrow would do much good against the fire-imp.

Elninya did not think so either. Did he remember how his sword had had no impact?

Exhilaration swept through both of them together. They were actually fighting the nightmare now! He *could* fight evil.

Noren hated the Lord of the Light! He had just spoken to him, and now he was letting him and his dragon be attacked by the nightmares and they did not know how to protect themselves.

"*NO!*" Noren screamed out loud. *Help me!*

"*Just ride me. Yes, I have to fight it too,*" Elninya told him.

Almost before he could prepare himself, she dove. Another ball of fire singed her wing. Yellow flame made a halo around her head and neck. Noren felt the warmth of it. Burning cold was replaced with burning heat.

Why? WHY?! Noren complained. Even as he asked the question, he felt like he could not resist the waves of evil. Interwoven through his thoughts were bitterness and other things he recognized as evil but could not fully identify in the moment. He felt infested by them.

His stomach lurched. Elninya was climbing again. The presence and strength of the evil was diminished.

Elninya's emotions soared as her wings bore her up. Her fire was great! She had not known that, and the Lord of the Light be praised for it, but when the fire of the enemy went into her fire, her fire rendered it harmless and consumed it.

Noren barely hung on as she banked hard, her body going almost side-ways, pulling her wing in, to avoid an orc arrow. He would not have been able to stay on if she had not been his dragon, if he could not feel every motion of her own body and mind almost like he felt his own.

She was going to dive again. She was sure that an orc arrow would not be a problem if only she could touch it with her blaze before it got to her. It would, quite naturally, burn up in her fire. Even if some charred remnants reached her, they would not do more than a small amount of burn damage.

14

The High Pass

When Elninya landed, she flinched and limped. Noren jumped off of her to examine the scratch in her paw. It was not deep, but he could see how it would be very painful on her footpad.

Perhaps the oil will help it, he thought, *and it won't take that much.*

Noren took a small amount of oil and carefully poured it into the wound. Then he lay down next to her warm side and she put her wing over him. Lying next to her and benefiting from the warmth of her body Noren felt as comfortable as ever.

The next day they made the highest point of the pass. It was painful for Elninya. She would have been comfortable flying and only walking a little, but she had to walk for hours and hours. To her dragon's body, it was cold enough to hurt but not cold enough to numb.

At first, Noren did not feel the thinness of the air enough for it to prevent him from seeing and admiring the view a great deal. A deep valley was cut between two peaks which rose high and white above them. The height was tremendous and appeared at once precarious and as unmovable as the world. It felt surreal. However he soon grew weary of it, perhaps because he was the thinness of the air was affecting him.

Finally, the mountains dropped away below them in the Steep Descent he had heard about. The dragons spread their wings and took off, generating just enough thrust to get them off the steep, nearly-cliff like mountainside.

Noren gasped when the ground first dropped away under him and Elninya. Even Silmavalien and Keya's descriptions had not prepared him for the reality. The mountains were really like a huge wall or rampart, webbed with cracks out of which grew trees! Awe filled him, and when he looked upwards, the highest peaks seemed to reach as high above them as they were high above the clouds, sheerer and sheerer the higher they rose and covered in mantles and avalanches of snow, dazzling white in the light of the sun, blue in the shadow.

This world really was *made by Love!* Noren thought.

If Elninya had not been so tired, Noren would have asked her to hover there, so he could admire the beauty and the grandeur. Instead, they glided down wearily to a lower level and circled to land.

How could there be a world bigger than this one? Noren wondered.

S

That night, Silmavalien finally fell asleep for an hour or so, just as the dawn began to grow in the eastern sky – which was scarcely visible from the high valley in which they rested.

She woke, looking on Minth, her thoughts a mixed-up jumble.

What was best for one must be best for all! Love ruled. Love was stronger than anything and victorious over everything. There could be no way, could there, that in order for one to have the best another must not have the best, that what was good for one was bad for another?

For a moment, in horror and terror, she had thought that was how the world was! Then she had realized it could not be. That would be a defeat for Love – for Love must *love* all and each. If that were so, then Love could not have the final victory, could not have Love's will, *could not be Love even!* So it must not be that way.

The idea of Noren dying and the idea of Minth dying had gotten mixed up in her head. She was re-living her ancient terror of being discovered with Minth and both of them being burned together. Silmavalien felt as if her heart would stop beating for the horror. She was rather sure it *did* skip a beat. At least it felt like it had stopped for a moment or two.

For a moment, she had been about to ask – perhaps she even had asked – *But what if it's not best for me? Whatever happens must be good for me, too! And that is not a good for me. That is an evil for me.*

Instantly she realized the absurdity of that thought. It was absurd on so many levels. If suffering such a horror, such a torture, such a death turned out to be a good for Noren, then any basis on which she might argue it an evil for herself was proved invalid.

Even thinking about this made her feel like vomiting, made her feel like passing out, yet she had to continue with it.

What was good for Noren – or anyone else for that matter – must be good for Silmavalien. She wanted his good and the good of everyone else too.

She remembered how she had asked to be made good. What if things like this were part of that process of being made good, being made incapable of bad? She saw, now, how that could make sense! She also recalled her struggle to surrender to the Lord of All Light, her fear that surrender to goodness – to Love – might bring a horror or suffering or something she was not, at that moment, willing to endure.

What if – what if Noren was right?

What if *he* might have to suffer because of her failure? Elninya had suffered because of his!

But Love was more powerful than anything else. Love was victorious. If that were so then, however inconceivable it might be, that suffering was a good to Elninya, would be a good to Noren?

Had not Minth already suffered because of the evil in her? It was she who had made him afraid, who had terrorized him with her fear. He might have fed her fear, but he knew nothing and could not help it. She had started it. Who knew, horrible thought, but maybe she had contributed to helping him be less good than he might have been, making him bad!

But, oh, it was such an inconceivable thought that all this evil, all this horror, these abominations could be good for each one and everyone. It must be so, for Love ruled, but that did not make it more comprehensible, more believable. It sounded like pure absurd nonsense.

Then she heard Elninya explaining to the dragons what had happened in the night, and all these thoughts dropped right out of her mind. "What?" she gasped.

"*Yes. What.*" It was Onyxalis' voice. "*I am the Obsidian Guardian. I have come to protect you and fight with you. What were you doing not waking me? I would have come and helped you.*"

Silmavalien did not hear Noren's response, but she heard Elninya express something to the effect that she did not know that Onyxalis was ready to fight yet and, at any rate, he could not have come fast enough to do them any good, so there would have been no reason to wake him anyways.

"*I was born to fight them. I may not have the powers I will have when I am fully prepared, but I have power enough to match orcs and imps. You are fools, you humans,*" said Onyxalis. "*You do not know how to recognize a thing or know what a creature is.*"

"Look," said Silmavalien, "I'm sorry I didn't know you were a good dragon and that I wanted to take your egg to the blacksmith to have it smashed, but that is hardly the same thing as this."

"*They go together,*" said Onyxalis, but Silmavalien was laughing at the absurdity of her mistake. The blacksmith?! That part was just funny. The rest might be too horrible, and too close to having happened to be funny, but the *blacksmith?!* What sort of an idea was that?

"We need to get over the pass," said Keya. "You guys don't need to quarrel right now. The sooner we start the better. It's rough, in case you Onyxalis don't know, though then again maybe it's not so rough for you, since you're so different. But it'll be an ordeal for the rest of us."

Thanks, thought Silmavalien.

As it turned out, the high pass was not as difficult as it had been in the winter. The air was warmer. The snow was hardened and easier for the dragons to move through. However it was still freezing cold, and the air was so thin that breathing was difficult even for the dragons and there was a tightness and pain in everyone's lungs. Except for Onyxalis, as Keya had nearly predicted. If he was affected by the rarity of the air, he was either less affected than everyone else or so much stronger that the effects he suffered did not matter for what they were doing.

15

The Shadow Rises

Silmavalien woke suddenly in the middle of the night. Beside her, Noren sat up as if he had been wakened as suddenly as she had, but he looked as confused as she was in the moonlight.

"An earthquake is coming."

She could not ignore the urgency in Onyxalis's voice, and now she felt a barely perceptible shiver in the ground underneath her. She stood.

I'd love to saddle you this time, Dance.

The earth was shaking more violently before she finished getting the saddle on Dance. It made her feel really weird, especially when she stepped under Dance to fasten the straps.

"Fly!" Onyxalis' warning-command was very urgent now.

She responded without even thinking about it. In a moment, she was in Dance's saddle. Already, several of the dragons were in the air above and around her. Dance pushed off the shaking earth and unfurled her wings.

Something cracked, echoing across the mountains, and then boulders fell.

She reached out to Elninya and Tanz to make sure that they and their riders were all right. Then she spoke to Naklath. She knew nothing about earthquakes except that they were rare and huge and violent, and she wanted Veyan and Naklath and Keya's family to be fore-warned in case the earthquake affected them too.

Onyxalis flew ahead of them.

What now? she wondered, as the dragons rose in the air and flew away from the mountains. The sounds of breaking rocks, rocks being rent, and falling, and clashing, was nearly continuous now, and she knew from Onyxalis that a ripple passed through the earth, splitting more cliffs. Huge pieces of rock fell, so huge and massive and so quickly that the dragons flew faster – away from the mountains. She felt the dragons' awareness of the animals' terror. They had no idea what was happening or what to do or where was safe.

O Lord of Light, she thought, *can't you do something for them? Can't you help them not to kill themselves in their fear, running off a cliff or something like that? Can't you protect them?*

Why is there so much death? Why is there so much destruction? Why is there so much suffering and fear? But I thank you that we're alive and safe.

They flew for hours, away from the mountains, and the dragons slowed down and relaxed when they were far enough away they no longer fearing being crushed under a falling cliff or hit by large pieces of rock flung out from the shaking Deep Descent. Several hours later, they landed on the plains and everyone went back to sleep as soon as the Dragonriders had unsaddled the dragons and made themselves comfortable next to their friends. It was not yet morning.

Several times that night, Silmavalien woke to the feeling that the ground was shaking or lurching under her, as if some restless creature were moving underneath it. Sometimes it felt like she was falling. However, there was no warning from Onyxalis, and when he noticed her fear, he just told her to go back to sleep.

She woke again in the middle of the morning, and got up to help Noren and Keya prepare and cook the deer Airrock had brought back during the night. Meanwhile, those dragons who were hungry, among them Onyxalis, went hunting. It was then that Silmavalien first learned that dragons could be scavengers. They would settle on deer and other animals large enough to attract their attention who had fallen or jumped from the cliffs, or been crushed by the rocks or otherwise injured or killed in the earthquake.

Looking towards the mountains, Keya said, "There is something wrong."

"We all know there is something wrong," said Noren, "so what do you mean in particular?"

Keya pointed and said, "Look."

Silmavalien stopped what she was doing and looked first at Keya and then in the direction she was pointing.

Keya was right. A shadow out of huge cracks in the mountains. It undulated, flickering like fire that was dark instead of bright, and the earth looked dull and dead through it. Something about it made Silmavalien think of the Fire Shadow, though this was only something like it, and it was also so much better.

Be careful! The message to her dragons was almost a scream.

She did not need to worry about that. None of them were going over *there*.

She fought the rising panic inside of her. *O Lord of the Light, please protect us from it. Please protect us from anything that will not help us to love and help everyone else to love.*

N

Noren flinched when he found the shadow Keya pointed out. It reminded him of the imps who had bones of shadow. Could it see them? Would it throw an absolutely *huge* fireball at them? If it did, how would they survive? There was no way the dragons would be able to breathe enough fire to block it. *What was it?*

"We *need* to get to Ellen Island as fast as possible," said Silmavalien.

The near-panic in her voice irritated him, like a thousand bugs crawling over every inch of his skin, and Noren struggled to keep his level as he replied. "We have to be able to eat, and the dragons have to eat, too. We're going as fast as we can, and we won't get there at all if we fall out of the sky and starve in the ocean."

Light, please don't let the Shadow control me!

"I know that," said Silmavalien, and now she sounded depressed.

Noren ground his teeth together. Why couldn't he *help?* Why couldn't he protect and love her the way he wanted to?

"Our love is imperfect," said Elninya, responding to his thoughts or to something of which his thoughts reminded her. *"There are ways you cannot help because you yourself are irritated. And there are ways in which you feel in a manner very much like the way she felt when you were talking about death in the snow."* He felt her shrink away from him and then respond to a movement in his mind of which he had been scarcely aware, confessing that she had been irritated at him and responded to him in ways that were less than perfectly loving.

He did not want to continue the conversation.

"We're going to fly tonight," said Silmavalien. "I don't want to stay here a minute longer than we need to. Such a thing can't be good."

Once again, he felt himself extremely, disproportionately irritated, even to the point of anger, at something about the way Silmavalien spoke. Several thoughts competed in his mind. *Is the Shadow in me, too? Do the nightmares have power over me because they are in me – because I am part nightmare?*

It is a good thing all this has happened and we did not get married back then. I think I would be flipping out, and trying to flame like an imp, if I hadn't come through all that. At least, I wouldn't be able to keep myself from flipping for long. Would I even be aware of it and that it isn't right, or would I be certain I was in the right and not even notice?

Don't let the nightmare get into me. Deliver me from the shadow inside me. You told me that you are Light and that you have the power of both Light and Darkness, so free me from the darkness. Make me all light.

To Silmavalien he said, trying to speak in as neutral a tone as he could, "That sounds fine."

S

Silmavalien felt the conflict and antagonism in Noren, and tried to keep her attention on slicing the slabs of meat. But what was wrong Noren? She found herself repeating, *I'm not married to him, so I shouldn't care. I'm not married to him. I'm NOT married to him. I'm not married to him! So. I. Shouldn't. Care.*

I don't want to feel this way. I don't want to feel upset. What do you think, Minth?

She was silly. He liked her. That was what Minth thought.

Silmavalien laid her knife and walked away for a drink. While she was opening the water-skin she looked up and saw, hovering right above eye-level, a tiny and beautiful bird. She had seen the creatures before, but in a moment like this, the beauty struck her as if fresh-born from the fountain of life. The creature's wings beat so quickly they made a blur, and her shining emerald feathers, very dark on the top of her head and back and lighter down her sides, were their own world of beauty. She looked like a winged and living jewel, stupendously beautiful.

The tiny hummingbird hovered there, looking at Silmavalien for a few moments, and then zoomed away. Silmavalien watched her and just saw her tiny, dainty body alight on the branch of a tree.

She found herself thanking the Lord of Light. *Love, you are so beautiful. You make, or keep, or take care of, or whatever, such beautiful creatures. I don't know why you let them and us suffer and die, and have to kill each other for food or to defend ourselves, but I'm sure you will take care of all of us all the way to the end in the best way possible. The best way imaginable, right? For what's best is possible, for Love is strongest, Love is victory.*

To her joy and peace, Jareth agreed with her. Yes. Love was victory.

Throughout the day, the ground continued to shake and undulate. Whenever it began to do this Keya, Noren, and Silmavalien would put down any dangerous tools with which they were working and step away from the flames.

Soon all the dragons came back, having eaten their fill. Silmavalien was relieved that Onyxalis did not want to try to fight the Shadow. She did not know why, and she did not ask him, fearing that if she did he might think about it and decide that he did want to fight the Shadow.

Looking at him, she was again amazed by the speed at which he was even still growing. How long would it take for *him* to be full-grown? How big would he get? When would he breathe fire?

As the day passed into evening, the shadow grew. Another shadow formed above it and spread out, falling down in something like dark rain. Silmavalien did not understand what was happening, but it horrified her. None of the dragons understood what was happening either, and neither did Noren or Keya when she asked them.

Then Onyxalis spoke to them all. *"It is the Enemy making ready for war. He has long waited for this day and now he is preparing to spread desolation over the whole land, destroying those whom he has long been working to ensnare and anyone who else who happens to be in the way."*

Silmavalien shuddered. *Lord of Light, be merciful. You must be better than the gods of the stories. Love cannot abandon anyone to destruction, right? So I am confident that you will not abandon anyone to evil and hatred.*

She wished she could have the comfort of the presence of the Ellenari, but she tried not to complain, even in her own thoughts, about it. Never mind the fact she could not complain only to herself or in her own thoughts. Her dragons would hear and know. She told herself that the Ellenari must be doing all they could to protect them. How else, with such a horrible Shadow looming over them, had nothing happened to or around them yet?

As soon as they were done cooking the food, they really *must* go. She wished an Ellen would come to them and tell them the fastest and best way to Ellen Island. The beginning of the way she knew was far east of where they were. Was there a more direct way, or at least a way which was not longer but would take them farther away from the Shadow more quickly?

She asked the Lord of the Light to send them guidance.

16

Ring of Flame

As night fell, Silmavalien noticed that her ring was glowing. It glowed brighter and brighter until it surrounded them in a pure light. When they flew, all fifteen dragons were in light at least as bright as the daylight though it was not strong enough to illuminate the ground over which they flew.

Throughout the night now and then a huge hunk of rock would come hurtling down on them from the mountains, even as far away as they, making them dodge it. Other times it would be a ball of flame or other things more sinister. Once a flock of arrows descended on them. The arrows had slowed in their flight and, though they were not easy to avoid, no one was seriously injured. Many of the dragons dealt with it by burning the arrows. Dance caught one in her talon. Onyxalis took several on his scales.

After that, they tried too fly still farther north, away from the mountains, and it seemed after a while that it might have worked, even though they could not imagine how they were not already far enough away.

During the night the dragons learned that one of the eggs Silmavalien had left with Keya's family had hatched to Nereis, the youngest boy. The dragon's name was Tryph, and he was an albino dragon with scales.

Then the light came, and they saw more of the effects of the earthquake. The hills between the Steep Descent and the plains of Arosië had shifted and torn. Rock spurs of the mountains had been broken. One piece had slid past another and then continued. Streams were jagged. Hills were split or had crumbled and one could see layers of earth long hidden now exposed. Fallen and broken trees were everywhere.

What a strange, strange thing, thought Silmavalien.

The weaker dragons were quite tired and they were looking for a good place to spend the day when they sighted a stone giant stomping along the land. The demon and its stride explained the broken trees and some of the crumbling of the ground. Then they watched it stoop down and tear a large boulder of the ground, which it hurled at them with amazing strength.

The dragons swerved and flew higher.

Then they tried to think about their problem. Airrock might think she could fly forever, but Minth and most of the others definitely could not. They did not know if there would be any demons to threaten them in the sea, but they could not make it to the sea without stopping to rest anyways. Even if they could, there were demons that could fly over the sea.

Silmavalien realized that Keya's family and Veyan were threatened, too, and she wondered why she had not thought of that sooner. How had she been so stupid and so occupied with their own problems.

She reached out to Tryph and Naklath. *"There are demons on the plains. At least, we've seen a stone giant that could break a huge boulder off the rock under the dirt and throw it high into the sky at us. I've no idea what you or your riders and their family can or should do."*

Naklath understood her fairly well. She knew Tryph was confused and scared. The earth shakings had been confusing and scary enough. The earth was still moving around.

Does that mean more evil is being let out or coming out, or whatever it is, or does it have nothing to do with it at all? thought Silmavalien. *I know so little. I don't even know if any of the earthquakes had anything to do with the Shadow and all these demons. It might be totally unconnected. Or it might be the earth fighting against them.*

Onyxalis responded, including all the dragons and Keya, as well as Noren. *"The earthquake and the rising of the Shadow and emergence of so many demons are related,"* he said.

She did not let him hear what she thought next. *How much* does *he know? I know he knows a lot, but I don't know if he never imagines he knows things he doesn't really know.*

"As for rest," Onyxalis continued, *"you can find a place to land and some of the dragons can scout the land. If they see anything they will tell you and you can all fly away. I know it will not be what you would like best, but it might do."*

ℵ

Noren growled to himself as Onyxalis spoke. The obsidian dragon acted as if the idea were entirely his, and maybe it was. Maybe Onyxalis had thought of it before he had. Maybe Onyxalis *would* have thought of it if he had not. Nonetheless, Noren *had* thought of the idea, and he did not like Onyxalis making Silmavalien think that he had not thought of it. It was just harder for Noren to speak to Silmavalien! Even Elninya was quite tired, and he did not want to tire her further relaying messages.

So he held his tongue, until they landed, and then when he was fairly certain that Onyxalis had fallen asleep, he told Silmavalien.

She looked at him and said, "It's the kind of idea I thought you could have come up with."

S

It was only a few hours later that Veine reported that she saw one of the nightmares heading in their direction. The tired dragons – and Dragonriders – woke and they continued on their way, flying higher than they usually preferred so they would be out of range of the stone giants.

After flying for a while, they settled down to try to catch a few more hours of sleep, and then when evening fell and Silmavalien's ring started glowing again, they took to the air. Minth was terribly tired, and he was also getting hungry. He flew almost in a daze, and Silmavalien felt sorry for him.

Why did things have to be this reason? Why did there have to be so much evil, and why did it have to be so strong?

Even though she knew there had to be a good reason, and even though she was fully convinced, and even at peace, in her knowledge that this reason would be entirely good once she understood it, the questions still hurt.

They flew through the night, and in the early morning they found themselves surrounded by winged demons, horrible and disgusting. Some of them seemed to be turning into stone, yet somehow they could still fly. Others were more nimble and dripped blood, and seemed a lot like ones Silmavalien had fought before. Looking out over them, she knew there were far too many for them to ever fly through or hope to defeat.

The dragons gathered themselves together so they would be able to protect each other with their fire, and Silmavalien felt a wave of cold and dry despair.

This was the end. They were defeated. They would not be helped or rescued. Love was defeated. Apparently Love never had been. There never had been any Love. There had only ever been an illusion of Love. No, there had never even been that. All was nothing. There was no beginning. There was no end. Formless grief assailed Silmavalien and then she wondered, if none of those things had ever been, if Love not only was not victorious but did not even have a meaning, what there was to grieve?

The light gleaming golden off Lighter's scales recalled her. She felt a wave of heat as he drew himself together and then breathed out a blast of flame.

There must be Love. How had she ever doubted it, even for a moment? It was preposterous. It was senseless! Yet still the despair clutched at her with knife-like talons. All certainly seemed hopeless. How could they possibly be rescued? And if ever Love failed, then Love was not, for Love must be victorious!

Love was. Love was the meaning. It was all nonsense about Love not existing. Love was existence. Love was the necessary and only possible root, source, or meaning for existence. It was all absurd.

What Noren said and thought about death, or something like what Noren said and thought about death, *must* be true. She did not really know what it was Noren meant. He had never been clear. But something like that *must* be true. They were going to be horribly defeated. Love was victory. Somehow this *must* be the way to Love.

Around Silmavalien the light grew brighter, at least to her eyes. She became aware of Onyxalis trembling in the center of the dragons, furious that he was useless and could do nothing to fight the demons because he could not yet breathe out his fire, a fire to which none of the other dragons' fire would have been comparable. He was reacting with fury against despair. They were going to be defeated, himself with them. They were going to fail. He was going to fail. He could not protect the two Dragonriders who were his charge. He certainly could not avenge the dragons! The whole world must be evil.

His senseless rage almost choked her in the noxious fumes of demonic despair. What if Onyxalis was right and everything was evil?

What if everything was not?

Love! Silmavalien cried out.

"So you are the Avengers of the Dragons? You are the ones who are going to avenge the blood of the dragons on those who killed them before and would kill them again if they had the chance? You have come to invite me to join your ranks and lead you for I am the Avenger of the Dragons, without whom you can do nothing?"

Silmavalien heard Onyxalis and was horrified. She remembered at once her encounter the medusa who had invited her to try to be queen of the world. What if the same offer were now being made to Onyxalis and he was falling for it?

It was Aelaza who had saved her, then! What could be done now?

Once again horror tried to enter her. What if Onyxalis was right? What if –?

The thought of Aelaza's command to the medusa remained in Silmavalien's mind. A thought crystallized in her mind, even as she felt that she was falling and some of her dragons with her. Certainly it could do no harm. *If you don't want me to, tell me so, Lord of the Light! But what else can I do? If this is wrong, forgive me. Do what is good. Bring us all into Love.*

Silmavalien raised her hand with the ring glowing upon it like a band of white and unchanging flame.

She did not even have to speak. The intensity of the light grew so bright that she had to close her eyes and cover them with her other hand to make it endurable. Just before she closed her eyes, almost involuntarily against the flood of light, she saw flame everywhere, all around them, as white as the band of harmless flame upon her finger!

The nightmares were bursting into flame as bright as day.

Thank you, Silmavalien thought. *Thank you, for Onyxalis.*

A few moments later, she was listening to Linol and Elninya sharing something they had got from Noren. Perhaps they would have peace enough to rest for a little while now? All the dragons – except for Onyxalis and Airrock, and maybe Dance and Tanz – felt like they were going to fall out of the sky. The last minutes had been so intense.

Though the light was now dim enough to be bearable, it was still very bright. They had to rest sometime. They descended directly to the plains and everyone fell asleep within minutes.

17

Fire and Stone

When the light of morning threw its delicious, cool, and gentle life-reviving grayness upon the plains, Coroneth and Lighter woke. They resumed their watch while the most weary of the dragons continued to sleep, until they had slept so much that they could no longer sleep for hunger. Then a few dragons remained with the Dragonriders, while the hungriest of them went hunting.

The dragons saw some nightmares, mostly of the kind of the stone giants, walking the plains, but none of them came closer to where they camped, and so they did not move. Keya's family apparently had no issues. They did not even notice anything besides the quaking of the earth, which still continued, though it was less often and less strong.

Airrock rose, rather hungry, from her sleep and went out to hunt. She quickly found her meal and devoured it, and then Linol who had just finished his joined her on their way back, then they saw a stone giant. She was about to ask if Linol was up to flying any faster, since she detested its presence, when she saw it had just thrown a fawn against the ground, killing it, and was stooping again to do the same to another.

Airrock did not think. She felt. Her memories and her feelings pulled Silmavalien into themselves, as she dove out of the sky, Linol behind her. Hot, hazy fire came from her maws and with it she bathed the head of the giant until its arms came up to grab her. She was fast and darted out of its way, and she and Linol breathed fire on its hands which it thrust out to grab her.

Silmavalien pulled herself part-way out of Airrock's feelings, so she was still aware of them but they did not flood her, while Tanz, Dance, and Songeth hastened to her aid.

Linol retreated and confirmed that the herd of deer were fleeing as fast as they could.

Airrock expressed jubilation that it looked like her fire was having an impact on the stone!

The demon stooped to tear open the ground for a missile to hurl at the flying dragons. Airrock recognized her opportunity. She swooped, breathed out her best and hottest flame, landing upon the stone head, and began gouging it with her claws. It certainly made an impression. Linol, following her direction, landed on the stone forehead and began to attempt the same operation.

One of the stone hands made for them and both dragons took to the air, breathing fire into the horrid fingers. When the giant made to throw the rock at them, they dived to gain enough speed to avoid it at such close range, then climbed rapidly.

So the battle against the stone giant went on. On their next attempt, Airrock and Linol mingled their fires in an attempt to better melt the rock of the giant's head so that they could do some real damage to it.

Silmavalien sat down and told Noren, narrating what the dragons did as they made their moves. She could see his pride in them, and then when she paused for breath, he told her his own Elninya wanted to go, but he had told her not to. Her presence would not make the others safer, and they could flee whenever they wished, but she was still too tired and hungry to fight well. She needed to recover.

Keya, too, seemed delighted. "Isn't this wonderful?!" she said. "We're actually fighting for the good!"

Eventually, Silmavalien stopped narrating it. The other dragons arrived, and it became a slow, drawn-out battle. It was soon clear that the head was not as important to the stone demon as it was to humans, dragons, animals, or even orcs, which meant that they had to destroy much more of the stone giant in order to vanquish it. But at last, as evening fell, the dragons had the victory. They returned, triumphant and weary, to rest while other dragons scouted.

Then they continued on their way towards the sea. The next day, they reached the beach in the early afternoon, and dropped down on the sand, completely exhausted except for Onyxalis.

Then Silmavalien saw Aelaza, standing upon the waves rolling into the shore and rising and falling with them. She smiled at them, and Silmavalien thought her smile was directed especially at her, as she said, "So I am able to lead you!" Then she turned to include everyone and said, "It is well for you that you rest here. You do not want to take on the sea tired. It will be long enough and weary enough for you if you are all well-rested. I must lead you by the fastest way we can go."

Then she stepped onto the sand and turned to Airrock. Silmavalien sensed a certain likeness between them, as the dragon approached the Ellena. Airrock dipped her head and touched Aelaza's forehead with her shining snout.

"Well done, dragon," said Aelaza, and Silmavalien had the sense that something private passed between them. "It is about to begin, and you have begun well. Do not presume that you are the mighty one. Even I am not mighty, Airrock, and against my natural might yours is as nothing. In this battle, my own might makes me no more secure than yours makes you."

Airrock nodded her head.

Onyxalis' voice rang out defiantly. *"But my might is, or at least will, be something to yours!"*

"That is beside the point, child," said Aelaza. "Did you not hear what I said to Airrock? *In this battle, my own might makes me no more secure than yours makes you.* Only in Shallim-Araldor can any of us stand firm against this enemy."

Onyxalis uttered a low growl and withdrew into himself.

"I will stay here and watch over you with Hazalel," said Aelaza, "so that you will rest comfortably." She turned to Keya. "You and Tanz should rest here also, but it would be well if you went to your family."

Silmavalien knew she would miss Keya. The following day, when they parted, the two embraced. "I don't want to leave you, either," said Keya, "but it is probably for the best that I go to my family. If there is trouble, they may need Tanz. Tryph is just a hatchling, and while Naklath is almost a year old, Tanz is much older and bigger and stronger. But I don't want to leave you. I love you."

"I love you, too," said Silmavalien.

𝓢

The journey over the sea was more of a stretch for the dragons than the return from Ellen Island had been. Silmavalien could tell that the Ellenari were in a very real hurry – or what would have been a hurry for her. She did not sense any hurrying from them. Yet they were evidently in haste to reach the volcanic island as soon as possible. They did not let the dragons hunt at all, and they provided food for Silmavalien and Noren, cooked when it was the kind of food that need cooking. They even helped to oil the dragons' skin.

Everyone was always exhausted, and the Dragonriders shared in the exhaustion of their dragons. Even Airrock did not feel like she had extra energy, though Minth felt much stronger than Silmavalien had expected, as well as several others of the weaker dragons, and she suspected the Ellenari were putting something helpful into the food they gave him. Maybe it was some of that oil!

Sometimes they flew in the wind and rain, though the Ellenari led them on whatever path was calmest or had the best winds for flying to Ellen Island. When they finally reached it, Silmavalien noticed the effect of recent volcanic activity right away. There were new bays and beaches of black rock and black sand. Scorched land was just beginning to sprout, and Here and there were active flows of lava.

But they were all so sore and tired that, except for maybe Onyxalis, they took little notice. The dragons glided into a beach where there were some old, tall trees near the ocean, trampled down the underbrush, and lay down.

18

The Sword and the Volcano

In the morning they were met by Aelaza and Hazalel. "Do you have the Dragon-sword?" Aelaza asked Silmavalien.

"No."

"Then come with me and we will get it."

S

About an hour later, Silmavalien and Noren walked up the side of the volcano. She carried the broken Dragon-sword in its magnificent sheath, while Aelaza and Hazalel lead them to a point higher on the volcano's mountain than the point to which Aelaza had previously brought her.

Standing on the peak was Oaeiae, and Silmavalien was certain she was larger than the last time she had seen her. Fire burned in her eyes and her own black sword was naked in her hand. "It has begun," she said. "The battle is about to be joined."

As Oaeiae spoke, a thrill like the energy of the volcano surging up in expectation to break through the earth went through all the dragons and the two Dragonriders. Aelaza and Hazalel continued up the mountain and stood on either side of the Ellena of the volcano.

Oaeiae turned to Silmavalien. "Cast the Dragon-sword into the volcano."

Fearfully, she mounted to the edge and dropped the Dragon-sword over it. Then she hastily stepped back.

"Don't be afraid," said Aelaza. "You are safe here."

Silmavalien nodded, still shaking. Onyxalis perched on the peak, trembling like a cat about to pounce on its prey. Beneath them the cauldron bubbled. Sprays of lava shot into the sky and fell back into the lake of lava. A few long minutes passed. Then Oaeiae turned to Onyxalis. "Dive into the lava and bring us the sword."

The black dragon had no hesitations. Wings folded, he sprang off the edge. As soon as he entered the lava, it began to move in earnest.

The earth moved and lurched, undulating. Silmavalien fell on the black volcanic rock and scraped one of her hands. "Don't fear," came the voices of the Ellenari again. "You are safe here. The lava will not come here."

The ground was still moving. Silmavalien sat up and said, "But what if we fall?"

"You won't," said Oaeiae. "Not where the lava might come. *I* will take care of that." The way she spoke assured Silmavalien completely. Something about her voice and something more than her voice made it sound like she was the volcano itself or at least its mistress, perhaps its governing and animating spirit.

"Look!" Noren called to her, pointing. She crawled to him and looked. Following his finger, she saw what looked like waterspouts of a brilliant luscious red substance erupting out of the ground. The lava-spouts grew and multiplied and streams of lava flowed from them and connected them, so that they made a brightly glowing and slightly squiggly line.

Yes," she said. "It's beautiful, but I wouldn't want to be near it. What if one sprouts up underneath *my* feet?"

"Yes," said Noren, "but what if we could be made such creatures that it wouldn't harm us? Elninya is rather fond of the idea."

"*She's* a dragon," said Silmavalien. "Maybe, in the ideal and perfect world, all dragons will be such creatures. After all, it's not ideal or perfect for any of them to have skin problems. Also, it seems dragons can be obsidian dragons. I don't know if I told you about Tiela's egg, but we put it into the volcano. The dragon will be an obsidian dragon."

"Elninya's nothing like Onyxalis," said Noren.

"Well, Onyxalis is *one* obsidian dragon. And this is not the ideal and perfect world," said Silmavalien.

They looked above their heads then, and Silmavalien saw the volcano spouting, like a much bigger lava-spout, far above their heads. It dissolved in red droplets, beautiful but scary. "What if one of those falls on us?" asked Silmavalien.

"It won't," said Oaeiae. She stood now with her back to them, watching the volcano. "I told you, *I* will make sure of that."

Images and sensations from Onyxalis reached Silmavalien. The sun-like brilliance in the hot depths of the lava. The strength of the lava surging up and flowing out of the pressure underneath. The essence entering into his body. He was still searching through the thick brightness for the Dragon-sword.

"What if Onyxalis comes out of this with all that power and still like he was?" asked Silmavalien.

"That's not our business," said Noren, "but we don't know most of what's going on in him, or what is in store for him, and for us, and for the whole world."

Songeth flew to a ledge of rock just below them and began to sing. As the first notes rose out of his great throat, Silmavalien felt her fear of the volcano turned into something else. She joined her voice with Songeth's, adding human words to his dragon's song, and then Noren added his voice, too.

> Fire of the earth, fire of water
> Flame of our watching, flame in earnest
> Roar that breaks down the gates of the mountains!
> Roar of the flame in the black heart!
>
> Challenge is meeting challenge at last!
> Earth heaves in travail and fire is born!
> Fire of dark meets the lake full from the sun!
> Blackness by black is overcome.
>
> Obsidian fresh from the flame
> Pledge of the battle, pledge of two hearts
> Earth is swimming on seas of tossing flame
> Suffocating heat in the sun's heart!
>
> Sun in the earth, sun of our life
> Sun hid in darkness, sun of our death
> Power is clothed in plumes of deepest shadow
> Triumph proceeds to predestined throne!
>
> But first the battle is fire's delight
> The fire in struggle bright glows indeed
> Flow down the mountain's sides scouring the green earth!
> Burst from the ground, be leaping fire!
>
> Sun from without, sun hid in earth,
> Sun that gave us birth, sun of re-birth
> Pledge of the battle, pledge of two loving hearts
> Triumph proceeds to predestined throne!

Finally, Onyxalis clutched the Dragon-sword in his fore-claws.

He emerged from the volcano, a cloud of black smoke preceding him, all the brown scales now a brilliant red like cooling lava. His wings swept down and raised him up. The lava-lake rose and overflowed its basin in the lower parts, making a wide river of lava that rolled down the slopes and then through the forests. The foliage broke into flame before it and then was covered.

As Onyxalis rose from the lake of lava, Oaeiae grabbed a hand of Silmavalien and of Noren in each of hers and lead them up to the peak. On the other side of Noren stood Hazalel and on the other side of Silmavalien stood Aelaza. "Look!" said Oaeiae, pointing.

Onyxalis rose above them. Silmavalien thought he was even bigger than he had been a few minutes ago. He opened his mouth and what looked like a river of fire poured from it. He roared in exultation.

Pointing out to them the rivers of lava, and places further down the slope where rivulets of lava were breaking out of the black rock of the mountain and carrying bits of it with them, crumbling as they went, Oaeiae said, "You might think that is death and destruction. It is not, or if it is, it is the death and destruction that brings about life and restoration. Without the lava continually breaking out of this volcano and replenishing the island, Ellen Island cannot survive. Much of this is hidden to you now, and I do not want you to try to understand it or to make too much of it before you understand it. I want you to be able to remember that things may not be as they appear to you and others. Indeed, they may be very different and you do not know what they are."

Onyxalis came towards them. Silmavalien knew now that he was rather bigger than he had been just that morning. In fact, he was bigger than Wydth or Lighter! Oaeiae made them all step backwards and the obsidian dragon laid the sword, still glowing with the heat of the volcano, at their feet.

Oaeiae picked it up and held it out for Silmavalien to take.

"It's too hot," she said. "It will burn me."

"Not when I give it to you," said Oaeiae.

Silmavalien glanced at Aelaza, who nodded to her. Then she held out her hands to take the sword. Oaeiae had spoken truly. It was warm, but it did not hurt her.

She looked around nervously. Was she supposed to do this now? All three of the Ellenari looked at her with waiting, watching smiles.

Silmavalien approached Noren and held out the

Dragon-sword. She smiled nervously. "I don't know ... I don't know," she began, then collected herself. "This ... This Dragon-sword is supposed to be for the champion of the Dragonriders. I don't know if that's you ... but I hope you will be *my* champion." She ended feeling really nervous.

Had she just proposed to him? Had she just asked him to propose to her?

If she had, she meant it. It had to be sometime. They were obviously meant to be together. He might wonder about it, but it was clear. Everything pointed in that direction.

Noren took the sword, his hands trembling a little. "Thank you, Silmavalien," he said. "I don't know either, but I too hope to be that for you." He looked at the Ellenari.

"Go ahead," said Oaeiae.

Noren finished taking the sword. He was a little afraid. Champion of the Dragonriders? What did that mean? He did not want to be like Onyxalis.

"Do not be afraid," said Hazalel. "You are to fight demons. Onyxalis is to fight demons. You are to combat evil together. It is nothing anyone should be loath to do."

"The sword is still broken," said Oaeiae. "Do not take it out of its sheath, on no occasion, for nothing whatsoever."

"All right. I won't take the sword out of its sheath," said Noren.

"Go and rest," said Aelaza. "Tomorrow we must fly back for the mountains. No. Do not be afraid. We are not yet to confront the demonic powers."

19

Halls of the Ellenari

Aelaza and Hazalel came to them the next morning. "Get ready," they told them. "We're going to fly straight for one of our abodes, high in the Greater Aravin Mountains."

Silmavalien wondered how they were going to make that flight without rest, but as soon as they were in the air, a strong wind arose underneath them and at their backs. It carried them far faster than even Airrock could have ever flown, so that the sea and the islands blurred together beneath them. Aelaza and Hazalel went before them, Aelaza in the form of a storm bird that Silmavalien had seen before, and Hazalel in a shape that resembled a very large emerald hummingbird.

In the evening, the Ellenari led them down out of the current of air and into an island that Silmavalien recognized as being the first one Aelaza had brought her to, when they had first flown to Ellen Island. The next morning, they were caught in the same current of air again and wafted high into the Aravin Mountains. Airrock told Silmavalien that they were now much higher than she had ever been able to fly before, though she felt no thinness in the air, either in her lungs or under her wings. They were surrounded now by dazzling white snow and sheer shining cliffs.

Then they entered a wide valley, flying between slopes and shoulders of the mountains that towered still higher up – it seemed as high above them as they were above the sea.

The world was not shining white and blinding light anymore. Wide spaces of green grass alternated underneath them with groves of trees that were as much bigger as the ancient sequoia trees as the sequoias were bigger than other trees, though more of them were not conifers than were. Lakes of startling blue were connected by rivers that wove between and under the trees. Bridges of white stone spanned both rivers and lakes, connected by paths that led to towers of the same stone. Throughout the valley and around its edges were cliffs, most of them also white, but not all. Stairs led up the cliffs, and towers stood atop them or rose from their feet, while rivers poured over them in dazzling waterfalls into the lakes.

Silmavalien thought it was like nothing she had ever seen before, though it looked a little like the home of the gods in some of the stories, when the Ellenari led them down to land on the shore of a lake, beside the white bridge that crossed it. On either side of them rose white towers, strong and firm and high, and the sand on the shore was shining and silvery.

As they landed, Silmavalien noticed the clearness of the lake. Much nearer to the water, it was so clear that one could see in perfect detail, through the tiny ripples, the sand and the pebbles and the waving reeds, and the colorful fishes that swam over and among it all.

She dismounted the dragon and stepped down on the sand. Was it made of tiny pearls?

Silmavalien took her gaze from the water and the sand and looked at Aelaza, who stood beside her in her human-like form on the side. "Come," said the Ellena.

Silmavalien followed her over the blue-green grass towards the path of white marble. Looking around, she saw several Ellenari coming towards them over the bridge. These Ellenari were also in their human-like forms, but they were as different and unique as Aelaza, Hazalel, and Oaeiae. One of them looked like a tall and large woman who grew a bodice and short skirt of black scales. Her hair was white, and so long and thick that it fell almost to her feet and curled about her shoulders and entire body. She inclined her head in courtly greeting.

"Valoria Eni! Long have we awaited your presence here, Dragonriders, Keeper of Dragons and Champion of the Dragonriders. Now the Dragon-sword shall be re-forged and we will go to war. My name is Lisila. What are your names?"

Noren stepped in front of Silmavalien, and bowed. "My name is Noren. I am the rider of Elninya."

Silmavalien followed Noren's lead and curtsied. "I am Silmavalien, rider of Minth, of Veine, Songeth, Dinora who is gone, Wydth, Coroneth, Tiela, Airrock, Jareth, Daurth, Lighter, Linol, and Dance."

"Welcome to the halls of the Ellenari," said Lisila.

"We have long awaited your hatching, also, O Obsidian Guardian, Avenger of the Dragons."

"My name is Onyxalis, obsidian dragon to Silmavalien and Noren," returned the black dragon. He walked forward and the ground trembled under his weight.

"Well-met, Onyxalis, newly come out from the Ellen Volcano," said Lisila. "Here you will all be equipped as best as we Ellenari can do for the coming battle, and here you will be taught that you may fight well and live.

"Follow me … Do not be afraid. The bridge will support Onyxalis with ease."

Silmavalien stepped onto the white stone next to Noren, and the dragons followed them, led by Onyxalis. The bridge was long and wide and strong, and it did not tremble under them. Across it, the land seemed to be a garden. Hedges of flowers, groves of trees, and beds of aromatic herbs lay everywhere. Between these, and even through them, the Ellenari led the two human Dragonriders and the fourteen dragons.

Their eyes were everywhere, on the birds which flitted to and fro, twittering and singing, some of them with bright foliage, some of them with muted foliage. The flowers were all small, at least compared to the general size of things in that high valley. Some of them were very bright indeed, but others were colors of green and brown which scarcely stood out from the rest of their plant's foliage and branches, and Silmavalien would not have noticed many of them if she had not known Dance. Many ground creatures such as squirrels and chipmunks raced around their feet, between the flowers, through the beds of herbs, and up and down the trees. They may have been wild, but they did not seem at all frightened, though they were shy. Silmavalien even saw a skunk which peeped out its head from under a bush to discreetly watch them as they passed.

It would be a shame to have to eat these animals, she said to the dragons.

None of them were interested in the issue. Only Onyxalis felt like eating anything and, curiously enough, he wanted to eat rocks. Those crumbly, porous, black volcanic rocks felt best to him.

The Ellenari led them to a bed of some plant with a mild but interesting scent. The foliage and branches looked soft and springy. Lisila gestured to indicate the entire maze of beds with pathways of grazed grass between them, and trees interspersed throughout. "Choose wherever you wish to sleep here. The dragons can sleep on the beds also. The plants will not be harmed."

"Th-th-thank you," stammered Silmavalien.

"This is not much to us," said Aelaza. "All is by the direct command of Shallim-Araldor concerning you." She turned to Lisila. "I think the Dragonriders will be hungry."

"*I am certainly hungry,*" said Onyxalis. "*What may I eat?*"

"What do you want to eat?" asked Lisila.

"*... Rocks.*" Onyxalis communicated a vivid picture of the kind of rocks he wanted.

They taste like that?! Silmavalien asked, incredulous....*I never thought of rocks like that before.*

"*I can drink lava,*" replied Onyxalis. "*I can even breathe lava.*"

His words woke strange feelings woke in Silmavalien like long-distant memories. She saw again the rivers of lava flowing over the island and the lakes of it spreading from the feet of the lava-spouts. Something she could only think of as hunger woke in her at the memory, as if it had been present then, though she felt certain it had not been present then. She certainly had not been aware of it. Yet she did not exactly want to eat or drink the stuff. She did not want to eat or drink the stuff at all. She wanted something which was *like* it in some mysterious, indefinable way.

Lisila raised her arm, white like snow but blushed with the hue of roses, and pointed across the wide valley to a shoulder of the mountains on the far slopes. "A cave is prepared for you there, Onyxalis, where you can find rocks which you may eat of any variety you desire."

The great obsidian dragon bowed his head. Then, with an earth-shaking push-off, he lifted his bulk into the sky and flew in the direction which Lisila had pointed.

"Are you hungry, Silmavalien or Noren?" Lisila asked.

"A little," replied Noren, "but if there is anything we should do first, I feel quite well."

"The time of the night or the day does not matter for us here," said Hazalel. "We can easily have lamps for your sake when it is needful for you to be able to see in the night-time."

"It is of no consequence," said Lisila. "If they wish, food can be brought to them while we set about the beginning of our work." Turning to the Dragonriders, she said, "Follow me if you will. Your food will be brought to you. Any of you dragons who wish may come, but only Silmavalien and Noren are required for this."

After unsaddling the dragons and leaving their packs there, the Dragonriders followed Lisila across the garden in a winding path between and over the plants, much like the one they had just followed to what would be their beds. Though their sleeping arrangements were strange to them, they were not worried that they might be uncomfortable. So far they had only ever received the best from the Ellenari. Whatever the Ellenari gave far surpassed anything they could have gotten for themselves. Probably this valley would be as strangely temperate as it was strangely filled with good air.

In one of the cliffs, which now showed to be polished smooth, there was an opening. They entered it and found themselves in a white hall. Light emanated from Lisila so that they could easily see their way so she led them deeper in. They passed through several passages and entered a hall on one side of which burned a many-colored fire which somehow burned differently from any other fire. Around stood several Ellenari whom they had not yet seen.

20

The Re—forging Begins

A closer look revealed the fire to be a glow, a solid nimbus, of colored light, both rainbow and pastel. Around the edges it flickered and shimmered like the edge of a fire.

An Ellenar stood next to it with his back towards him, watching over it and apparently doing something with it which they could not see. His hair was dark gray and in the hollows and shadows of its locks and curls glowed flickering nimbi of colored fire. His body emanated an obscuring nimbus of shifting red, orange, yellow, and green light.

He turned to face them.

Oaeiae stepped out from among the other Ellenari and smiled at them. Her eyes flashed with the light of her volcano.

The Ellenar who had been tending to the fire beckoned to them. "Come, Dragonriders, Silmavalien and Noren."

They walked closer, slowly. The heat of the fire was intense around them, like a glaring sun.

The Ellenar led them to a white table which stood beside the fire and against the same wall that the fire glowed. Then he held out his hands. "I forgot. My name is Ululhumben. Will you give me the sword?"

Noren unbuckled his belt and handed the sword, sheath and all, to Ululhumben.

The Ellenar took the sword and laid it on the table. Then he slowly drew it from its sheath. In his hands the Dragon-sword remained in one piece, but Noren, watching, could clearly see the break in it. He felt Silmavalien staring beside him, as he took in the unsheathed sword for the first time ever. He could not name the feelings that coursed through him, almost as if he were somewhere far, far away, and he could not make sense of the engravings, which glowed with a dim red light, like cooling lava. Somehow, they knew they ought to fit together into a complete picture, though he could not see what it was.

Beside him, Silmavalien turned to Oaeiae. "You told us you control the volcano on Ellen Island. How does it work when you're not there?"

"Time for the Ellenari is not like time is for you," said Oaeiae. "I could not answer your question. I do not very well understand what you just said. But hush! Now is not the time for these conversations." She stepped up beside him, where Ululhumben laid the sword down carefully on the table.

"This is for you and Noren," said Aelaza, and Noren glanced from the sword to see her handing platters to Silmavalien. Then his attention went back to Oaeiae. She stood at the table now, and tapped her finger on the blade. The dim red of the engravings momentarily flared up with the almost-sun brightness of the hottest lava. She stepped back. "Now!" she said.

Ululhumben delicately picked up the sword, holding one side of the blade in one hand and the cross-guard in the other. "Noren, will you let us put your hand on the hilt?"

"Umm, yeah," said Noren. He lifted his right hand.

Hazalel took his hand and placed it carefully on the hilt. Noren consented without any reluctance. The sword was in a fragile state. Why they needed to have his hand on it, he did not know, but there was so much he did not know. These people were so different.

Noren glanced slowly around him. Hazalel and Ululhumben stood as still as statues. Aelaza, Lisila, and four more Ellenari whose names he did not know watched him with a silent, still, almost restful, intensity. The air felt like a string stretched almost to the breaking point.

His eyes met Silmavalien's. She watched him intently but with an attitude wholly different from that of the Ellenari. What she saw and what the Ellenari saw was largely different. It was perfectly obvious from the differences in the way they watched him. There was a kindness, a tenderness, an intimacy, in her eyes which was unlike anything he saw in the Ellenari. She was his own Silmavalien, wasn't she?

S

Silmavalien broke the eye-contact. It felt precarious carrying the platters. She looked around the vaulted room and saw what looked like a bench against one wall. "Aelaza?" she asked, for the Ellena still stood next to her.

Those enigmatic sapphire eyes turned to her. "What is it?"

"Can I put this down over – there, against the –?" she began, stammering a little. How was she to point out what she meant?

Aelaza clearly indicated the same stone bench. "Yes. Do what you like with it – Oh, I should tell you. Any of the water you find here is good to drink."

Silmavalien nodded. "Thanks," she said, but the Ellena had

already returned her gaze to Noren. Silmavalien walked to the bench, laid the tray down, and looked at the food. There was a substance which looked like bread on which were set bunches of very small red berries. It looked good. She sat down on the bench, tore off a piece of the bread with some of berries on it, popped it in her mouth, and returned her attention to Noren and the Dragon-sword.

Several different thoughts chased themselves round in her mind. She and Noren were obviously meant to be together. They should be married! But did they really know what that would look or be like? The world was so very strange! Apparently, Noren was the Champion of the Dragonriders who would wield the Dragon-sword and with it kill the Fire Shadow that guarded the Riders' Passage. But what did it mean? If he was to be Champion of the Dragonriders, if he was to fight, would he be wounded? Would he be killed? Would he be captured again – and this time *killed*? She definitely did not want that!

Would it be her fault? Was it she who had made him Champion of the Dragonriders? Had it belonged to her to choose who received the Dragon-sword and became that champion? Was he destined because she had chosen him and could have chosen another, or had she been destined to give the Dragon-sword to him because he already had been destined to bear it?

There was so much she did not know! What if she had made the wrong choice? How would she know, either way? Silmavalien suspected she would be able to ask the Ellenari, but they often did not give answers. She suspected there were a number of things they knew no better than she did. This might – or might not – be one of those things. Even if they did know, they might still refuse to answer.

𝒩

"That is good," said Oaeiae. She turned, and in a streak of what looked like the smoke of a volcano and a dash of lava, though both vanished quickly, she left the room.

Noren looked around and opened his mouth to ask a question.

"Just take your hand off the sword," said Hazalel.

Noren did so. He looked around him for a moment and saw Silmavalien beckon to him.

"Go ahead," said Hazalel.

He walked across the room and sat down on the other side of the tray from Silmavalien. He took a piece from the untouched plate and began to eat. He turned back towards the Ellenari just in time to see Ululhumben laying the sword in the fire. He and Lisila exchanged a glance and a few short words which Noren heard but could not understand. Somehow, they did not sound like any human language.

Then Lisila left the fire and approached them. "You can finish your meal here," she said. "After that, go out and do as you please. Rest mostly. Return here tomorrow morning."

A low resonant hum emanated from the fire. It throbbed in the stone under their feet, against their backs, and on which they sat. Elninya told him she felt it, and so did the other dragons who were not in the sky.

Onyxalis, who was chewing rocks, said, *"It is beginning. I have waited for this thrum for so long. The whole world has waited for it so long. The war is about to begin. We will answer the Dark Lord's challenge. A new age is born."*

Noren did not, at that moment, have any taste for Onyxalis' grand pronouncements. He felt Silmavalien's half-exasperated half-resigned sigh beside him.

"I love you," said Elninya to her rider.

I love you too, replied Noren, comforted, though he noticed that he felt a little strange without the sword. He had grown accustomed to having a sword at his side since it was given to him when he was a courier, and he had missed it when he fled with Silmavalien. When the Dragon-sword had hung there, it felt right. Now that space was emptier than ever.

"This is so delicious, but it's really different," Silmavalien whispered to him.

"Everything here is really different," he said, glancing at the Ellenari who stood around the fire. Some of them were watching the sword and the fire intently. One had hands in the fire. Several had tools of some sort in their hands, and a few were talking to each other. "In fact," he continued, "everything is really different. It's not just here. It didn't start with Onyxalis, either."

"No, it didn't," said Silmavalien.

He felt Silmavalien shift next to him as if she did not really feel comfortable, and he realized he did not feel like he belonged here anymore either. He started to stand, and Silmavalien stood next to them. Lisila appeared in front of them as they picked their food up in their hands, and she glided in front of them to lead the way out.

"I think I might have been lost in there if I had not been able to follow her," Silmavalien said to Noren, when they stood under the sky again. "How are we going to go back tomorrow?"

"I *think* I could find my way back, but there was a place where I wasn't at once sure which way to go," replied Noren. "But I think the Ellenari will see to it that we can and do go back when they want us."

"They're *so* different!" she said. "Do you think they would know that we would need their help?"

"They don't seem incompetent," said Noren. "They've always done well seeing to our needs even where, I'm sure, our needs are very unlike theirs. Aelaza and Hazalel have probably watched us for long enough to know enough about what we're like and what we need."

That discussed, the two Dragonriders found places to sit down on the grass and finish their meal.

21

The Watching

After finishing her meal in silence next to Noren, Silmavalien meandered over to one of the lakes. She walked slowly along the shore until she came to a bridge which she walked along for a while before sitting down on the edge. Then she admired the clear water and the world she could see through it.

Drifts and piles of sand lay in the bottom. Plants, mostly reed-like or with long leaves, grew up from the bottom, green or purplish-pink or purplish-green or purplish-brown. Pebbles lay on the bottom, of many colors and shades, among larger rocks that were shaped almost like castles with holes in them. Water-snails crawled across the bottom or clung to the sides of these larger rocks. Fishes of different sizes, colors, and shapes swam through the tight, twisting channels between the larger rocks, or in the dark shadows. Sometimes they swam across the open, their bodies undulating in harmony with the flow of the water. Shoals of fish wandered among the plants, grazing – at least, it reminded Silmavalien of the way herds of deer or horses moved from one place to another foraging. Once, she saw a fish come out of one of the holes in a rock.

Watching the fish fascinated her. They varied so much in size, with some of them no longer than her thumb and very slender. These were mostly a brownish-and-whitish color and were hard to spot among the rock or browner plants, but that only made glimpsing one more delightful. She saw one fish, as long as her arm from finger-tips to shoulder, which was also a subdued color – brown with purple spots. Others of the fishes had feathery fins of every color of the rainbow or all the colors together, and many of the fishes were pre-dominantly colors of coral or purplish pink, mints, teals, and aquamarines, or jade green, and shades of purple from royal to lilac. Other fishes were pre-dominantly bright reds, yellows, or orange, sometimes coral or peach tones of pink, and now and then almost fiery greens or purples interspersed among the other colors.

It looked like a whole underwater world, as bright and beautiful and diverse as the one above water, something she had never thought about before, but then Silmavalien realized how tired she was. Watching the fish had almost distracted her, but she really did need to sleep.

She rose, almost stumbling, and was going to make her way back to the place where the Ellenari told her they would sleep.

Linol came to her before she was even off the bridge, and lay down to make it easier for her to climb on him. He would carry her to the sleeping place. Then he was going to come back here. He wanted to watch the fish and play in the water. He was certain the water would feel *so* nice on his skin and body.

I bet it will, too, she told him, settling herself on his shoulder. *Maybe tomorrow, depending on what they want of us, I will come and swim with you. I'm sure most of the dragons will want to swim, too. The water just looks like it's nice and will feel nice.*

Minth was already laying down in the beds when Linol landed, and after climbing off of Linol, she lay down next to Minth. He hummed contentedly.

A soft laughing watery thrill passed through Silmavalien.

Yes, Minth. You are so much bigger than me, now. I think you are more bigger than me than I ever was bigger than you.

Yes, it is so wonderful!

𝒩

Noren had his own thoughts. He climbed up onto a knoll from which he could survey the meadow-garden in which he was to sleep. Looking out over huge trees, over beds and shrubs of the gardens, and over the blue, blue water, he organized his thoughts. The Dragon-sword. There was power in that sword. He knew it. He had felt it when he first received it from Silmavalien. He had felt it more strongly with his hand on the hilt just half an hour earlier. The whole thing with the Dragon-sword scared him a little.

What was he called to do? What did he have to do? What if he failed?

Onyxalis' grand pronouncements only further worried him.

Elninya's thoughts brushed against his. She was laying in the shallows of one of the lakes, enjoying the cool, refreshing feel of the water. It felt nicer than anything she could ever remember having felt on her skin. Drinking it had made her feel so alive and clear. *"Don't worry, Noren. What you need to know in order to love will be made clear as it will help you. The Lord of All Light will guide us. He loves us. We are loved by Love.*

"Noren, I love you."

I love you, too, Noren again responded. *But that's not all.*

He was certain that Silmavalien had been asking him to renew their engagement and marry her with the words with which she had given him the Dragon-sword. He had seen that attitude in every look and word of hers since then.

Unlike her, he was not at all concerned about not knowing what marriage was or what it was about. When he had first asked her to marry him, he had been well aware that neither of them really knew what they were getting into. His idea had always been that they would discover what it meant as they lived it. Certainly, it meant they would live together and love each other always, or at least until one or the other of them died, and that they would do the things married people do with each other and love and take care of any children they had. Nothing either he or Silmavalien had learned since their engagement had changed any of that. What more was there to know about the thing until one was doing it? In order for such a thing to work out, they had to be able to trust and know each other. That was very important to Noren.

Anything the mythologies or stories or religion had taught about marriage or roles in marriage or anything else had never mattered to him. He had learned from watching the marriages of others to the extent that he could, and he counted this a very imperfect method of learning. He would not expect his and Silmavalien's relationship to be modeled after that of anyone else, and certainly not of others whose lives were informed by all kinds of nonsense, some of it quite evil, which he had rejected. He had thought, himself, about what marriage necessarily and inherently required, what its consequences would be, and what would be necessary for all of that to work well. He had thought even more about Silmavalien and how he loved her, and he had tried to think about her and how she loved him and what she would want. They would talk about everything and find out together. That was actually one of the things he had always wanted to do with her.

What concerned him was that he could not see how marriage could possibly work if their lives were to be involved in such a battle against evil. How would he be able to protect her? How would they be able to have or raise children – and if one was going to marry, one certainly had to accept and deal with the possibility of children! Marriage, more often than not, caused children, and sometimes it caused quite a few children.

That was one of Noren's concerns, and it was directly related to the Dragon-sword. He still had the other concern relating to telling Silmavalien what he had done and also to whether she really trusted *him* or not. The thought occurred to him. Did he trust *her?* If he did, would he be willing to tell her what he had done, trusting that she would continue to love him? Could he trust her after how she had lied to him? Perhaps, if he desired her, he should start with his trust of her.

If he told her what he had done and, of course, that he had completely repented, repented of the very way of thinking about life and death which had permitted him to do it, and she told him she loved and trusted and wanted to marry him still, would that establish that she did in fact trust *him?* Noren thought it might.

But that only solved one of their problems. Did the concept of trust and his new world-view have any bearing on whether or not they could or should marry before what looked like the certain – or rather completely uncertain – circumstances and entanglements of their lives?

Noren decided that he was too tired to think anything more through that afternoon, and he, too, went to the beds where they had been told they should sleep.

S

Early in the morning Silmavalien woke and stepped out from under Minth's wing. She felt quite refreshed. The high snow peaks in the west gleamed a coral pink in the light of the growing dawn, and she felt as if her soul was borne on wings to some celestial and perfect region. As simple as the beauty was, it was all the more beautiful and grand, all the more full of promise and assurance. Something – everything – was going to be well, in fact, was going to be perfect.

For a long time she stood watching, as the coral light increased and changed shape. The dragons watched with her. Then she spread out her arms as if to welcome the dawn, only she spread out her arms to the light in the west, for the light in the east from which it came was quite invisible.

"O Lord of Light, O Love," she said, having no more to say. Her hope and assurance was too great even for expressed and articulated gratitude. Her soul hushed in reverent silence before the dawn that told of the greater and perfect dawn, before the promise and assurance – almost vision – that all was very well, by the power and being of Love.

Another minute passed. Minth stirred and spread his wings. He had lain and slept for a long time and felt the need to stir his huge body, to move and to fly.

She went down to the lake and drank. At once it reminded her of the water of the Spring of Nerya. Though it was not nearly so potent as that water, it had something of the same effect. A few sips satisfied her thirst and also made her feel stronger.

N

Noren sat on the soft grass, lounging against the beds which formed a soft cushion to support his back. The whole valley was filled with a soft, indirect light that made it seem entirely peaceful, and Silmavalien was half-sitting, half-lying beside him. She muttered something about how she was hungry, and he asked if she thought the Ellenari knew they were hungry.

"I'm sure they do," she said, still sounding a little sleepy. "Maybe they mean for us to find food for ourselves here."

"Or maybe we're supposed to go back to the caves where – it was Aelaza, right? – gave us those trays yesterday, and they'll give us breakfast there again today."

She said something to the effect that she doubted she could find her way back to that room.

He suspected he could do it, but there was such an air of mystery about the place, an aura of power and something more, that he did not want to risk getting lost and finding himself somewhere they did not belong. It might even be dangerous. "We could just go to the entrance, and see if we're guided from there or they bring us breakfast there," he suggested.

She mumbled something that sounded agreeable, and he sat up straighter. Just then he heard the softest rustle of a branch that stood out from the sounds of the slight breeze and turned his head to see Hazalel and Aelaza stepping along the path, bearing plates with food of a different sort from what he had last evening.

The Ellenari separated and went different ways along the path after giving them the plates, but Noren had the sense they stayed near. He went with Silmavalien to get another sip from the lake when they were both done, and when he stood up from that, both the Ellenari came to them again and led them back to the same room with the mysterious fire.

As he passed through the opening in the cliff, he felt something from Elninya which made him stop completely, at least in his mind.

"Noren."

Yes?

"Don't worry. The power of the Dragon-sword will be no more yours than the power of the ring is Silmavalien's."

He felt like cuddling up against his dragon and hugging her. *Thank you,* he thought. *I love you.*

S

Once in the vaulted room, Silmavalien did not know why she was there. The Ellenari did not seem to need her at all. They again had Noren hold the Dragon-sword, and they instructed him to perform a variety of different actions, sometimes with props that they provided. Some of the actions required or revealed strength, others flexibility. Silmavalien did not understand most of them or what was going on, and she did not try to understand.

As the time passed, it became increasingly clear to her that they would not need her at all. She wondered if bringing her there had been an oversight. Some of the time she spent watching Noren, but most of it she spent conversing with her dragons and sharing their experiences while she sat on the bench. Linol admired the fish and other creatures in the lakes, and the other dragons were playing and swimming with him in the lakes. None of them had been in the least disappointed by the water. It turned out to be even better than it had promised.

When Silmavalien watched the Ellenari, she noticed that they seemed to gather something from the exercises they had Noren go through. They would continually turn to him, sometimes only to look at him, and then do something she could not see to the Dragon-sword. Then they took the sword out of the fire and off the table for him to hold again, and she saw that it flashed even more than before. The lines of fire in it were extremely bright and she turned her eyes away. The jewels flashed, too, but she thought that they flashed with reflected light.

A couple hours later, Aelaza and Hazalel took them both out. Aelaza said to her, "Do whatever you like. When the time comes, you will find your dinner. You and the dragons should both do as you please. Rest or play or practice whatever you like as you feel like it. We will tell you when something else is required."

Silmavalien was about to respond when the Ellena nodded in a kind of curtsy, then jumped to the cliff and ascended it with her usual speed and grace. A moment later, Silmavalien saw Hazalel finish speaking with Noren and leap up the cliff in the same manner.

She told Noren what she was going to do, then went to play with the dragons in the lake as she had promised them.

N

The days which followed were strange. Noren and Silmavalien always found their breakfasts and dinners, usually near the place where they slept. When any of the dragons became hungry, he or she soon came upon a freshly-killed and brought meal.

Both he and Silmavalien were constantly, sometimes intensely, aware of the feeling that they were being watched, that the Ellenari were near them and among them, watching them, though they did not see or hear them. Only once or twice did any one of them, even the dragons, see an Ellen, yet they felt as if certainly tens, probably hundreds, and maybe thousands of Ellenari were around them, constantly focusing their attention on them. At the same time, there was a kind of background of immense silence and solitude, as if they and their dragons were alone in the world. The whole was slightly uncomfortable, especially when they were most aware of it, and Silmavalien told him that the dragons experienced this even more strongly than they did, but it did not make them uncomfortable.

She and Noren both thought that Onyxalis continued to have interactions with the Ellenari, but the obsidian dragon, who continued to grow rapidly, did not tell either of them anything about it.

Noren did not speak to her about marriage or about the crime he had committed. He felt that he must speak about it to her privately, and he did not have the necessary privacy while being watched, even scrutinized, by a whole city of Ellenari.

22

The Receiving of the Dragon—sword

Throughout this time, Silmavalien and Noren explored as much of the valley as they felt comfortable exploring. They decided that they really had nothing to fear, since the Ellenari had told them to do as they pleased, and since they were certain they constantly their watchful eyes, the Ellenari would tell them if they got to close they weren't supposed to go.

In fact, Silmavalien pointed out, Aelaza had implied as much, and Noren agreed that Hazalel had as well.

For the most part, Silmavalien's interest was focused on the streams and rivers, the waterfalls and lakes. One morning, she was sitting on the bridge spanning another lake when she noticed some creatures that were much larger than fish and did not really look like fish either swimming in the lake. They had eyes and snouts and mouths that looked far more like those of wolves' or other animals than fish, and their hides were not scaled, but smooth like most of the dragons. They had different kinds of fins and tails, and then one of them jumped out of the water and spouted water out of the tops of its back, behind its head, before spinning around and diving back under.

She was intrigued by the creatures, and Linol glided over a few minutes later, alerted by her excitement. He had not found these amazing creatures yet! They watched them for a while, admiring their beautiful bodies and the way they swam, as well as way they jumped and made themselves into short-lived water fountains.

The creatures stayed near the bridge for a while, and she and Linol slowly and gradually made friends with some of them. Later, she and Linol often went swimming with them. Most of the other dragons were less interested in swimming and, besides, the dolphins were still scared of them, or at least very shy around them. Silmavalien did not think they were really scared the way that animals outside this valley were frightened of predators, and Linol agreed with her. It was something much more like shyness.

While she and Linol befriended these water-creatures, Songeth gathered together and befriended most of the songbirds in the vale. He organized amazing symphonies and orchestras of bird-song, leading them with his own fantastic voice, and he often found ways for the other dragons to be part of his songs as well. Silmavalien could tell that he was really happy. It had been a while since they had been able to stay in one place long enough for him to make friends with the shier, more frightened birds of the world below, and there were times she thought he would have preferred to migrate with his bird friends.

Meanwhile, Airrock continued to practice her acrobatics. She scared the water-dwelling animals by flying as high as she could in the sky and then diving into the deepest part of a lake. She also copied the acrobatics of the water-creatures Linol and Silmavalien loved, folding her wings in tight and spinning around several times before re-opening them.

Dance, for her part, explored all the flowers and shared them with Silmavalien, and despite what loomed over her, the imminent war, her worry that any and all of them might be hurt and killed, and even that she might have doomed Noren with the Dragon-sword, she was happy and relaxed. She got to spend all her time with the dragons, getting to know them, and she did not even have to prepare oil for them, since the oil jars were always re-filled by the Ellenari.

Onyxalis' size continued to astound Silmavalien. When he soared over the valley, a tremendous black bulk with red wings, it only further showed just how large he had gotten, especially when his hgue shadow eclipsed the sun at high noon. He was well more than twice the size of Wydth or Lighter now, and when he breathed a sheet of fire across the sky, she understood what he'd meant when he thought that the other dragons' fire would not compare to his. It looked just like the lava – almost sun-like white-yellow radiance that faded to orange, and then a deepening, darkening red as it cooled – and there was so much of it that she and Noren wondered how even his massive body could contain it.

At night, the dragons sometimes perched in the trees. Even Wydth and Lighter could find branches big enough to easily support their weight, so they almost looked small in the trees, and Songeth usually sat on a branch when he sang with the birds. Silmavalien often found sheltered nooks to spend the night in with the dragons.

S

It was evening. A few thin streamers graced the deepening blue sky high above. Silmavalien walked along a path through beds of aromatic herbs. Tiny red flowers, each of their petals resembling the dual wings of a butterfly, graced the dark, deep green of the leaves with their shining silvery sheen.

She looked up and saw Aelaza coming down the path towards her. "Hello," she said, feeling awkward and nervous. A few days ago she had talked to Noren about asking the Ellenari if they knew what was hurting the dragons in their eggs and if anything could be done about it, and he had agreed they should ask the Ellenari.

"Sin elendri," replied Aelaza.

"Can I ask you something?" asked Silmavalien.

The Ellena only stood still and silent.

"There's something wrong with the dragons, isn't there? So many of them shouldn't be albino, and they should have scales," began Silmavalien.

Aelaza only waited for her to finish.

"Do you know what is wrong? Is there something I – or someone – can do about it? Do you know what it is?" asked Silmavalien.

"You're right that there is something wrong," said Aelaza. "Everything I know about the matter suggests that you and Noren will have something to do with putting it right. More than that I cannot tell you."

"Oh," said Silmavalien. She was going to ask, "Do you know if there is someone else I could ask about this who might know more?" but the Ellena came a step closer and spoke again.

"The re-forging of the Dragon-sword is now complete," she said. "I have come to lead you to it. Follow me." She turned, and Silmavalien followed her down the path.

The Ellena up a cliff this time. Steep and irregular stairs had been cut in it. Looking at it, Silmavalien asked, "Should I ask one of the dragons to come? That would be so much faster."

"No," said Aelaza. "This is for you to climb." With perfect ease and strength, the Ellena began the ascent.

Silmavalien struggled with it. Some of the steps were so large that she had to climb up them using both her hands and her feet. Aelaza frequently gave her some assistance.

She stopped to catch her breath after a particularly difficult step. "Why do I have to do this?" she panted.

"You need to be ready for what you must do," said Aelaza. "Your training has begun. Come." The Ellena sprang up the next step and waited for her. By the time she got to the top, her legs and lungs were burning and she had several scrapes and bruises.

Silmavalien straightened and looked around. A domed hill rose before her. More Ellenari than she had ever seen before were assembled on and around it. The sky was getting dark, and white lanterns interspersed among the Ellenari provided a plentiful glow that contrasted beautifully with the darkening, shifting purple and blue of the evening sky and the blue-gray of the shadowed snow-mountains surrounded them.

Aelaza led her through the Ellenari and up to the summit of the hill, where a large white rock stood out from the crown. A tightly gathered group of Ellenari circled and it, and Silmavalien saw Ululhumben and others from the room with the fire. Right outside the circle stood Lisila, standing like a guardian, a sword like a white flame glowing naked in her hand.

With pause or hesitation, Aelaza led Silmavalien right into the ring.

She saw that Noren stood there, too, within the ring. Hazalel stood beside him, and his slightly quicker breath as well as a few scrapes on his hands made her think that he, too, had been made to climb the stairs.

Her eyes met his as she stood beside the rock, not quite across from him, and she saw uncertainty on his face. It was not a disturbed or uncomfortable kind of uncertainty; he was not worried. He did not know what was happening or why, and he was content to wait for all to be revealed.

Over their heads all the dragons circled, Onyxalis included.

Aelaza stepped past her, right up to the rock, and she turned to watch the Ellena draw the Dragon-sword out from under a purple cloth that was lying too flat on the rock to conceal anything. But it was not the cloth that drew her attention. Her eyes drank in the sword. The shape of the cross-guard resembled out-spread dragon wings and the jewels, blue and red and green, sparkled fiercely. They had never been so bright before, and the sheath shone so brilliantly that it was almost a perfect mirror.

Aelaza glanced at her, as if in question, and Silmavalien held out her hands. Aelaza placed the sword in them, and as soon as the hilt and sheath touched her hands she felt a tingling vibration of power. She looked at the sword again, overcome by the beauty of its jewels, and walked around the stone to where Noren waited. There was a flash in his eyes that told her that he was at once excited and somewhat nervous and afraid.

She held out the sword to him.

He took it. Hazalel belted it around his waist with what looked like a band of something like shiny black leather. Noren drew it from its sheath.

The jewels flashed. It looked like fire, in the same color as the gem, darted from them. The whole blade glowed like molten lava, bright orange-red. The lettering glowed with all the stabbing brilliance of fresh lava, white-yellow, as bright as the sun, stabbing out light. Silmavalien turned her eyes away.

The excitement of the dragons felt like thunder throbbing in the air.

"The Dragon-sword!"

Noren had spoken the words aloud. Silmavalien did not know if they were audible, or if they came to her after the manner that the dragon's thoughts, including Onyxalis' thoughts, came to her, both from all the dragons and from the host of the Ellenari.

He sheathed the sword, and she saw the light pass. "So what comes next?" he asked.

"Challenge is meeting challenge at last," said Onyxalis. *"The battle is indeed about to be joined."*

"That is true," said Lisila, "but we do not issue our challenge just yet, O Obsidian Guardian, Avenger of the Dragons, though doubtless the Nightmare Lord knows something of what is passing here. Certainly, he must know that you have been to Ellen Island and that you have disappeared in the heights of these mountains. That is enough for him to guess, and he too is making ready for war. But we do not join the battle just yet. In answer to Noren's question: you train and are more fully prepared. For him, that will largely involve training with this sword, but it will also involve other things. You, Onyxalis, must train too, as will the other dragons and Silmavalien. *Then* we will meet their challenge and the battle will be joined. But it will be fiercer than any of you know, or perhaps shall know."

A cold thrill went through Silmavalien's heart, as if the air itself changed. For a moment even Airrock felt the cold shrinking.

What was coming to them? It was so much bigger than they

were! What did it all mean?

Silmavalien bowed her head and spoke silently to the Lord of the Light. She did not know what she wanted to say, but she asked, *Will you protect us? Please protect us from becoming evil or being marred by evil. This is so frightening! But you are Love and you must win. Does that mean we must win, too? In the end, and always in some way, I'm sure it does. You are making us good. Are you making everything good? I hope so.*

23

The Training Begins

All of them, both the humans and the dragons were fully occupied with the training exercises the next day, and they were exhausted by evening. When he laid his aching body down to rest, Noren remembered that he wanted to have an important conversation with Silmavalien, but he could not remember what it was.

The days that followed were intense for everyone. As Lisila had said, most of what he did focused on the Dragon-sword. Having been trained to wield a sword as a courier so he could defend himself and his messages from robbers and the like, he was already far from a blundering idiot, but there was still a lot to learn, especially since the Dragon-sword was a little different from the swords he had used as a courier.

The sword did not shine and glow when he drew it in training, like it had that evening. The blade shone like a polished silver mirror, but it did not glow red as if molten. The engraving glowed a dull red, but it did not flash out with the brilliance of the fiery heart of the earth which is a piece of the sun.

But he was not the only one being trained, and his exercises were not so intense that he did not get a few moments to watch the others, still less to notice Elninya's training. The Ellenari directed them constantly, pushing their endurance, showing them tricks for what they could do with their fire breath and how to extend, and teaching them new maneuvers and how to perfect maneuvers they already knew. Even Onyxalis was not exempt from this training, even the training related to fire, and he noted Elninya's amusement that Airrock was not exempt from being shown new acrobatic moves or how to do ones she already knew better. Somehow, that pleased her immensely.

She laughed in his mind at that thought. Airrock marveled at her prowess in the air, and she enjoyed testing her abilities to the limits and even to the point of serious danger simply to see what she could do, and she told him Silmavalien – and the Ellenari – were often cautioning her to be careful. It was amusing to watch.

He got to watch Silmavalien's training more. In fact, they were often together. They shared many of the exercises to help them grow stronger and faster, and while her training focused on the bow, his did not entirely ignore it. Somehow, it was more comfortable being close to her in this sort of environment, as if the physical and mental challenges shoved aside the awkward questions that plagued their relationship. It was somehow familiar, too, as if learning and getting stronger together was similar to the way he had taught her the bow, except now they were both learning together, and that was even better.

S

One afternoon, Aelaza led Silmavalien up one of the shoulders of the encircling mountains. They stopped, high on the mountains' slope where more of the sky was visible than Silmavalien had seen for months. It was evening now, and between two mountains she could see the saffron pink, the orange and gold, of a sunset, fading every minute into a pink ever purpler and then a purple ever bluer. It was ethereal and beautiful, and for several minutes she gazed at it, just drinking in the beauty. The day had not been as exhausting as usual, and many of the dragons soared nearby, likewise enjoying the colors.

"The sunset is so beautiful. Praise Shallim-Araldor, Lord of the Light," said Aelaza.

The world must be made by Love. Thank you! She hardly registered the Ellena's wonders, but the scene struck her with renewed certainty and gratitude.

There was so much to be thankful for, far more than just this view of unspeakable and immeasurable beauty. She and the dragons were together. Minth was stronger and healthier than ever before. She and Noren and all the dragons were training to rescue people from the power of the nightmare creatures.

But that thought turned a darker turn. It seemed so impossible that evil could ever really be made right. It was just too horrible! She turned to Aelaza.

"How is it that Love can be victorious and yet there is so much wrong? How can what's wrong ever be good?" she asked the Ellena. "How can Love allow evil? I mean, I really *know* that Love is real, that Love is completely victorious simply for being Love, that all the bad will be conquered and made to serve Love, but how? It seems impossible, evil is so horrible, so undoable. How can evil ever cease to have been at all?"

"I do not know that, either," said Aelaza, looking for the first time at Silmavalien with what the human woman clearly understood to be surprise or astonishment. "I did not know that you humans would wonder that! I thought you knew. I thought you would know easily. I did not think that all of you knew all the time. How would you know that, while you were doing all you could to avoid thinking about the issue? But I thought it would be clear to you! I do not understand how anyone who has been wrong can be wholly good."

"Oh," said Silmavalien. She did not know what to do or say now.

"I think," said Aelaza, "that you will understand this before I do and as I never will. Already I think you know things I do not know."

The two stood in silence for a few moments which felt very long, as the colors in the sky subtly changed. Then Aelaza said, "Tomorrow, you and Noren are to set out for Aros Cor in Dragonsong Forest by way of the Riders' Passage. It is there that you will find the wood you need for your bows. You will meet Keya and Veyan and that family and will conduct them also to Dragonsong. You all are to rest well tonight."

"How will we meet them?" asked Silmavalien. At that moment, she spoke to Tanz. *"Tanz."*

The blue dragon only barely responded. She had more important, more pressing things to think about. She had no attention to spare. Briefly, Silmavalien spoke to Naklath and to Tryph and received the same response from both of them.

"They will fly to you. We will make sure that you meet one another," said Aelaza.

"Do you know what is happening to them right now?" asked Silmavalien.

"You will meet them and they will be well," said Aelaza.

Suddenly Silmavalien remembered when she had been told that she would have no trouble if she fled at once and yet she was attacked by winged vampire-like nightmares. "Aelaza," she said, "once you told me that if we flew at once we would not be troubled, but we were still attacked by nightmares. Will we really meet them tomorrow? Will they really be all right?"

"I never said you would meet them tomorrow. I said you would meet them," said Aelaza. She spoke roughly and curtly, and Silmavalien knew she had somehow displeased the Ellena. "You will meet them, Silmavalien. And I told you, 'If you go down at once, you will face no trouble in doing so.' *Did* you face any trouble in going down?"

"No," said Silmavalien, "but we were attacked."

"And the attack did not in any way hinder you from going down, foolish Dragonrider," said Aelaza.

"Did I do something horrible?" asked Silmavalien, cringing.

"You know what you did," said the Ellena. There was no comfort or reassurance in her voice.

There was a pause during which the air felt like it was full of knives. Then Aelaza said, "Go down, eat the meal prepared for you, and sleep well. You must still fly tomorrow." With that, the Ellena sprang to the edge of the cliff and began leaping down it.

Silmavalien stood still, all her pleasure in the beautiful evening dashed to pieces. She called Airrock to her and, while she waited for the dragon, fell down face first on the ground. "O Lord of the Light," she begged, murmuring out loud, "must I go through this again? I don't want to. I want to trust you. I want to obey you."

For a moment Silmavalien felt like making excuses. *What did I do wrong?* But she knew. She knew her desires in asking that question and complaining, as if she had met any real difficulty in going down or as if the Lord of the Light or his servants had lied to her, were not right. Exactly what they had been she was not sure, but she knew they were not right.

"O Lord of the Light, please forgive me! I want to be good. I want to love," she whispered into the ground.

The Voice spoke to her then.

"Rise and be good, then. I have never forsaken you and never will forsake you. I am always for you as long as you want to be for me. Do you not remember what I have always done when you have run from me?"

Airrock was drawing near and Silmavalien stood.

The meal waiting for her below tasted like there was something unique about it.

ℵ

Noren was sitting on a grassy sward with the Dragon-sword laying naked across his lap, when he received much the same news from Hazalel. His first thought was if he would have the time and privacy he needed to speak to Silmavalien in the Riders' Passage, but what he asked was, "Do I need to be prepared to fight?"

"You must always be prepared to fight the demons," said Hazalel. "Exactly when a fight will present itself to you I cannot tell you."

Noren nodded. He was reminded of how he had lain in a dungeon waiting to be burned. Somehow, though his circumstances could not have been less like that prison, with stars coming out in the sky, a gentle breeze blowing on his face, and the scents of flowers and herbs in his nostrils, he felt similarly. He ran his finger down the blade. Did he now walk towards his death with more freedom and more truly than he had, when walking bound between those guards towards the stake? Was to bear this Dragon-sword, perhaps to victory, against the nightmare also to be condemned to die?

But this was all foolishness. All men died sometime. In that sense everyone was always walking towards his or her death, willing or unwilling.

Noren desperately wanted to tell Silmavalien. Somehow, he felt like he had to tell her before one of them died. He had to tell her he still loved her, he was still interested in her. But when? Where? He couldn't do it in public!

At the same time, he felt a thrill of excitement at the thought of leaving this secluded vale and going he had no idea where and doing he had no idea what. Oh yes, he did know a little bit of what. It had something to do with getting a bow.

"I have a bow already," he asked, looking up at Hazalel. "Why do I need a new one?"

"For what is ahead of you, you will need the bow and arrows you will receive. What you have now is not what you will need for the battles ahead of you," said Hazalel.

"Is it kind of like how the sword I was given as a courier will not be able to do what this Dragon-sword will? My new bow isn't even as good as the one I lost when they captured me," said Noren.

"It is enough like that," said Hazalel.

Noren nodded. He thought for a moment of asking why the Ellenari could not get the materials needed for the bow and even escort them there, but thought better of it. He sat for a few moments longer, staring at his sword, and feeling too weary to get up and find his meal and go to sleep. He had worked much less hard today than in the previous days, but it would have taken days of rest for him not to feel tired.

Noren shook himself out of his dazed and distant state. It would not do to not eat the food provided – he was certain that it had special qualities – and it would not do not to sleep either.

Of course, the dragons needed the rest more than he did, for they would be flying, which was much harder work than riding. But most of them have been given the entire day to rest. At first, none of them had thought anything of the changed routine, but now Noren wondered if it had to do with this. The Ellenari may have known about this not only that morning but days ago – or even longer. Who knew how the Ellenari lived or worked or knew things? Noren and Elninya certainly didn't know.

24

The Shadow's Lair

The Ellenari brought them breakfast in the morning, along with extra dragon saddles and packs full of food, water-skins, and oil, as much as could hang from the saddles. While they ate, the Ellenari gave them more detailed instructions about the trees and branches to use for their bows, and a few other bits of information. "In case we are not able to be there at that time," said one of the Ellenari.

"Why can't you do this?" asked Noren. "You know what is needed and you are much faster than we are."

"It would not work for you if we did that," said Lisila. Her sword was free in her hand and appeared to be an unwavering white flame. "There are many things you do not know. Now, the sooner you fly the better. And remember: if you must enter the battle before you return here, to Shan'Dala, for further training, let Noren ride Onyxalis and let Silmavalien ride Airrock, Tiela, or Lighter. No dragon without scales and any less ease in the air than Airrock possesses should be burdened with a rider in the battle that is to come. But you must fly now."

That sent shivers down Silmavalien's spine, but they were finished eating and the Ellenari helped them saddle the dragons and attach the packages. Silmavalien felt reassurance by Aelaza's instructions and by the way the Ellena helped her with the saddles and packs. She had been so terrified last night that it made for her to sleep. What if Aelaza was going to be angry with her forever? She did not think she had ever made the Ellena so mad before. But she spoke to her today as if it had not happened.

They flew out of the valley. Minth told her he did not know what the Riders' Passage was even though he felt like he should have, but Airrock, Tiela, and Coroneth were all confident they did, and that was enough. As they flew the valley, the world they entered felt strange to Silmavalien. At first, she thought it was just the contrast between that world and the heaven-like city of Shan'dala, but then she saw that the world had changed, too. Fire and smoke ascended from the plains of Arosië, and she had the feeling that the evil of the nightmare was not very far off. The dragons felt it, too.

Silmavalien and the dragons kept in touch with Keya's family through Tanz and Naklath and Tryph. She made sure they still had the eggs she had given them, and learned that they were actually ahead of her and Noren. They were journeying towards the Riders' Passage as the Ellenari had instructed them, keeping on the lowest tier of the Steep Descent and the sea shore whenever they could.

Before long, the smoke made her throat scratchy, and the dragons told her they did not like it either. At least they were sometimes able to fly above it, something that made them grateful for their training by the Ellenari. Otherwise, only Airrock and a few of the others would have been remotely comfortable at those heights.

The smoke shrouded everything below them in gray clouds, and that night they searched to find a place as sheltered from the smoke as possible to rest. While the dragons settled down to sleep, Silmavalien pulled out and a packet of food and sat looking up at the sky, wishing she could see a star, when she felt Noren move up beside her. He stood next to her for a few moments and she enjoyed his silent company. Then he broke the silence. "Do you know anymore than I do about this whole business about new bows?"

She shook her head. "I know Lexamarian, about whom I've told you, had a bow that looked to be made of a wood I don't know and which was engraved. It was too heavy for me. She told me she herself came from Treas, I don't know exactly how long ago."

She did not tell him what she had realized that morning. They were going towards the Riders' Passage which was guarded by the Shadow. Noren now possessed the re-forged Dragon-sword. Was now the time when the prophecy would be fulfilled and the warrior among the Dragon-riders would slay the Shadow with the sword? It looked like it to her.

ℵ

Noren pulled himself together in preparation to tell Silmavalien when he noticed a flash of movement out of the corner of his eye. At least one Ellen was with them. He wanted complete privacy.

He would have to ask the Ellenari to give them that privacy.

He left Silmavalien, still eating her dinner, and went to the other side of the camp. He waited for a while, wishing he could have seen the stars through the smoke. As it was, it was very dark and he had to walk carefully. He drew the Dragon-sword, so he would be ready if any nightmares attacked. The red glow of the engraving did not disturb what little vision he had.

It was early winter, now, and he felt certain that the nightmares must have something to do with the fires. The wind that came down from the heights was very chilling. Noren waited for a while until he was certain Silmavalien had fallen asleep. Then he raised his voice and called, "Ellen, will you speak to me?"

He saw movement again and lifted the Dragon-sword just in case, though he did not feel the close presence of a nightmare creature. He knew that no Ellen would be threatened by him or by that sword, and he was certain that they saw as much better than he did in the dark as they moved faster than he could move.

"What do you want?" asked a voice that was not familiar. He might have heard it before, but it was one of those he knew.

"I would like privacy to speak to Silmavalien and not be overheard," he said.

"That may not ever be possible," said the Ellen. "I do not know, but you might have such privacy in Aros Cor. It is too dangerous for us to give it to you now. You may however have to either not speak about whatever this is to Silmavalien at all or do it when you may be overheard by us."

"Thank you," said Noren, bowing. "I will wait until Aros Cor, if no opportunity arises before then."

"Is that all?" asked the Ellen.

"Yes," answered Noren. With that, he felt the Ellen move away from him, though he did not know how far.

A rift opened in the smoke and Noren saw a few stars, still hazy through the smoke but quite visible. He watched until the rift closed and thanked the Lord of the Light. Then he went back and lay down under Elninya's wing after sheathing the Dragon-sword.

S

Dread lingered over Silmavalien, stealing her appetite. Finally she finished her meal and lay down to sleep, but sleep took a long time coming. Instead, the dread buzzed in her mind. How long would it take them to get to the opening in Dragonsong Forest? The last time she had fallen into the Riders' Passage she and the dragons had almost starved. First, they had almost died of thirst. She did not want to go through it again. And what if Noren with the Dragon-sword killed the Shadow and the Shadow also killed him? There was, apparently, so much that was so uncertain. It would be better, she supposed, than him being burned alive, as she feared from time to time, but she did not want it to happen. She wanted to get to live with him.

She had hardly slept when the time came to fly on again. By evening, the smoke was definitely much thinner. The air was still hazy, but she could see the mountains beside them, the forests and cliffs beneath them, and the sea. The next day, in the late morning, both Silmavalien and Noren and the dragons with them and Keya and her family with Veyan and their dragons approached the area of the Riders' Passage.

She saw that the earthquakes had changed the land. The cliffs rose up without any passage down them. The sea was choked with fallen pieces of land and rock, some of which had fallen nearly upright and still had trees and bushes struggling to grow on them. There was a long crack in the cliffs up which ran an inlet of the sea.

Tanz told Silmavalien Keya wanted to know if she should start bringing her family up.

No, Silmavalien responded. *We can fly all of you up at once, and that should make us visible from the crack for less long. I think this is very close to the abyss in which lives the Shadow. We want to be careful.*

Elninya, tell Noren this is where the Shadow dwells. We're going down.

Keya says to tell me now she can get an earth-star? Yes. That's cool. I can't think about that right now.

A few minutes later, the two larger dragons, blue and purple, were visible on the shores of the sea. Soon after that, she could see Tryph, who was not yet learning to fly, and the ten humans.

Keya had already mounted Tanz and Veyan sat on Naklath when the dragons with her and Noren landed. They were helping the humans onto the saddled dragons, one dragon for each human, when a dark shadow fell on the land.

At once, Silmavalien knew what was coming: the Shadow of the abyss. She dropped what she was doing, went to Noren, and whispered to him, "I think you have to fight this."

"Fight what?" he asked.

"The Shadow. It's coming."

"I've not been trained to fight shadows," said Noren.

"You have the Dragon-sword. None of the rest of us have a weapon that will do. And you have been trained for this. You just don't know it yet," she said.

Don't fly, Silmavalien said to the dragons. *Stay here.*

A wave came out of the sea with such force that it pulled the dragons towards it. They unfolded their wings and hovered. Above the chasm rose the Shadow, dark wings unfurled, flames flickering in its body.

"*I, too, can fight it,*" said Onyxalis. He circled, climbing higher.

The Shadow dropped into the chasm. Its whip of flame whirled.

Don't be afraid. Don't be afraid, Silmavalien repeated in her mind. *You will never forsake me. You are always for me. Love, Lord of the Light. Don't forsake me to fear. Don't forsake me to hate. You are always for me. Help us now!*

Rocks fell from the cliffs. Trying to dodge the rocks, the dragons moved towards the crack. Silmavalien and Noren were both on foot, picking their way along the rocks they had climbed onto to get away from the wave. Noren led, towards the cliff. But it was no safety. The Shadow was trying to lure them there and capture them. What else could they do? They could not fly into the barrage.

"*Actually, you might be able to,*" said Onyxalis. "*I might be able to melt it for you.*" He was still climbing. He breathed out a flood of lava-like fire.

The Shadow retreated deeper and farther into the chasm, nearer to Noren and Silmavalien and the rest of the dragons.

Between the cliffs it was very dark, and colors were muted and almost gray. Noren stood on a rock at the edge. The dragons were trying to dodge the missiles, some of which burned from the touch of the Shadow's whip of fire, without going into the chasm. The Shadow loomed above, terrible and threatening. It came down, swinging the whip of fire.

Noren leapt from the rock on which he stood to a patch of sand and pebbles under the darker shadow of the cliffs. He drew from its sheath the Dragon-sword. A little more cautiously, Silmavalien followed him.

As soon as it was free of its sheath the Dragon-sword shone as it had on the day when Noren first unsheathed it. The engraving shone like the sun, white-hot, like the hottest, uncooled lava. The blade glowed a brilliant, blinding orange, only less bright than the engraving. The jewels in the hilt and cross-guard flashed as if flames were imprisoned within them. Flickers of fire licked the edge of the blade.

Silmavalien looked from the Dragon-sword to the flaming whip of the Shadow, which looked as if it were now retreating from Noren and readying itself to fight Onyxalis. "A sword for the Dragons to match the whip of the Shadows!" she cried.

Noren did not acknowledge her, but then she was not really speaking to him. Silmavalien stayed as close to him as she could, followed him up the rocks more by feel and sound than sight. She kept her eyes on the Fire-Shadow above and the obsidian dragon. *I hope Onyxalis is okay.*

Apparently he heard her. *"I will be,"* he replied curtly. *"In fact, I'm going to make it go down back towards you."*

Silmavalien watched as Onyxalis turned back on his tail. He was far too big to descend into the chasm, but he thrust his face into it and breathed out that lava-like fire. It did look more like lava than like fire, though flames flickered around it, much as they did around the Dragon-sword. It poured.

I wonder if the Shadow also knows the prophecy about the Dragon-sword and that's why it now prefers to fight Onyxalis. Perhaps it did not know we had the sword before, thought Silmavalien.

At the same moment, Onyxalis warned them all, *"Be careful. I don't want you being hurt by any molten rocks I send down."*

S

Noren barely heard Silmavalien. His eyes were everywhere. He stepped forward over the sand, eyed the foaming sea, and then climbed back up the rocks away from it, vaguely aware that Silmavalien was following him, putting her footsteps in his. When he had got far enough he thought he was safe from the sea, he stopped.

He watched, taut and still, as the Shadow rose into the obsidian dragon's flame. Onyxalis swerved, then breathed out another flow of fire. Noren did not see or understand what happened. The Shadow came back down, very quickly this time. Onyxalis flew over the edge and dived.

Somehow, Noren knew, between him and Onyxalis, they had to keep the Shadow from attacking the other dragons. He, being bound on the ground, could not do it by himself.

He was glad he had had that experience of being sure he was going to die and being unable to do anything at all. He needed that now, while he watched and waited. The Dragon-sword felt light in his hand.

The dragons gathered into a tight huddle underneath Onyxalis, who twisted and breathed out streaks of flame, melting the rocks so that they proved harmless to himself if not to those he sheltered. As the Shadow came towards him again, he directed the rest of the dragons and breathed out another flood of flame. It retreated and came towards where Noren waited, Silmavalien behind him.

He stepped out onto the sand.

S

Silmavalien grasped her knife in her hand and stepped behind him. When the time came for him to fight, she would give him the space he needed. Glancing at the ring, she saw that the engraving on it glowed white-hot. They would both have what they needed.

"Lord of the Light!" she whispered out loud. Her heart beat violently. The seconds and half-seconds seemed to last forever. Dread filled her breast.

You will never forsake me, she whispered again. *Don't forsake me now. Fight for me.*

"A scorching death to higher life. Fire of dark meets the lake full from the sun," she muttered.

It was now so close. She was struggling against the memory of her previous confrontation, not that time at the bottom of these cliffs but at their top, with this nightmare shade. She saw its flaming eyes, full of poison, full of hate, nothing like the deadly flame of the volcano which had entered into the blade of the Dragon-sword.

"Lord of the Light, protect me!" she cried, this time almost a scream.

25

The Guardian of the Riders' Passage

No fear chilled Noren's heart as he stepped forward, as calmly as he had stood tied to the stake that day. The Dragon-sword seemed almost to raise his hand and he thought that maybe it really was winged. At a certain point he stopped and waited for it to come to him over the dark, gray water.

Nearer and nearer the Shadow came. Noren saw the malice and poison in its flaming eyes, but he was neither cowed nor horrified, not for the moment. The hilt was warm in his hand. The dark wings overshadowed him and seemed almost to close around him, cutting him and Silmavalien off from the rest of the world. Like death. He heard her scream behind him, reminding him that she was there. It was a strange comfort remembering that she was with him. Elninya touched his mind with the barest touch, so he would know she was there but not be distracted by her.

The whip of flame made a pass over his head. He barely crouched for a moment, then leapt at it, passing the Dragon-sword through it.

There was a flash of white light, and the Shadow retreated. The next it came closer, and the skirmish began in earnest. The Dragon-sword amazed him, seeming to move almost of its own volition, to know where to strike and where to parry, to almost pull him where he needed to be.

It flared like a flame whenever it passed near the Shadow, and once, during a brief pause in the play, Noren wondered where the Ellen had gone. Did they not intend to be here for this? He had the feeling that none of the nightmares he had ever fought before were anything to this one. It gave him a feel similar to that of the shadow that had risen out of the earthquake.

He had to be careful not to slip into the sea and even not to slip on the pebbles and sand. He wondered how Silmavalien was doing. It was well the Ellenari had made them practice doing so many strange things. If he had ever wondered if they were wasting time, he knew they had not been wasting time now. One or the other, or more probably both of them, would have fallen by now and they would both be dead, if not for all of that training.

Noren took a step forward, then a darting leap.

S

Silmavalien backed away from Noren and then closer to him, watching both his moves and those of the Shadow. She did not want to make things harder for him, either by getting in his way, or by being too far away from him to protect easily.

His bright, glowing sword encouraged her as much as the ring whenever she saw its flaming light. The tune to the song they had sung on Ellen Island played in her head, as she almost danced to Noren's beat. Once she found herself humming, "Triumph proceeds to predestined throne." Somehow, that, too, encouraged her.

Then Noren stepped decisively forward and leapt at the Shadow. She stood frozen for a moment. Should she follow him? Would she get in his way if she did?

The Shadow twisted around and came down. Deep darkness fell over her. The ring and the knife glowed white-hot, but she fell to her knees. "You said you would fight for me," she said out loud. She felt all of the Shadow's evil coming to surround her and envelop her soul in the darkness of hell. How could she fight it? It bore down on her mind and soul, snuffing out her thoughts, her loves, her dragons. She felt Minth's terror and attempted reassurance and aid, as well as that of many others for a moment. Then even that seemed to be swallowed in darkness.

"Love, you said you will not forsake me. You cannot. You are Love. You cannot lie," she said.

N

Noren saw the Shadow move. He turned around, the Dragon-sword leading the way. He felt himself cut off from Silmavalien, but it seemed that the darkness over him lifted. He stabbed and slashed.

The whole body of the Shadow flared up in one white-hot flame for a moment. Then it faded, cooling, reminding them strongly of the way that lava cooled.

Silmavalien rose to her feet, dizzy and shaking. She stepped across to him, stumbling as if she was about to faint, and leaned on his shoulder. He stood watching, relaxed, the Dragon-sword still glowing in his hand.

Then many things happened at once. A shiver which sounded like a crack ran through the earth. The water sang. Up the cliffs on the far side of the inlet went leaping what could only be one of the Ellenari, but it was definitely neither Aelaza nor Hazalel. He thought it might have been the Ellen to whom he had spoken in the night, but he could not be certain. He still wondered why the Ellenari had not helped them, especially if they were so close.

A song rose out of the earth and air. Songeth's voice gave form to it.

> Challenge is meeting challenge at last!
> The Shadow is slain and its victory
> Has now been turned to defeat long awaited.
> The Dragon-sword has at last appeared.
>
> The Dragon-sword is arisen at last
> Re-forged in the flame and light of old.
> Winged in the hand of its bearer it rises;
> Through death and life and death again he lives.
>
> The stars in the earth are freed at last
> And their Guardian arisen in light.
> The war is begun; the war shall now be won!
> Through death and life and death again earth lives!
>
> Long has the challenge of Nightmare reigned;
> Now we answer it with the sword unsheathed!
> This war, thought lost, shall be won, though fierce indeed
> And fire proceeds to predestined throne!
>
> The flame and whip of the Shadow's pit
> Has been defeated; it has met its match
> And been found no match for the flame of the earth
> The light and flame of the Dragon-sword!
>
> The fire of darkness is overcome
> By the fire of light in the darkness' depth
> And the whip of Nightmare by the Dragon-sword:
> Triumph proceeds to predestined throne!

Noren stood, his blood still racing, and listened. Silmavalien leaned against him, her eyes closed, and listened too. He put his arms around her and felt her body quake.

The song faded out of the ken of their senses. After a few moments of silence, except for the pounding of the waves, Silmavalien stepped away from him. They looked at each other for a moment, still feeling dazed.

"I'm alive," stated Silmavalien.

"Funny you should say that," said Noren. "I feel the same way."

"Really, it's that I'm free," Silmavalien said. "I thought – I thought – I don't know what I thought, but it's not been like that since so long." She shuddered.

"I don't know what you mean," said Noren. He looked around him. "This place is still dark."

"Of course it is," said Silmavalien. "Look at the cliffs above us! How much light *can* come in here? But it's not dark like it was."

"You're right," said Noren, looking up. "I can see stars."

The sky was not nearly as dark as it grows at night, but still dark enough for a few stars to be visible between the cliffs.

"Your sword is not glowing like it was," said Silmavalien.

Noren sheathed the sword. "Let's go to the top."

Minth and Elninya had already landed nearby, their bodies half in the water, for their riders to mount them.

S

Silmavalien patted Minth before he took off. *Yes, thank you. I'm glad we're well. Yes. That means I'm glad you love me and I love you.* He turned his head back to croon at her for a moment, and then took off.

At the top, the rest of the dragons were arrayed, except for Onyxalis whose black bulk hovered above them. It was difficult to find places where he could land. Keya stood waiting, and when Silmavalien slid off of Minth she embraced her.

When they stepped apart, Keya said, "I missed you so much! I'm so glad you and Noren are fine."

"I don't feel fine right now," said Silmavalien.

"Well," said Keya, "shall we go? Would a walk in the woods be nice? These woods are so nice."

"I guess," said Silmavalien.

She and Keya joined hands, and the whole group walked the short distance to the opening of the Riders' Passage, except for a few dragons who flew most of the way.

Standing on the rock out of which the Riders' Passage opened was an Ellenar. He was tall, and his hair was divided into many colors which looked to Silmavalien like the colors of the glow-stones of the Passage. One strip of his hair, from where it grew out of his forehead to the ends was one color, and another strip was the next color. In his hand was a sword set with gems of every different color, but in that lighting it was not obvious whether or not they glowed. His skin was a pale color, his long tunic looked like plates of greenish rock joined together, and his eyes were pools of milky light.

As they approached, he bowed to them. "Thank you for defeating the Shadow, Noren, warrior of the Dragons, bearer of the Dragon-sword," he said. "I am now the Guardian of the Riders' Passage. You may all pass."

Like Oaeiae is the Guardian of Ellen Island and its volcano? thought Silmavalien.

It was the first time an Ellen had ever bowed to either of them. Silmavalien stood still and watched, too dumbstruck to speak, as Noren walked right up to the creature.

ℵ

"Why did we have to fight alone?" Noren asked. This was the same Ellenar who had spoken to him in the dark, and he had been here all along.

"Because you had to fight it alone. I could not fight for my place," answered the Ellenar, unperturbed. "I cannot tell you why. The reason I know you cannot hear now."

Noren bowed himself then. He felt unbelievably strange. He had never before thought of the Ellenari as people who might need *them* to do things for them. What could they *do* that the Ellenari could not do? The Ellenari were stronger, smarter, faster. But apparently the world was very unlike what it appeared to him for the most part. "Y-you're welcome," he said, feeling awkward, but like he must say something.

It was still only about noon, and the Ellenar gestured for them to go on. The company entered the Riders' Passage, which was big that even Onyxalis to fit, and Noren found himself walking in what seemed like a tunnel through the night sky.

Elninya said to him, *"Do you remember what we thought about being free of the sky and flying among the stars?"*

Yes, said Noren. *I know what you are thinking. Here, already, we are enclosed in the earth and yet flying among stars! Perhaps we really will get to fly among the stars in the sky, as already we can fly among the stars in the earth. But, when we are free of the wide spaces of the sky, will we still be free of the earth?*

How many times must we die, or hatch, or be born, or whatever it is?

Perhaps forever? It depends what you call dying or death. Yes. I agree with you.

Maybe we won't mind. Already I'm beginning to think I don't mind as I did. Yes, it doesn't really matter whether we mind or not. But still, I'd like not to mind it.

S

Silmavalien, too, felt strange. She also had thought of the Ellenari as helping them, never of them helping the Ellenari. But she remembered the conversation she had with Aelaza watching the evening, and though she was surprised, she was not shocked. And, somehow, the Riders' Passage was inviting. There was something gentle and welcoming about its light that chased away the dread and fear she had been fighting this whole way.

N

The Nightmare Lord roared and dark flames flashed out from his body, the shadow of a fire that no longer burned. His messenger cowered in fear, certain it would be killed to await greater torment.

"The Shadow that guards the Riders' Passage is defeated? The Ellenari have won it again? The *Dragon-sword?!* But I broke the Dragon-sword so that it should never again be whole and so that, if it were re-forged, it still would not have the flame it had once! *I made sure to do it right! This cannot be!*

"Tell them all to fight harder than ever. We were so close to complete victory! We will not be defeated now!"

The messenger bowed. "Yes, lord."

"And go to that witch and make sure she captures these Dragonriders and these dragons – including the Obsidian Guardian. Do *not* forget him. Silmavalien should not have been permitted to rescue Noren last time. She was supposed to trap and kill them both. Tell her she must not fail now and to prepare her spells for the Dragon-sword. If she fails now, it will be all of hell for her.

"*TOTAL DOMINANCE IS WITHIN MY REACH NOW! I HAVE SENT MY ARMY FORTH!*"

26

The Spring of Nerya

In most places the Riders' Passage was big enough for the dragons to fly comfortably, and so they were able to make better time carrying the humans and their provisions that if they had all had to walk. But sometimes they stopped for Onyxalis to crawl through one of the places too tight for his bulk.

During one of these stops, Keya found herself an earth-star, as she called them. "I found it in blue to match Tanz," she told Silmavalien, "kind of like you found one in mint to match Minth's eyes!"

"Nice," said Silmavalien.

"Do you want to see where I took it out of?" asked Keya.

"Sure," said Silmavalien.

When they got there, Keya said to Silmavalien, "So are you and Noren married yet?"

"No," said Silmavalien.

"Do you want to be?" asked Keya.

Silmavalien looked over her shoulder at the others, then turned back to Keya. She spoke quietly. "Noren knows I'm interested if he is. But for some reason he won't talk to me about it. I get from the dragons that he's waiting until he has enough privacy to tell me whatever it is he thinks he has to tell me. I'm not sure if he fully knows himself yet."

"Oh," said Keya.

"The other thing," said Silmavalien, "is that this is so dangerous. Apparently, there's going to be some kind of huge battle. I'm really scared. What if one – or more – of our dragons die? But one of us might die, too. Or maybe even both of us. But I'm so scared. I – I – if one of the dragons dies …" Her voice trailed away and she began to cry.

"Oh, Silmavalien," said Keya. She had no idea how to go about comforting her friend. Her own heart quailed at the idea of being separated from Tanz. And she knew that Silmavalien knew everything she could possibly tell her about Love.

S

Suddenly, she felt all the dragons pressing against her heart and mind, pushing away the dreadful thoughts of losing them with their real, immediate presence, and enfolding her in their loves with all their voices twined together and crowding each other.

Yes, I know we'll all love each other, no matter what happens. I know you all love me, she replied. *I just feel this way. And I know you all feel this way too, more or less.*

Before long, the group continued on their way again. Silmavalien was amazed how much faster they were able to go than she had been able to last time, even though she should not have been. Not only were they all well-fed and watered, instead of starving, but they were mostly flying. In what could not have been more than about several days they reached the lake of Nerya, and she was struck anew by the beauty of the water that looked like it glowed because of all the glow-stone buried beneath it. Near the edges one could see, diffused by the water, the light of individual earth-stars under the surface, but further in the water was all a soft radiance.

The others were amazed, too, especially Keya. She took a long look at the water and then exuberantly declared she was going for a swim. She took her outer clothes off right there and dove in, and Silmavalien thought she had never seen anything quite like the way her body disappeared into and shone in that liquid light. Her little brother's dragon, Tryph, waded in after her.

Noren looked across the water at Silmavalien. "You?" he asked. He would not be surprised if she did not. Apart from the ripples made by the swimmers, the water was so dreadfully still. It made him think about death and life.

"I don't feel like it," said Silmavalien, "but this water is extraordinarily good. It's better even than what the Ellenari give us."

"It is," said Noren. After a short pause, he said, "I miss the free air, the sky, and the sun, but this place is really beautiful in its own way. You were right when you said it was like traveling among the stars, like stars buried in the earth instead of hanging in the sky. Of course, we don't really know what the stars in the sky are like. We only know what we imagine them to be like."

His words made Silmavalien think of Malchoris, the star Aelaza had shown her. Truly, she did not really know what Malchoris was like. She wondered if she really knew anymore about what he was like for knowing more about the appearances of his body than Noren did or than she had previously. It was quite possible that either appearance, that of the stars from Areaer, or that which Aelaza had shown her, was true in its way, but did not suggest all the truth. Aelaza had said as much.

She decided to tell Noren about Malchoris. She was not sure if she should tell him that what she was telling him was true, so she started out by asking, "What if stars, too, are more different and unique than we could ever have imagined? What if stars are burning globes of fierce and exultant fire and joy, a flame as different from both the fires we know as the lava that springs out of the earth is different? What if stars are person-like and engaged in the battle with the nightmares, too? What if once there was a star, and the matter out of which he was to be formed was scattered far away from all the other stars and spread too thin for him to form himself, and an Ellen helped him form himself, and he is all the happier and more joyous, his flame the brighter and fiercer, for burning alone in the dark skies with nothing to distract him from his Lord, the Lord of All Light, including his own light?"

Noren did not say anything at once. Then he asked, "How did you come up with such an idea? It truly is different and beautiful. But you're right about things being different than we think. Goodness, the Ellenari, about whom we never had any conceptions at all except from themselves, for no stories told us of them, are really different – not only different than we thought, but as we thought they were not! At least, I don't know about you, but I would never have thought that an Ellen would need me to fight a nightmare for him."

"Well," said Silmavalien, "maybe that Shadow could not be killed except with the Dragon-sword and maybe no Ellen can wield the Dragon-sword."

"That's possible," said Noren, "but I hadn't thought it." He paused for a while, looking at the milky water gently rippling on the rock, then said, "It's amazing these experiences the Lord of the Light gives us."

"You mean this, right here, right now?" asked Silmavalien, looking up into his face eagerly.

She did not see there what she had expected. "No, I wasn't thinking of that, though this *is* amazing, too," he said.

Silmavalien could tell that he did not want to talk. She got up and worked on oiling a few patches of Minth she thought might benefit from it, while conversing with her dragons. Then, she lay down, near the shore of the liquid light, and thanked the Lord of the Light for bringing her safely to this place. She was overwhelmed with a sense at once of the insecurity and strangeness of her journeys and adventures and with gratitude. So many good things had happened to her.

After everyone got out of the shining lake, they decided to stay there for a little while. The dragons would drink as much as they could before they went on.

N

Noren spent a lot of time with the two young Dragonriders, Veyan and Nereis. At first, it was difficult for him to speak to them, since though he had picked up a little of their language from Keya, and Keya had taught them far more of his language, neither of them spoke the other's language competently. He taught them as much as he could about using the sword without any practice weapons. Eventually, they decided to use arrows as make-shift practice swords. If they broke too many arrows, they would stop using them, since they might still be wanted, but he did not think they were likely to need the arrows again. He talked to Silmavalien, and she agreed with him that the new bows were likely to use different arrows, and the current arrows were certainly useless against many of the nightmare creatures.

But she did not want him to use her arrows anyways. "Your arrows are yours," she told him. "Break them pretending they're play swords if you want to, but you won't use mine. Mine are at least useful against orcs, even if none of the other nightmares, and I don't know that we will be able to make our new bows, still less that we won't have to fight again before we get them. But I guess you don't feel much need for a bow such as you have anymore, now that you have that awesome sword."

"I won't break all of my arrows," said Noren. "And we're going to try not to break any of them."

"All right then." Silmavalien rolled her eyes, and he could tell she did not believe him.

He wondered if there was any way to tell her what he really wanted to tell her. He had not seen any Ellenari near, but that did not mean they were not here. It was hard to get away from the rest of the group, and in the silent, closed passages sound carried very far, usually somewhat distorted, but sometimes amazingly clear. What he had to say he wanted no one but his love to hear.

S

They stayed for what Silmavalien thought was about two days around the lake of Nerya. All the dragons swam and played in the water, and they enjoyed the fact there was plenty of space for everyone to fly, even Onyxalis. Then they went on, and this time they took a passage that was new to everyone, including Silmavalien, since they were talking the way that opened out into Dragonsong Forest, further west than she had ever been before.

They found the actual Spring of Nerya, where the water bubbled up from a crack between two glowstones or earth-stars. They all knelt and had their last drink straight from the waters, and when Silmavalien rose from the waters, she said to those around her, among whom were Noren, Keya and Veyan, "I wonder where the Hall of Dragon Eggs is. From something Aelaza once said, I know it must be somewhere around here." Were the dragon eggs still protected there, and had she just not found them, or had they been killed, as the Ellena feared?

"Do you think we should try to find it and put our dragon eggs there?" asked Keya.

"I don't see why, and I think we would have been told if we were supposed to do that," said Silmavalien. "I haven't even the least idea of how to find it."

She lingered for a moment before they went on, looking at the Spring, at the gentle, bubbling curve of the waters and the lights shining through and reflected in the ripples that were ever-changing yet always-the-same. Her heart felt cold with a kind of horror or terror. What if she had ended up, in her confusion and ignorance, going the wrong way around the lake and trying to take this passage? None of them would have survived. The way to Dragonsong Forest was much longer. They would have all died before they were half-way there.

"Thank you, O Lord of the Light," she whispered. "How many disasters have you prevented? How many times did I walk on the edge of a cliff without falling and I did not know it, yet you kept me safe?"

She knelt down and touched the waters with her finger. Then she turned and climbed onto Minth's shoulders, flying after the others down the passage. This one turned out to be not only the longest, but the widest of them. It rarely even grew thin enough to force Onyxalis to land, though twice it grew so thin that all the dragons landed and let the humans walk through, while they flew up to find another way around.

27

Riders of the Obsidian Dragon

A cool breeze blew against his face. Noren almost shuddered with the pleasure, as it reminded him again of when he'd been led out of that stifling cell into the sky and air that moved and was alive.

A couple minutes further on, Elninya saw a light which was not that of the glowstones. In a few moments more the opening became visible. Through it they saw the peaks and shoulders of mountains, splashes of red light and blue shadow across them, against a sky from which the stars were not long vanished. It must have been the time of sunrise.

One by one, the older dragons, very hungry by now, soared through the opening. Even in the light of dawn, the glowstones still visibly glowed out of the rock as they passed over them.

Below them lay a large forested valley ringed by mountains. North and eastwards they were the sky-piercing, impassable mountains of the Greater Aravin Range, but on the south and west they were the much lower, though still very high mountains of the Lesser Aravin Range. The valley was full of hills and meadows, with sparkling lakes and winding streams, and the sides of the mountains were clothed in trees, too. As Noren and Elninya flew further into it, he saw they were in a valley which descended and opened up into the greater valley of the Dragonsong Forest.

The tired and hungry dragons flew down the valley and descended into the warmer air below. It was still colder than the Riders' Passage had been, and very chilling.

It soon became clearer just how immense the trees were. Most of them were bare and they were not conifers, but they had to be at least as large, and thick, and tall as the sequoias of the Steep Descent that Silmavalien and Keya had told him about. The meadows were also large, and it did not take Onyxalis long to find one where he could land. He was the one dragon who was not hungry, since there had been plenty of rock for him to eat in the Riders' Passage.

Noren quickly unsaddled Elninya and then sat down to eat the food he still had in his pack before going to sleep, while she flew off with the rest of the dragons to hunt the deer she told him were everywhere and bring back food for Tryph.

It was about noon when he woke to the cries of a hatchling dragon. He sat up and saw that Silmavalien had woke before him and was already watching the ugly white hatchling snuggling in the arms of one of Keya's brothers, the one called Kenaja, he thought.

Silmavalien saw him, and they acknowledged each other with their eyes, but did not move any further. Together, he knew, they rejoiced in the new life. It was almost two new lives, for the dragon was newly hatched and the rider's life would be new. Yet it was one new life, too, for the dragon and the rider would share their life. Watching brought back his own memories of bonding to Elninya and those first moments together.

After a few minutes, the dragon crawled out of Kenaja's arms to lick up the remains of his egg. Kenaja turned to Noren and Silmavalien and said, "His name is Karphathph."

"Dragons always have such interesting names, don't they?" asked Silmavalien.

Noren could not see what was interesting about the name Karphathph. It was hard to pronounce, that was all. But maybe it was so hard to pronounce because of the language Kenaja spoke. Kenaja had spoken to Silmavalien in his own language, and she had replied in the same language. Now that he thought about it, he was a little surprised that he had understood what she said.

Just then she turned to him and translated.

"I knew that was what you said," said Noren, "but I don't see what's interesting about the name Karphathph. It's hard to pronounce, though."

"Do you want me to tell Kenaja that?" asked Silmavalien, raising her eyebrows.

"No," said Noren. He stood up. "Though we should probably get about our work."

"We have to find Aros Cor first," she said.

"We know how to begin doing that," said Noren. "We know it's hidden in the Greater Aravin Mountains. We can ride Onyxalis. He isn't tired or hungry."

Onyxalis came to them, and while they saddled him, Silmavalien said to Noren, "I'm glad Karphathph hatched for Kenaja. He was always meant to be a Dragonrider."

"How do you know such things?" asked Noren. "They tell me you hoped Tanz would hatch for Keya and she did, and that you thought Nereis would also make a good Dragonrider."

She shrugged. "How many dragons am I bonded to? Eleven, no, twelve, thirteen if we count Onyxalis."

"Onyxalis is bonded to us," said Noren. He did not look up at her, but busied himself checking the ties. Then he said, "We're ready. You first."

Silmavalien climbed onto Onyxalis' back, and he climbed up after her. They secured themselves in the saddle, and then the obsidian dragon took off.

"I don't think he would have wanted to be ridden prior to whatever happened to him in the volcano," Noren whispered into Silmavalien's ear, hoping that Onyxalis was not paying attention to them at the moment.

"No, I don't think so, either," Silmavalien replied.

It was not long before they found themselves flying through a narrow valley. The sides of the mountains on either side were steep, and yet the trees clung to them and covered them though covered in snow themselves. A stream ran babbling down the ravine, and green grasses and herbs fringed its path.

Soon, the ravine opened up into a wide vale that was much smaller than the main valley of Dragonsong Forest. Most of the trees here were smaller, though some of them were even larger than most of those in the greater Dragonsong valley. Herbs and bushes dotted the vale here and there, sometimes forming clusters. Despite the altitude, there was very little snow. Dozens of little trickling streams ran here and there, and most of the greenery was lush and bright.

Onyxalis found a place to land, and the Dragonriders dismounted. His black bulk, with those red wings and accents, made a beautiful and interesting contrast to the green and white of Aros Cor, for Noren and Silmavalien were certain that this was Aros Cor. It fit the description they had been given.

"*This is Aros Cor,*" said Onyxalis.

They both knew that he knew. They looked into each other's eyes and Noren thought, *Surprisingly enough, I'm comfortable telling her around him.*

Then, looking around him, he thought, *This place feels very private. It gives me a feeling the exact opposite of the feeling Shan'Dala gave me.*

Now or never. I have to tell her. What do you think, Elninya?

"*Do whatever you feel like you should do,*" she said, and her voice embraced him in unconditional love.

Noren noticed then that there was a smell in the valley, very dim and faint but present, which reminded him a little of the volcano of Ellen Island. He dismissed the thought for the moment, and again meeting the eyes of his love said, "Come, Silmavalien, my love."

Her eyes sparkled as she looked up at him. Stepping as lightly as a dancer she stepped forward. The two trod fragrant and aromatic herbs and grasses under their feet.

"Silmavalien," said Noren, "I won't touch your hand just yet. First I have to tell you something."

She looked at him silently, but with eyes that begged him to continue.

"Shortly after Elninya hatched, I was afraid for my life and hers, and I shot and killed a little girl without looking or thinking."

She nodded gravely, without speaking, and he knew he did not need to tell her that he was really sorry. She knew it already. She knew well enough what had happened to him in the dungeon and at the stake.

After a few moments, she said, "Why do you tell me this?"

"Because if you are going to be my wife, you need to know it, what I've done. I can't hide myself from you and yet ask to be one with you, *ask for you.*"

She nodded. "So you'll marry me?" she asked.

"That's what I just said I'll do, if you will marry me," replied Noren.

This was at once so different and yet so like the past. He could hardly believe it was happening. It felt like a dream, yet too lovely and real to be a dream.

She did not say anything for a while, and he wondered if maybe she had not been expecting this, or if what he had just said impacted her more than she'd implied. Then she stepped towards him and took his hand. He grasped it lightly and kissed her.

"But, umm, I don't know how to get married," said Silmavalien. "Or when. And what will happen, since we're in a war?"

He kissed her again. "We're in this war *together*. Why don't we go and find the wood for our bows together now, my love?"

Silmavalien giggled. "And herbs. We want to gather the herbs here."

"I never heard about it before," said Noren.

"That's because Aelaza taught it to me. I never learned how to use a sword. But she told me about lots of herbs that have excellent properties, and I can just see and smell that this vale is full of them, every different variety and kind."

"And it's a good thing the Ellenari didn't try to teach this to me," he said, following her through the grasses. "I couldn't have learned anymore in that short time, and I *needed* most of it to survive our fight with the Shadow. I hope we get to go back to Shan'Dala and learn more."

"Yes," said Silmavalien. She knelt and plucked a sprig from a bush. "But perhaps we should look for the right tree, first?"

"That sounds like an excellent idea. Then we can gather herbs together. I think I can learn a little bit about that now," said Noren.

28
Not Yet

Silmavalien and Noren soon discovered that the vale was full of hot springs, interspersed here and there among the trees and groves of herbs. The water in the stream which ran out the ravine was drawn from these hot springs and from snowmelt, which explained why it was so warm and flowed freely. The rocks and dirt under and around the bubbling hot water were often splashed with terrible and brilliant colors of red, orange, yellow, and sometimes pink or green. The water was very hot, and even the rivulets that flowed away from the streams were often too hot to immerse theirs hands in. The water steamed, filling the vale with a light, warm mist.

Neither one of them wanted to waste time exploring the hot springs. They took a moment to note them, and then they found the trees they had been told to use for their bow staves. Using the tools the Ellenari had given them, they had most of the work done by nightfall, and Silmavalien managed to gather a fair amount of herbs as well, laying them on a rock near where Noren worked in between the tasks she could help with. They only had one of certain tools, and some things were much easier for Noren to do.

It was getting too dark to see well, so they put away the tools and Noren covered the bow-staves and then he turned to her and asked, "So, how shall we sleep tonight?"

"The way we've been doing," said Silmavalien. There was no mistaking what he meant. "We're not married yet."

"When will we be married? Why aren't we married yet?"

"We have to get married somehow," she insisted.

He rolled his eyes, clearly thinking she was ridiculous for caring about this, and she looked him in the eye, so that he really looked at her in return, and then said, "I'll ask Keya's father how he and his wife married. But, look here: we're about to go into a battle. We're going to have to fight. Do we want to bring babies into that? And what if I get pregnant? I won't be able to fight if I'm pregnant or nursing. You will, but I won't. And I think I'm needed almost as much as you are."

"Oh my goodness," said Noren.

He plainly looked exasperated, and she leaned forward to kiss him. "I love you," she said. "Later. Just a little while. Remember how close this is to being right on top of us? We don't even know if we'll be able to go back to Shan'Dala and finish our training."

"What*ever,*" he said, rolling his eyes again.

"If that's how it's to be, love, then let's go back down to where everyone else is, right now."

They took the bag of tools, the staves and the herbs, and mounted on Onyxalis.

As they flew out through the ravine, Silmavalien looked up at the stars peeking out in the blue-purple sky strewn with clouds. Mist was filling the valley below. She felt like she could have floated with the mist. She and Noren were *almost* really together now. It was almost as new a life as bonding to a dragon! It was hard to believe, working together in Aros Cor, riding together on the back of a huge black dragon, that they were in a war-torn world preparing to go to battle against a mighty force of nightmare demons. It seemed so jarring, so impossible. She suspected Noren felt that way, too. Did he really want to repeat something like the battle with the Shadow with a pregnant Silmavalien or one with a baby in her arms behind him? She wouldn't even be able to keep her feet and balance like that.

But if the world really were what it felt like it was right now, it would be perfect to marry now.

As soon as Onyxalis landed, she scrambled down his body as quickly as she could and rushed across to Keya. "To answer your question," she said, "I and Noren are going to get married as soon as this big battle is over … if we both survive, that is."

"Congratulations," said Keya. Then, "It really is going to be big. Bigger than you can imagine. We were chased out of our home by what looked like a limitless horde of horrors. Some of us thought we were going to die just from seeing and being near those horrors. They burned everything as they went. We wouldn't have made it if the dragons hadn't been out flying and seen that army hours before it reached our home, or if the Ellenari hadn't protected and led us." She spoke in a low voice, apparently overcome by the horror.

Both women were silent for a little while. Then, Keya said, "I think it was worse even than … remember the time you ran away and I and Tanz flew after you?"

"Yes," said Silmavalien. She, too, paused for a moment, before saying, "Maybe, it was kind of like how I felt under the wings of the Shadow. I don't think Noren felt it like that. But I don't want to talk about it."

"I can understand that," said Keya.

Silmavalien looked around. She tore a chunk of some fruit the name of which she did not know out of the same sack from which Keya was eating. "I promised Noren I would ask your father how he and your mother married each other."

"He's told me twenty times," said Keya. "At least. I'll tell you."

Keya had barely begun telling Silmavalien before one of her brothers heard them, and in a few moments all her brothers and her father and her grandfather had gathered around to hear her tell Silmavalien. She had chosen to tell about it in her native language, which meant that only Noren could not understand. Silmavalien was not sure if any of the men knew *why* Keya was telling her, though.

It was a simple ceremony, mostly involving some flowers which the couple would wear as clothing, a few dances, and then some prayers while the couple said their vows to each other under a tree in private, after some public declarations before their parents and siblings. Keya finished, saying, "If you and Noren want to get married that way, we'll help you. I'm sure we will."

Her brothers excitedly proclaimed their willingness, and Keya went on. "It won't be exactly alike though, for obvious reasons, such as that we're not Noren's parents or relatives! So, we'll have to change some things. But we can do a ceremony for you anytime you like. If you want to do it right now there aren't very many flowers, but I bet in a few weeks there'll be a lot more, if you can stay here that long. How long do you think you'll be here for?"

"We have no idea," said Silmavalien. "We really have no idea about anything."

"And, of course," added Keya, "we know a lot more about the Lord of the Light and who he is, so we can pray to him to make you one in Love better than we could – well, not I, but other people – for my father and mother."

"I don't think we know that much about him," said Silmavalien. "Mostly, I think we just *think* we know more about which names to use."

"I guess," said Keya. "I know a lot more than I did when I was born." Her eyes sparkled and shone, and Silmavalien saw it even in that light. She knew that Keya knew plenty that she could not say. Most of what Silmavalien knew she could not say, either. She knew that most of what Noren knew he could not say. It was only fair to assume that others might know or have known much more than they could say or at least than they did say.

"I know a lot more than I did when I was born, too," said Silmavalien. "But that doesn't mean we know more than your grandfather or your mother did."

Keya shrugged. "That's true."

Silmavalien went to Noren and told him as much about it as she could remember. She could not remember all the details, but she tried not to leave out any than she did remember.

"It sounds beautiful," said Noren, "but, really, what matters to me is whether it pleases you. I could care less about all these things. Goodness, for all I care, we could even do the ceremony after we get together. You can decide what you want to call 'marriage' but all the marriage I care about is us choosing that we will love each other forever, and take care of each other, and never leaving each other, and then acting like we're married. But all the time, *I love you.* If you promise to marry me if you live long enough, you're my wife right now."

"All right," said Silmavalien, "and I do promise, but I told you I have other objections to acting like we're married just yet."

"Yes, you did," said Noren. "I wish you didn't, but they make sense. In a way. I still think you're assuming that you know more than you do, and you should know better by now."

"Don't you do the same thing all the time – assume that you know things you don't know when you know better?" said Silmavalien.

"If I do, I don't notice it, not when I'm the one doing it. I doubt you do either," he retorted.

They walked further into the woods. Then he stopped, and after they listened to the nearest stream for a few moments, he asked her, "Why on earth did you suggest to me that you wanted me to renew our proposal and engagement – an engagement that was about to culminate in marriage – if you didn't want to be married yet?"

Silmavalien stiffened. "I don't know. Because I'm stupid? Because I wanted to know that you still wanted to marry me – like, really wanted? Because I *do* wanted to be married now. I just don't want to be married now under the circumstances or at least the expected circumstances."

"You *are* stupid," said Noren. "You really should have told me about Minth and married me, instead of running away. Then we wouldn't have this problem."

But we don't know what would *have happened,* she thought, but she did not say so out loud. She would not want Noren to fear that she had gone back on her decision that it was wrong of her to betray his trust.

Above them fifteen dragons performed a graceful aerial dance.

Both of them looked up, watching the dragons circle against the stars. For several minutes they stood in this way, silent. Then Noren said, "I'm sorry. I'm not mad about it, just frustrated. Though it might have been even more frustrating if we had done that. As we were just pointing out, there's so much we don't know."

29

The Herbs and the Bow

Early the next morning, six Dragonriders and all the dragons flew up to Aros Cor. The rest of Keya's family remained in the lower lands of Dragonsong, some of them hunting, and others of them improving their camp, which they intended to make into a real dwelling under the direction of Shilchu, who was old and weakening, but still capable of advice.

Silmavalien would have loved to watch and be part of that, and she knew Noren wanted that as well, but they still had to finish their work on their bows. She was just about to finish on her bow when a young boy's squeal made her turn.

"The hot water isn't boiling Tryph!" Nereis was yelling. "He likes it. Look at him. He's paddling around in it!"

She and Noren both down their work and came to look. She stood above the hot pool, arms crossed over her chest, watching Tryph paddle, when she felt Minth's yearning.

You want to try it too? You're sure it won't hurt you because it doesn't hurt Tryph?

All right. But be careful. Go in slowly. I don't want your whole body covered in blisters and half your skin burned off.

Minth made a jubilant croak and wheeled in the sky. He had found one which might be big enough for multiple grown dragons to bathe at once!

A few minutes later, all the dragons except Onyxalis – who was too big – and one-day-old Karphathph were bathing in the hot springs.

She and Noren finished their work and laid out the staves for their bows, and then she asked all the Dragonriders to come to her. One of the reason she had asked them to come today was to help her collect the herbs growing here. Now she gave them detailed description of the herbs she wanted, what parts of them to pluck and the best stages of growth to get them, along with descriptions of plants that might look similar but weren't. Then she assigned specific herbs to one person or another, and gave that person more detailed instructions, taking him or her with her to see an example of their herb. It would take too long to teach everyone even half the herbs which the Ellenari had taught her.

Inwardly, she was jumping up and down with excitement. She

had gotten to see more of the herbs, and just how many, there were in the vale. Last night, she had gone to sleep thinking about all the things Aelaza had told her about the properties of the herbs. Several of the dragons had reminded her of things she had half-forgotten. Hidden in this Vale of Aros Cor were some of the most potent healing herbs in the world, though Silmavalien thought they might exist in other places, too. She thought some of these herbs she had found here also grew on Ellen Island, but she had not known about them when she was there. She had learned from Aelaza that certain herbs might make it less likely for Veine's (for any other dragon's) off-spring to be harmed while developing in the egg inside her body, but she had learned the herbs were rare and never expected to find them. Now they were here, in comparative abundance.

The herbs won't undo the curse, but they will lessen its effect. That's what she told me, and that's enough to be exited about!

It was certainly enough to make her so excited she had not been able to sleep well last night and she had been the first one up in the morning.

When you get out of your hot bath, she asked, *would you like to eat some herbs and grasses fresh? Goodness, you can even graze a little if you like!*

Yes, I know. This has been much too much like it was when you were all hatchlings and growing up. It was rather nice in the Riders' Passage, since we weren't doing anything except moving, so we were free to converse the whole time, but at first I know we were all really tired. It was no rest from the training in Shan'Dala flying to the Riders' Passage and still less fighting the Shadow.

I hope that this is over soon, too, and all goes well, so that we will be able to go back to just being together and playing together. Since coming back over the High Pass with Noren, there's been no rest or space for anything. Even when there's time, we're all too exhausted.

I know you don't understand it, but I am horribly afraid. I can't imagine that we'll be involved in a war and a great battle and none of us will die, still less that none of us will be seriously hurt!

I know you're not afraid, Veine. Yes, Airrock, Wydth, all of you, I know most of you are not afraid either. It doesn't seem to be in your nature to be afraid. But I can't help it, and I can't argue myself out of it. I wish I could.

Yes, Minth. I know that Love is in control. You're so good at reminding me of this, Veine. I know we're loved. But Dinora died. So many have died. Lexamarian's Lelarina died long before she did. Horrible things have happened to so many people. I can't help but see them as horrible and be afraid of them. Everything will be good. Everything will be well. Love is always completely triumphant. Thank you, Lighter. I know that. But I don't feel, I don't see it, right now. I'm not even sure how much I know what it means ...

In the afternoon, everyone gathered together again. Silmavalien looked over the herbs others had collected and asked them some questions about their gathering. Then they all sat down on the grass and took a meal out of the bags they had brought with them. Conversation was awkward and stilted because of the language barrier.

She noticed Keya's eyes on the staves for their bows, and then she noticed Noren watching Keya. She leaned over and whispered, "She doesn't know how to shoot. At all."

"Really?" Noren whispered back. "I'm surprised. I'd think she'd be interested in learning and that her father or brothers would be willing to teach her – or you. You could have taught her."

"No, I couldn't have," whispered Silmavalien. "I hate killing."

"You could have done target practice, silly," replied Noren. Out loud, he asked, "Would you like to learn how to make a bow, Keya?"

Kenaja leaned over and asked, "Sister, what did he ask you?"

"If I want to learn how to make a bow," answered Keya. "The fact is, I *would* be interested. But I'm more interested in this battle against the nightmare creatures, and I think that is what these bows are for. I want to be trained for it, and fight too. Not people. Not animals. Demons." She gave Noren the same answer in the language he understood.

Silmavalien and Noren shared a glance with each other. She was one of the people who, fluent in both languages, had to hear everything twice.

"If I have time here, then I can show you how to do what I and Silmavalien have done," said Noren, "and then how to finish it into a bow, but I think the end result depends a lot on things the Ellenari have not yet shown us. And whether you get to be trained for it certainly depends on the Ellenari. If you cannot ask them yourself, we can ask them for you. There's so much about the battle that I don't think even the Ellenari know." He leaned towards Silmavalien again, and asked, "Do you still have the bow you told me about? Lexamarian's, I think it was?

The one you think our bows might be like?"

"Yes," said Silmavalien, "but I don't have any arrows for it. At least, I *think* I still have it. I haven't checked in a long time."

"Why don't you check? And, why don't you see if you can draw it now? You might be able to!" asked Noren.

"Yes, I should do that. I should have thought of that a long time ago. But I don't know whether it's in a pack I have here, or one I left down below," said Silmavalien.

"Why don't you go and look?" asked Noren.

She stood. "I'll do it, right now."

While she and Noren had been speaking, Keya had been translating so that Kenaja could understand and so that Veyan and Nereis could understand more easily and better.

In a few minutes, her eyes flashing, Silmavalien returned with Lexamarian's bow. "Look!" she said. While everyone's eyes were still turning to her, she bent the bow, struggled with it for a moment, and strung it.

"Not easy," she declared, "but a lot easi*er.*"

"Cool," said Noren. Keya translated.

Silmavalien proceeded to raise the bow and draw back the string. Shaking, she slowly let go of the string. "I think I could learn to use this," she said.

At that moment, two things happened simultaneously. Everyone stood. Aelaza's voice – it took Silmavalien a heartbeat to recognize it – rang out, saying, "How do you have that ready already?"

"I don't," said Silmavalien, as she saw the Ellena springing towards her from one rock to the next. "This is Lexamarian's bow."

In a few moments there were several other Ellenari among them. "Do you by chance have any *others* of our bows among you?" asked Aelaza. "Why didn't you show me this a long time ago?"

"Because I forgot about it," said Silmavalien. "No, I don't have any other bows around. But this is one of *your* bows?"

"Not the kind we use ourselves," said Aelaza. "But does Noren or anyone else have any such bows?"

"No," said Noren. "I never had any, but even if I had, I wouldn't have it now. I lost every material thing I owned except for some clothes when I was captured."

Keya came forward nervously. "I don't know which of you I'm supposed to ask for this," she said, "but I would like such a bow for fighting the nightmares and to fight beside Noren and Silmavalien."

"Do you have any of Lexamarian's arrows?" asked Aelaza.

"No," said Silmavalien.

Hazalel turned to Keya, "All of you must have some training. I think Lexamarian's bow will be perfect for you, but you will have to learn how to use it, and we will have to make new arrows for it, unless we can find the one who would be able to find Lexamarian's arrows. Even so, I think it is better for you to have your own arrows, Keya, and I think Lexamarian's bow will be the right size and weight for you. Kenaja, Veyan, and Nereis will get new bows, and they will help make them as Noren and Silmavalien have." He turned to Lisila.

"Whether you and Tanz will be able to fight in the battle alongside Silmavalien and Noren, we don't know," said Lisila. "I would advise you not to ask for it, Keya."

"But I want to, and they will need help. That's going to be the fiercest part, isn't it?" asked Keya.

"We *think* so," said Lisila. She turned to Noren and Silmavalien. "Tomorrow you will begin the return journey to Shan'Dala."

Yes! thought Silmavalien.

"Through the Riders' Passage?" asked Noren. "We do not have the provisions we would need for that."

"No. You will take the High Pass. Aelaza and Hazalel will guide you into Shan'Dala as they did previously."

"Are we to take the High Pass because that way is faster?" asked Noren.

"No," said Lisila. "I have brought you some more provisions, and I would have brought you more and asked you to take the Riders' Passage, since it is much safer, except that a fierce battle is being fought in the place you, Noren, slew the Shadow. The Nightmare Lord is desperately fighting to regain the Riders' Passage and we might not be able to protect you from its mouth to Shan'Dala."

"He won't win against your Guardian and install another, will he?" asked Silmavalien. "We would hate to have to do that battle with the Shadow all over again," she added.

"Do not worry about that," said Lisila. "If the Nightmare Lord gains the Riders' Passage again you and Noren will both die."

"Why is that something not to worry about?" asked Silmavalien.

Looking around her, she perceived that this was something which was obvious to everyone except herself, Ellenari and humans included.

She perceived nothing from any of the dragons, though she thought several of them, among them Veine and Minth, were laughing at her. "What?" she asked.

At that moment, she understood from Minth. If they all died together, her worst fears would not come to pass. *But there's more to it than that, isn't there?* she inquired.

It depended on how one thought about it. Who could say it? But something it was *not* something to be afraid of.

Silmavalien was used to that kind of response from dragons.

Aelaza addressed her then. "You have done well with the herbs. You and Noren are to leave tomorrow morning. In the meantime, you may as well finish what you have begun so well. I am glad you have found so many and so good herbs."

"Thanks," said Silmavalien, blushing. Aelaza's tone and manner had been more intimate than she had ever thought they could be. It scared her a little. Why? What was going on? Was something somehow wrong?

The Ellena bowed, then sprang away. Some of the Ellenari remained, continuing their conversations with the people they were talking to, but Silmavalien handed Lexamarian's bow to Keya who, engaged in conversation, scarcely acknowledged her, and then left to get a drink. She felt strangely disconcerted.

Hopefully, the return journey would give her enough energy and enough space to herself and time with the dragons to settle herself.

That evening, Keya came and sat next to her. "I hope they let me go with you tomorrow," she said. "Whenever we're separated I really miss you."

"I hope so, too, I guess," said Silmavalien. "I miss you, too."

"You guess you hope so?" asked Keya.

"I don't know, I don't know so," said Silmavalien. "I really want everything to go my idea of *well*. But I asked the Lord of the Light to make me good, and I guess that involves this kind of thing?"

"Something like that, too," said Keya.

30

Spell of the Night

Noren rose in the night and went to Elninya. He mounted her without the saddle, and she took off and carried him to one of the spurs of the mountains to be alone with themselves. When they settled down, he said out loud, "Elninya, sometimes it *does* seem like we died. If every time we die, we're freer than we were before. I didn't really mind fighting the Shadow. I'm not afraid of fighting it again. And we're not afraid of losing each other temporarily, either. I mean, we are, but not the way other people are. I wish Silmavalien and Minth and Veine and all the others could have the experiences to make them not afraid that we've had."

"I wish so, too," she replied. *"We're really together now, and nothing can separate us. We have the same purpose, and the purpose we have is real and triumphant, so why fear?"*

But Silmavalien wants the same thing, too. To be good. To obey Love. To love. She wants the same thing you told me you wanted for me at whatever price, even death by flame, and which I now want in the same way, thought Noren.

"Yes," said Elninya.

"Not that we're – or I'm – that great either," mumbled Noren. "I'm miffed that Silmavalien first opened the door to me and then doesn't want to step through it with me. I told her I wasn't mad at her, just frustrated, but I don't know if that's completely true. I *am* frustrated, but I'm not sure I'm not a little bit frustrated *at* her. Maybe, I wouldn't be able to learn how to be really good unless I have to learn how to be really good to someone who's not perfect."

He rose to his feet. "Let's fly some more, Elninya," he said into the cold night wind.

S

Several hours later Silmavalien woke. She knew by the position of the stars where they were visible between the clouds rolling in that it was just after midnight. A few moments later she was wide awake and aware that Elninya had left sometime in the night.

What are you and Noren doing, Elninya? she asked.

"Flying."

Something is wrong, thought Silmavalien. *I want to go south, too. What about all of you?* she asked the dragons.

South was not the way to the High Pass. There was no reason to go south.

Could there be dragon eggs southwards?

The dragons did not know. How would they know?

Elninya, does Noren have the Dragon-sword?

No? Then either you're turning around right now or I'm coming to you. In fact, either way I'm coming to you with it. You should never be without it anymore than I should take off my ring.

They did not want to turn around. Apparently, Elninya had heard her question to her dragons. If there were dragon eggs, they wanted to find them before the nightmare hordes got to them. Did she remember hunting the orcs and finding Jareth and Daurth's eggs?

All right. I'm going right now. Silmavalien had gotten to her feet and was filling a pack with things. *And I'm bringing Elninya's saddle, too. Onyxalis, what do you think?*

The black dragon did not think anything at the moment. *"Going south is a strange choice, but there could be dragon eggs in the Lesser Aravin Mountains if there were dragon eggs in all the different places you found them, Silmavalien. I will go with you."*

All right. Thanks, said Silmavalien. She put Elninya's saddle on Airrock, saddled Tiela, attached her and Noren's personal bags to the saddles, and mounted Tiela.

We're coming to you, Noren!

At dawn, Elninya and Noren landed in the Lesser Aravin Mountains, but still took a couple hours before Silmavalien reached them.

Silmavalien silently dismounted Tiela, found the Dragon-sword, and presented it to Noren. Then she said, "Noren, I've given this sword to you one too many times. Don't leave it again."

Noren said nothing as he took the sword and buckled it around his waist. Then he said, "What are we doing here?"

"I don't know," said Silmavalien. "Well, I know what *I'm* doing here. I had to come and give you *that.*" She pointed at the sword hanging from his side.

"Don't rub it in, Sil," said Noren. "I know it was dumb of me to leave it, even just for a short flight to the hills to be by ourselves. You don't have to keep reminding me. I won't do it again."

"Okay," said Silmavalien. She paused for a moment, then said,

"So there's two options now. We sleep here, or we fly back to Dragon-song. Either way, we're a day behind to the High Pass and Shan'Dala."

"I'm going to keep going south," said Noren.

"Does that mean we are going to sleep right now? Because none of us is flying any further south before sleeping," said Silmavalien.

"Yes, we can do that," said Noren.

"And why are you going south?"

"There's something there. I want to go south. We aren't even out of the mountains yet. As you mentioned, there might be dragons eggs in the Lesser Aravin Mountains."

"I suppose," said Silmavalien. "But what if you get to the foothills and still want to do crazy things?"

"We'll discuss that when and *if* we get to it," said Noren.

"Do you *want* to get captured and burned alive?!" yelled Silmavalien.

"No, of course not," said Noren.

Silmavalien turned red in the face and opened her mouth, but the words she wanted wouldn't come. Noren held up his hand. "I'm going to try not to get captured, Silmavalien. Onyxalis is with us. We have both the Dragon-sword and your ring. I don't think a net will hold all of that."

"Neither of us knows what we might be dealing with. I don't think even Onyxalis knows," said Silmavalien.

"No. Neither of us knows what we might be dealing with. So, I am going to sleep right now, since you insist."

"I do," said Silmavalien. "I will go to sleep too. I am tired, and you and Elninya must be more tired than I or Minth are."

I hate fighting with you, but this is just stupid, she thought.

𝒩

Noren woke in the early afternoon. All he could think about was an obsessive desire to go south. He had never experienced such a thing before. He knew no reason for it and he found himself distrusting it. He woke Silmavalien, intending to fly back to Dragonsong Forest with her.

When he had roused Silmavalien she rubbed her eyes and said, "You know what? I really feel like going a bit further down myself."

"You do?" he asked. "You were dead opposed to it in the morning."

"I do," she said, quite clearly. Noren was convinced she was fully awake by now.

"All right then," said Noren. They saddled the dragons. If she felt differently now … it was not as if he could stop her if he could or wanted to try, and he did not forget how she had appeared out of the sky to rescue him. If she wanted to do something, she might have a reason.

S

When they reached the lower foothills after dusk, Noren and Elninya circled down and landed. However, the farther south Silmavalien went the more she wanted to fly south. She was surprised that the dragons, all of them except for Onyxalis, felt the same way. There was something exciting ahead of them! Even Elninya felt it. She asked her.

She dismounted Minth and walked to where Noren stood next to Elninya. "Noren," she said, "I'd like to go further tonight. So would the dragons."

"How will we hide Onyxalis during the day? He's huge," said Noren.

Silmavalien wondered if humans were really going to be their biggest problem. What about the nightmares? "How populated is the region just ahead?" she asked.

"It's not that populated," said Noren.

"Might we be able to take a risk? Find a field for him to lay in? If Onyxalis is all right with this, he can lay somewhere other than where others of us do, that way if he is discovered he can fly into the air and we won't be discovered right away?" asked Silmavalien.

"*I don't object to the arrangement. I am here to protect you two,*" said Onyxalis.

"It might work," said Noren. "I guess we can if you really want to." He shook his head. "I only wish we had the bows we and the Ellenari were going to make and the arrows. I'm really not sure what those bows and arrows could do, but I'm sure it would be something helpful."

"I do, too," said Silmavalien, "but I don't think it would have helped to keep Lexamarian's bow but have no arrows for it." As she spoke, she thought of Keya and Tanz. She spoke to Tanz, asking her if she also felt like there was something good and exciting in the south.

No, she did not. Why?

We're south, and we feel like that, said Silmavalien. *We're not sure why.*

"Well, if we're going to fly, we might as well fly now," said Noren.

31

Call of Dragons

In the evening, when they were preparing to fly again, Noren said to Silmavalien, "What if this is a trap?"

She looked at him steadily and asked, "You think it is?"

"I can't rule out the possibility," said Noren.

"I don't think I could rule out the possibility, either," said Silmavalien. "There are very few possibilities either of us can rule out."

"But the Ellenari told us to fly to the High Pass, not to wander about south of the Aravin Mountains," said Noren.

"Even the Ellenari don't know everything," said Silmavalien. "When I first met Aelaza, she had no idea that I had so many dragons and she thought they had come from eggs in the Hall of Dragon Eggs near the Spring of Nerya."

"I'm still uneasy," said Noren, "and it's really strange how first I wanted to go south and you were absolutely opposed, and now you want to go south and I don't."

"I would have been opposed to any other direction you'd decided to take except for towards the High Pass," said Silmavalien.

She paused for a moment, while she worked at getting the saddle onto Lighter's back. Then she turned to Noren and said, "How about we go this one night more, and if we don't find anything we'll go back towards the High Pass? It's not like we're even going straight away from the High Pass. We're going east as much as south, and the pass is east."

"All right," said Noren.

When morning came and they circled down, Noren said to Silmavalien, "I want to take a walk and look around."

"All right," said Silmavalien. "Onyxalis is not far off. The other dragons are here. If we don't go too far, it should be pretty safe. You are going to take your sword, right?"

"Yes," said Noren, reaching for the sword and belting it on. Why had he been about to forget that again? "We should take our bows, too, as little use as they are against most foes."

"Sounds good," said Silmavalien, quickly grabbing her quiver. "Shall I string it?" she asked.

"If you want to," said Noren.

Silmavalien strung it. Noren decided he might as well string his also. He looked at her, "And you have your ring on, right?"

Silmavalien looked at him strangely. "Are you teasing me? You know I have my ring on. The only time I ever take it off is when I speak to the Lord of the Light and I always put it right back on."

"Yes, I know that," said Noren.

S

Something is really strange, thought Silmavalien, *yet I want to go on. Something or someone is calling me.*

She led as they meandered through the plains, mostly south. After about an hour and a half, her wandering path took them past a grove of trees to a recently plowed field. A slight rise on the ground stood on one side of the plowed fields, and between the fields and the top of the rise rose a few trees beside which stood a little cottage.

Silmavalien stopped dead still. "I feel the presence of evil."

"I do, too," said Noren. "Should we go back?"

I know you're ready to fly to us the moment we need you. Thanks.

"I want to go and see that house," said Silmavalien.

"Do you still feel like someone is calling you?" asked Noren.

"Kind of. If I think really hard and pay attention," said Silmavalien. "I feel like it comes from somewhere over there." She pointed to the rise in the ground and the cottage.

"All right," said Noren. "We'll go there. Should we ask the dragons to be in the sky, ready for us?"

"Yes," said Silmavalien. "There. I've done that. I wish we'd left them saddled."

"Should we go back and do that, and then come back?" asked Noren.

"We might as well," said Silmavalien. "But I don't want to eat."

"We won't eat then," said Noren.

Walking straight, the journey was about three quarters of an hour. In a little over two hours, Noren and Silmavalien were standing in front of the door in the cottage.

"There is evil in here," said Noren.

"There is," said Silmavalien.

"My hands want to touch that door," said Noren. "Whether to knock on it or to break it down or what I don't know. I think we should flee."

"No," said Silmavalien. "We should go in. Someone in there

needs something. Look! My ring is glowing." She held her hand in front of Noren's face.

"You're right," he said.

"Open the door," said Silmavalien.

N

Noren stopped to pull the Dragon-sword from its sheath before opening the door. *Good!* he thought. *The spell, or whatever it is, must be broken. I am remembering the sword on my own now.*

L

Within waited the witch, Luvine. She was shaking. She had felt the approach of the two Dragonriders and then had felt the distance between them increase again. Had Noren suddenly remembered that he had forgotten the Dragon-sword and gone back to get it? She did not want to deal with both the Dragon-sword and the ring, even though the ring was the more incalculable of the two. Then she saw the door open and the male Dragonrider stepped through, the Dragon-sword burning in his hand. Behind him followed the female Dragonrider, about whom she had been more afraid. She had seen both Dragonriders who came to rescue Noren from the fire, but she had not known which was the keeper of Dragons, the companion of the warrior of the Dragons.

N

Noren stepped through the opening into the stuffy darkness of a room far bigger than he had thought. Instantly the blade in his hand lit up. He felt Silmavalien step in, right behind him, and then heard the door close behind them.

They stood on dark blue-gray stone. Near the back of the room stood someone who seemed to be bent with age but they could not see much of the person, who was arrayed in purple veils that largely obscured his or her shape. The walls of the room were hung with purple curtains and lined with tables cluttered with bottles and scrolls and a host of other instruments. Silmavalien and Noren could not take it all in, in a glance.

"Greetings, Dragonriders," said an old, cracked, female voice. "Welcome to my abode."

Both Noren and Silmavalien started at the sound. Shivers ran down their backs. Neither of them answered. Silmavalien stepped out from behind Noren.

"My name is Luvine. I would welcome you to my service and teach you the secrets of power, power greater than your masters, the Ellenari, can give you," said the witch.

Silmavalien did not answer. Neither did Noren. He continued to watch her as she took slow steps, first one way, then another. Finally he said to the witch, "We don't want your power."

"But if I am aware, the Obsidian Guardian has hatched and is with you. Why is he with you unless you want power from him? Perhaps, he would be interested in my offer? What do you say, keeper of Dragons?" asked Luvine.

Silmavalien still did not answer. She continued to move back and forth, across the room, with no pattern or purpose that Noren could see.

L

Luvine's fear and trepidation grew greater and greater as she watched the female Dragonrider perfectly navigate the maze of traps and spells she had created to capture her. Almost every step was the only one which would not land her in an invisible trap. Luvine eyed Noren's sword with fear, also. She knew something of what it could do. Watching the female Dragonrider, she remembered what her dark masters had told her about how the Dragonrider came across dragon eggs. She wanted the female Dragonrider to speak. If she did, she might gain some power over her. As it was, everything was going wrong.

Luvine almost flew across the floor towards the female Dragonrider.

N

As soon as he saw the witch move towards his beloved, Noren stepped forward to intercept her. He could see the malice and danger in the way she moved. He could feel the energy of her witch-craft in the air. Holding the point of the Dragon-sword before him and the blade across his path, he advanced.

The witch stopped. Evidently, she did not want to be anywhere near his sword.

"Have either of you ever been afraid of death?" she asked. "If you let me, I will use my power to protect you and your dragons, your loved ones."

Neither Silmavalien nor Noren spoke. The witch's words hung in the air. Seconds passed while Silmavalien moved, back-tracking, going sideways, turning about, walking forward, often re-tracing her path. Noren stood where he was, his eyes darting between the witch and Silmavalien. He did not know what his love was doing, but he would not distract her.

Silmavalien stood before one of the tables.

L

Luvine stood, frozen in fear. The female Dragonrider stood with her hand inches away from the bottle that contained one of the old witch's most powerful and precious spells. She had to do something!

The witch moved. Noren's sword burst into flame. Whirling darkness and terrors filled the room. Unerringly, the female Dragonrider's hand guided itself to the bottle. She picked it up and crashed it on the ground. Luvine could not believe it, even after all she knew and had seen. How had the female Dragonrider known to do exactly *that?*

S

As soon as the bottle shattered into a thousand shards on the rock floor, the curtains and walls on one side of the room seemed to dissolve. Out of the darkness coalesced and resolved the forms of dragons, growing larger and more complete and more solid every millisecond.

In a moment Silmavalien's mind made sense of all the impressions she had received. Dozens of dragons, bereft of their riders, imprisoned in a nowhere no-space no-light of witch-craft! Now she felt their minds spinning all around her. She felt them reach out towards her as soon as they had space to think enough to do so. She reeled from it all.

L

In that moment Luvine knew that the female Dragonrider had come primarily not in answer to her summons but to the dragons.

32
Release of the Dragons

For a few moments everything was confusion and chaos, roaring and flickering lights and darkness. Silmavalien still did not speak and she was for a few very precious seconds completely overwhelmed by the thoughts of seventy-one dragons.

𝒩

Despite all the chaos, which made it feel like the world was revolving and spinning around him, Noren, after leaping once again between his love and the witch, stood still. He thought he was going to fall; he thought he was being tumbled head over heels; he thought the ground was falling out of underneath his feet. He stood still, scarcely moving even a finger on the hilt of his sword.

S

Silmavalien, too, did not move. She was too overwhelmed by things outside the witch's control to do so. When she could think, she remembered something. She took the quiver off her shoulder and reached into it. She pulled out a sprig of a precious herb she had found in the Vale of Aros Cor, the only sprig of its kind she had. Next, she took an arrow and speared it through the sprig. She took her bow in her hand, fitted the arrow to the string, and saw through all the chaos the flaming Dragon-sword.

She knelt, taking careful aim. Then she released the string. *Twang* went the string. *Zip* flew the arrow straight to its target, the blade in Noren's hand, before the witch knew what was happening.

𝒩

Noren was startled by the impact to the sword and to his hand through the sword, but he did not know at once what it was. In fact, only long afterwards did he put together what he knew and come to the understanding that that sensation, out of all the chaos, was real and what it was. Nonetheless, he remained still.

As the sprig and arrow caught fire, the herb exuded an intense fragrance which instantly cleared their minds and senses. Silmavalien moved very quickly, back and forth, jumping sometimes, and in a few seconds she was with Noren. The witch stood, reeling from her own spell, three and a half feet away.

In a moment Luvine had produced a long knife in her hand. She sprang at Silmavalien.

Noren moved forward holding the point of the Dragon-sword before him. Luvine impaled herself on the blade and caught fire.

"It was you two whom I meant to burn alive!" she screamed. A moment later she was consumed completely in the flames.

The room cleared. Noren and Silmavalien looked at each other.

"We did it," they said simultaneously.

"Did what?" they asked, once again simultaneously.

S

Silmavalien drew herself together to answer. It was almost too horrible to speak, but that it had happened was far more horrible, and it had to be dealt with now. "She killed Dragonriders and captured and enslaved their dragons, assaulting their minds with bitterness and hatred. She tended to capture the dragons while their riders were being burned alive. In fact the dragons themselves burned, but under her witch-craft instead of dying the essence of their bodies was transported into a place somehow connected with that bottle I broke."

"Horrible!" said Noren. "I suppose this is what she meant to do with me and Elninya?"

"I would presume," said Silmavalien. She looked around her, then said, "Let's put all of this stuff to the flame with your sword."

"That sounds like an excellent idea," said Noren. "Is it safe to move through the room?"

"If it isn't, we'll never get out of here, right?" said Silmavalien. "You've got the sword."

"Why don't you get the door, if you can find it?" said Noren. "We don't want to breathe this stuff as it burns. If you can get any windows, get those too."

Silmavalien easily found the door through which they had entered and opened it. She could not find any windows and Noren was right. The place was filling with an air and smoke that seemed poisonous.

Yes, Dalis, why don't you do that, please? Thank you, Silmavalien responded to a suggestion from one of the dragons.

In a moment several of the dragons had broken a hole in the roof. It began to fall around them and they scrambled out to rest on the hillside.

As soon as Noren had set everything in the room on fire with his sword, she fled with him through the door. They hurried into the middle of the ploughed fields, and the seventy-one dragons gathered around them. From there they watched the witch's house burn.

The dragons around them were many colors, blue, blue-gray, red, orange, green, yellow, and countless variations of these colors. Their scales shone in the sun, and both their scales and their colors shone ever more brightly as the witch's house was consumed in flame. However they were weak and gaunt and they flinched from the sunlight. Two of them were albino.

"We're going to have to flee *fast*," Noren said to her. "There's no way this fire can go unnoticed."

"First I must give the dragons the herbs I collected in Aros Cor, but I wonder what you are afraid of, Noren. Nightmare creatures may find us as well wherever we go, for all we know, and we have little to fear from humans. This is probably the same witch whose witch-craft bound Elninya. Without her, who do you think is going to assault a company of nearly a hundred dragons with Onyxalis?" answered Silmavalien. She called Airrock to her.

After Airrock arrived, in just a few minutes, Silmavalien rode her back to their camp. She tied their bags to Airrock's saddle and they flew back to where the seventy-one dragons newly released from a curse rested. Then she made everyone clear a space for her, tore off her cloak, laid it on the ground, and assembled the herbs on the cloak. When she had all the herbs arranged on the cloak in order of type, she dumped the rest of the contents of the bag on the ground and spread it too on the earth. Those types of herbs the uses of which she could not imagine being helpful here she put all together on one hand. Then she divided those which remained into seventy-one more or less equal portions. She instructed Noren to help her with this.

While she worked, she said, "I'm sure some of these dragons would benefit more from one herb and some more from another herb. I bet some of these dragons need more period, and others need less. But I don't know enough to tell for certain, and I certainly don't have the energy to figure out what is best for everyone in the time we have. So, I'm just going to give them all as nearly the same thing as I can, since I can't think of anything better."

"I'm not criticizing you about this or asking you for an explanation, Sil," said Noren. "I'm glad we did this, though."

"Me too," she said, when she realized a minute later she had not responded. She was too busy with the herbs, trying to keep track of them and to divide them as equally as she reasonably could. Meanwhile the dragons who had always been free mingled with the newly-freed dragons and spoke with them.

"It's horrible," said Silmavalien to Noren. "Think of losing your rider and then being tormented and enslaved like that! I'm so glad I came here."

"Have you told the other Dragonriders?"

"Airrock told Tanz, I know," said Silmavalien.

Neither of them spoke again for a few moments. Then Onyxalis called their attention to the flames consuming the witch's abode. *"The curse is broken,"* he said.

He jumped into the air and landed amidst the ruins, of which little was left apart from the floor of dark blue-gray stone, polished smooth.

It took her a few moments to realize the full import of what Onyxalis had said. *The curse is broken? The curse?* The curse that weakened all the dragons? The curse that had killed Dinora and so many others before they ever hatched? The curse that damaged the dragons in their eggs, making them albino, making their skin crack, messing up their minds?

"We need to thank the Lord of the Light," said Silmavalien to Noren. "It's he who's done all this, helped us with it. We couldn't have done it without him."

"Do you need to stop what you're doing or to speak out loud?" asked Noren.

"I don't think so," said Silmavalien. "We'll thank him better later, but he will know we thank him now. He's Love."

She could not, however, understand it. Her soul burned and writhed with the thought of the pain of the dragons. She felt crushed by their agony. *Help us love. Help us not to hate,* she prayed. *Deliver us from the nightmare. Don't let us be enslaved by the nightmare, reduced to nightmare ourselves. Rescue me and all these dragons completely. Don't let us be consumed by fear and hate. You are for us.*

Silmavalien clung to the fact that she had asked to be made the kind of creature who really was good, who could only do good and could never do evil. The same best thing she had requested for herself must be the best for everyone else. Surely that was what all of this was working towards.

"All right, Noren," said Silmavalien. "Let's give this to the dragons. It isn't much, but I think it will help."

"How shall we do it?" asked Noren.

"Umm," began Silmavalien.

"Make them form themselves into two lines, one of thirty-five dragons, the other of thirty-six dragons, and present themselves to you and to me? We'll give the herbs to each of the dragons, and when a dragon has had his or her herbs, he or she goes over there," Noren pointed, "by the grove to be with your dragons – you can ask them to go there – and the next dragon comes for his herbs, until they are all done?"

"Yes," said Silmavalien, "I think that will work. Thank you, Noren."

"It's really nothing."

33

Answering Song

They were preparing to fly for the rest of the day. Silmavalien leaned against Minth's neck and stroked his jaw. *I know you were thinking about me and watching me the whole time. I love you so much.*

Yes. I know. The rest of you love me too. You were all paying attention to everything you could without distracting me. Thank you so much. Who even knows who remembered the plant in my quiver?

ℕ

I'm sorry, Noren said to Elninya, hugging her around the neck as tightly as he could when she was so much bigger than him. *That's horrible. But it didn't happen to you – us – though.*

"But it happened to someone else!"

I know, said Noren. *It's really sad. But I love you. You love me. We're going to love them. I'm sure their riders loved them and love them still. But I can understand why you're upset.*

I know. It would be so horrible if someone's rider or dragon didn't love him or her.

He leaned his head against Elninya's shoulder. Noren could not think of how to comfort his distraught dragon. He had never known his friend to be so upset or, more accurately, upset like this, before. She had been pretty upset at him sometimes. Now she was in turmoil. Always before she had been confident.

Songeth's voice began on a low thrum and rose. Noren scarcely noticed.

𝑆

Silmavalien felt every muscle in her body jump. One by one but very rapidly, three more dragons' voices joined Songeth on a chord of throbbing anguish.

Words materialized in her mind, but she did not join in. The anguish of the song wrapped her into itself before she even thought about the fact that three of the dragons were singers. At first she listened in heart-broken silence, then began to weep. If ever words or a song were put to the way she had felt before her surrender to the Lord of the

Light when it seemed as if the nightmare would steal her soul, or to the
way she had felt embraced by the wings of the Shadow, this was it.

> Shadows fall on a lonely sea as we struggle in pain
> The night upon us is thick and heavy; who looks for light?
> Chains bind us in futility and we struggle in vain
> The sea wails and our hearts are failing; who can still fight?
>
> Love is broken and it flees from us
> Our thoughts are crushed and we die in pieces
> Wandering through a choking waste of dust
> Weighed down by a thousand curses
> Our souls withering in shreds
> Torn in two by a fire of the night
> Caught in a hundred mortal dreads
> Enslaved beyond the last glimmer of twilight
>
> Powers fail and we writhe in torment; who can still arise?
> A flame of destruction; we are dragons no more
> Souls are dissolved in nightmares' horror and we have no eyes
> What can set us free from a prison with no door?
>
> How can we be loved, we who never were and are not?
> All is one impossibility of torment.

N

Noren touched Elninya gently. He understood her horror. He himself
reeled. So there was a void into which all answers fell and could not rise,
a void out of which not even an echo returned of the question.

S

Silmavalien felt the last note of the song, if such a cry of anguish could
be called a song, fade away. She hoped it was the end. She spoke to all
the dragons present. *I'm sorry. I couldn't come sooner.* What else could
she say? To her, what the song conveyed was no surprise. She had
encountered it in the dragons' first moment of freedom while the witch
still lived. It was one with her fear of losing her dragons.

Silmavalien spoke to Songeth. *There is an answer. You can't end it there.*

I know that no words I say will answer it. But there is an answer. You can't end it in a finality of the impossible, of despair. It can't just be dropped there. It's a lie like that.

I know that's how they – you – felt, to some extent still feel. She was speaking to all the dragons around her now. *But it's not the truth. Not if you leave it there. If you leave it there it's all wrong, even though it* does *feel like that sometimes. But how can we put wrong feeling into a song to be felt over and over forever and ever? It's not distressing like the song about the prison of ice and the smothering that is freedom is. That song is impossible to bear if you aren't willing to go through to the freedom; it feels like this one then. But it has hope in it! It is hope! This is not hope. This is despair. This is a lie. Love is a person and Love is victorious. Love must be victorious, simply by being itself. To love is to triumph over the nightmare. Don't you remember when I first really realized that? It was after we buried your clutch-mates, Songeth!*

Even this one has at least a possibility of hope in it! I know that the song for now cannot be like this, for your anguish and despair is greater, but this we could leave it for it was true: what you just sang, if you leave it, is a lie.

Silmavalien gathered herself together and sang as softly as she could the final two verses of the song she and Songeth had sang when they buried the hatchlings:

> We find all here are lost
> In this land beneath the sun
> None the falling night and shadows of the past
> Can outrun
>
> Beyond the storm what wait
> All of earth to grasp e'ermore?
> Unlooked for light? Else a dark, haunting fate
> All t'swallow

"It *is unlooked for light,*" Silmavalien whispered out loud. "*Except that we've all been looking for the light all our lives.*"

𝒩

Noren, to whom Elninya had told the entire conversation, stepped forward. "Silmaválien," he said, "I *like* the way those verses end. I think they *are* appropriate."

She smiled at him. He could see the tears wet on her cheeks and pain in her eyes. She spoke out loud now. "Songeth, don't tell me you can only sing what comes to you. Sing something better. If nothing else, we will sing the Dragon Song. Though," she added, "I think my and Minth's bond-song would be better. Songeth, we will do the best we can to sing *that*, even though what we sing will be only a mockery of what I and Minth experienced and know we shall experience again. Only when we experience it again, it will be so much better, so that what we experienced then will be to that as this attempt to sing it will be to the first time."

Through Elninya, Noren felt her reach out to the newly-freed singing dragons, asking them to sing with her, and he felt the one named Dalis respond.

A moment she lifted her voice again, and he recognized the song from which she had sung him a few verses almost a year ago now. In one way it was so much fuller and better with the accompaniment of the singing dragons. In another way, Noren thought, it was not. Silmaválien knew what she sang, and that made her song as full as a song could be. Even if he had not thought her voice was as beautiful as a voice could be and nothing could ever add to it.

> Swift and fiery, wind immortal,
> Running beyond all mortal sight,
> Now made one, undying in unity eternal
> Beyond the everlasting fire and light.
>
> Before the worlds were born
> This was and is a world of its own;
> Only those to love forsworn
> Know this world to which no eagle has flown.
>
> Now see and behold, lo!
> This world more deep than eyes may see.
> Come and find what no mind may know
> Where all may dwell and as one be.
>
> The streams here are pure and clear.

The winds are born with a flame living.
Never can one come to the end of me here.
There is fulfillment and yet no end to the seeking.

Come and find all your desire
To be made one ever closer.
Soar on winds of fire,
Fly beyond all you ever were.

This is where your heart can learn to fly;
These are the lands of true flight
Where there is no end or limit of beauty and sky
And you can race flame, soar on light.

This where you may run
As fleet as deer;
This where you will soar to the sun
Find there is no fear.

Swim through the rivers,
Ride upon the crest of the waves of the sea.
The winds here are stronger
Than all you can ever be.

Yet there is no harm;
Even pain will be life in love.
Find only peaceful charm,
Join the joy of all winged life above.

Do what you cannot do.
Race the wind swifter than you.
Find her in your heart, too
In strangest ways all your desires come true.

Elninya, Noren asked excitedly, *do you recognize our own bond here?!*
   Yes, each is unique and yet alike!

S

Silmavalien walked through the dragons and touched the pink scales of one dragon's shoulder. The dragon, Dalis, snaked her head around and blew her hair into disarray. *I know you miss your rider,* Silmavalien said. *What was her name? Oh yes,* his. *Fornake. But you have hope now. You have joy. Your bond with him is the truth. The witch's magic was the lie.*

Yes. I'm not mad at Songeth. That first song just couldn't be left like that. Even you, Dalis, I think needed to sing first that song, and then this one, because this is the answer to that.

"*Fly now. It is not time to fight the Nightmare,*" said Onyxalis.

The *now* was so urgent that Silmavalien leapt up Dalis' foreleg and seated herself on the pink singing dragon's shoulders.

34

Fly!

In a few moments all eighty-five dragons were in the air. Silmavalien thought that such a vast array of creatures as large as dragons and as colorful could not fail to be missed by anyone in the region, certainly not anyone who was looking.

If we're to die, you wish I was on your back, so we could die together. I know, Minth, and I love you, but I don't think you need to be afraid of that. We love each other and we'll die together, just like we live together, even if we aren't physically touching.

Now she felt the presence of the evil Onyxalis had mentioned. For a moment she thought perhaps they should have taken Noren's advice and flown at once. Then she thought that even already the herbs were probably beginning to have an effect. Flying would have been dangerous to the dragons in the state in which they had been. More importantly, if there was to be a battle with the demons it was absolutely necessary that the dragons be convinced of and loyal to Love. If they were wallowing in despair and bitterness they were defeated already. What had delayed them had to happen and, perhaps, it could only have happened then. It had to happen before battle with the nightmares.

Yes, Songeth. I love you, too. I love all of you. You know that. I'm not mad at you, Songeth.

Silmavalien felt Dalis rock under her in a gust of wind. She was riding without a saddle, and she could fall far too easily!

Dalis was sorry. She was definitely struggling with the alternating winds, even though even Minth wasn't having any problems.

I know. It's not your fault. How long has it been since you were able to fly or move at all?

The air in her face felt cold and wet. It was going to rain. And she was so tired. She guarded her thoughts from Dalis, even as she thought they would have to land and she would change to Airrock. She let the silver dragon know.

Silmavalien looked down, around, and behind her. She saw a few winged monsters behind them and some things she could not see very well in the fields below them. Clouds were beginning to form above them.

I have questions, too. He told me he will never forsake me and will fight for me. But the evil is unbearable. She spoke to all the dragons around her. *Don't give in to the questions. Don't give in to the despair. Fight against it, not for it. Why did such horrible things happen to you? I don't know. But don't give in to the evil. What can happen to us? I don't know. But always fight for Love. Never give in to evil, never give in to fear, despair, hatred, bitterness, or the lust to dominate and control. Fight it. Call upon the Lord of All Light. The Ellenari call him Shallim-Araldor.*

She spoke especially to Minth and Veine and several others of her dragons, but she did not shut the others out. *We don't know much about death, but we do know it is part of the journey deeper into Love. It won't be final separation. It won't be final horror.*

Yes, I don't know what it will lead through. It might lead through something as horrible as what these dragons – you've – experienced, something as horrible as what I felt I might enter under the wings of the Shadow. I don't know. I hope it doesn't. But I can't be sure. After all, Love let these dragons suffer this. But, if it does lead through horror, it will lead through. *Of this I am certain. The world beyond, the final world, is what we've glimpsed in impression and in love of one another. And I don't see any reason to think it does lead through something like that. I just don't know.*

Half the reason she was speaking was to combat her own terror. She did not know whether she was so terrified because of the nightmares around her, or because of what had happened to the dragons.

𝒩

On Elninya's back, Noren fought fear in his own way. He cast back in his mind and remembered when Silmavalien had told him that he did not know what he might really think or feel while being burned alive and repeated his reply, applying it to his present fear. *It doesn't matter what's it's like. It's really stupid to feel about what I feel. It becomes a lie. If there's one thing I know, it's this. That song is like death. A once-frozen life gives way to death as cold as ice – death can break life's death, turning living death to dying life. To die, to rise high – to touch the grave and touch the skies. Bright the blackest flame, a scorching death to higher life! Death will evermore be release to the regions bright. That last line reminds me of the song Silmavalien just sang. I don't know any better way of saying it. Do you, Elninya?*

"*I do agree with you,*" the dragon replied. She impressed images upon his mind: a sunset and thoughts about dying away into beauty: her feelings about fire when she was young: the openness of the sky.

Yes. There is no reason why I should be disturbed by this prospect more than by anything else. What I saw and know holds true. Even if it does not, I can and will trust the Voice. The Lord of the Light and of the Dark. Love is Lord and has the power even over these horrors that sound too much like the hells and cursed existences of the myths. He promised that what he is doing is making me good. He is Love. I can only trust him. I can only believe the Voice. Yes, I will do that, resolved Noren.

S

Silmavalien's thoughts turned to the fact that she had not yet properly thanked the Lord of the Light. That would be a way to resist the nightmare's assault on her mind. *Thank you, O Lord of the Light, for Dalis. Thank you for leading us to these dragons. Thank you for protecting us and helping us so that we, too, could remain free from the witch and free your dragons and defeat her. Both the ring and the Dragon-sword have their power from you. And I remembered the herbs and my bow. Thank you. Thank you for helping me and Songeth sing to the dragons. Thank you that we've got to experience love through each other. Thank you for Minth.*

Dalis was having a hard time keeping up. She was not last yet but she had lost her place. Vampire-like nightmares and other winged horrors were behind them. The wind was rocking her precariously.

Maybe I should've dashed across and got on Airrock, thought Silmavalien, *but Onyxalis's cry was so urgent. How could I know?*

N

Noren looked behind him. Out of the ground rose horrors. Winged nightmares, some of them looking more like rotting corpses, some of them reminiscent of the stone giants, gained on them. He remembered the last fight in the air he had endured which had ended in a ring of flame. It had seemed so hopeless. It had been so hard. He and Elninya were tired. The freed dragons could hardly be in any better shape. He did not want to do that again right now. But he was not really afraid. He had been able to see cause for only despair then. Their situation could hardly have been more hopeless. Yet they had not been defeated. The Lord of the Light had given them victory through Silmavalien's ring.

Onyxalis wheeled back over the group. *"You have not yet seen me in battle. You will be amazed."*

S

There's Ellenari ahead? They're coming towards us? Oh, Minth! Silmavalien clung to Dalis as she fought to navigate the winds. Her whole body was sore despite all the various ways in which the Ellenari had trained her. She did not feel like she could cling to Dalis much longer.

I know, Dalis. If worst comes to worst, we'll land.

Yes, I'm more comfortable with Onyxalis between us and our pursuers, too, Dalis, Veine. I think I might feel less of the evil, even. He has something of the same effect on me as the Ellenari often have. Or is it their approach that I feel instead? I don't know. It doesn't matter. It's good, either way.

It really was misty now. They were flying in and out of forming clouds. The winds were getting even more chaotic. It might be *their* presence she was feeling, as the storm fought the nightmare. She was thrown forward on Dalis' neck one moment and lurched backwards the next. Dalis told her that her whole body hurt. The moisture in their faces felt like rain.

A flood of heat. A flash of lurid red-orange light. Silmavalien was too weary and exhausted, on the verge of tears, to look over her shoulder.

Dalis swerved and almost rolled over. Her wings beat staggeringly.

What was that? Silmavalien asked.

Dalis shared a blurry image of a barbed arrow.

Oh! We're being shot at by orcs? Can we climb?

Dalis did not know if she could climb. The winds might be more violent.

Through the ranks of the dragons shot an arrow like a shooting star. In that cloudy sky, it seemed like lightning and their skin tingled as it passed them.

I hear you, Veine. The Ellenari are here. Thank goodness!

Aelaza says to tell me we did well? Umm, well, we need to do well now!

Dalis did not think she could breathe fire. She could not fight. She only just remembered that dragons like her should be able to breathe fire.

Aelaza says it's all right? Just fly. I'm not sure how much longer
we can *fly.*

𝒩

Noren looked over his shoulder. Onyxalis dove through the clouds in a
haze of molten fire mixed with steam. Flashes of flame and dark smoke
went up where the nightmare horrors collided with or were caught in the
stream of his lava-like fire. His mighty tail swept more out of the sky.

Noren bent low over Elninya's neck and drew the Dragon-sword.
He was not sure if it would be helpful, but he thought that just in case he
should have it free.

Onyxalis, should we come back and help you?

"No. You're much more vulnerable. Elninya does not have
scales."

Noren sighed. *Let's go back to Silmavalien and Dalis, now.*

35

Towards the Mountains

So I should come and fight with you? asked Noren.

"Now, yes," said Onyxalis.

All right. I and Elninya are coming. His heart beat dreadfully fast and hard.

Elninya turned one way. The rest of the dragons, except for Onyxalis, flew past them. Noren experienced a sickening moment of terror and was glad that Silmavalien had suggested they not eat that morning.

Around them, mostly on the ground, several Ellenari engaged the enemy. Their arrows took out winged horrors; their swords, gleaming in the misty darkness, cut down orcs. Onyxalis moved this way and that in a haze of fire and mist.

Several bat-like creatures dripping with blood and gore came towards Noren and Elninya. Noren felt faint and overwhelmed with horror. Elninya dipped and swerved. One came right overhead, dropping towards Elninya's neck. She tilted. He stabbed. The vampire went up in flames. Only then did he know he struck it.

Elninya spun around and breathed fire. An arrow from the Ellenari took down another vampire. Noren caught one with the Dragon-sword as it tried to avoid Elninya's fire.

"Go with Silmavalien now," said Onyxalis. "The Ellenari will take care of the rest of this."

That disappoints you, Elninya? Noren asked as she turned.

"Not really. I'm tired and hungry. But I did enjoy scorching them. We both scorch them." The glee in her voice felt like a thermal under their wings.

In a few minutes they circled down and landed where Silmavalien and the others waited for them on the ground. It was raining in earnest now.

Noren slipped out of the saddle and saw Silmavalien running towards him with a roll of food in her hand. She had a half-eaten one in the other hand. As soon as Elninya folded her wings, she came right up to him and stretched the roll towards him. "I thought you might be hungry now," she said.

Noren bent over and took it. "Thanks, but I'm glad I didn't eat earlier. I don't feel too sick anymore, but those were sick nightmares."

She nodded. "I know."

Noren still was not sure he could eat, but he did not tell this to Silmavalien. He stuffed the roll in his shirt. He could eat later while they flew.

"It took us two nights' flying to get here," he said to her. "It won't take us less to reach the mountains again. Can the dragons hold out that long without food?"

"And Airrock and the others of mine who are strong can't hunt for seventy others!" said Silmavalien. "There's probably not even enough food for them around here. Otherwise I'd ask Onyxalis if there was something he could do."

She paused and looked around. Noren thought she looked bewildered and flustered. Then she said, "But we can't stay here. We have to keep moving. The faster we move, the sooner we can eat."

"No," said Noren, "but as you said, a few humans are probably not much of a threat to us. They probably wouldn't even think of attacking so many dragons with less than a full army. And the dragons might feel better after they've slept."

Silmavalien nodded. Then she said, "I don't really want to scare people out of their wits."

"They're probably scared already, if anyone saw anything of that battle, which I bet someone did. Or if anyone saw us fly overhead, which they might have. We didn't get very high. And someone probably saw the witch's house burn," said Noren.

"Yeah, I guess," said Silmavalien.

Her replies were becoming more and more dull. She looked weary and unfocused. "I'm sure that was more intense for you than it was for me ..." Noren began.

He stopped short. Silmavalien did not look as if she heard him at all. She swayed, pressed her hand to her head, then fell.

She fainted, didn't she? Noren asked Elninya. The dragon responded in the affirmative.

Silmavalien sat up. Noren swung himself out of Elninya's saddle and landed heavily. He retrieved the roll she had dropped out of the wet grass which was wetter every minute and handed it back to her.

Like a streak of starlight, Aelaza rushed up to them.

Seeing her, Silmavalien asked, "How many of you came to help us?"

"More than just I and Hazalel," said Aelaza. "As I told you, you did well. You can rest here for the few hours left before nightfall."

"All right."

Silmavalien rose, still taking bites from the roll, and stumbled across to where Minth had lain down. She sat against his side to finish eating, drank again, and lay down next to him. In a few moments she was fast asleep. So was Minth.

Noren smiled, hearing the exchange between his love and Aelaza and seeing her get up to rest.

Aelaza turned to him and said, "She'll be fine."

Hazalel stepped with long strides over the wet grass and came close.

Were they worried when we disappeared south instead of going the way they told us? Noren wondered and then suddenly felt strange in the presence of these beings. Did they worry at all? Was it even a possibility to them? "When did you know where we'd gone and why?" he asked them.

"I could not tell you that," said Hazalel, "but I will tell you: we know why you went before you knew why."

Noren nodded. He took the roll out of his shirt and had a bite. "When we fought just earlier, how did I and Elninya do?"

"We did not have the luxury of scrutinizing your movements as we do in Shan'Dala," answered Aelaza. "You should probably go to sleep, too. You might not be as exhausted as Silmavalien is, but you will be if you don't sleep."

"I'm hardly ready to eat yet," said Noren. "I can't sleep."

"Then walk, and you'll be tired soon," said Aelaza. "There's no more for us to tell you now."

A couple hours before midnight, the Ellenari woke them. They had brought enough meat for each of the seventy-one to have little more than a bite just before nightfall and had given it to the dragons and told them to go back to sleep for several hours. Now it was time for them to fly.

They flew through the rest of the night and the following day. Most of the time it rained. A gentle wind helped them forward. By the time they dropped down to land at the very edge of the foothills, Noren could feel Elninya's stomach grumbling. The last time she had eaten was the day after they emerged from the Riders' Passage in Dragonsong

Forest.

The dragons alighted, spread out over an area of at least thirty acres. Most of them felt like they were too hungry to sleep and too tired to hunt. Eventually everyone went to sleep except perhaps for Onyxalis.

An hour later, Noren woke to the exhilaration of the dragons. There was humming and croaking and even a little singing. *What is it?* he asked Elninya.

"Two deer."

That's not very much.

"There will soon be more. The Ellenari have brought them. Airrock says she is going to sleep and rest her wings for another hour or two and then she will hunt, too. I don't think Onyxalis is very good at hunting in a place with lots of trees or rocks. He is too big and so he can't get down to catch anything. It's too easy to run where he can't get his big body or even his big neck and head attached to his big body. Refuges are always in range."

Noren could hear a kind of snorting or gurgling sound which was Elninya's laughter. He found himself laughing, too. Of all the things Onyxalis could do, that was the one he could not do! It was then a very good thing that he could eat rocks. Who would want – or be able to – catch enough to feed such a huge dragon?

"Silmavalien says it is funny ... I told her."

This only made Noren laugh more.

36

Fighting the Nightmare Within

Silmavalien woke a few hours after dawn. She and Noren were just having breakfast together when they saw above them, coming from the direction of the mountains, white wings flashing as if with flame in the light of the rising sun. Before long the creature was much nearer and clearly visible. It was Lisila and she was not flashing so much with the light of the rising sun as with the white flame that was her sword, held drawn in her hand.

As she came rapidly nearer, Hazalel and Aelaza also appeared and stood on either side of Silmavalien and Noren.

Lisila alighted brusquely and folded in her wings. At once there was no evidence of them at all. Except for the drawn sword she appeared as she first had to Silmavalien and Noren. "The Nightmare Lord undoubtedly knows that you defeated the witch and that you are south of the Greater Aravin Mountains. A fierce battle is still on-going at the mouth of the Riders' Passage in the Steep Descent. Given the circumstances, the Riders' Passage is too slow for us now. The demons are collecting to do battle for the High Pass. If you think everyone is strong enough, the best thing is to fly for the High Pass as quickly as possible. You will have to fight. If everyone is not strong enough to fly for it now, the battle will almost certainly be much harder."

"I don't think anyone is remotely strong enough. Most of the dragons are on the point of collapsing," said Noren.

"We flew harder than we did when I rescued Noren and Elninya," added Silmavalien. "Some of the dragons are saying they think they would fall out of the sky if they flew today. They don't know if they could take off."

"You don't need to tell me what the dragons say," said Lisila. "I hear them as well as you do."

"Oh, sorry. I forgot," said Silmavalien.

"No matter," said Lisila. "In that case you will not fly today and we will bring you more food."

Both Silmavalien and Noren thanked her.

All three of the Ellenari inclined their heads. Aelaza and Hazalel sprang away. Lisila re-sprouted white wings and flew back the way she had come.

Silmavalien lay down under a tree, looking up into a blue sky, scattered with the remnants of the clouds. The spreading branches of the trees split it into a lace-like pattern, and as she examined the branches she saw the first beginning of green buds that indicated it was coming out of winter dormancy and the sap was beginning to flow.

She could hear the despair, bitterness, and clamor of so many dragons. They were all affected by the venom and poison present in the thoughts of their companions. It made her feel sore and sour and in general ill herself. She could not tell whether the dragons did not want to fight at all or whether they wanted to take out their loss and misery on anyone whom they perceived as responsible, imagining that they could fight the nightmare by killing people under burning or crushed cities and buildings. She could not tell whether it was different dragons who wanted to do nothing, and who definitely did *not* want to fight, and who wanted to burn cities and crush houses and slaughter, or whether these two tendencies were conflicting expressions of misery in the same dragon. She wanted to get away from it all.

She tried to block out the thoughts and clamor of the dragons, but she could not help feeling it. She felt sorry for the newly rescued dragons who did not want to indulge in misery, hate, and despair. It must be so exhausting for them in their current state and with their experiences, so similar to those about which the other dragons were complaining and raging and despairing. In a sudden flash she thought that it must feel to them so much like fighting the nightmares themselves. The attitudes, and therefore even the presence, of their fellow dragons might feel to them like the presence of the nightmares.

𝒩

Noren was aimlessly scratching at bark, when Silmavalien burst in on his bubble of quiet. "I feel so sorry for dragons like Dalis and Tubon!" she said. "They can't get away. They're so tired themselves. Between that and the horrible things they've experienced, they must experience the hatred and misery of some of the other dragons like the presence of the nightmare!"

Noren nodded. His love's words brought his mind back to when he'd first wondered if the nightmare was inside of him and that was why it had so much power over him, shortly after he had almost been killed by fire imps. *I wonder if Elninya ever felt that way with me,* he thought.

"*I love you. All that is over now. We're together,*" she replied, noticing his thoughts. She was not going to answer if he asked her how it was, and Noren knew it.

"What can we do?" Silmavalien lamented. Her emotions grated on him. "How will they recover like this? It's got to be horrible for them!"

"I don't think there's anything we *can* do," said Noren. "They don't so much as feel well enough to take off, let alone fly a few miles, and I don't know if that would help given the way dragons speak to each other –"

"It would definitely *help*," Silmavalien interjected.

"*It would help*," said Elninya. He was aware, was he not, of more or less how much she spoke to Tanz or others when they were in the same place and of how much she spoke to them when they were not?

Yes, but a few miles is different from a hundred miles, said Noren.

A separation of a few miles' distance would allow them to block or ignore much of what another dragon radiated, though strong feelings would often get through.

All right. I'm not the smartest man in the world. Out loud he continued, "And there's nothing we could do to help them move anyways, unless they want to walk away, which I don't know. There's so much we don't know, too. If we have to fight nightmares to gain the High Pass, what they're fighting now might help them then more than anything else could."

"But we can't do nothing about their pain!" Silmavalien almost squealed.

Help me not get mad! thought Noren. He was tired himself and had been scratching at the bark to relax so he could take a nap. "What can you do?" he asked, trying to speak as kindly and neutrally as possible. "If you can't do anything then you can do nothing."

S

Silmavalien heard the irritation in Noren's voice and wondered what she could say to do better. To try to fix that. She was sure it was not what she was saying, but how she was saying it, that bothered him. "That can't be. It's just – I can't. I can't ignore it."

"I don't know everything. I don't know what you can and can't do or should and shouldn't do," said Noren.

Silmavalien nodded. "I could sing. But I don't feel like it. I'm too tired. And I don't know if it would help. I can't sleep around this. I don't think the dragons who want to sleep can sleep around it very well either."

"It is bothering Elninya," said Noren. "If you wanted, maybe you and some of your dragons could find a hill a couple miles away and you could sleep there for the day?"

"I'd feel bad," said Silmavalien, "leaving the others."

Noren sighed. "I really don't know what to do for you."

She stomped her foot.

"I'm going to take a nap myself. If you wanted, maybe I and Elninya could go with you and whoever wants to go with you," said Noren.

"No," said Silmavalien. "I'd feel wrong doing it that way."

"All right. Well then, unless you have something more to say, I'm going to take my nap."

"I don't think I do," said Silmavalien. She stood there for a few moments while Noren turned and continued whatever it was he had been doing before taking his nap. Then she walked into a little copse in the middle of the resting dragons and climbed into the lower spreading branches of a live oak. From there she spoke to the dragons.

I know you don't want to give into bitterness or despair, Tubon. I know you don't want to give an opening to the nightmare, Dalth.

I know what that feels like, when you feel like you simply cannot keep fighting the evil, you're too tired and worn-out.

Yes. You know to think about Love, to focus on the good, to think about and cry out to the Lord of the Light, but it's so hard to do that, so hard to resist the tendency to think evil, nasty thoughts … It feels like flying into a headwind that's blowing – or at least gusting – faster than you can fly. Yeah, I guess. Maybe.

Would it help if we sang, Dalis? It might. It'll almost certainly help while we sing. The question is whether the effect will last after we stop singing. That's the thing. We can't sing constantly. We can't fight constantly. So how to rest in the middle of the battle without being overcome? Can we fight literally always? At least we don't feel like it.

Let's try to sing. What shall it be?

I have to make it up? That's strange. Helping a singing dragon to sing, to make up a song. I thought it was always the other way around – a singing dragon helps a human to sing, teaches her a song. No, don't feel bad, Dalis. And I've only known one singing dragon: Songeth. How stupid of me to think all singing dragons are alike! And, how stupid of me not to consider how tired and shaken you must be and think that might affect things.

There's so much you've forgotten in that darkness and you don't know if most of it will come back to you? Well, I don't know what to say. How about we sing?

But she just could not think of a song or any way to start a song. It made her so nervous she was not sure she would be able to speak if she had to speak out loud. It was just awkward trying to think of a song, to start a song, for a singing dragon.

Then Minth showed her a memory.

You're right! I used to sing songs to you, Minth, and to the others sometimes, just because. You say to do it like that?

But this is different, so different ... Yes, I'll try that, but I don't think it will make a difference.

Silmavalien chucked. *The song doesn't have to be any good. Thank you all! I feel much more comfortable now. But, of course. Why would the song have to be – not what you'd call any good, and you're right. It* will *be some good, but it doesn't have to be ... well, whatever it was I was thinking. You probably never think it at all.*

That helped. She made up a line in her head and then opened her mouth to sing it. As dragons joined in, those who were not singers still contributing their thoughts and understanding, the song grew. Most of them tried to contribute vocally, if only with an out-of-sync crow or by humming.

> Love is what we need right now
> Love is why we fight and why we do not fight
> Love is what we sing so loud
> We do not hear but rather drown out the night
>
> Love is breathing in the flower
> That we smell in sweetness on the wind that blows
> Love will mend the wrong we bore
> Even when we have no idea how it flows
>
> Love is why we can never rest
> Love is worth it all and we cling hard to Love
> Love must be our rest in stress
> Or bitterness will rain on us from above

Love is what we need right now
Love is why we fight and why we do not fight
Love is what we sing so loud
We cannot hear but rather drown out the night

Silmavalien yawned and nodded. *I think I'm too tired to sing anymore.*

Even if it doesn't work, *it has worked? It's worth it, since you're not alone. You're helped. We're together. I understand. I understand how much you need that. Together. We love each other. That's what matters. You can fight with that, even if this doesn't relieve the fight. Yes! I'm glad for you.*

She slipped off the tree and first noticed that she was sore. She also yawned again. *Thank you. I can go and sleep now. I still think I might find somewhere a little farther away to sleep … There's even too much commotion over some things … Yes, it's a good thing we came to rest not too far from a stream, so you can drink. I think it's not more than half a mile from the east edge of our encampment.*

We couldn't have alighted much closer to it. The trees are denser there and there's banks and all that. But I think all of you can walk there and drink in turns.

She was stumbling out of the copse now. *Yes. I really need to go to sleep …*

N

Noren listened to the song while he fell asleep. It was so reminiscent of some of his own struggles. He thought how lovely was Silmavalien's voice. He fell asleep to the sound of Elninya humming it and to the vibrations of that humming in her side and in the ground on which he lay. *You have a beautiful voice, too,* he told her.

So Silmavalien did find something to do to satisfy her need to help the dragons and not leave them unaided and uncomforted to their struggle. Well, I'm glad she did, was Noren's last thought before sleep took him.

37

Arrows

Silmavalien did not think she had slept that late, but when she woke the sun was just setting. It was not completely dark yet, but all was cast in shadow.

The darkness was thick and heavy, with a foul stench. Where was it coming from? What exactly was it?

She woke fully and knew that they were surrounded by the nightmare creatures. The dragons were awake and knew, too.

In a moment she was on her feet.

Orcs and stone-bats? Can we fly?

We brought no saddle and you don't know if I can stay on if you have to fight in the air. At least I remembered to bring my bow.

Silmavalien was already stringing it.

"I'm coming with Noren," said Elninya.

"I am coming as fast as I can," said Onyxalis.

All of her dragons were coming too, as well as the stronger and healthier of those they had freed from the witch's curse.

Tiela lifted her wing from over Silmavalien, and she took three running strides and leapt onto a rock. She pressed herself against another rock that rose higher from the first, while Tiela jumped into the air, battering with the wind from her wings.

The next moment Silmavalien felt the wave of heat from her flames. She grabbed an arrow and strung it.

She was a much better shot than she had once been. She drew the string back, saw a gnarled shadow move under the trees, and released. The arrow flew straight to its target which screamed.

Already she had another arrow on the string and then another in the air.

The three dragons – Tiela, Songeth, and Dance – kept the stony winged monsters in the sky at bay. The rock which overhung her sheltered Silmavalien both from the monsters in the sky and from the arrows of the orcs. She kept shooting them which kept them distracted. They still tried to shoot the dragons.

Several of their arrows bounced off Tiela's scales. Then one pierced her wing. Silmavalien almost fell at her dragon's cry of pain. Another arrow pierced Tiela's wing. She struggled to maintain consciousness through the pain. Every time she moved her wings, every time the air whooshed past them and pressed against them, the pain spiked and threatened to swallow her.

I'm almost out of arrows!

Dance told Silmavalien that was okay. There were not that many orcs left.

Noren and Elninya were almost there.

She looked up and saw them in the sky. The next moment they dived on the gargoyles. Noren's sword flashed in the darkness and looked like a fragment of volcanic fire in the night. Silmavalien cheered.

A warning from Dance. An orc closing in on her. Silmavalien strung and shot another arrow. The orc fell.

The others are fleeing, right?

Certainly the nightmares of the sky were dispersing. She felt the dark presence fade.

She looked into her quiver. *I only have two arrows left.*

She looked up at the sky. *I hope the Ellenari will help us with Tiela. I think one of the arrows went through her wing.*

Dance showed her the arrow. It had. Tiela was landing now. But Silmavalien like to come back on Dance's back?

The green dragon touched down and folded her wings. Silmavalien climbed down from the rock and onto her shoulders. A few minutes later they landed at the edge of the encampment. The newly-freed dragons landed too, exhausted but unharmed. They *were* getting better!

When Tiela landed, a few moments after the others, Silmavalien burst into the tears she had been trying to control. *I'm so sorry. I had such a horrible idea. It hurt you!*

The dragon tried to comfort her. Did they even know what idea was who's first?

Silmavalien did not see where the Ellena came from, but she looked and Aelaza was right there. She slid down from Dance's shoulder and approached her. "Is there anything I can help with?"

"Not right here right now," said the Ellena.

Silmavalien sat down, feeling horrible.

She did not know how much time passed, except that it was completely dark and there was no longer any glow in the west, when Aelaza stood in front of her. "Make sure you don't forget to eat yourself," said the Ellena.

"I'll eat after this," said Silmavalien. "But let me ask you something: did I do wrong in taking some dragons to sleep where we could?"

"You've asked me similar questions before," said Aelaza. "I can't answer it and I don't know why you think I should know everything you should or should not have done or that I should tell you if I did know. Do not judge the rightness of an action you have taken by what you perceive to be its consequences. Try to do what is right and don't blame yourself for an action, or feel good about one, because you think it had consequences you currently perceive to be for ill or for better."

"That's confusing," said Silmavalien.

"No it isn't," said the Ellena. "The way you think about consequences and time and actions is confusing. What I say makes perfect sense."

"Not to me, though," said Silmavalien. "What about the fact I only have two arrows left?"

"What about that?" asked Aelaza. "You shot well. You will be getting a new bow and new arrows soon. Remember to eat." With that she darted away.

Silmavalien rose and went to where they kept their bags. She found Noren had built a fire and was boiling water. She took a meal out of a bag and then turned to Noren and said, "I lost all but two of my arrows."

"We could look for them tomorrow if you want," said Noren. "Some of them are probably fine."

"Yeah, but what if they aren't? I won't have any arrows to fight with if something like that happens again."

"We don't know what is and isn't going to happen when," said Noren. "We'll look for arrows tomorrow if you want. Maybe we'll find almost all of them undamaged."

"I doubt it," said Silmavalien, "and I have to oil the dragons tomorrow. Given that we might be called to fly for the High Pass anytime, and I might not have time to oil them until we reach Shan'Dala, I should oil them all."

"Whatever you want," said Noren.

"All right," said Silmavalien and took her first bite. She was thirsty herself and would not eat any more until the water was ready. She felt like everything was a total disaster. Tiela was hurt. Was it, or was it not, her fault? How could she have known? *Could* she have known?

Should she have not done it for some other reason?

She could feel the dragons urging her not to think in this way but she could not shake the feelings.

Hey! Which of you wants to be oiled first? I'll work on oiling someone while waiting for this water to boil and then cool.

That suggestion made the dragons happy. It was a smart idea instead of a stupid feeling. How about Coroneth?

Silmavalien shook her head. No. Daurth. Would he come over?

The sun had set by the time she was done oiling Daurth. Silmavalien put away her grooming tools and stood, looking up at the stars. More clouds were massing themselves on the western horizon. She felt so desolate. *It is my fault. I know it is my fault. At any rate, something is my fault. It's my fault I didn't ask the Lord of the Light for help, either at the beginning, or when Tiela was first hit. It's my fault I didn't thank the Lord of the Light for the fact we survived. Well, I can't do the other things now, but I can thank him now, and I can say I'm sorry now.*

She proceeded to do so, but it felt strange and unreal. She sat down for a long time looking dully up at the stars wheeling above her. Sometimes she got up and paced. She shivered in the cold wind coming down from the mountains. It changed, growing wilder and wetter as the clouds rushed into the sky and covered the stars.

She was beginning to feel like this war would never end. It would become more and more intense and more and more impossible forever. She was so tired. Even when she felt strong and ready to do things, instead of like she just wanted to sleep and eat and sleep and eat and sleep again, she was so weary of fighting.

A strong gust of wind knocked into Silmavalien as wings passed over her. For a moment she was startled, fearing an attack. Then she knew that it was one of the dragons. He felt better and was tired of only standing or lying or walking. He felt like flying even though it was still hard.

Good for you, she thought.

She took off her ring and fiddled with it in her hand. Why was she feeling this way? She knew she ought to ask the Lord of the Light to help her, but she was not sure she wanted to be helped. She wanted to give in, to fight no more, to rest. She knew she should not be moping or complaining, but she was not sure she wanted help not doing so.

The thought charged into her mind: *What if the nightmare has gotten inside you? Do you not want to fight it and drive it out?*

I want to rest. I don't want to fight or strive at all.

What if it is not that you do not want to fight the nightmare, to be good, but that the nightmare that has gotten inside of you does not want to fight itself – and does not want you to fight it and drive it out?

All right, thought Silmavalien. *Lord of All Light, I'm not sure if I want you to help me, but I know I did want you to help me and make me good and loving so I can't do any evil, and if it's that I'm confusing what the nightmare is for what I want, then certainly make me good and loving and help me to not give in but keep fighting to be good and against evil. Make me want it, please. I really do want to love, to serve Love, never to fight against Love. That, even now, I know I want.*

The ring laying on her palm flashed briefly, and then glowed for a moments against her hand. She took that for his answer and slipped the ring back onto her finger. Carefully she walked through the night – it was almost pitch-black now that the clouds had covered the stars – and between the dragons, some of whom were stirring their bodies and taking brief flights. Without waking him, she slipped between Minth's wing and body and lay down next to him. Her own body felt sore and she wished for the beds in the garden of the Ellenari.

Above them, Onyxalis circled and wheeled in the sky.

ℵ

Noren woke early in the morning, before it was very light. The air and ground were wet, the sky was drizzling, and the trees were dripping. As he stepped out from under Elninya's wing he saw the dragons slowly and gracefully dancing in the sky. More than half of the seventy-one were above them as well as most of Silmavalien's dragons. Behind him, Elninya re-arranged her wings.

They're feeling much better, aren't they? Noren asked her.

"We're all feeling better. We had to rest for a little while to notice it, but all of us except Onyxalis feel like something has shifted and we're better. Everything is clearer, stronger."

Umm-hmm, Noren replied. *Tiela's not feeling much better, is she?* Noren wished they could move on from here and do something. He tired of having nothing to do.

Behind him, Tiela got up, turned her body so that she could take off away from him, unfolded her wings, and jumped into the sky. *"Even*

Tiela is feeling better in that *way,"* she replied. *"Her wings feel much better after Aelaza's treatment, too."*

Oh, said Noren. *I want to do something. I think I will go look for Silmavalien's arrows. She's still asleep, isn't she?*

"Yes," said Elninya. *"I want to dance. Can Wydth take you?"*

Sure. He knows where to go right?

Elninya would make sure of that.

Noren went with Wydth, and it felt strange riding a dragon other than Elninya. He found several remnants of broken arrows, but only one undamaged arrow. Most of them seemed to have vanished. That some would vanish he understood, but not how most of them did. The other curious thing was the absence of the orc bodies. Where had they gone? Who had taken them away? There were a few stains of blood in the ground but no bodies. Why?

Noren stood up from bending over and examining some marks in the soil, when he heard the softest sound. Looking up, he saw Hazalel standing before him. He straightened, waiting for the Ellenar to speak.

"Greetings, Noren," said the Ellenar.

"Greetings," said Noren. "What have you come to tell me?"

"Tomorrow you and the dragons should journey as far as is comfortable for you towards the High Pass," said the Ellenar. "There wait until you are told more."

"Is that all?" asked Noren.

"All for now, though if you have questions I may be able to answer some of them," said Hazalel.

"My first question is right here," said Noren. "Why are there no bodies left from the orcs?"

"When possible the Nightmare Lord recovers the corpses of his minions. I do not know why," answered Hazalel.

"Should we try to burn or otherwise destroy the corpses so he cannot do whatever it is he does with them?" asked Noren.

"You definitely should not do so if it doing so endangers you or requires resources and energy you need, or know you might need, for something else," said Hazalel. "You should not feel bad about the fact that you did not do so last night."

"And I should not try to make sure I do so in the future?" asked Noren.

"No. That is not your role."

"I understand that," said Noren. "Thank you."

"Do you have any more questions or requests?" asked Hazalel.

"I don't think so," said Noren.

"Then fare well," said Hazalel. In a moment he had again vanished into the landscape.

Silmavalien is awake now, Elninya? Tell her I found one arrow and that I'm coming back.

Noren walked back up the hill to where Wydth waited for him. He climbed onto the shoulders of the largest of the white dragons. Wydth was definitely bigger and stronger than his Elninya.

In a few minutes he was having breakfast with Silmavalien.

"I'm getting tired of this waiting," said Noren. "I want to do something – not sit."

"Are you?" asked Silmavalien. "I feel like I would like to never do anything again. I don't mean I don't want to ride dragons or things like that. But I'm sick and tired of fighting."

"Well, we're going to oil the dragons today, aren't we?" asked Noren.

"Yes," said Silmavalien blankly. Her shoulders drooped. She looked so dejected. "If we aren't attacked out of the sky or nightmares don't rise out of the ground. Or something like that."

Later, in a break between oiling dragons, Noren told her what Hazalel had said about leaving tomorrow. To his surprise she did not freak out. "It will be good for them to stretch their wings," she said. "Though Tiela – I feel sorry for her. Her wounds don't directly affect her ability to fly, but even though the Ellenari treated them they're still so painful," she added. "Did Hazalel say anything else?"

"I asked him why the bodies of the orcs had disappeared. He says the Lord of the Nightmares tries to retrieve them whenever possible," said Noren.

"Oh," said Silmavalien. "I suppose it's a good thing I burned those bodies ages ago in the cave. I was probably right they would attract more nightmare creatures."

38

Battle to the Height

The following day they flew for about six hours before settling down. The newly-freed dragons were tired and Tiela was in a lot of pain.

Silmavalien slept with Dance that night, and the flower-loving dragon was still asleep when Silmavalien stepped out from under her wing. It was still rather early in the morning and she saw Aelaza standing surrounded in a very faint nimbus of purple lightning-like light.

"Are we going to fly for the High Pass and Shan'Dala now?" asked Silmavalien.

"Yes – but Shan'Dala is not the only one of our cities, though it is the one most conveniently situated for us," said Aelaza.

To her surprise, the thought made Silmavalien rather more excited than otherwise. Her eagerness woke some of the dragons and she explained it to them quickly.

In less than an hour the entire company was aloft.

All of the dragons grew continually stronger, and able to fly farther and longer at once. In only two weeks they were climbing up to the High Pass.

While they were saddling the dragons that morning, Silmavalien said to Noren, "I wonder, why is it that we have not seen any demons? We've experienced no opposition. Nothing. No hint of the nightmare presence. Can they have left off guarding the Pass?"

"Don't you think instead," suggested Noren, "that they will be waiting to ambush us just where it is hardest? And, to give them still more advantage, they will not warn us of their presence until they cannot help it."

"Ouch!" said Silmavalien. "How will we survive? The High Pass is barely survivable as it is!"

"I don't know," said Noren. "Onyxalis will help us. The Ellenari will help us. The Lord of Light and Love will help us."

The next evening they were not quite at the peak of the Pass when they suddenly felt a strong, piercing sense of paralyzing horror and despair. It was like a dark cloud. Both humans and dragons were weary, so it took all of them a few moments to realize what was happening to them. It took Silmavalien a moment to understand even Onyxalis's sudden cry, *"Be ware!"*

In a moment nightmares dived down on them from the mountains above. Out of ravines, out of the snow, out of who-knew-where hordes of orcs and imps and stone ogres and giants emerged. Onyxalis provided some cover, but even he was far too small to cover nearly one hundred dragons. The scarce night air glowed bright with the lava that poured from his mouth. His tail swept vampires and other winged nightmares out of the sky.

Silmavalien had never before noticed what happened to Onyxalis' fire when it cooled, but despite the sluggish state of her mind, in the excitement of the moments, she noticed many things. Some of it was flung far and cooled rapidly; it fell down in still-burning-hot boulders and shreds on the nightmares, knocking them out of the air. Sometimes it split to reveal still glowing, molten cores and made the snow sizzle and stream. Some of it reached the snow on the sides of the mountains still hot rivulets of steaming water and slush ran down. Snow fell from the sides of the mountains in huge avalanches burying the orcs under its weight.

They wouldn't have survived for more than a few minutes without Onyxalis' wrath. The arrows of the orcs were few and scattered as their hordes were killed under the falling snow. Nonetheless it was a horrible battle. The dragons were hard-pressed, weak and tired as they were, to avoid the missiles from below and the darting, flying horrors around. They had to rise ever higher into thinner and thinner air, and there was nothing Silmavalien could do. Only wish she could somehow be lighter.

Noren, in Elninya's saddle, had the Dragon-sword unsheathed. It glowed like a piece of Onyxalis' fire, but even it did little more than discourage attacks on him and Elninya, from what she could see. Elninya was not strong enough or fast enough up here for them to help anyone else.

Then she heard the first bow-shot from the Ellenari.

The strife scarcely grew less intense. She felt several of the dragons wounded, but she had no attention to spare, as she struggled on the borderlands of nightmare. Disconnected and horrible shapes, emotions, and thoughts chased themselves around in her mind. When she was awake enough she called out to the Lord of the Light and tried to focus on her dragons and think about them. Between those moments she was subjected to alternating and mixing of waves and inarticulate, but no less horrible, fear and hatred, despair and bitterness, sickening, bloated fancies and utter loathing that encompassed everything or nothing.

In a moment of clarity, she realized Airrock, who she was riding, flew close beside Elninya and Minth. Struggling slightly less than the rest of the dragons, Airrock was trying to remind Elninya to stay close to Minth.

Suddenly Silmavalien saw Elninya's white body shining ahead of her in the darkness. Against her neck and the stars rose the dark silhouette of Noren's body. In one hand he waved the Dragon-sword which glowed like a bar of flame fresh-taken from the heart of a volcano. The beauty of it struck her and impressed itself on her heart.

"Oh, thank the Lord of All Light!" she cried.

She raised her hand and her ring shone and became to the others what Noren's sword had been to her.

They reached an altitude at which the tired dragons simply could not fly anymore. *"Land,"* Onyxalis told them. *"I and the Ellenari will protect you."*

Silmavalien felt the dragons' relief. It poured over her palpably. They landed, and an army of the Ellenari formed a ring around them. Her ring cast a light so that they could clearly see the ground or rather snow under their feet and around them. On the edges of the light, passing in and out of the darkness, they saw the forms of Ellenari, strange in the night and in the battle. The shining flash of a sword, the flight of an arrow like a shooting star, a streak of something like lightning, and other movements announced their activity, though Silmavalien did not know what they were doing.

Above them Onyxalis still fought, though he seemed to have less lava-fire than before. She did not know if he had less or if he was breathing less because they were on the ground and he did not want to hurt them on accident.

It was still cruelly exhausting for the dragons, some of them wounded, who had to trudge uphill through the snow.

Even she who was not doing anything except resisting, was on the verge of absolute exhaustion. She was hardly aware of her own body anymore, when a warm wind arose around them and the air became more breathable. Her lungs stopped burning, and every breath stopped aching, and it meant even more to Minth. A strange and utterly familiar scent tingled in her nostrils, yet it somehow seemed as if she recognized it, or as if her dragons did.

Slowly they revived, and then Lighter noticed – she thought it was Lighter – that some of the dragons freed from the witch seemed on the point of death. *Onyxalis, can anything be done?* she asked. *Can someone ask the Ellenari?*

They say they're doing all they can. O Lord of All Light, can you please do something?

Just then the lead dragons noticed that the ground began to lead downwards. They were on the very crest of the High Pass.

"Just a little farther, just a little farther," Silmavalien whispered, but she did not know if some of the dragons could hear what she tried to tell them. *Does this have to happen again?* she thought, thinking of the dragons dead in the egg. *Lord of Light!*

Elninya, ask Noren if he has any ideas.

"Nothing except for any herbs you might have left," replied Elninya.

I used everything I can think of that might help the day we fought the witch, responded Silmavalien.

The battle around them seemed to thin. There was a moment of calm, then a few moments later more calm. *"Yes,"* said Onyxalis. *"They are a lot fewer than they were half a minute ago."*

Silmavalien swung herself down from Airrock, stumbling as she fell into the deep snow. She trudged up the slight incline to where the wounded, exhausted dragons had lain down at the back.

Two Ellenari leapt down from the mountain-side and landed almost in her path. One of them she recognized as Aelaza. The other had hair that flowed down her back in waves and curls of gold. She wore a cloak with a pattern of red next to green next to white next to yellow next to red again. It was fringed with tassels of red, white and green. The Ellena's back was towards her and so Silmavalien could not see her face.

Aelaza tossed her a smile and beckoned. The three continued up to the incline to where the dragons lay.

When they reached the dragons, who looked dead already, the Ellena whom Silmavalien had not seen before turned towards her. She glimpsed a black robe under the cape. The Ellena wore a black mask through which glinted white eyes that reminded Silmavalien of Lisila. Silmavalien was taken aback to see that she covered her face with a mask.

"Call me Firutrilia," she said, holding out her hands with a mass of green in them. "Take these and place them in the dragons' wounds."

When Silmavalien did so she was surprised to find that just a touch of the herb completely staunched the flow of blood.

Perhaps they would all live.

39

Dawn of the Beginning

Weeping, Silmavalien dashed across the snow as quickly as she could to find where Firutrilia and Aelaza were tending another dragons. "Bona and Sulth are dead," she cried.

Firutrilia nodded. "Yes, Silmavalien. But I cannot discuss death with you very well." She held out more bundles of herbs. "Take these to Noren." She pointed to one bunch. "Take these yourself. Noren will take those and give them to all the dragons to sniff. You will divide these between them to eat."

"Can you do nothing?" she asked as she took the herbs.

"I can do many things but only those things I can do," said Firutrilia. "It is not mine to bring back Bona and Sulth. Now go!"

Silmavalien went. *Elninya, tell Noren to come to me.*

Half an hour later, the two Dragonriders found themselves face to face with Hazalel after giving the herbs to the last dragon. Hazalel took Noren's herbs and said, "Now you will fly for the Steep Descent and Shan'Dala."

"But we should give Bona and Sulth a proper burial!" protested Silmavalien.

"There is not time. They will not be harmed by not being buried as you would like. You must fly quickly before the Nightmare Lord re-organizes his forces for another attack," said Hazalel. "This is far from over yet."

Silmavalien opened her mouth to protest again. "But," she began when she heard Onyxalis' volcanic voice.

"Do not worry, child. I will take care of their bodies in a way which is quite suitable to us dragons," he said.

Silmavalien sent him a weary thanks, too tired even to be amazed that he was not tired. She and Noren went back to Airrock and Elninya, and despite the tremendous effort required, the dragons pushed themselves into the air. They struggled upwards for a few long, long moments, then tilted their wings and glided down over cliffs and terraces and hills covered with snow.

As they descended into warmer, thicker air, and the herbs of the Ellenari continued to strength them, they were able to think again and realize what had happened. Silmavalien felt better, too, and when she was able to hear them, she realized how much the fact that she cared for them meant to the dragons freed from the witch. They had been imprisoned, alone and separated from each other in that awful darkness of fear and hatred for so long that they had in a way almost forgotten their riders. At the same time they were desperate and sick for that companionship and friendship they had lost.

That she cared for them made them feel like love was reality, not a delusion, and life was worth living in a way that nothing else could. The fact that she cared about them even after they were dead for some reason really meant something to those who were still alive. What the dead knew neither she nor the other dragons knew.

The weary dragons alighted on a slope where thick, cold patches of snow alternated with places where it was melting. A few conifers stood mantled in the happy green of their own leaves and of moss, and between the white snow, grasses sprouted up and put on a shade of green that seemed to shout joy. Flowers opened in gorgeous colors of happy hope.

Silmavalien slid from Airrock. It was early morning. The light from her ring dimmed and went out. Somehow the earth felt like it was about to break into song, as if it was the beginning of a whole new universe unstained by any ill. Then the first bird chirped. It seemed to Silmavalien like it was the tentative first attempt at song of a world fresh-born.

She looked at Noren who had come to stand beside her. "Do you see what I see?" she asked. "Do you feel what I feel?"

"Who ever knows the answer to that question?" Noren shrugged.

One of the dragons chirped. Another chirped back. One began to hum.

Silmavalien felt a thrill, a quiver, something not yet born but on the very verge of birth, run through the dragons.

𝒩

As exhausted as he was from the previous and the night's battle, Noren felt invigorated by something in the air he breathed. On a second thought, he did not know if it was in the air. But he felt strangely exhausted to the bone and invigorated with life at once.

He looked around him. The world felt so fresh and new, yet they were still going to a battle, presumably a battle far more terrible than the one through which they had just passed. He no longer had any hope that he would come out of that battle alive. Yet everything around him whispered of life, of freshness and vitality of life. He would go through death and find himself as alive as ever. Of that he was convinced, for he could shake neither the certainty that he would die nor the certainty that he would live, nay, the certainty that he would soon be even more alive than he was now.

He could not sort through the way he felt about everything.

Noren put his arm around Silmavalien. He could feel her quiver with cold. He was shivering a little himself. The air in his face was terribly cold. He could see the first glimmer not of gray but of yellow and rose where the sun would rise, just north on the very edge of the mountain cliffs.

The air quivered with a mighty sound, a tremor of life that set the whole air trembling, cool and fresh and invigoratingly alive. It swept through him like a tidal force and he felt like the whole earth around him, and perhaps his own being, too, and Silmavalien beside him, were all being turned into the most perfect musical instrument that had ever been. The newness was overwhelming. It felt like the first song was about to be sung. It felt like they were the first musical instrument, or a musical instrument in the first assembly ever. Or else they were witnessing the first music in the world. It had all the grandeur of a rushing finale and yet the feel of a beginning, and the two were the same thing, not separable from each other.

The three singing dragons who were left sang together, their voices making a perfect harmony. The love they had experienced, the love they wanted, the love they shared, impelled them to sing.

Yet Noren felt certain he could not have sung the song they heard. He was too immersed in a listening, a breathless listening, and Silmavalien with him.

> Sing above the highest star!
> Sing in triumph ever-new!
> Sing, we are together for true
> And are nevermore to part!
>
> Rise on wings behind the sun!
> Rise on wings, spring's first thought!
> Rise to soar on the wings of dawn

And pass beyond world to world!

Soar and share the sun's own wings!
Soar on winds above the world!
Soar from earth to sky and sky to sky
And to the other side of time!

Fly as free as light's first strike!
Fly consumed in flames of joy!
Fly and find earth is sky for you
And your world is just begun!

Sing in joy above the sun!
Sing with voices of the spring!
Sing and find your voice in mine
As I find my voice in yours.

Above the sea clouds took on bright and fresh shades of yellow and gold against the gray-rose sky. Then the rim of the sun, slowly but almost visibly, raised itself above the sea, looking as it had just bathed in the waters of joy and was still dripping with literal happiness, fresh and radiant.

Neither he nor Silmavalien remembered the exact moment when the song stopped. It became indistinguishable from the air of the morning and the breath of the dawn. The song was no longer a distinct thing from the sunrise.

He turned to Silmavalien and said to her, "It's a foretaste of death – or maybe not a foretaste but a metaphor."

When she looked at him blankly, so blankly that the blankness of her expression nearly covered the horror in it, Noren realized he had been a flaming idiot to expect her to understand. Had he not just told her that no one ever knew when another saw and felt the same thing one did? But that very question of hers had made him think she would know. Well, he still did not know that she did not, but only that his words did not mean to her what they meant to him.

He saw her glance at the sun and then at the rose- and blue-tinged world around them, then back at him with an astonishment that showed that she knew that she knew neither what he meant nor what he did not mean.

"I've tried to explain this before," he said. "No, I'm not sure it's a foretaste of dying, which is, I think, what you mean by death. I mean it's a foretaste of what we'll find on the other side. All that's good and beautiful and free and fresh and alive is. Just a foretaste. Remember your own song about nothing ever before imagined?"

"Yes," said Silmavalien. "I think I have an idea of what you mean."

In near ecstasy, Noren said, "Everything we see as a beginning is a shadow of the real beginning and everything we see as an end is just the beginning of that beginning. It couldn't be otherwise, because, as you told me, Love must be and is triumphant! The world ends, our lives end, only so that they may truly begin!"

Silmavalien looked at him with wide open eyes. "But that doesn't answer my question about why so much pain and suffering is involved."

He did not answer but looked again at the dawn and the white snow and the green trees with brown or red trunks mantled in green moss and the grass and the flowers which were just beginning to open their petals. The whole scene whispered to him of something too beautiful to be told, something about to begin in the utter and fantastic triumph of a thing born flawless and fresh and effortless.

At last he turned back to Silmavalien, who had joined him in looking around on the world, and said, "I think you are better at talking about that answer than I am."

"Yes," said Silmavalien. "The dragons are just reminding me. Is a thing truly and satisfactorily good until no evil thing can turn it away from goodness or make it less good? At least, that's the kind of goodness I want. Yet that answer so rarely feels satisfactory to me, even though I couldn't be satisfied with less than that kind of goodness and asked Love to make me that truly good and loving."

Noren nodded. He could say nothing to her. He thought he knew what she meant, and if the answers he had given her before did not communicate what he knew, nothing he could say now would do better. But he did not know if she might know the answer to her question as well as he knew it. At any rate, there was nothing for him to say.

He found her as beautiful as the dawn with a beauty and loveliness that dazzled him. He suspected, somehow, that she found him similarly dazzling. Together they turned from each other's faces and watched the sunrise for a few more minutes while all the dragons fell asleep, except for Onyxalis who was only now catching up to them.

Then the two Dragonriders silently turned and went to sleep with their dragons.

In their dreams the song went on, something like this:

> Love will raise the dead to life.
> Love is dawn that brightens all.
> Love is complete, unhindered spring
> That wakens all to new life.

40

Unguided

"Noren."

It was Hazalel's voice. Noren sat up. He was so tired.

"Noren."

He had to respond. He stood and came out from under Elninya's wing. Looking around he realized it was about the middle of the afternoon. Probably of the same day as they had come over the Pass. That explained why he was so exhausted. He was extremely hungry, too. His stomach rumbled violently. He had had water to drink, but had not touched food since yesterday morning.

Several paces away stood Hazalel. Noren was a little surprised at the extreme weariness, a weariness different from any Noren had ever known but no less a weariness for that, written on his face. In one hand he held his recurved bow, which Noren now recognized as similar in workmanship to the bow which had been Lexamarian's. In the other he held his sword of shining steel.

While Noren straightened and yawned, Hazalel spoke again, "You and the dragons are to continue your flight toward Shan'Dala. There is no time for you to eat right now. That can happen tomorrow, though if you can do so on dragonback you may do so. I do not know how much guidance I will be able to give you, so I must instruct both you and Silmavalien on the way to Shan'Dala. When you reach that point beyond which you cannot fly unaided someone will come to bring you up."

Noren nodded. His hope for a few moments of comfort was dashed and he felt somewhat irritable, but he was not surprised. The desperateness of the war being fought had impressed itself upon him and he knew this kind of thing was involved in war. In fact he had anticipated this. The enemy must still be fighting for the High Pass and he expected that they would still have to fly. They were allowed to rest for the day as much as was essential, no more. "Yes. I understand," he said.

Looking, he saw Silmavalien making her way over the ground avoiding the patches of muck. She looked as tired as he felt. He noticed that her hair was in complete disarray, a mass of knotted tangles. The dragons were beginning to move around.

Hazalel now addressed both of them. "As soon as the dragons are ready, fly east. Tomorrow, eat and let the dragons hunt, unless you receive other instruction from us or circumstances make it apparent that you cannot halt to do so. Then, continue east, making as much speed as you may. When you come to a place where one of the high mountains juts out from the rest and there is a lake in a high valley and a stream that rises out of the ground at the foot of the cliff below that valley, then fly to the other side of the spur. You will find a very high cliff in which lays a pocket of soil in which grow trees and out of which flows a small spring that feeds a pool that trickles over the rocks. Fly above the cliff as high and as deep into the Aravin Mountains as you can. It is the way to Shan'Dala."

"All right," said Silmavalien. "I think we can remember that. At least one of us will for sure. Come, Noren. We can get food for us to eat while the dragons take care of their needs. Then we'll saddle the ones who will carry us today."

"That sounds like a good idea," said Noren.

Several minutes later, they leveled out over the cliffs. Looking down, Noren saw that while the fires no longer burned in the Greater Aravin Mountains or on the Plains of Arosië, their marks were still evident. In whole regions the flames had burned so hot not even the standing skeletons of trees remained. More commonly, there stood dead trees or trees whose tops were just breaking into leafy green again. Elninya showed him where, with her keener eyes, she saw green breaking through the ashes of the lower altitudes where there either had been no snow or it had already been melted or washed away by rain.

"I am so tired," she said, *"but, tired as I am, I must look around me."*

Silmavalien did well today, for someone who is tired of striving and fighting, Noren remarked to Elninya several minutes later.

On and on they flew. For the first several hours, while the sun finished setting and the sky turned darker blue and then black and the stars came out and shone brighter, Elninya spoke to Noren fairly often. They showed each other various things that caught their attention, whether a star or the shape of the mountains or the color of the sky. Then Elninya grew too tired for that. Noren was still fairly awake and noticing what little he could in the dark, but Elninya responded only sluggishly to anything he said. It was with an immense amount of effort that she kept on flying, kept herself thinking about flying, about the wind and where the ground was. Noren tried to help her with this.

Then he too wore out, and they landed in the early morning. Onyxalis said he was extremely hungry himself and flew up above the tree-line to burrow under the snow for rocks to eat, while the other dragons sorted themselves into those who were too hungry to sleep and were going to hunt, and those who were too tired to eat and had already fallen asleep.

Noren felt like he was only less hungry than the dragons, and Silmavalien soon joined him in tearing into their meal while sitting against a tree. They ate in weary silence, and then he found a thicket. It was rather beautiful, with many trees of different kinds growing close together and interlacing their branches like good friends, but what mattered to Noren at the moment was that it was dark and a good place to sleep.

He hoped Silmavalien had found something equally good.

𝒩

Noren was drowsing the next morning, trying to get his sleep schedule back together after sleeping most of the previous day, when Onyxalis' voice crashed through his daydreams like the thunder of rocks falling. *"Come. Awake. It is time for us to continue."*

He was on his feet before Onyxalis finished and starting to draw his sword. *Is the nightmare upon us?*

"No. But it is time for you to continue."

But not so urgently that he could not get a drink and breakfast. He found Silmavalien doing the same, and they ate hurriedly and drank the last of the water they had with them before saddling the dragons.

It was only a few minutes before they were in the sky again.

"Silmavalien says to ask you how long you think it will be until we reach Shan'Dala," relayed Elninya.

It took him a moment to think about that. Why would Silmavalien ask *him* that? She was the one who had lived in these mountains for months and might recognize the landmarks. All he knew was that it could not be as far east as the Riders' Passage.

"I'll tell her that," said Elninya, and Noren got the distinct impression she found relaying between him and Silmavalien like this to be amusing. Or was it the subject of the conversation?

A few moments later, she spoke to him again, but this time with the pattern of images that she shared when relaying another dragon's thoughts. Airrock had flown higher than anyone else and she thought she might recognize some of the landmarks. They could probably get there in a week, she considered, and now there were hints of Silmavalien's thoughts in the communication. Airrock could probably get there in a few days.

Over the days that followed, Noren rejoiced with Elninya in her new strength. She told him all the dragons were stronger than they had ever been before. The ones from the witch's prison were still getting stronger every day, but she was still getting used to her new strength and endurance. That was the only thing that was really fun about being pushed this hard. It was nice to be stronger!

Six days out from the High Pass, they flew along a mountain that jutted out from the rest of the range in high, sheers cliffs that formed sharper corners against the rest of the mountain range. These terraces and cliffs met in a jumble of many different lines of cliffs and land meeting, so that the deep corners looked almost like chaotic staircases, as if nature had put her own spin on some of the things he had seen among the palaces and mansions of those who ruled in Silrah.

At the foot of one of the cliffs, a stream flowed out from a large pool. They flew up the cliff, until they found another terrace, where a lake lay deep against the cliffs that rose high into the sky all around it, framing the hilly valley in an almost cup-like shape. The lake itself formed a triangular shape against the cliffs, and was very deep in the corner, but out against the land it was shallow and fulls of islands and reeds.

This looks like it, doesn't it? asked Noren.

"*Yes,*" said Elninya, but most of the dragons were too tired to try the flight up right now.

This does look like a good place to rest and eat, Noren told her.

A few minutes later, she was finishing in the lake along with a veritable rainbow of dragons, and he and Silmavalien stood at its edge. The wet sand felt nice on their bare feet, as they looked out over the water while the dragons hunted in it. Their colorful scales made strange reflections on the green-tinged lake.

"It's so strange," said Noren. He waved his hand to indicate the entire landscape, impossibly high snow-covered mountains rising behind the cliffs before them, the lake and its forested islands with rushes growing on the snows, the trees beside them, and the dragons around them. "Such a peaceful beautiful place and then a war raging which threatens to kill us all."

He turned to Silmavalien and took her hands in his. "I no longer believe I'll survive the battle."

"Oh, Noren!" said Silmavalien. He could not decide whether she was scolding him or whether she was about to cry.

"It's not just *me,*" he said. "And it's not like I have any fear that it will be lost. Another might, I suppose, see this peaceful beauty, this hope, this purity, and then the evil, the corruption, the strife and horror, and think the good is an illusion. I suppose. It doesn't make sense. It's the other way around. I just know it is."

"I know that too," said Silmavalien.

"Perhaps even before I did, right?" asked Noren with a smile. Then he said, "But if we do die, why does it bother you? I remember some line about 'lands more fair and fine than any we have yet come by.' That's what awaits us. Death's not an end to life but a beginning – an entrance into some state or place of such life we'll see this as but a shadow of life."

"But what if I survive you? What of living without you? What of living without *them?*"

It took Noren only a moment to realize that she was talking about the dragons. "There's a lot neither of us know," he said. "I can't say anything to comfort you about that."

"You feel the horror of it, too!" she scolded.

"I do," said Noren, "– to have part of yourself cut out of you, to be separated from one you love, who's lived in you and whom you've lived in –"

Silmavalien interrupted him then. "Several of the dragons are still bitter and angry beyond thought about their loss. They want to wreak havoc and destruction on all whom they deem responsible. I think one of them doesn't want anything and feels like destruction."

Noren waved his hand. "I didn't want to have such an uncomfortable conversation right now."

"We live in an uncomfortable world," said Silmavalien. "What did you want to talk about?"

Noren stepped away from her and looked down at his toes. It took some time for him to answer. Finally he said, "I want to be with you."

"I want to be with you too, but we talked about this," said Silmavalien. "I have to fight, too, and I can't if I'm pregnant or I have an infant. Also, what will I do if I'm a mother and you're dead?" At this point she really did begin to cry.

"Oh, Silmavalien, my love," said Noren. He stepped forward and put his arms around her, intending to comfort her, but she half-resisted. *That was a disaster,* he thought.

She wiggled free from his arms, still crying. *I wish I hadn't done that,* he thought. *I really did not mean to do that.*

Elninya's thoughts came into his. *"No, but you're not too good at thinking about what things will feel like from someone else's perspective."*

You knew this was going to turn out like this and you didn't tell me?

"No. I was tired and hungry and fishing. I wasn't thinking. I only just now noticed and looked through your memory to see how it happened."

Noren nodded. He walked away from Silmavalien, sat down on a log, and buried his head in his hands. She was right. So was Elninya. He did not understand what it was like for her. He could not understand what it was like for her. When he thought about it, he realized that he could not even imagine surviving the battle while Silmavalien died in it. He could not believe that such a scenario was enough of a possibility to have any idea how he might feel about it, or even the possibility of it. He had no idea what things might feel like for Silmavalien. He thought of how she had freaked out at the idea of him being burned alive, and he knew that the idea of that happening to her would make him feel like drowning the world in blood would be a small price to pay to save her. For him to live without her might be comparable for her to live without him the way things currently were. If she became pregnant, it was a whole different story, something which he could not even begin to fathom.

How my feelings do not line up with what I think I know, thought Noren. Considering what he was certain he knew about death and life, he thought, *Yet even when I keep all this in mind, I feel scarcely less fierce. How should I feel? It would be DISGUSTING for me to not feel upset, mad, angry, sad, something, I don't know what, about this. Come to think of it, if I don't even know how I should feel, how can I possibly help Silmavalien to know and feel the way she should?*

Noren sat there for several more minutes. Then he decided to get up and tell Silmavalien he was sorry for presuming to criticize the way that she felt and tell her how she should and should not feel. "I might be right you should not feel the way you do," he said, keeping his distance from her and his eyes downcast. "But I don't really know. At least, I'm not sure I even know *how* you feel. And I feel ways myself that I can't help but think must not be right, yet to feel any different way that I can think of feeling, even though I can't actually feel that way, would be even more wrong."

From his love's stance and eyes, Noren could tell that she was listening. When he stopped speaking there was an attentive silence for several moments. Then she said, "I think I know what you are saying. Thank you."

Noren acknowledged her and then left to be with himself.

41

The Question

"The nightmare is upon us. Fly."

Noren woke to Onyxalis' warning mingled with horror. The obsidian dragon soared out over the lake, a dark shape against the stars, and Noren leaned against his presence to keep from despairing, as a whole host of evil feeling mixed in his soul, combining into a maze of confusion. Hastily and clumsily he saddled Elninya, while Silmavalien saddled someone else beside him. He did not have the time or attention to care who.

He only knew they were the last ones in the air, and now he felt a little like what Silmavalien had described to him before the battle of the High Pass. He did not feel like he could fight any more, or like he even know how to fight. Defeat was all but certain, and the deepening darkness, even though it should have been early morning, the deadly, mind-chilling terrors, and the dark arrows and bolts of dark fire in the sky only added to his sense of hopelessness.

The song of the Ellenari's bows was too intermittent to provide more than momentary flashes of sanity and hope, yet somehow he did not find himself on the verge of succumbing to blind rage and madness. He could just feel the touch of it, but whatever this despair was, it was not that.

Then a wind arose out of the night. He felt the thrill that went through Elninya when she caught it under her wings, and the joy as she rode it around and over the ridge of the mountains among the rest of the dragons. Something like lightning flashed around them in every color of the rainbow and every shade, and it seemed sometimes like lines of fire ran through seams in the clouds. They burst through torrents of rain, and then through places of almost complete calm, and all the while the air was carrying them faster and higher, until they were far higher than Elninya could have flown on her own.

The air did not feel thin. Not even to him.

Then with sudden clarity, he recognized the valley of the Ellenari, Shan'Dala, spread out before them. The same mountains rose above them, the whiteness of the snow gleaming faintly in the light of the stars and the half-moon. The air was fresh, cool and alive and seemed to breathe life and clarity into them. The atmosphere felt almost surreal.

Elninya glided down and landed. She was not the first of the dragons, but she was not the last either.

He started unsaddling her, and a few moments later, he was aware of Silmavalien unsaddling her dragon on the other side of Elninya. He decided not to go looking for the beds, even though he was sore. He was tired, and it was dark, and this grass, before the first bridge, would do. The earth was softer than anything he had for days, and Elninya put her wing over him as usual. That was enough for the moment.

He woke to see the valley of Shan'Dala filled with the soft light of the morning. The sun was shone on the higher mountains but did not yet touch the valley. He stood, stretched, and could not believe he had only been asleep for a few hours, given how rested he felt. He did not recall even the air of Shan'Dala being that powerful.

"*It might be,*" Onyxalis said, in the tone of voice he used when speaking to both him and Silmavalien, "*but that is not why you feel refreshed. You have slept for a day and a night.*"

That explains why I am hungry, he said.

"*You will not be hungry for long. I have told the Ellenari that you are awake, and they are coming to bring you food.*"

S

Silmavalien rose and kissed Minth's very large nose. Then she went through the entire gathering of dragons, greeting each one with a touch and a kiss. Things had been too wild and rushed for that this last week, but she did not want a single one of them to think maybe they meant less to her. She could not forget how much it had meant to them that she cared about them even when they were dead.

She felt their love and gratitude enfolding her in return, but it was not enough to satisfy her questions. If anything, it only drove them deeper. After kissing the last dragon, she walked some ways away and right up to one of the huge trees. She placed her hand on it, waiting and thinking. Though no one had died in the flight of two nights ago, though it felt like last night, it had felt to her a little like the battle of the High Pass, in which two had died. She remembered, too, the promise of the Lord of the Light that he would tell her why there was death, why death was what it was, what death really was. How she wanted that answer!

An immense silence surrounded her. Out of it, in it, she heard the

Voice, and the Voice was not different from the silence. *"If you must go through death to know what death is, that law of the universe of which it is the corruption, are you willing? Do you still want to know?"*

Silmavalien froze. Her blood felt like ice. Her heart felt like it would stop beating. Could she?

She could not say no. Neither could she say yes.

The whole forest around her felt like something she could not name. The air felt colder than ice. No. It was not the air. It was something else. Perhaps it was space itself.

She did not now want to rant or yell at the Lord of the Light that there had to be another way. This way made sense. He had told her before that she must go through the surface to find the Meaning. He had told her he had been helping her to do so and would continue to help her. Now a new meaning, yet one evident all along, to those words appeared to her. She must go through death to find that of which death was the corruption or surface. She must go through death, she must die, to receive the answer promised her. If she wanted to know what death was, she must die. She could hardly complain that it was unfair, that there had to be another way. It had never occurred to her that what she was asking all along, as she rebelled against the horror of death, was to die!

Silmavalien felt like an icy vice gripped her heart. At least, she must be willing to die. Was there a difference between dying and being willing to die? Well, one could die unwillingly! But she had known she would die all along. She had never had any idea that she, alone of all men and women and creatures of which she knew, would not have to die. But when the Lord of the Light had promised to answer her question about why life must be fed by death, he had promised her that she would die. The idea that he was helping her to die, bringing her towards death, was chilling.

To die was one thing. To be willing to die was another.

"If you must die to know what it really is to die, are you willing? If you must die to receive that good of which death is the corruption, do you still want to know that good? If the surface is death, do you still want to find the Meaning which is Love?"

The question was clearer now. It was not was she simply willing to die. It was, is this worth death to you?

She could not answer.

I want there to be no horror. I want the horror and loss to be recompensed. I want to know why. I want to know a reason which explains everything adequately. I want to see that it is all worth it.

"If you must go through the thing you perceive as horrible to know that which satisfies and washes away the horror, are you willing to go through the horror? If you must die to know why there is death, do you still want to know? Do you want the Answer?"

Silmavalien bowed her head against the tree. There was no arguing she could do. Of course, to really know what it was to die, she might have to die. Of course, to really understand what death was and was not, she might have to suffer it. Was she willing?

Is there a question of whether I am willing or not? Silmavalien asked. *I want to love. I want to be good. I want to know why, I want to know what's right and good. And I will die. There's nothing I can do about it. So why the question of whether or not I am willing? Willing to receive your answer? Yes, of course. Willing to die? Is there a meaning to the question?*

She could not escape the feeling that she was only confusing things. On purpose.

"If you are unwilling, you shut your eyes against reality. Unless you are willing to go through the surface, the surface is all you will ever get, and you will not find the Meaning. More than that you cannot now begin to understand."

Silmavalien shivered. Unless she was willing to die, she would die forever and never live. Was that the point? *Help me,* she pleaded, but she did not know whether she was pleading for help in being willing to go through anything to find Love, to find Goodness, to find the Meaning, or whether she was pleading for help to avoid the issue and run away – where to, she could not say! Only to go through agony and death was not something she wished!

"I am helping you. Why do you suppose I question you?"

I don't want that kind of help! Now she felt like screaming. It made sense, of course. She must know whether or not she was willing in order to be willing. To answer this question was the next and necessary step towards the things she had asked of the Lord of the Light. But that was not the help she wanted.

But did she even know what she wanted? If she did not know what she wanted, how did she know this was not the help she wanted?

She wanted everything to become clear and easy! The help she wanted was to know, comfortably and clearly and easily, what she wanted.

"I am helping you to know what you want."

Isn't there any easier way?

"No. You are not willing."

Why did it have to be this way? She leaned against the tree, cold in her heart and soul. Was the only way out of confusion right through confusion, into the depths of confusion?

"If what you want is the confusion, or something the confusion protects, yes."

But I don't want confusion.

It sounded like everything she had been hearing. The way into life was through death. Noren said that a lot. The way to the Meaning, the interior, the heart, was through the surface.

Silmavalien stepped away from the tree and realized that the dragons, even Minth, only barely glimpsed what had just happened at best. It was private. It felt unspeakable. It felt impossible. Yet it was real. It remained present in her, a coldness in her heart and a chill in her bones.

42

Bows of the Light

When Silmavalien came back from the tree, she found a very large and delicious breakfast on the shores of the lake. Noren joined her in eating it, and after that he helped her oil the dragons who needed it. In the evening they went to the beds when they had slept the last time they were here, and the next morning they found their breakfast beside them again. They finished the dragons' hides that day, ate again in the evening, and slept again, all without so much as glimpsing an Ellen.

On the third morning Silmavalien went down to the stream separately from Noren to get her morning drink. When she straightened, she saw Aelaza standing on the other side of the bank.

"Come over, Silmavalien," the Ellena said.

Silmavalien backed up several paces so that she could make a running leap across the stream. Barely clearing the water without drenching her boots, she scrambled up the far bank and stood in front of the Ellena.

"Here is a little breakfast," Aelaza said, holding towards Silmavalien a cluster of fruits. "Now, follow me."

The Ellena turned and Silmavalien followed. Aelaza led her through a part of the gardens that seemed almost like a wood. Next to one of the trees a white rock rose out of the ground. The tree's roots were visible, twining around the rock.

As Aelaza led her towards the rock, Silmavalien saw what soon revealed itself to be a bow and quiver leaning against it. The Ellena stooped next to the rock and picked up the bow.

Silmavalien's eyes drank it in. It was slightly and beautifully recurved. All along it were engravings of flying dragons, trees, flowers, and various wildlife. There was a textured grip and noche for the arrow. Though it was not exactly the same as the bow which had been Lexamarian's, the resemblance was great.

Aelaza handed the bow, along with its string which was made of some strong silky strand, to Silmavalien, who took the bow and success-fully strung it in a few moments. She stared at it, marveling at its perfection. She and Noren had done only the smallest part of making this wonderful weapon against the powers of darkness. Then she raised the bow and drew back the string to her cheek, right into the area where the pressure to hold it was least. It was heavier than her previous bow, but not by much. She could quickly get used to it, and it felt like it was made for her, almost as if it were a part of her body and would respond to her wishes like her own muscles did. She held the bow for a moment, marveling at the perfect fit. Then she slowly released the string.

Aelaza's eyes glowed. "Very good," said the Ellena. The quiver was now in her hands. She drew out one of the arrows and offered it to Silmavalien, who took it and examined it.

The arrowhead looked like it was made of a white diamond cut to a perfect point. The shaft was a silvery light-gray substance. Exactly what it was Silmavalien could not be sure. It felt more like wood than anything else she knew, but not exactly like wood. Probably it was wood specially treated by the Ellenari, but here was a crystal-like quality to it. It was fletched with white-silver feathers that glimmered in every hue depending on which way the light fell upon them.

She felt the dragons paying attention to everything she saw and felt. This bow and these arrows were very like indeed to those of Aelaza and the others of the Ellenari.

You're right, she replied. She balanced the arrow in her hand. It felt light for the bow, but she could not judge what the right arrow weight might be for that bow. Clearly, both bow and arrows were different from those she knew.

She took the bow, nocked the arrow on the string, and drew it back to her cheek. Yes. The shaft was a perfect length. She released the string and looked again at Aelaza.

"Very good," said the Ellena again. She handed the quiver to Silmavalien.

Silmavalien took the quiver and inspected each of the arrows. There were twenty-four more arrows in the quiver, and the only difference she could see was that the arrowheads were tinged different colors. Some were more white, others were tinged with blue, still others with red, others with purple, and yet others with green.

She slung the quiver, which was made of some special cloth, over her shoulder.

Aelaza stepped forward and tapped the bow and arrow which Silmavalien still held in her hand. "This bow will shoot these arrows much farther and faster than you would think, from your experience with the bows and arrows made by men. You may shoot other arrows with it, but they will not fly so fast, so far, or so true as these will. The arrowhead is as sharp as the point of any sword or dagger. Most nightmare creatures will be destroyed by the touch of these arrows shot from this bow. Other arrows will not have this effect."

"Will you replace these arrows when I lose them? For in a battle I will certainly lose arrows," said Silmavalien. "Twenty-five is not that many."

"You will not lose them. Or if you do, you will be able to find them," said Aelaza. "That is one of the things we will teach you."

"This is going to be really strange," she muttered, and then realized she had said that out loud.

"Everything is 'strange' as you say," replied the Ellena. "But before we teach you to find your arrows, we are going to start teaching you to use the bow. Come."

They approached a wide, grassy area at the same time as Noren and Hazalel approached it from another side. Noren held up his bow, waving it above his head, and she squealed in response and raised hers in the air. "You're right!" she yelled. "I wasn't going to need my old bow and all those arrows I lost!"

Silmavalien could see Noren smile at her. He waved his bow higher.

She darted out from behind Aelaza and raced across the grass to him. The Ellenari remained where they stood and watched.

"I've twenty-five arrows," she said.

"I have fifteen. I wonder why that is. Let's compare them."

Silmavalien drew an arrow out of her quiver and Noren drew one out of his. They held them side by side. Noren's arrow was longer, in keeping with the longer draw appropriate to his larger frame. Otherwise, the two arrows looked no more different from each other than two arrows from Silmavalien's quiver might have looked different from each other or than two arrows from Noren's quiver might have looked different.

"They're mostly the same," said Noren, "but mine are bigger and heavier and stronger. And," he added, "less."

"We could ask the Ellenari why you have less," said Silmavalien.

"Maybe it's because I have bigger and heavier and stronger," Noren joked.

"Yeah right. I don't think so," said Silmavalien.

At the moment Noren turned to Hazalel, standing several paces away from them. "Why do I have fifteen arrows when Silmavalien has twenty-five?" he asked.

"You have the Dragon-sword. That is your primary weapon. Silmavalien's only weapon is her bow," answered Hazalel. "That is why."

"Could you not have made more for one or both of us?" asked Noren.

"That's not a question we answer," said Hazalel, with just a note of humor in his voice. "Come. It is time to show you how these work."

The Ellenari directed them to take an arrow and shoot for the highest branch of a nearby tree.

First Silmavalien's arrow, and then Noren's, arced into the sky. Their bows did not sound quite like the bows of the Ellenari, but they sounded beautifully like them. The arrows also sounded like, but not quite like those of the Ellenari. Silmavalien almost dropped her bow as the arrow sped from it, glinting in the light. She saw it only as a streak that sped through the tree. She did not see whether it hit the target exactly.

She glanced at Noren, smiling, and saw him look at her with the same look of wonder of his face. These bows were amazing!

"Now," said Aelaza to Silmavalien, "look for the arrow."

"How?" asked Silmavalien.

"Just look."

That was easy enough, and she ran off. About a quarter hour later, she came back with the arrow in her hand. Even though the Ellenari had told her the arrow would fly, she had no idea what that really meant, and she thought she would have found the arrow faster if she had known. It was almost like it drew her straight towards itself, but at first she had resisted the thought it might have flown so far.

Aelaza gave her an unhuman smile as she brandished the arrow, but though Hazalel stood beside the Ellena, Noren was nowhere in sight. "Can I help Noren look for his, if he hasn't found it yet?" she asked.

"No," said Hazalel without looking towards her. "You could not find his arrow the way you found yours. And you each must learn to find your own."

That made sense enough, more than most things did. She lay down on the grass under a tree and stretched on her back to wait and talk to the dragons.

A thought occurred to her and she sat up. "May I ask a question?"

"Of course. Ask any question you want. Only, you are not guaranteed an answer," said Hazalel.

"I have the ring of light. Noren has the Dragon-sword. So why do I have more arrows?"

"The ring of light is not the Dragon-sword," said the Ellenar. "Noren's primary weapon is the Dragon-sword. The ring of light is not exactly a weapon. Ten arrows do not equal the Dragon-sword!"

"I suppose," said Silmavalien.

Hazalel continued. "Noren will be fighting mostly with the Dragon-sword. You will need more arrows than he will."

Silence reigned again, and it was some time before Noren returned. The Ellenari had them repeat the process, and Silmavalien continued to find the arrows much more quickly than Noren could. By the third time, she would have thought he would be used to how far these bows could shoot.

Then it grew dark, and another Ellen brought them a meal and vanished, while Hazalel and Aelaza stayed with them to tell them more about their bows and what they could expect their training to look like. Hazalel took one of Noren's arrows and showed them the point, running his finger along the edge which did not cut him. "With this point and the power of your bows," he said, "this arrow can pierce multiple enemies in a row and continue its flight, destroying every nightmare through which it passes. Learning how to use this to the best effect possible will require special training, which will begin soon, at least for Silmavalien, but not quite now.

"Tomorrow night, you will shoot and look for your arrows in the dark."

Noren sighed.

Silmavalien leaned over towards him. "Don't worry too much about it. Just walk."

"All right. I'll try that," he whispered back. "And hold the image of the arrow in my mind. They told me that, too. But I'll try to do what you suggested at the same time."

43

Filianth

Once more the training became intense and the time passed, without Noren really noticing it. Silmavalien's training progressed similarly to his, but not the same, and the dragons continued their training as well. The Ellenari pushed them near the limit of their new-found strength and endurance, and Elninya's excitement in her new strength alternated with frustration. There were times he was certain that, if she had been him, she would have said she would rather they had not undone the curse so she would not have to do this, but she was not stupid enough to express, or even think, such sentiments.

Of all of them, Noren thought Onyxalis found his training the most frustrating of all, especially when the Ellenari taught him to breathe fire that was like the fire of other dragons, in addition to his lava fire. Noren was not entirely certain why Onyxalis needed to know this, but he was too tired to bother asking and suspected if he were not so tired he could have come up with reasons himself. What was certain, however, was that Onyxalis whined about it a great deal, and Noren could not decide whether the obsidian dragon was simply that arrogant and opposed to having to do things like everyone else, or whether he was trying to distract his riders and the other dragons from their exhaustion and provide a source of amusement.

Probably both.

After a few weeks, Noren noticed that he was constantly attended by a green and gold dragon. The lithe male watched his training whenever he was free from his own, and always slept near him and Elninya. He woke very late one morning when he had been given the day off to rest, and peaked out from under Elninya's wing to see the other dragon's emerald wing, shimmering with gold where the dappled light struck it, and he wondered if maybe the green and gold was trying to court Elninya. If so, perhaps his mind was still confused from what the witch had done to him, because he was pretty sure Elninya was nowhere near being in her mating season. He was not sure how he knew, but it was the sort of thing she would know, and so might he.

The green dragon's head snapped out of under his own wing then, and Noren marveled at his beauty. He was glorious lying in the dappled green light, as the little bit of sunlight Shan'Dala got during the noon hour filtered through the giant trees and landed on his scales, making them glint with every shade of green and gold.

His golden eyes bored into Noren's own, and suddenly Noren felt as if he were falling, falling, falling. Falling through a riot of gold and green, glinting with edges so sharp the colors themselves could cut him.

Whatever the green dragon wanted, he did not think it was to mate Elninya, unless maybe he was trying to ask Noren's permission first.

The dragon shook his head fiercely.

It was not to mate Elninya then. But he did not want to wake her up to ask her to relay for him, and Onyxalis was asleep, too, or at least not paying attention to him. Besides, Noren suddenly did not want Onyxalis to be part of this, and he had no idea why.

He only knew that he was confused, and he was going to go see if Silmavalien was awake and he could ask her.

He found her watching the water-creatures with Minth and Linol, and when he asked his question, her eyes fluttered closed as she reached out to the dragons. A moment later, they snapped open. "His name is Filianth," she told Noren, "and he says he likes you."

Her words were heavy with meaning, and Noren's head spun as he tried to process it. "He likes me? Do I remind him of his rider? And he wants to be around me?"

Silmavalien laughed. "You make him feel good," she said, spluttering, and then refused to tell him anymore, as if it were some secret he had to discover on his own.

Somehow, when she did that, it did not feel at all like when the Ellenari did. There were times Hazalel and the others frustrated him to no end, but *she* made him feel good.

He turned around, intending to go back and find Filianth, only to see the dragon watching him from the tree line, partially concealed by the herbs beds and the branches of a sprawling tree. When he saw Noren looking at him, his gold eye closed and he ducked away.

Noren turned back to Silmavalien. "Is he playing hide-and-seek?"

This time, she actually told him something. "I believe he is shy," she said, "and he is worried he scared you."

"He did, kind of," said Noren absently, watching a glitter of scale that showed between the leaves. He wondered if Silmavalien knew more than she was telling him, or if she was almost as confused as he was and refused to give him any ideas because she did not have any that she was sure of.

He waited a few minutes, and when Filianth did not show his face again, Noren walked towards him, making sure not to go too quickly if he was shy. He wondered if the presence of other people, even if it was just Silmavalien, who Filianth certainly liked as well, and two of her kindest, gentlest dragon friends made him shy, or if he was just shy from having almost scared Noren. He certainly had not been shy this morning, and he had not been exactly discreet about watching Noren train, or eat, or sleeping near him for a while now.

A rustling sound alerted Noren to movement once he was well under the trees, and then a line of whitish spines appearing and vanishing between the leaves told him what direction Filianth – or at least his tail – was going. He waited, not certain if he was supposed to follow – he did not want to scare the poor dragon next, and it suddenly occurred to him that Filianth might be as confused as he was – but then a glowing eye peaked at him from between several branches, and stayed open just long enough to make sure he saw it, before winking and disappearing again.

If Filianth did not intend that as an invitation to follow, he was stupider than Noren thought he was.

Elninya's sudden chortling in his mind almost made him lose his balance and fall, and then she withdrew just as suddenly, leaving him leaning against a giant trunk for support.

What? he asked after her.

It took her a moment to respond, and when she did her mind-voice was still bright with something almost like laughter and full of a strange joy, but it was much more subdued. *"This is private,"* she said. *"I do not belong."*

He pressed his forehead against the bark and ran his fingers over the ridges in it. *How could you not belong in something I am part of?* he asked her.

She laughed again, and he felt her mind enfold his for a moment, tightly, communicating she would never let him go. Ever. *"I will be,"* she said, *"but not just yet."*

Shaking his head, Noren followed after Filianth.

Why had he not eaten before getting absorbed in this game or whatever it was? Filianth had waited until the morning, and he probably could have waited for Noren to eat.

Or not.

Finally, the dragon led him into a meadow where he crushed aromatic plants underfoot, filling the air with a sharp, sweet smell. Noren sat down on a patch of spicy-smelling moss between two tree trunks, and decided it was time for Filianth, if he wanted to. He had followed the dragon for long enough, and it was his turn to approach now, and Filianth clearly heard his thoughts well enough that even if he was too stupid to understand the body language – which Noren was certain he was not – he had to know what Noren meant.

Noren was not afraid of him, just confused, and since he was evidently too shy – or confused – to let Noren approach him, he could approach Noren instead.

It took a while before he did so, coming slowly nearer and nearer, until Noren felt his breath on his skin and could smell the smoky scent of it, mixed with the herbs Filianth had been eating here. Then Filianth came nearer still, and Noren still sat still, even when he felt the soft scales of the dragon's nose on his knuckles, which he had clasped over his knees.

Then Filianth sat back on his haunches and rearranged his wings over his back. He looked half-intimidating like that, half-shy, uncertain, and even vulnerable, and Noren could have sworn there was a gigantic smile on his face.

Had he *ever* seen one of the dragons rescued from the witch this happy? He was not sure he had seen very many dragons this happy at all, ever. Elninya, once or twice perhaps. Maybe one of Silmavalien's. But like this?

Not that he could remember, and it seemed like Filianth was daring him to step forward and touch him now.

Noren complied. He stood, stepped forward, and reached up to touch the dragon's jaw.

Laughter filled his mind, distant, and bright, and golden, filled with foresty light and flashes of flame, and it was definitely not Elninya's laughter.

Noren's eyes widened and his fingers clutched at the dragon's scales. He had never heard a dragon in his mind, except for Elninya – and Onyxalis. And he was bonded to both of them.

Silmavalien was bonded to many dragons, though. So maybe ...

"Yes," said Filianth, his voice suffused with unutterable pride, but also something Noren detected after a moment as some sort of

hesitance overlaying a deep fear and vulnerability, and a still deeper hope. *"You are … my rider."* The dragon imitated a hiccup, and began again. *"I want you … to be my rider."*

"I am willing," said Noren, his voice breathless. It was his turn to be uncertain. "If I may ask why?"

Filianth did not answer. The dragon crouched down, dropping his neck and curling it around Noren, before touching his face with his snout. Emotions crashed over Noren, and he would have fallen if he had not had an arm over Filianth's neck, nestled between the spines, to lean against. The image of another man. Not a man, a little boy who squealed with delight as they rode a thermal, or as Filianth ruffled his hair and lightly knocked him over into the grass. The joy of their relationship overwhelmed Noren, and he once again wondered that Filianth had chosen him for a second rider.

But the joy mingled with other emotions. Fear and pain. Filianth fighting to protect his boy. Both of them captured. The mean humans hurting his boy. Then both of them burned alive. A flash of the pain. Filianth's knowledge that his boy was all right, waiting for him in a fire that did not harm but only healed, and clinging to that knowledge in the far, far worse ordeal of his captivity in the witch's bottle. Clinging to the knowledge his boy was not going to rest until he was rescued, too, and that the healing fire would not abandon him forever either.

Then the vulnerability. The hesitance. To bond another was to risk another who could be torn from him, a pain that made the torture of being burned into nothing. But that fear was a lie, and the joy redoubled and surrounded Noren, pulling him into its greater dance.

He still did not understand, but then again he did not understand why Elninya had chosen him either, and he was honored beyond delight. He would love Filianth to the best of his abilities, just as he now endeavored to love Elninya and Silmavalien with all his soul.

And that was enough for Filianth.

Then Elninya joined their minds, and the joy re-doubled.

44

Before the Battle

That evening, Hazalel told Noren he would have half of every day, alternating between the mornings and evenings, off to develop his bond with Filianth for a week or two. The Ellenar also explained that as his bond with Onyxalis developed it opened up certain faculties of his mind, so that in cases of extreme necessity, he might even be able to speak to almost any dragon.

Spring passed into summer and summer into autumn, while they trained. He continued to practice with the Dragon-sword, and sometimes he got to watch the Ellenari train Silmavalien in the use of her knife, so she would not be completely defenseless on the ground. Soon, most of their practice was moved to dragonback, and they learned to shoot moving targets, and to line up moving targets to shoot many with a single arrow, all on the back of a diving or swerving dragon. Noren practiced with Elninya, and even occasionally with one of Silmavalien's dragons or another of the newly-rescued ones, but mostly he and Filianth practiced together. It was Filianth Noren would ride into battle, since now that he was fully recovered from his ordeal in the witch's bottle, he was even stronger than Elninya, but more importantly, he had scales to protect him. But there were times when an exercise they did together forcefully reminded Filianth of the happy times he'd had with his first rider, his little boy, and crushing grief would overwhelm the dragon. He would often land and cry, keening his loss and desire to the skies. Even though he knew his boy was waiting for him, sometimes the loneliness was unbearable.

During these times, he often wanted Noren with him, sometimes just to be there, to be with him and remind him he was not alone, and other times to talk to him, to remind him of the things he knew. He told Noren once that was one thing he had when imprisoned by the witch: there were times when he almost gave into despair, when he'd felt his boy's touch, not the way he had when they were alive, but definitely there, definitely his boy, and definitely in the hold of a conquering joy, though he still felt for his dragon. But once or twice, he asked Noren to leave him alone, to let him deal with things alone, just to himself. After the second time, it was as if he had recovered something. The loneliness, and the grief for what was not, was still there, but it was no longer able to eclipse the things Filianth knew or drown his hope – or his joy in Noren, his new rider. After that, they were able to be together more fully, to share what they did in a way that was more complete, and revel in their shared skills.

A few weeks after Noren and Filianth finally got the hang of it, he and Silmavalien were given armor, all of which was white and bore the insignia of a black dragon rising upwards with wings outspread. Silmavalien's was less all-encompassing, but Noren's covered most of his body and the helmet almost completely concealed his face, restricting the visibility he would need to use his bow to best effect, but also providing much more protection. They were given white cloaks that bore the same black dragons, and could be wrapped around them for warmth or thrown back to be cooler.

S

A few days after she and Noren received their armor, Silmavalien woke up to Veine telling her that she was carrying eight eggs and she was going to be ready to lay them soon. After breakfast, she walked with Veine to the training field, and together they told Aelaza.

"You will leave Shan'Dala in time for Veine to fly to Dragonsong Forest, lay her eggs, and return in time to fight," said Aelaza.

Since she was there early, she ended up talking to Aelaza, and telling the Ellena more about her life. Apparently, the Ellenari could be curious in their own way, and Aelaza was interested in what it was to be a human and have a human experience. She asked Silmavalien to start at "whatever is the beginning for you," and when Silmavalien got to the day she had tracked down the orcs to Daurth and Jareth's eggs, Aelaza told her she was the Ellen who had protected her that day. She had hunted down many nightmares monsters in the mountains during that time of Silmavalien's life, so that it would be longer before the Nightmare Lord could learn of her existence and that of her dragons, and more importantly, be able to attack them.

"Then why didn't you know who I was or where my dragons came from when you rescued me from the Fire-Shadow that used to guard the Riders' Passage?" asked Silmavalien.

"Time for us Ellenari is not like it is for you," explain Aelaza. "That was when I met you. Don't try to understand it. You'll get it wrong if you do. Also, you know, the dragon eggs in the Hall of Dragon Eggs are not harmed. I was able to check when you went through the Riders'

Passage to Dragonsong Forest. It must simply have not been the right time for them to hatch, and I can see why. But what is not is not and cannot be known."

Two weeks later Ellenari woke her and Noren and called them and all the dragons together in the early hours of the dawn. The armies of the nightmare were amassing and it appeared they were assault Kranah. The only hope of the people in the city to survive the rage and fear that the nightmare would bring was for them to go to war now, and their training was now complete or close enough to it. There would always be room to improve and more to learn.

Silmavalien's heart constricted at the news. It was outside Kranah that Noren had almost been burned alive two years ago. They would be caught between two enemies, the nightmares against which they fought, and the people of Silrah for whom they fought and risked their lives?

But she could not back out. She knew the Ellenari would not make her, and she knew that Minth would not judge her. He would always accept her and he would always love her. But she could not turn away from the Lord of the Light's call. That would be worse.

Nor could she ignore the people's need. She could fight. She knew the truth, she knew that Love was real and must always be finally victorious, and she could fight in that. Not everyone else knew that. And her dragons wanted to fight, too. Airrock was excited to go.

She would go and fight. All the reasons she might do otherwise came from fear, and fear was the nightmare. She had already messed up so much with fear. She had already hurt Minth so much with fear. She was not going to let fear rule her again.

She was not going to let fear rule her relationship with Noren either.

Even as she made her decision, the Ellenari continued to outline the plan they would follow. As soon as they had eaten and saddled the dragons, they would fly for the High Pass. On the other side of the Pass, Veine would turn west and fly to Dragonsong. Given that the nightmare was concentrating around Kranah, it was unlikely there would be any threat to her, but Keya and Tanz would fly out to meet her.

Silmavalien listened, and she and Noren ate while the Ellenari finished packing their bags and saddled the dragons. They flew out from Shan'Dala before the sun had risen, and landed at sunset. Silmavalien dismounted Minth, unsaddled him, threw the packs which had been attached to Lighter to the ground, and strode off to see Noren.

N

Noren straightened from laying out a blanket to sleep on. Silmavalien's eyes glinted as she walked towards him. "What is it?" he asked.

"We've been thinking about each other like we're married since forever," she said. "We *are* married. I don't know when or how, but it's obvious that we are. We don't need a ceremony to marry us. We don't need to get married, since we are."

"Yes," said Noren. "I know this. I am glad you do, too. But why are you saying it?"

She drew herself up very straight. "This battle is going to be huge. And it's going to be soon. Either we will die in it, or we will survive it. If it doesn't end with this battle, it will never end, and we might as well act as if we are married now, instead of waiting for an opportune time!"

"But if I die and you survive?" asked Noren. He could not believe the change in her attitude.

"I want to be with you," Silmavalien said. "And if you die, I want to be with you before that happens." Her voice almost broke, and he could hear the tears in it.

"My love," he said, himself full of joy.

At that moment Elninya swept her wings into the air and took off, throwing up a cloud of dust and leaves, some of them half-decayed. Noren had to close his eyes against the debris she kicked up in his face.

An instant later he knew what was happening: she and Minth were mating! For a moment, he wondered if their dragons mating had something to do with Silmavalien's sudden change in attitude, but then he knew it had coming all along. It had just lain dormant under so much else, pushed to the side by the exhaustion and companionship of their training, until this brought it out.

Still, he could not shake the feeling that there was some connection between Minth and Elninya mating, and the two of them coming together.

He felt it as joy surged through the dragons. The air and earth hummed with it, and Filianth flung himself into the sky in ecstasy. Something about a mating flight further restored the minds and hearts of the dragons who had been tormented by the witch, and the joy of that union that brings new lives in the world was healing.

Silmavalien stepped up to him, her face radiant, and he put his arm around her. She leaned into him, and he knew she felt the joy and the healing even more than he did.

In all the excitement, neither of them were hungry that night.

S

The next day, they continued towards the High Pass. The dragons were stronger than they had ever been before, though now that their progress was measured in the ground they flew over together, she thought that most of them still were not as strong as they should have been. Even Tiela, who was large and bulky and not a wonderful flier by nature, had more strength and endurance than most of the albino dragons, Veine, or Linol. However, most of the dragons freed from the witch were strong. At least physically, they seemed to have recovered almost completely from their imprisonment, and none of them flew with the ease Airrock had, several of them were close enough to give her a great deal of joy in flying with them, and most of them flew better than Elninya and most of her dragon friends.

Tanz reached out to let her and Veine know that she and Keya were already on their way, and to tell her that the dragons in Dragonsong had also grown stronger since the curse was broken, though it did not seem to have any effect on how often they needed their skins oiled.

Just over a week later, they had made it over the High Pass, which was still an ordeal, but it was not as awful as it had been in the past. Silmavalien was certain the dragons could breathe, and even fly, easier in the thin air than they had before, and she did not think it was because the Ellenari were doing anything. But it was still exhausting, and while Veine flew straight for Dragonsong Forest, the others rested to regain their strength.

The second day they were resting, Lisila came to them, like a flash of snow-white wings out of the evening sky. They all turned to see her approach, and she did not even come down between Silmavalien and Noren. "The nightmare rises Kranah now," she told them. "Fly to Kranah and be ready to fight every step of the step." Then she flew on, moving through the skies with all the speed that Aelaza scaled the cliffs of the Steep Descent when she protected Silmavalien from the Fire-Shadow so many years ago.

She did not stop to stare, but when to saddle Airrock and tie the bags to Tiela's shoulders this time, but despite Lisila's warning, they did not encounter any resistance. In a couple weeks, they alighted in a field that was a morning's brisk walk from the walls of Kranah, though the dragons would cover that distance in a few minutes.

A tall Ellenar with hair as black as coal, armor that came down to his knees made of a shining blue metal, and a sword in his hand, came to them a few minutes after they landed. "I am Naragon, Captain of this battle," he said. "Fly over the surrounding areas and harry the enemy. It is here, though it is only beginning to manifest itself. When you find nightmare creatures, destroy them utterly if you can. Guard your hearts and minds against hate and fear and bitterness." He looked over them keenly. "If any of you harbor any hatred in your heart towards the people of Silrah, leave the battlefield now."

"I do not. At least, I think I do not," said Silmavalien.

"Then you are well. Do not begin to do so," said Naragon.

She heard all the dragons assure the Ellenar that they had forgotten any hatred they might have. They would defend the people against both their enemies, even when the people served those enemies with as free a service as any such service could be. She was pleasantly surprised. She knew that until that moment many of the dragons had not decided whether or not to hate those who were responsible, or would have been willing to be responsible, for their most horrible slavery and torture. She was glad with a calm steady gladness at their unanimous choice to stand with Love and the Lord of the Light. But she also noted their emphasis that the people served their enemies with as free a service *as any such service could be.* They saw them as slaves, too, and slaves who might go to the same torment they had suffered if they were not rescued, and she was not sure how they had all arrived at the freedom and compassion to see that, but it seemed to mean everything to them.

"I do not," said Noren.

"All of you are well," said Naragon. "Fix your minds and hearts on Shallim-Araldor, the Lord of All Light. Do not waver from your resolve to Love. Fight valiantly!"

He vanished, before Silmavalien could ask how the nightmare creatures could be here and yet not be here.

"That is not something for you to know," said Onyxalis. *"The demons are near. They are positioned so they can come quickly. However, not everything is yet in position for them to pour out in a horde of unmitigated evil. It is our job to keep that from happening for as long as*

possible – for long enough. It will happen. How and where they are near, how the Ellenari know where they are and what the dangers are, is not something you can know. You, Silmavalien, will remember when the rock ogre seemed to come out of the rock to confront you when you were descending a cliff of the Steep Descent. Do not try to understand them. It is more foolish than to try to understand the Ellenari or myself."

She accepted that, and went to help Noren organize a dragon patrol over the region. A few hours after night fell, it began. Before dawn came, a party orcs with a medusa was found. The dragons who discovered it harried the group with their fire, while Noren, who was nearer than Onyxalis, rushed to their aid with the Dragon-sword.

That company was completely defeated, but over the days that followed more companies composed of various nightmare creatures crawled over the land. Sometimes the dragon patrols who found them were able to completely obliterate them, but often at least one of Noren, Silmavalien, or Onyxalis came. Silmavalien found that it was a bit different using her bow to kill three or more nightmares with a single arrow in reality than it had been in practice, but she and Noren both grew quickly competent both at that and at finding their arrows.

They compared notes after every encounter, sharing their failures and successes, as well as discussing what they could do better, and sometimes even bragging. And, in between engagements, they treasured the closeness between them which they had finally accepted. Even under the storm-clouds of coming battle, their union made the world seem like paradise around them, and it did not feel so much like they were fighting a war against horrible creatures, a war that was likely to be their deaths, but like they were living life and overcoming odds together.

Then came the evening when Veine laid her eggs. She told Silmavalien she was coming straight back, and showed her riders the eggs. Four were a rich brown, three were white with brown webbing like hers, and one was white. All the dragons within were alive and healthy, and she was so proud to be their mother!

Keya and Tanz were coming back with her and bringing more herbs from Aros Cor.

Silmavalien smiled at that. Tanz had already told her directly.

And still, no one moved to attack them, though the people of Kranah knew they were there, whispered about them, and feared them.

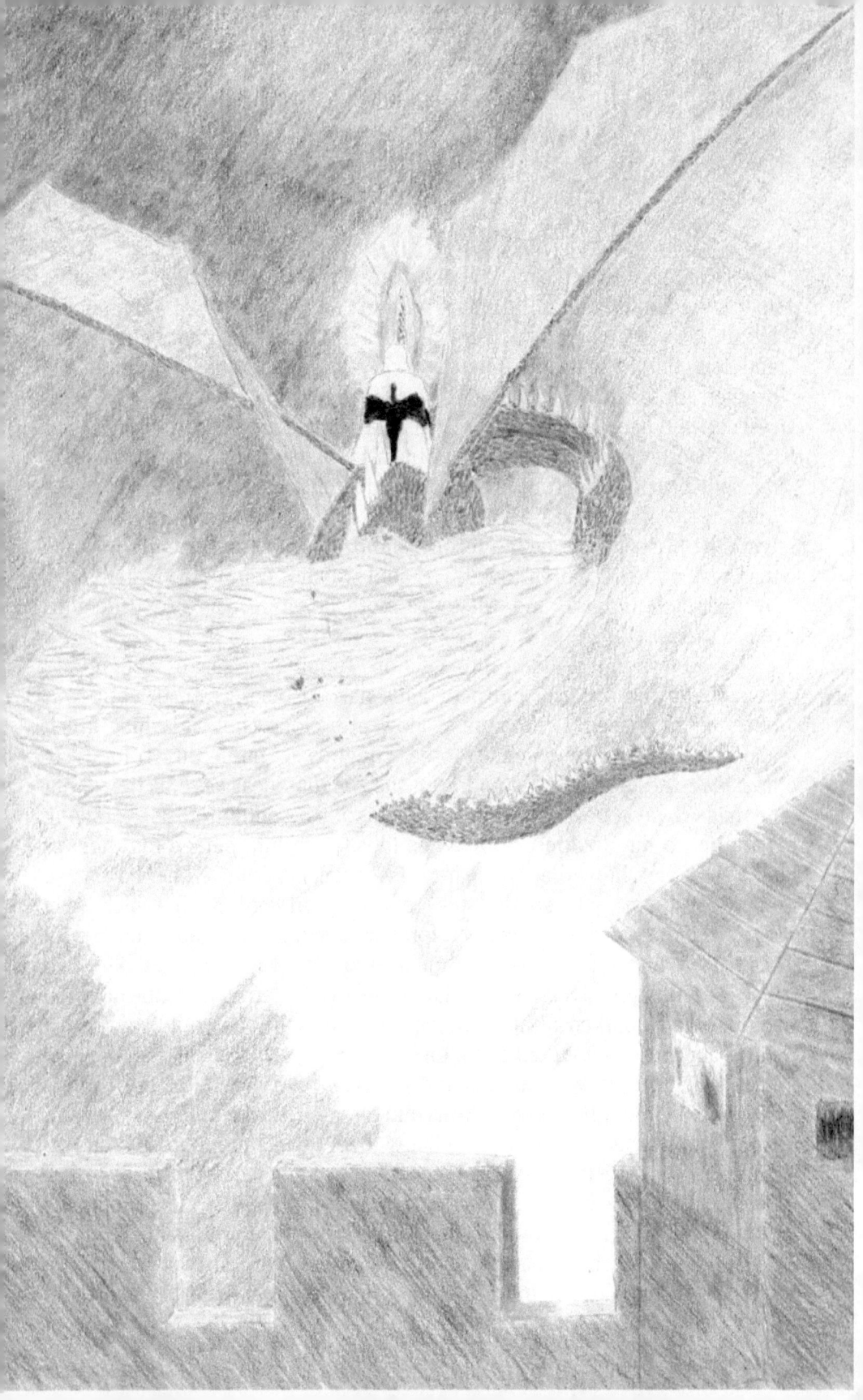

45

Flame in the Clouds

Elvorn sat on Victor's back. He had done his work as quickly as possible so that he could have a little time with his horse, the gift of a man hated by all. He remembered vividly how he felt about that man being killed and how glad he was at the news which had terrified his countrymen, his brothers, his family, his friends, at the news that the man had been rescued and had flown away with his dragon and more Dragonriders.

Before he met Noren, Elvorn might have thought the tales about the evil Dragonriders and the dragon-demons were true. However the look in the man's eyes as he searched for a good owner for his horse while he himself was facing torture and death had convinced Elvorn the man was not evil. Noren loved. His soul was not completely eaten away by hatred, bitterness, and whatever more horrible lusts drove demons and witches.

Elvorn urged Victor into a gallop. Topping the rise of a slight hill, he stopped the stallion and patted his neck. Looking up, the boy was once again amazed. Out of the shadow of a cloud shot a flashing green and gold dragon followed by other dragons in numerous colors! He treasured the moment. He had seen the dragons near several times, but he had always been near others and so he could not risk drawing attention to the dragons. Sometimes those with him cursed the dragons and spoke of how their appearance – especially since there were so many of them – foreboded the return of an evil from which they supposed the world to have been forever saved. Elvorn had to be careful not to give himself and his contradictory views away.

The sight which would have been only terror and horror to so many others sparked in him awe and wonder. Only he could speak of it to no one. He often talked to Victor about his old master. He had done so back when Noren was languishing in prison very often. To tell anyone else how he thought about dragons and Dragonriders would have been to risk death himself. To let anyone know that the wealthy man who had no more need of Victor was the hated Dragonrider would probably have been to lose the horse. And even if Elvorn had not loved Victor, he would have felt that he owned it to Noren to take care of his horse.

The next moment a senseless, irrational fear fell over Elvorn. He felt Victor tense under him. Then a strange darkness fell on both earth and sky, unlike any darkness he had ever seen before. He looked, trying to find what terrified both himself and the horse, and saw horrible creatures fill the skies. Winged bat-like things of an ugly, eerie green, whose wings dripped poison and blood, stony bat-like creatures of a granite gray, and other things so horrible he could take in their shapes dropped out of the clouds. He sat, stunned almost to death with fear and horror.

Then Victor sprang forward underneath him, and the horse's movement roused Elvorn and pulled him out of the grip of the nightmare. He clung to Victor as the horse carried him towards the still-open gates of Kranah.

He looked up again, and this time hope and beauty touched his heart. The dragons charged the demons and colored flame ran amidst the clouds heavy with rain!

𝒩

Noren felt the darkness fall, a thick miasma of hate and fear, and he took a moment to steady himself. The world opened into light upon light. Dying away into beauty. He reached for Filianth and Elninya together, and they each folded each other in their own strength, surviving together when they might have fallen alone.

How was Silmavalien?

On Airrock's back, Elninya told him. They were just taking off the ground. All the dragons would be in the sky in a moment.

Noren looked down and saw the mounted figure racing for the gates and the cloud of horrors descending from the sky to pounce on him. He fitted an arrow to the string of his bow, took a heartbeat to aim, and released. Not as quick as the arrows of the Ellenari, his arrow nonetheless became a streak of light in the dark sky. It pierced horror after horror before burying itself in the ground right beside the gates of Kranah, and every nightmare it passed through went up in green flame.

Elation passed through Noren. Though he had known what to expect, it was still wonderful. He had never pierced so many nightmares with one arrow before or seen so much of that holy flame. The sight was beautiful. He marveled too at how the arrows took care of the problem of making sure the Nightmare Lord could not recover the corpses of his minions, since that was what he was certain happened to the vanished bodies, and Silmavalien agreed with him.

Of course, the Dragon-sword had much the same effect. Indeed, how perfect were the weapons of the Lord of Light! Truly the Light was Lord over the Darkness.

A moment later an arrow from Silmavalien whizzed through the air shooting far over the city of Kranah, into which nightmares were diving at that moment. Trying to stay clear of the arrow of light, they knocked into one another and he rejoiced as her arrow took out even more than his. Nightmare after nightmare exploded into blue flame, and any monster that swerved or fell into the flames caught fire too.

The battle was not hopeless at all.

He looked down again, and saw several Ellenari defending the gate and walls from the hordes of nightmare creatures who could not fly. Once again he was amazed with hope. He had never seen the Ellenari fight before, and they moved even faster than he would have thought. Their swords flew back and forth with the speed not of an arrow but of one of their own arrows, and he would have loved to watch, but he did not have the leisure for that. He and Filianth had to give their undivided attention to the battle around them.

A few moments later, the battle was truly joined.

In a few more moments the battle was truly joined. Dragons darted among the nightmare creatures, their fire dealing death. It took all their skill to keep themselves away from claw or tooth or poison or other weapon of the demon creatures. This way and that arrows flew, both from the Ellenari and from the two Dragonriders, and the sky, overhung with clouds, glowed with lines and streaks of colored flame in addition to the flame of the dragons.

Noren slung his bow into his quiver where six more arrows waited. He pulled the Dragon-sword from its sheath and at once it throbbed and glowed. Red and white light flashed from it and flames flickered down its blade. Filianth roared in exultation and anticipation. With three dragons, one of them Elninya, close behind them Noren and Filianth rode into the midst of the battle.

S

Glancing to one side, Silmavalien got a glimpse of Onyxalis opening his maw wide, crunching a stone bat between his mighty jaws, and swallowing it. She was so shocked she involuntarily reached out to him.

"I have to eat rock to maintain my lava," he replied. *"Those nightmare creatures based on rock will do as well as anything else."*

Oh. So that was why he had been taught to breathe fire like her dragons! If he had to fight for a long time, and he could get enough stone or metal to maintain his volcanic flames, than he would still be able to breathe some sort of fire.

She put these thoughts aside, nocked an arrow to the string, sighted down it carefully, and let it fly. Never before had she seen so many nightmares fall to a single arrow. It was almost an inferno of white flame that leapt into being in the midst of the sky.

Over there, Airrock. I think that's where most of my arrows are.

The dragon raced for the spot Silmavalien indicated. A score of dragons went with her, forging a path through the winged nightmares.

Airrock dived, her head surrounded in a halo of vaporous white fire. Then, abruptly, she snapped her wings open. The world tilted around Silmavalien. A moment later the dragon landed. She swung herself down from the saddle and landed heavily in the soft, wet earth. A few yards away was one of her arrows, buried head-down in the ground. She pulled it out. "This way," she said out loud, motioning to the dragons to come with her.

The earth heaved up, cracked, and ruptured. A horrible looking head of soft folds of blotchy snake-like skin that had no eyes but did boast antennae and fangs appeared, almost underneath Silmavalien's feet. She leapt backwards and fell on her back as she struggled to draw her hunting knife. The worm came towards her.

Airrock leapt past her, forcing her back onto the ground with the blast of air from her wings, and flamed the worm.

Silmavalien rose, feeling horribly shaken. She launched herself forward, clearing the patch of earth from which the worm had emerged, and ran towards where she suspected another arrow to be. Around her the dragons fought, clearing a path for her. Onyxalis left where Noren was fighting to aid her.

𝒩

Noren and Filianth fought their way right through the hordes, guarding the gate and that section of the city. Together they were a force to be reckoned with, and both dragon and rider exulted with pride together in the awesome team they formed against the nightmare. Filianth protected Noren, moving when he had to, flaming. Noren protected Filianth, his sword searing any nightmare that came within reach. The dragon was extremely flexible, so that if a nightmare dove for his tail or back he could often move or twist around, bringing either his flaming maw or

Noren's sword down upon the monster.

"I'm glad I get to fight these things," Filianth told him. *"It's not like even Luvine was better off than we were. Who knows what she endures now, if what's left can even be called Luvine. I don't wish that void on anyone, and I am so glad to be fighting this war! This is a battle worth dying in."*

I hear you. You've told me that before, Noren replied. He scrambled half-way out of the saddle, his feet still tied in, his knees on the dragon's back, and held his sword across his legs, waiting for the monster he saw coming for them. For some reason the Dragon-sword did not burn him though he felt its warmth.

The large monster dove on them. Filianth spread his wings flying upwards right into it, then rounded his body and pulled himself together. The momentum of both winged creatures drove the monster right onto Noren's upheld sword. For a moment it felt like the weight of the monster would either tear the Dragon-sword out of his hands or his body out of Filianth's saddle. Then it took flame.

Filianth dove forward, trying to gain as much speed as possible to take Noren away from the burning monster. Even so and even through his armor, the heat singed his arms and face.

As soon as the burning monster fell behind them, Filianth changed his course to gain as much altitude as he could. In aerial battles, the higher one was, the better. Maneuvering and fighting from above was much easier and much more effective.

There's nothing I can do about that, Noren responded to an image from Elninya. The city was beginning to burn. *It's all I can do to keep most of the nightmares out of it. You can tell the Ellenari, though. I don't know what they can do, but they can do things we can't even as we can do things they can't. And we can pray the Lord of All Light that the clouds start to pour. That should help them fight the fire. If it's enough and early enough it might even put the flames out by itself, and I don't think it will make our fire less powerful against the nightmares.*

You're right. It might affect dragonfire a little. I don't think it will affect the fire of our arrows.

At that moment, Filianth directed his attention to a flight of obsidian dragons flying out of the thick bank of clouds in the west.

A moment later the rain began to fall.

46

Between Two Enemies

Silmavalien was again on Airrock's back, eight arrows in her quiver, when she saw the black dragons drop out of the clouds.

Are they really black or do they just look like it in this lighting? she asked.

"They're really obsidian dragons," said Onyxalis. Silmavalien had never sensed him so distraught before. Something must be terribly wrong, if even he felt defeated.

"Onyxalis, you are prepared to fight them," said a voice that seemed to fill the whole plain. Instantly Silmavalien recognized it as the voice of Oaeiae. "Only you have the Gift of the Volcano. Do not be afraid to fight them. These obsidian dragons did not wait for their appointed time but sought the vengeance which they thought was their right. For this reason none of them are the Obsidian Guardian they dreamed themselves to be. They fell to the enemy, as you so nearly did, and they are horrors of the nightmare. Fight them as if they were nightmare creatures, for so they are, and so you would have been if you had yielded to the invitation of the Dark Lord."

There was a pause during which Silmavalien knew that Onyxalis said something to Oaeiae which she did not quite hear.

"It is you who must fight them, Onyxalis. Go out to meet them and keep them away from the others. It is your place," said Oaeiae.

"It is my place," repeated Onyxalis, as he flew out to meet them. *"Silmavalien, I will help you get to your arrows after this."*

"Thirty-one," replied Onyxalis, and Silmavalien knew Noren had asked how many there were.

In respond to his riders' concern, the obsidian dragon said, *"Don't worry about me. They're not a match for me. No heat can hurt me now I have been through the volcano. Both of my fires will harm them. They cannot breathe lava. The biggest of them is not half my size. I will defeat them. I am the Obsidian Guardian. They are not."*

At that moment the black dragons split into many groups. It looked like they were going to flank Onyxalis.

Silmavalien kept some attention for her black dragon, but she had to return most of it to the battle around her. *I'll start using my arrows again, but I'm still looking for opportunities to drop down and pick them up,* she announced.

Then the sweeping wall of rain hit them.

Silmavalien saw a dark monster, very like the Fire-Shadow, sweeping down over the city with hundreds of lesser demons. She knocked an arrow and sent it flying for the Fire-Shadow. From other quarters, several arrows of the Ellenari also flew through the descending company of demons.

The whole cloud of darkness went up in many-colored flame. Noren was right. The rain did not dampen the fire of light.

She sent another arrow flying out over the city. Then Minth spoke to her.

Aelaza is waiting for me? All right. Tell her I will be over there in a moment.

While Airrock was flying towards where the Ellena waited, Onyxalis announced, *"The black dragons are dispersing. I cannot keep all of them from getting to the main battle."*

She acknowledged him and caught the echo of Noren's similar acknowledgement.

Then Airrock landed and Aelaza darted right up to her. The Ellena held up seventeen arrows towards her, and Silmavalien slipped them back into her quiver. "Thank you," she said. "I'm now back to twenty-three arrows."

"That is well," said Aelaza. "But are you well?"

"I don't know," said Silmavalien. "I still cannot get the worm out of my mind."

"Death-worm," said the Ellena. "It is well it did not touch you. Remember whom and what you love. Remember that Love is triumphant. Think of and call on Shallim-Araldor." She smiled. "Remember Malchoris?"

Silmavalien nodded.

"And here is something to refresh you in more ways than one." The Ellena lifted a cup of sparkling water up to her.

She drank it all. "Is it – is it from the Spring of Nerya?"

"Yes," said the Ellena. "Wait here for the moment, while I give all the dragons here a taste of it. Then we return to the battle."

They're shooting at you and Noren, Filianth? Can't they see that you're protecting them from the demons?! Oh no!

Silmavalien gasped. She saw Aelaza a few paces away, moving away from her. "Aelaza!" she called.

The Ellena stopped. "Yes, Silmavalien?"

"The people of Kranah are shooting at *us!*"

"Well, try not to be shot by them then," said Aelaza. "You knew it would happen."

"Why can't they tell we're fighting to *protect* them?" asked Silmavalien.

"They're deceived. You know what they think you are. There's not time for this conversation now. Remember: if ever you hate, you give victories into the hands of the nightmare."

Silmavalien nodded gravely.

Aelaza waved to them and Airrock rose into the air. The other dragons followed. An arrow which must have been Aelaza's rushed past them, taking out a black dragon rushing towards them. The dragon fell on one of the towers of Kranah, crushing it and anyone nearby.

𝒩

The hours wore on. Noren grew tired, and seeing what his arrows and sword could do was no longer exciting. Elninya and Filianth were just as tired, maybe more so, and so were all the other dragons, except maybe for Onyxalis. Lava kept pouring from his mouth, and he kept on munching on stone nightmares. He melted and then devour stone giants.

Noren wondered how they would win. They grew ever more weary, and the monsters kept on coming. There were never any less of them, and by evening several of the dragons had died. He saw Silmavalien briefly and could see that she was far more bothered by their deaths than he was, which was only natural. He did not know them, and he could not even keep track of all their names. He probably would not have noticed on his own that they were gone. She spoke to them all at least once a day and knew each of them.

He wished he could comfort her, but he was so tired himself. Hazalel had given him back his arrows and given him a drink from the Spring of Nerya, but it was not enough to completely refresh him or the dragons.

At least the black dragons were defeated, but it was so difficult to keep the nightmares from coming into the city from the sky. The arrows of the Kranahians did no harm at all to most of the demons but could wound, or even kill, any dragon. How could they be so foolish? At least, Onyxalis had defeated the black dragons and he spent most of the time guarding the city from above. No one was comparable to him in battle, and he did not seem worried about the Kranahian's arrows.

Sometime after the sun had set Ellenari told him to go to a field and rest. They would fight through the night, and they had told Silmavalien and the rest of the dragons to rest, too.

Gratefully, he went to the field. Silmavalien seemed to have got there just before him, and she was moving among the wounded dragons with the black-robed Ellena who was the Healer, Firutrilia. He joined them, holding whatever they wanted for them, and when they were done, Firutrilia stepped away, and he and Silmavalien ate and drank the food and water they had been given in silence. They were too exhausted to talk about things they usually did.

Silmavalien stood. He looked up and then away. Her ring flashed on her finger, providing an umbrella of light, and his eyes watered if he accidentally looked at it. "Coroneth is arranging some of the dragons to watch for the night," she said. "He'll make sure they all know to wake you if something too strong for them comes."

He smiled wanly and stood. She followed, as he trudged through the sheets of pouring water and the slick mud that sucked at his boots to go to Elninya. Filianth was with him the whole time they were fighting, so he always slept under her wing.

He knew what the dragons called him. *Warrior of the Dragonriders.* But he did not feel like such a great warrior, and it was not what he aspired to be either. He was just trying to do the best that he could.

I love you, Elninya. I love you, Filianth. I'm grateful for both of you, he said, as he curled against her warm body, and felt Silmavalien beside him. In a few moments he was fast asleep.

Onyxalis continued to do battle.

S

Silmavalien lay down with Noren, but tired as she was, she was still distraught to sleep. After a while she stood and went out from under Elninya's wing.

She could not look at the ring of light on her finger for it shone too brightly. She could not stop thinking about the dragons who had died and the dragons who still might die. And Noren. And Minth. Minth could die so easily. He was sound asleep, but he was weakest and more exhausted.

Life for life. Some must die that others might live. Why? It was so horrible. She sat down on the ground, her bow sheltered under her cloak, and wept. Why did life have to be bought with death?

She needed the answer *now*. Before this battle was over, so many more would *die*.

"*Child,*" said the Voice, "*love. Love.*"

Eventually, exhaustion forced her to sleep for a few hours. Firutrilia shook her awake scarcely past midnight. "Breathe this," she told Silmavalien, forcing a sprig of leaves into her hand. "Then give a scent of it to all the dragons Noren is about to take into battle. Then we will tend the wound again."

Her head spinning with weariness, Silmavalien rose. *Oh, don't die, Noren,* she thought. As soon as her mind cleared, she spoke to Filianth, *Take care of Noren.*

The dragon responded with irritation. What did she think he was going to do? Of course he would take care of Noren as best as he could. He loved Noren as his own rider.

47

The City Falls

After Firutrilia gave Silmavalien more instructions on how to care for the dragons, she left. Silmavalien was still going round and round, trudging between them and doing what she could, with only Minth and a few other unwounded or barely wounded dragons with her, when she felt the approach of Veine and Tanz.

She had just finished what Firutrilia had told her to do when the two dragons landed. She rushed to Keya. "I didn't know you were coming all the way," she said to her friend.

"Of course I was," said Keya. "I begged to be with you. And I knew you would need them. Veyan, Kenaja, and Nereis all have bows that they use well. The Ellenari have given us a lot. And the main battle isn't there. There's some fighting on the edges of Dragonsong Forest, as they try to make sure no nightmares enter Dragonsong and that no nightmares escape after encountering them, but it's nothing to here."

Her blue eyes gleamed with a warm, soft light as she looked into her friend's face. "I want to be close to you. I want to fight with you. Even if it's all they warned me it could be, horror and death, this is where I want to fight. So I asked. And here we are."

"Thank you so much, Keya," said Silmavalien. "Excuse me for a moment while I touch Veine."

She and Veine shared their affection for one another. She pressed her forehead against Veine's cheek, and Veine nuzzled her in return. After a few minutes, they broke apart, and Silmavalien turned back to Keya. "I think it's my task to stay here and protect these wounded dragons. I don't know what you want to do, but ... but, Keya, did I tell you? I can't bear it. Why must life be bought with death? Why must some die so that others may live?"

Keya held her tormented gaze for a few moments, and then said, "I can only speak to what you know, and what can I say? I only know you asked to be made good and loving no matter what. Could that be part of it? Could that be why the world is the way it is? I don't mean that you asked, but the thing you asked for. What if to love perfectly we must know how to love to death, to give our lives for what we love? What if death is how we learn love?"

"But how can you learn love by being separated from the one

you love!" Silmavalien almost screamed. "Or the ones," she added more softly.

"What can I say?" said Keya. "Nothing I say, though true, though you know it is true, will comfort you, will it? No, you must *know* something I cannot give you. There's so much I don't even want to try to talk about. But even in that separation, do you not see how you might learn to love in a way that might not otherwise be possible ..." Keya's voice trailed away.

"No, I don't," said Silmavalien.

"Are you being completely honest with yourself?" asked Keya. Her own eyes were moist. She held up her hand. "No, Silmavalien. I'm not judging you. I'm just asking you a question for you to consider the answer."

It's just like a question the Lord of the Light asked me, thought Silmavalien. *Or rather, almost just like.*

At that moment one of the dragons alerted them to danger.

Silmavalien raised her head and saw the horrors diving down on them. She had her bow out and an arrow on the string. A moment later it flew up, striking the nightmares and sending them up in white fire. Keya's arrow was only just behind hers, and blue fire was added to the white.

After the skirmish they found that none of their arrows had fallen far. They still had twenty-five arrows each.

ℵ

The Ellenari were elsewhere. Noren did not think they had deserted him, but they were elsewhere and neither Filianth nor Elninya could speak to them. His arrows were all gone and he could not look for them. A huge horde was approaching the gate. It was the hour of the dawn.

Land, he told Filianth. *The only way I can defend this gate is on the ground with the Dragon-sword. Otherwise they'll get through and over between your dragonfire since I'm out of arrows. Just keep me safe from above.*

The dragon landed and Noren dismounted. The sword glowed in his hand, sending forth all the light of a volcano.

Almost before Filianth was in the air, a horde of orcs and other demons came on. Noren's armor protected him well. Orc arrows bounced off his helm. Fireballs from imp minions were rendered harmless on his breastplate. Though he was incredibly weary and his arm felt sluggish, his sword was winged in his hand and fire darted from it. Wave after wave of nightmares came up to the gate and wave after wave of nightmares fell back in defeat, destroyed and burned up by the power of the Dragon-sword.

Again and again Noren felt like he could not fight another wave, and again and again he fought and was victorious. The weary dragons fought above him, occasionally lending him assistance against the land-bound nightmares but mostly doing as he asked and protecting him from above, while Onyxalis protected the rest of the city.

The dawn grew brighter in the east. With a sudden shock Noren noticed that though the sun was not yet up, it was now light. Then another wave of nightmares were upon him.

Behind him, through Filianth and Elninya, he was vaguely aware of Jareth falling to the ground, pierced through with a dozen arrows. Others of the dragons were wounded by arrows, but not too badly to fight and fly and live.

S

Silmavalien felt Jareth's dying pain. She looked at Keya and her friend saw the fire in her eyes. *Oh, Jareth!* cried Silmavalien. He had only just reformed from his cruel ways and there had not been time to get to know the real dragon! She swung herself into Lighter's saddle. *"We're going,"* she said out loud and to all the dragons.

Several of the less wounded ones rose behind her.

Why, O Lord of All Light? she screamed in her heart.

N

Noren's sword flew and wove a fiery dance. Then, abruptly, there were no more nightmares in front of him. He wavered, hot, thirsty, and tired. The cloud cover had broken in the east, though the air was very wet. It felt like it might pour again any moment.

The gates of the city swung open.

E

Elvorn stood, holding Victor by the rains. He had been watching the dragons fight, wishing he could help them and wishing he could stop the men from shooting at them. He had not slept all night, but in the crowded, terrorized city he had not left his horse for a moment.

Then he heard the white dragon scream. He felt the earth shudder as his body hit the ground. He knew he was dead. He knew who had killed him. Not the demons, but the men the white dragon had been protecting from the demons.

He walked down the small street towards the gate. He heard the great gates of the city opening and then saw that the white dragon had fallen on a house. That street was blocked by rubble. He looked briefly at the gleaming white body stained with red and was about to cry. He wondered if this was Noren's white dragon or another one. There was no dead rider with the dragon, but he had noticed that most of the dragons flew and fought without riders on their backs. He turned and took another way to get to the main street.

When Elvorn reached the main street he stopped dead-still. Soldiers walked down it. Between them they held a captive who still wore a white cape and armor with a black dragon upon it. The captive's helmet had been knocked from his head. Dark hair framed a sweaty face which Elvorn saw well enough to be certain whom he saw. Noren the Dragonrider! He could tell that Victor recognized someone, too. The position of the horse's ears and a very soft nicker told him so.

Somehow he *had* to rescue Noren. In the state of the city right now, they could kill him so quickly. That Dragonrider had been risking his life to protect them and this was the payment he got! Elvorn was mad. Why could they not tell? How could they be so stupid? This was just wrong. One had only to look in that man's face to know he was not a witch or a servant of demons.

Further, thought Elvorn, unless that man were quickly rescued, the demons would destroy them all. The Dragonriders were not here to bring the demons and destruction upon them. It was the Dragonriders who stood between them and those demons and that destruction and horror.

Besides, he could not let that man be tortured and killed because he had tried to protect them all. Elvorn would risk his own life to rescue Noren. It had been bad enough when he had almost been killed before. Elvorn would do something now, even if it might only result in both of them dying. Something had to be done. Otherwise everyone would be enslaved by the demons and tormented by them forever. Well, that was not quite certain. There might be someone stronger who could rescue them. But Elvorn would do everything he could, no matter the risk to himself, to rescue Noren.

Still leading Victor, he followed the soldiers down the street.

48

The Victory

Noren fought despair as he was marched through the street. There were things he had to do that were yet undone, and there was nothing he could do. His bows and arrows were gone. He still had the Dragon-sword, since they had been unable to remove that, but his hands were bound.

How would Areaer be saved now? The demons would come into the city and there would be no one to resist them. Kranah had essentially fallen.

Somehow, the Lord of the Light would be victorious. Love must be victorious. But maybe that victory would be in another world and on the other side of death. Maybe this was the end of Areaer.

Even now, he could not doubt the ultimate triumph of the Lord of All Light.

His captors dragged him into a cell and tied his hands to one side and his feet to another lest he get his sword free. But he was so tired that, despite the uncomfortable position and the stench, he barely heard the bang of the door as it was shut enclosing him in utter darkness. A moment later, he was fast asleep.

After all, there was nothing he could do, so why remain awake?

S

The gates of the city clanged shut again. Silmavalien thought she had never been so terrified before. *So Noren will be burned alive,* she thought, *and this time I won't be able to do anything about it!*

She felt reckless now, though she remembered that even in her distress, even if her husband was tortured and killed, she must not hate the people. But hating the people would not save him, or them. She translated all her agony into hatred for the nightmare. For this monster of hatred and horror, of fear that fed blind terror and rage. *That* was why Noren would suffer and die.

Over the city and above its gates she and the dragons prepared to make their last stand. She had no idea how to rescue Noren even if they brought him out to burn him instead of killing him in the dungeons under the city. Any dragons who entered the city would be shot full of arrows. Even a scaled dragon would almost certainly be killed outright, though she realized Onyxalis might be able to do it. Maybe.

ℕ

Several hours later, Noren was rudely awakened. He was jerked up by the ropes and out into the corridor of the dungeon. He was not yet fully awake until he found himself in another room filled with horrible instruments.

Somehow, they tore his armor off and held him down, binding him again. He kept trying to get to the Dragon-sword which was still attached to his belt and could not be removed. But his hands were held too tightly for him to so much as touch the hilt.

"Now," one of them said, "tell your demons to leave."

"They're not my demons," said Noren. "I've been fighting them this whole time."

"Lies! Do you think to seduce us? We are protected by the power of the Goddess of Light and Queen Valiena herself. Everyone knows that Dragonriders are lords of the demons and bring them wherever they go." The man motioned to another.

Noren cried out as pain ripped through his body. What could he do? He had to do something! How could such stupid people be rescued?

But then, in the midst of the pain that threatened to steal his mind and sweep him away, joy almost took his breath away. He did not hate. He did not want to hate. He could not imagine why he ever had ….

He was free.

𝒮

Elninya and Filianth told her what happened, and their rage joined her own. She bit her lip, looking out over the city. All she wanted, all she had wanted since Noren had been taken, was to fly in there and rescue her husband. But no matter how much destruction they were willing to wreak, there was no way she would get to him. It had been demons, but the humans' arrows that killed Jareth, and they would have to fight through both demons and humans.

And then … he was held under the ground or somewhere deep in that massive building. She would never get to him.

Silmavalien turned her attention back to the battle and sent the arrow she had knocked flying. She scarcely looked as flame took hold of nightmare after nightmare. There had to be something they could do. If only they could defeat the demons and make them all go away, Noren might live!

With nothing better to do, they continued to fight and protect Kranah, the city which killed its protectors.

Not that she could judge everyone within it so harshly.

Then a darkness without substance coalesced and progressed down the main road entering Kranah. As blackness gathered around it, making it appear as if it were a gap in existence, Silmavalien recognized it for one of the feared Abysstreaders that annihilated whatever they touched.

Both she and Keya released arrows right for it as it approached the gate, but somehow the arrows of light passed through the Abysstreader and did not harm it. It seemed like it was so fast that, for a moment, its nothingness was not in the arrows' path.

It continued towards the gate.

The dragons scattered every which way. Above them, Onyxalis continued to fight keep as many nightmares as he could from entering Kranah. Then the Abysstreader entered through the gates, which disintegrated into nothing the moment it touched them, and nightmare monsters materialized out of everywhere. The sky and earth was full of them.

She and Keya used every one of their arrows trying to fight towards each other, and then Onyxalis abandoned the city to help bring the dragons together and to the place where the wounded still lay. Dragons died as they fought towards each other, more quickly than Silmavalien could keep track of. One whole band was overwhelmed and slain, and then she screamed in rage and fear as Minth took wound after wound.

Somehow, he made it back to the place where they regrouped, but he barely landed before passing out.

She could, *COULD NOT,* lose both Minth and Noren together! Already she had lost Jareth and more were on the brink of death. Minth *had* to live!

Lord of All Light, why?

"Soon, perhaps, you will begin to understand that I answer you, Silmavalien."

She hardly heard the voice.

E

Elvorn inserted the key into the lock and swung the door open. "Noren, I've come. It's taken me this long, but I found a key in all the chaos – Oh!"

He stepped in. "I see I'm too late."

He heard Noren mumble something but was not sure what. He pulled a knife out and quickly cut the ropes that bound the man.

Noren rose, limped across the cell and picked up the cloak that had somehow been left in one corner. He wrapped it around himself and drew the Dragon-sword from its sheath.

"Thank you," he said to the boy.

"It's nothing. I thank you, Noren. I –" stammered Elvorn. He pulled himself together. "Follow me. I know a way out."

Noren followed Elvorn as quickly as he could. Elvorn felt his urgency and led the man faster, despite the pain that must have caused. "What is it?" he asked.

"An Abysstreader. I must –" began Noren.

N

Abruptly, the boy swung a door open and led them into the street. Victor waited there for them and seemed uncertain which to greet first. He looked first at the boy and then at Noren, and blew in the wounded man's face. He could not help but recognize the horse and kiss his nose back. He knew now who had rescued him.

He also knew that Filianth was not far. The dragon, covered in wounds, fought desperately and valiantly to stay near his second rider, unwilling to lose his rider again even if he could not fight through to him. Even though the connection between them was in some ways less close than what Noren had with Elninya, he had been more affected, and Noren felt the anguish as he remembered losing his boy. He fought as he could, unwilling to put any more distance between him and his rider. While Noren was about to die, his would not try to save his life apart from his rider's.

Noren looked down the street and saw the Abysstreader. At least, he would not have to go far to find it and risk his strength giving out before he got to it. He staggered forward to meet it.

The boy sprang in front of him. "No, Noren! You are too hurt. You have fought enough for us. I will fight it. You cannot."

"I can,"
said Noren. "I
have the sword."

"Then give
me the sword. I'll do it,"
said the boy.

"Both I and the Dragon
-sword were prepared for this," he
said. "I may die. I *will* be victorious."

Noren dodged in front of Elvorn. The Dragon-sword flamed and its heat permeated his whole body, giving him new strength. He felt it draw him towards the Abysstreader.

For a moment the demons were distracted by the battle about to take place. Filianth took the opportunity to launch himself closer to his rider. There he fought to ensure that Noren had only to fight the Abysstreader and not the rest of the horrors above.

Noren was aware for a brief moment of Elninya's concern. Then, biding her and Filianth love, and through them biding Silmavalien love, he put all distractions out of his mind. The burning pain became a dull backdrop as he walked resolutely and confidently forward. There was no doubt in his mind that he would come out of this fight the sole victor, whether he died or lived.

The Abysstreader came forward too. Noren held the Dragon-sword before him and flames ran down its blade which seemed so hot it would have melted apart from the magic of the Ellenari.

"You will fall, Noren of Treas," spoke the prickly, flat voice of the demon.

"You are nothing," said Noren. "By Love and by the Lord of the Light and by this flame you will perish."

Then he was upon the Abysstreader. Though when he moved his wounds tore him, none of that distracted him. Several times it touched him and there was more pain, but still his sword moved almost of its own accord and he successfully fended it off.

Then Noren stumbled. The Abysstreader was upon him. He fell backwards, then pushed off and fell forwards, his sword before him.

Somehow the Abysstreader passed over him. He spun around,

almost passing out from the pain and the effort of the combat, but he thrust his sword into the nothing of the demon.

The flame of the sword reached out. Noren pulled his hand, still holding the sword, back, but not before all the skin on it had blistered. He fell backwards upon the stones.

At that moment the demons began to disperse. Vaguely he heard Airrock telling him – or Elninya telling him what she said? – that she and Silmavalien were coming as quickly as they could. Above him, Filianth fought off the last of the demons attacking him and landed next to Noren. He reached his long neck forward and blew on Noren's face. *Don't leave me.*

"*I won't, Filianth,*" Noren whispered *through the haze of darkness and pain.*

𝓔

Elvorn came forward, leading Victor almost in a daze. Why had he let such a wounded man fight such a monster? Then he remembered. He could not help it. And it was a horrible monster. Maybe he could not have fought it at all. Maybe the Dragon-sword would not even have worked for him.

49

The Impossible

Silmavalien was weeping freely by the time Airrock landed. She slid down the dragon's shoulder and knelt over her husband. Kissed his bloodied face. "Noren."

"My love," he said, sitting up with a monumental effort. She flinched at the sight of the torture that crossed his face. "My love," he said again.

"Don't die," she said, crying.

Filianth raised his head above both of them, looking down on them with one of his gold eyes. Then he lowered his head and breathed into both of their faces. *"You'll be together again. You won't be overcome or destroyed. I know,"* he said, then laid his head back down on the stones.

Silmavalien knew he was almost as wounded as Noren. Elninya landed beside them in another flurry of wind. A boy stood watching, still holding a horse's reins.

Noren reached out and touched her face. "I love you. I will always love you. In that we'll always be together."

She could not say anything. She could not bear how hurt he was. Her face crumpled into tears again.

Their eyes locked for a moment, and then his glazed and he fell back to the stones. For a moment Silmavalien feared he was dead, but Elninya assured her he was not yet dead and then she saw his breathing. "We can't stay here forever," she said. "They'll come again and –"

The boy stepped out of the shadows. "I know," he said. "Why don't you take him wherever you think is safe on one of the dragons? I'll follow you on Victor. But I don't know what to do about him." He pointed at the wounded Filianth.

"We can't move him. And they might not even notice he's alive. Still, I hate to leave him," said Silmavalien. "I'll need to take his saddle off, though. I can't hold Noren in my arms and ride bareback." She struggled to get her words out of her throat. "And we only just discovered we were married," she said under her breath.

"Don't worry about leaving me," said Filianth. *"He hasn't left me. I really do not mind if you physically leave me."*

That made her more comfortable. She took the saddle off Filianth, glad her fingers did not fumble. He moved just enough so she could pull the straps out of under him. Then she saddled Elninya and got in her saddle, then asked the boy – Elvorn, Elninya told her – to lift Noren up to her. Then Elninya spread her wings and was in the air, flying up as quickly as possible so she could get beyond the range of the arrows.

Elvorn mounted Victor and followed Airrock, who flew low enough he could follow her and high enough she could dodge missiles if she had to.

Silmavalien cradled Noren, trying to cause him as little pain as possible. Her tears fell on his face. How could anyone do this to the man she loved? She restrained herself from wailing, not wanting to distress him if he wandered on the borderlands of consciousness.

Elninya landed, and Keya took him from her and laid him on a bed of soft grass. She was at his side in a moment, and then Firutrilia came from tending one of the dragons and knelt over him beside her. "There is nothing even I, the Healer of the Ellenari, can do to keep him in this world as you understand it," she said, and there was more kindness or understanding in her voice that Silmavalien had ever yet heard in the voice of an Ellen.

She nodded, unable to bring herself to speak.

"If this is any comfort to you," continued the Ellena, "Minth will live."

Silmavalien nodded again, staring down on the face of her beloved. "Noren," she whispered.

His eyes fluttered open at her voice, then closed again.

Quietly, Firutrilia left.

The sound of a horse galloping made her turn her head briefly to see Elvorn reining in Victor. She turned her head back to watch Noren, as Keya took Victor and Elvorn walked up and stood beside her.

"He gave me his horse," the young man said quietly. "I knew he couldn't be a witch and be thinking about the welfare of an animal when he was about to die. And he fought for us. And that's what we did to him."

"Not you," said Silmavalien, wanting to assuage the boy's torment even in the midst of her own. "Never you. You didn't do it."

"No, but maybe if I'd been less cautious I might have been able to free him before it happened."

"And if you'd been less cautious, maybe you would have been killed and the Abysstreader would have vanquished," said Silmavalien.

"No, you did what you thought was best."

Elvorn shook his head and said nothing for a few moments. Then he said, "I really admired him. I wanted to get to know him. I wish I'd been more courageous years ago, the first time." He stopped himself from talking, then began again. "But you're his wife, right? Here I am, talking to the man's wife like this. What a fool I am."

"I'm not mad at you," said Silmavalien miserably. "But I'm going to ask the Lord of the Light why. I think he might finally tell me."

Elvorn could not restrain himself from asking, "Who is the Lord of the Light?"

"Love. At least, I think he told me he's Love," said Silmavalien. "I know that Love must be victorious simply by being Love. The Lord of the Light is ... well, he's the source of the only power that can defeat the nightmare. How can I say? Ask Keya. She's so much better about this than I am."

She bent down over Noren and kissed his face. *It's not possible,* she felt. It had to be a nightmare, a dream, since it was just the sort of thing that couldn't be. Her Noren couldn't be lying here like this, all wounds, dying. It. Just. Couldn't. Be.

Firutrilia returned with water and gently bathed his wounds. Then she gave him some to drink, speaking softly to Silmavalien as she dripped the water down his throat. "Don't deceive yourself. He is not going to remain."

Silmavalien nodded. Tears trickled down her face again. What could she say?

Elninya touched her mind, and the calm in the dragon's mind-voice amazed her. Elninya was his dragon. She couldn't be ... like this.

"Death is like hatching," said Elninya. *"It hurts that we do not all go through death together, but it is like hatching. We will meet again as we could never have met here. We will not be dead; we will be vividly and vibrantly alive. The separation is torture, but the horror you imagine is a lie. You yourself are not even clear on what the horror is; you only imagine it must be a horror, and that is a lie."*

Silmavalien nodded. *But I just can't believe he's dying!*

"He is in pain, to the extent that he is conscious. Can you not believe that? He is going where we cannot yet follow. We will be, in some measure, separated for a time, yet I know even that separation will not be total. Can you not believe that? But he will be alive. More alive than he is now. Than we are now. The world dies away into beauty, into

life. The egg will break and we will all be free of all that of which we are free now and more. Deeper and deeper into the heart of life. We will meet each other as we cannot now. We will be together as we cannot now."

I'm not sure I can believe he's going away, replied Silmavalien. *And I can't believe anyone could do that to him! He was fighting to protect them. Even so ... how could anyone? I LOVE HIM! And I'll miss him so terribly. How? How? This can't be reality.*

"Maybe it isn't. In a way, but not in the way you imagine, you know," said Elninya.

At that moment Noren's eyes flicked open. "Silmavalien," he whispered.

"Noren," she replied.

They stared into each other's eyes. What could she possibly say to him that would be appropriate? "I love you."

"I love you, too."

"I'll miss you," said Silmavalien.

"I would, too," said Noren. He remembered that he would not try to argue her out of the only way she knew how to feel. Nonetheless, he had to share one of his last thoughts with her. He forced himself to sit up a little, and again Silmavalien flinched as she saw the torture of the effort. He reached out and touched her face gently. Keeping his hand there, he said, "I don't think you will understand me, and I don't expect you to, and I won't be hurt if you don't. I love you. I don't want to part with you." He paused, closing his eyes, recollecting himself. "I cannot say this right. Try not to misunderstand me." He paused again for a long time. "There is a reason the world is made this way ... Unless there were a death for us to fear and suffer, I could not have loved you, or this people, the way I do now – the way Love has given me to love. I'm ... no, you won't understand that. Believe I love you. I love you so much. It is well that I was given this ... this way to fight, to love, to ... die ... you, my love."

He collapsed from the effort and lay back down, his eyes closed. He opened them again and fixed them on hers. "You get to share in that ... love ... freedom ... through me. I can't say it better. Try to understand. I don't expect you to. I love you ... My love ... Forever."

"I love you," she repeated.

Minutes crawled by while they looked into each other's eyes. In the background Elvorn and Keya conversed quietly.

"Filianth has gone," said Noren.

The thought flicked through Silmavalien's mind that perhaps Filianth's death and Noren's dying had something to do with each other. Perhaps Filianth needed not to be separated from his rider again. Then the thought passed, leaving hardly a trace in her mind.

Into her thoughts about the impossibility of what was happening, Elninya spoke again. *"Perhaps the thing you imagine to be happening is in fact impossible, and is not what is really happening."*

The minutes passed. Locked in that intimate gaze, for a moment Silmavalien forgot her grief in the union she and Noren shared. There was solace and joy simply in being together, and she nearly forgot about the world around her as she dove into their. For a little while the only moment that existed was the Now in which they were together. Then his eyes glazed. The time still passed at once too slowly and too quickly. His breathing slowed and became rough. Her heart twanged. Then she knew that he was dead – gone.

She fell on his chest and wept. She was vaguely of Keya sitting down next to her.

After a while she looked up and saw Elvorn standing on the other side. The pain written on his face launched her into fresh weeping. Why he cared about her husband so much she did not know, but he did. For some reason Noren mattered so much to him.

Eventually, she realized that it was time for her to tend to the dragons again as Firutrilia had directed. She could hardly tear herself away from Noren's dead body, as if she could not believe that he really was dead.

She lifted her head from his chest and looked at his face. She loved him so much. She couldn't bear it. Gently, hesitantly, she reached forward and closed his eyes, but then decided the gesture felt wrong somehow. "I love you so much. How can you leave me?" she said and wept again.

She forced herself to rise. She had to take care of the dragons.

Keya stood before her. "I'm sorry."

Silmavalien just nodded and gulped. She turned away. "You can help me. And you can show Elvorn how if he wants. Or he can go home."

"No, I can't go home," said Elvorn. "People might well know that I freed him. And, even now, they might hate him still. Besides, I want to go with you and the dragons."

She said nothing to that.

Silmavalien tended to the wounded dragons and then wandered a little ways away. She wanted privacy, and she soon found a small green hill that suited her purposes. Standing on the top, she said, "Lord of All Light, you told me you would give me answers soon. Will you answer me now?"

"I have been giving you my answer since you were born," said the Voice. *"First, let me assure you that I, the Lord of the Light, am Love. I suffer in you all that you suffer, and I say this not to you only, but to all that is."*

She stood still and silent.

"I will not now completely answer you, not as you understand it. In some sense I, Love, am the Answer – you know this already and have known it for a very long time. Your entire existence is, and will continue to be, about going deeper and deeper into Love. In that sense, you will never be fully answered. But you asked me why it is such that one must die for another to live.

"Many answers, all true enough in their own way, yet none of them fully true, have been given to you. You will not understand now. But Noren is not dead as you imagine dead. You shall see him again in the vibrancy of life, not the shadows of death. Try to believe what he understood and told you.

"There is more. There is so much more. I am Love. I suffer with you and in you and all the rest. All will be well. You have tasted that. You shall be with Noren, and with all whom you love, and with all that is made lovely and good, as you have never yet been with anyone."

"It is still so horrible," said Silmavalien.

"It is that horrible.

"You are loved. All are loved. What you desire shall be."

Silmavalien nodded, and some part of her realized that Noren was right. Through her love for him, through bearing the loss of him, through continuing to love all those in some sense responsible, through so much she could not name, she could learn a love triumphant over every horror that could be and could not be. She could be what she had asked to be. But in that moment the knowledge had no sweetness, even if her grief left no room for the invitation to a hatred that, she saw so clearly, would never fix or mend anything. Not her own heart, and not anyone else's.

No, there was no temptation to renounce the invitation to

triumphant love, even if right now it meant nothing to her.

What she could hold to was the knowledge that she and Noren would be together again, and the whole world would be healed and brought together in a union of wonder and beauty and joy to which the wonder, beauty, and joy she glimpsed in her bond to Minth was but a shadow.

And this union would never be broken.

Yet though that knowledge went as deep in her soul as the bone-deep knowledge that hate would never heal her heart, she was overcome by grief. There was so much yet to be answered. Though the song she and Noren had heard in the dawn was true, and though she knew they would live it together forever and everything they had begun would be true and fulfilled, with no shadow of loss, still for a time she could only weep.

Sing above the highest star!
Sing in triumph ever-new!
Sing, we are together for true
And are nevermore to part!

Rise on wings behind the sun!
Rise on wings, spring's first thought!
Rise to soar on the wings of dawn
And pass beyond world to world!

Soar and share the sun's own wings!
Soar on winds above the world!
Soar from earth to sky and sky to sky
And to the other side of time!

Fly as free as light's first strike!
Fly consumed in flames of joy!
Fly and find earth is sky for you
And your world is just begun!

Sing in joy above the sun!
Sing with voices of the spring!
Sing and find your voice in mine
As I find my voice in yours.

Love will raise the dead to life.
Love is dawn that brightens all.
Love is complete, unhindered spring
That wakens all to new life.

As he had before, Noren still called her to seek fuller and fuller life with him. This was not the end. The joy they had tasted together would be theirs in full. Their union was not destroyed.

Epilogue

Onyxalis made sure that the people of Kranah did not harass the healing dragons. Silmavalien was unwilling to bury Noren there. She left Keya with the wounded dragons, after teaching her how to do what Firutrilia had showed her, and took Noren to the ruins of Treas with a few unhurt dragons. The dragons helped she buried him in a hill of the Aravin Mountains and she covered his grave with the herbs of winter. One of the dragons placed a rock over the grave to mark it, but Silmavalien did not think she would ever be back. She knew he was alive somewhere and that one day she would go to meet him.

For the burial, Dalis and Songeth, who had come with her, sang the song of the dawn, and she felt the first touch of healing on the raw edges of her soul – it would not be finished in that world, but it began. She knew that the song was true and would be true, and she began to feel it. They *would* dance together in joy like never before, and in that knowledge she foretasted the joy of that dance, the dance they had never been able to dance on Areaer as it now was. But all of Areaer that was good and mattered, that was loved, would be renewed and perfected, and in that sense they would not leave Areaer behind. Areaer would pass through death into life with them, for Love could not be defeated in the smallest thing.

Though he was heavily scarred, Minth healed, though less than half of the dragons freed from the witch survived. Many of them died from wounds less severe than those from which Veine and Minth and Dance recovered. Elninya remained with Minth as long as she lived, and the two dragons even mated again.

While the dragons healed, many young people came out from the city and the surrounding towns, to ask if they could go with the Dragonriders wherever they went, and perhaps become Dragonriders themselves. They had seen the nightmare and seen how the dragons protected them, and a few of them even formed bonds with some of the dragons from the witch's prison who survived.

Within a couple months the entire group started to make their way towards the Greater Aravin Mountains. Once they reached the mountains they would travel west and into Dragonsong Forest.

The Dragon-sword was not buried with Noren. Instead, it was

taken to Dragonsong Forest where it was kept in a cave in the Vale of Aros Cor until the time it would be needed again. Despite the defeat to the forces of the nightmare on the plains of Silrah and at Kranah, those who wished to remain free of its influence had to be ready to fight it unto death, lest its fear and hate gain a foothold in their souls.

Elvorn offered Victor to Silmavalien since she was the wife of Noren, but to his great delight Silmavalien told him to keep the horse since they evidently got along well and Noren had given Victor to him. (Silmavalien continued to refer to herself as Noren's wife or bride, never as his widow.) When they passed through the region around Treas, some of the young people caught and tamed Victor's off-spring. Under Elvorn's direction they learned how to ride and trained their new horses, and brought them through the mountains to Dragonsong Forest.

When they reached Dragonsong, Silmavalien allowed the youth who had come with her to be presented to the dragon eggs they had. Several eggs hatched, including one of Veine's. The dragon was white with a gold head and neck very much like Veine's purple head and neck, and his name was Feryanth. He chose Elvorn, and when Feryanth was full-grown, Elvorn briefly visited his family to inform them that he was alive and well.

Only a few of the dragons who had survived from the witch's prison mated, but Dalis and Coroneth mated the day after they reached Dragonsong, even before Feryanth hatched. Airrock mated Daurth a year later, and Songeth and Tiela mated again. This time Tiela laid ten eggs, most of which were brown.

Silmavalien soon discovered that her fear had come true, and she was pregnant without her husband around. In Dragonsong Forest, she gave birth to a son whom she named Noren after his father, her husband. Elvorn and Veyan remained close friends to her and were always like elder brothers to her son, who eventually bonded to a dragon hatchling and even later married another Dragonrider. Keya was always close to her also. As soon as they reached Dragonsong Forest, Keya and Tanz gathered provisions and went again into the Riders' Passage to get the dragon eggs from the Hall of Dragon Eggs, for Aelaza had told them that they were still there. Keya never married, and Tanz did not mate for a couple decades, but she did eventually mate a dragon named Korbath who was as blue as she was, if a lighter, more electric blue.

Silmavalien left Dragonsong Forest, though Elvorn taught her to ride Victor. Some of the youth liked the horses and ventured out to buy more horses of the same kind, and eventually Elvorn gifted to Silmavalien a colt from Victor and a courser mare. He kept horses from Victor's line all his life as well. When the Dragonriders ventured out, they often brought back more young people whose outlook about dragons had changed. Many of these became Dragonriders and the population of the dragons grew. Though the laws of Kranah remained as hostile as ever against the Dragonriders, many people were no longer so certain about the Dragonriders and the laws were enforced with less rigidity. By the time that Silmavalien died and went to be with Noren in the world beyond and continue their ever-fruitful but never-finished quest for trust and ultimate union with love and beauty, it was reasonably safe for Dragonriders to travel openly in the more rural areas of Silrah, as long as they were careful, though the cities were still very dangerous, and some people made it their vocation in life to hunt dragons.

Eventually it became clear that the budding new population of dragons and Dragonriders could not remain solely in Dragonsong Forest, but what they did about that and where they went involves many stories which are all their own. Some of them, however, remained in Dragonsong Forest for millenia and it became the home of the Dragonriders. Ellen Island was also often visited by them, and now and then one or two of them would choose to live there for a while. The Greater Aravin Mountains, especially the Steep Descent, both where it overlooked the sea and where it overlooked the Plains of Arosië, became another place where dragons and Dragonriders dwelt.

It was also discovered that, somehow or other, the mountains around the opening of the Riders' Passage on the south side of the Greater Aravin Range had shifted again, and the whole passage was now open to dragons. Silmavalien thought it probably had something to do with the Ellenar that was Guardian of the Riders' Passage.

For many years Onyxalis the Obsidian Guardian protected Dragonsong Forest from all unwelcome intruders. When Silmavalien died, he was still strong and fresh and no one had any idea how long he would live.

Dragon's Home
A Short Story

{*Dragon's Home* is a slice of life sequel written from Keya's point of view a little over six years after the events of *DragonSword* (not counting the epilogue, of course). Keya sometimes seems like she has everything together, but she's immature, too. Here's her perspective, her struggles, and a bit of how her thoughts and her relationship with Silmavalien have developed over the years. Also meet Silmavalien and Noren's only child, Noren. (Writing this made me feel a little sad for Sil that she only gets to have one – she clearly enjoys being a mom so much.)}

Noren sobbed. "He dumped me! He made me fall off! He never does that to you!"

Silmavalien picked her growing son off the trampled grass and hugged him quickly. "No, Noree. Risen did not want that to happen. You wanted him to jump the log, didn't you?"

Noren nodded vigorously. "Yes! It looks *f-f-fuunn!!*"

Keya loved the way Noren pronounced 'fun', like he was mixing up the two languages they spoke, even when he did not decide to emphasize the word and drag it out as much as he could.

"Keya," Silmavalien called, "will you catch Risen before he rolls?"

"Sure thing." Keya stepped down the hill, the grass swishing aside and pulling her skirt aside with it. She would certainly *try,* but she was not horse-crazy like Silmavalien, Noren, and Elvorn all seemed to be, and she did not have a good touch with the animals. She could not catch Risen if he was feeling frisky or naughty.

Meanwhile, Silmavalien continued explaining things to Noren. "So Risen did what you wanted him to."

"I wanted him to do it like he does it when you ride him! Not make me fall off."

"I can give you some advice on how to do that, but mostly you need to practice more. Then you'll get to be a much better rider than I am!" Silmavalien explained, as Keya stepped past them, wondering if she *would* be able to catch Risen. No matter how much Silmavalien or Elvorn coached her, she never developed the instinct for when to approach or back off, how to move or stand, to get a horse who was not feeling like it to let himself be caught.

In the back of her mind, Tanz chuckled.

Why do you always think it is funny that I'm not ridiculously obsessed with a creature you would be willing to eat? asked Keya. She did not really expect an answer. Her question just made Tanz laugh at her more.

Keya did not really like horses, but it was not just about the horses. Certainly, they did not capture her attention the way they captured the others' – and some of her brothers' – attention, but Tanz had once told her that she might have managed to get by a little better if she did not have another reason for disliking them. Or at least having confused feelings about them. She had seen Silmavalien work through her grief and loss, and be a lot happier, because of playing with Risen. But she also knew that Risen reminded Silmavalien constantly of her dead husband, Noren. There was a fragility in Silmavalien because of that. Sometimes, Keya thought it would be better if they had not come into this love of horses because of the first Noren and his horse, Victor, who was now Elvorn's. Then it would be all pleasure and escape to Silmavalien, and not remembrance.

As it was, Keya was confused about what she felt, and there were times she hated the way Silmavalien would get. Years and years of living with someone did that to one. She fought a struggle she regularly lost to keep patience with faults of Silmavalien – or just things that annoyed her, Tanz reminded her – that had not been a problem between them when they were young and had only known each other for a little while, and nothing bound them together.

Now Keya was almost another parent to Noren, and Silmavalien was much harder to deal with. Keya loved her as much as anything, but it was hard to know how to respond to her. She believed Noren was somewhere that, in a sense, was not too far away, and that they would be reunited, but the grief and loss was always there. That it had to be such a way. And often, the questions of why. Why could it not have been different? And was it Silmavalien's fault? Could she have chosen someone else, and then would it have been another who died defeating the Abysstreader, and they could all live together in peace here? A crying Silmavalien often confided in Keya late at night after an exhausting day with the younger Noren's shenanigans.

Keya centered herself and looked around. These thoughts were probably part of what made catching the horses harder. Sure enough, Risen wanted to roll, but with his nose in the grass looking for a patch of dirt to lay down in, it was not that hard for Keya to approach him and grab his reins before he could shy away.

She led Risen towards where Silmavalien was leading Noren, his hand in hers, towards Keya and Risen. Silmavalien took the horse from Keya, and then gave Noren a short half-hug around the shoulders. She half-picked him up and helped him back onto the horse's back. "Now, to make sure you and Risen remember the right way to do things, just have some fun doing something easy and safe."

Noren smiled happily now. "And tomorrow you'll teach me how to jump the log?"

"Maybe not that fast," said Silmavalien, "but yes. Like Elvorn taught me."

Noren waved and gave a slight nudge of his heels to Risen's side. "I'll see you soon! You too, Keya!"

Keya smiled and stuck out her tongue at him. She felt Silmavalien move closer to her, though they did not touch.

Keya crossed her arms over her chest. As Noren rode Risen away at a lope through the huge trees, with branches big enough for the biggest dragons, excepting the gargantuan Obsidian Guardian, to perch on, she commented, "He really loves the horses."

"He does," said Silmavalien, and the tone of her voice told Keya what she had suspected, but had not known. Silmavalien was in one of those moods again. Keya found herself wishing for Tanz's physical presence behind her back.

"I'm coming," the blue dragon answered.

You should be hunting. You're hungry. You were grumbling about being hungry last night.

"If you want me, I'm coming."

I don't. It was a stray thought.

Tanz did not quite believe Keya, but at least she knew she would never hear the end of it if she did not get something in her belly before coming back. But having Tanz in her mind reminded Keya that she did not need to be so morose. She might not have what she wished for in her relationship with Silmavalien, but she had Tanz. Her relationship with Tanz was wholly mutual and without grief.

"I miss him so much," said Silmavalien. "I wish *he* had gotten a chance to teach me how to ride. I wish …"

Sil had always been easy for Keya to understand. It was part of why she learned her language so quickly. Now Keya had known Silmavalien for so long she did not have to guess what Silmavalien did not say, though half the reason Sil did not say it was because it hard to put into words. It was at once too expansive and yet defined.

Keya tried to keep herself from sighing. It would not help to remind Silmavalien what they both knew. She knew that. And sometimes when Silmavalien said it, said she knew Love ruled, there had to be a reason and things would turn out well, it got under Keya's skin in a way she did not fully understand, so she did not even want Silmavalien to say it.

Instead, she turned around and hugged Silmavalien. Keya was not usually *that* huggy, but it seemed to help Sil sometimes.

After a minute, Sil stepped away. "I … Keya, just, thank you."

Keya shrugged. She tried to make it feel natural. "It's okay. It's nothing."

"It's not, is it?" asked Silmavalien, her dark eyes wet.

Keya paused. How could she tell Silmavalien what she meant? She could not burden her best friend with her irritations. She was not even sure how to describe them, except that when she first met Silmavalien, she had thought their relationship was mutual. It had taken time for it to develop, but that had been her first joyous instinct. They had done everything together. They had loved and enjoyed each other equally. But then Silmavalien had run away on a stormy night and Keya and Tanz had gone after her, and things had never quite been the same again, though there were times Keya thought they were.

Then Noren the first had come back into Silmavalien's life, but things had not changed much. That time of their lives was very rushed in some ways, and Keya expected Silmavalien to be occupied with getting to know Noren again. It had only been a few months, and her feelings had never risen to annoyance. She had rather liked Noren. But in death, Noren took Silmavalien away from her in a way he never could have had he lived. Silmavalien and Keya would never love each other only as friends and equals again. Silmavalien needed, grieved, mourned, questioned. Keya stood there, trying to support her, aching for her to again be the young girl she had taught to swim in the lake.

And as Noren the second grew older, it got worse. Things had been almost good the year he was born. His baby-needs and joys distracted Silmavalien almost completely, and while it was exhausting caring for him – though it was actually pretty easy, since by the time he was a few weeks old the dragons, who doted on him, *always* knew what he wanted – it was a kind of exhausting that seemed to be emotionally fulfilling and satisfying for Silmavalien.

"It's not," said Silmavalien.

Keya felt Tanz move in her mind on that level that she was not quite aware of, but seemed to be instinct and first nature to the dragon. Tanz opened and cleared things that Keya could never have opened on her own. "No, it's not. It's complicated. Remember the day we first met?"

"By the well?"

"By the well. And how we learned to communicate, and how we interacted, and I taught you how we lived, and I learned who you were, long before we could speak the same language, and I told you I felt like we were twins. I showed you how we gathered salt, taught you to swim in the lake, and you did things with me."

"I don't, anymore?" Silmavalien pursed her lips and furrowed her eyebrows a little. "I know I do. It's cold to go swimming in the lakes now, I know, but we went swimming just a few weeks ago, that last warm day."

"No, it's not that," said Keya. "It's that it's not the same. Remember when you fled that stormy night, because you thought maybe I would come with you even if Love didn't want me to, didn't have that purpose for my life, so you fled so I wouldn't be able to, but I and Tanz found you anyway?"

Silmavalien nodded. Keya hated the look on her face. She felt … afraid? Like she had done wrong? Keya just wanted them to be … friends again.

"I was afraid that I was … attached to you, like I shouldn't be. Might get unwilling to leave you even if the Lord of the Light wanted me to," explained Silmavalien, before Keya could stop again.

"I said –" Keya started, then stopped. It would not help. It would not help to get mad. But she was so upset. Thinking about it again brought the feelings she had had that night, and when she had met Silmavalien again and Silmavalien had said some truly stupid things, alive in her again, and some of it was not pleasant. Some of it, particularly what she had felt about the stupid things Silmavalien said, felt stronger now than she could believe it had been then. She closed her eyes and took a deep breath. *Tanz.*

"I'm here." Keya felt Tanz stop devouring her kill to pay attention to her rider. The dragon radiated calmness, a new perspective.

"What do you think Love means?" asked Keya.

Silmavalien stared. "What?"

"What does Love mean?"

"To want the best for everyone. Everyone to be good, to be finally happy, to be the sort of creatures that can never do wrong."

"When you love someone," asked Keya, "how do you feel about them?"

Silmavalien's eyebrows furrowed more. "I don't want them to be hurt?"

Keya hated the question in Sil's voice. She wanted Sil to say what she thought, not to worry about Keya getting mad. *Why* was Silmavalien even responding to her this way? Sure, Keya had snapped sometimes, but she never got really angry. She had certainly never demonstrated anger in any way other than a poor or unkind choice of words or a tone of voice that really was not what it should be.

"Silmavalien, I love you. I'd do anything to be with you, to fight beside you. I'd never abandon you, never leave you to face the nightmare alone, as far as I can help it. And I and Tanz feel the same way about each other."

Silmavalien cocked her head slightly. "But what if I must fight the nightmare alone? To be – good, incapable being wrong no matter what? Sometimes, it's like that."

"Sometimes it is," said Keya, in a soft voice. She remembered. And no matter how much two were together, in some things one was sometimes very much alone. There were battles that, even if Tanz was with her, yet were hers alone, and she suspected the same was true of Tanz. "But it doesn't mean I'd ever abandon you. It doesn't mean I don't want to go with you, and that it's not a valid choice for me to want that. It doesn't mean *anything* can deter me, or should.

"Silmavalien, if Love is Lord, then should I ever not follow my love for you? Have you ever gone wrong by loving?"

Keya saw Silmavalien considering that, thinking. Doubtless, her dragons were adding their thoughts. Keya just had Tanz in her mind. She could not imagine what it must be to have eleven or twelve dragons always in one's mind, and many more who spoke to one regularly.

"No, I don't think so," said Silmavalien slowly, in the tone she used when she started speaking while still sorting through what her dragons told her, if it was telling. "I hurt Minth, but that was not by loving him, that was by being afraid of us dying. Being k-killed." She blinked rapidly, another characteristic of such conversations that Keya had noticed. "No, I don't think so. Never by loving. Often by fearing."

Now Keya felt as disorganized as Silmavalien sometimes looked – or as Silmavalien sometimes talked. It happened when Tanz got too involved in her thinking. She lost track of how she got where she was, and what she was trying to talk about, or think about. But, while she tried to remember what she had been thinking, it often made her ask questions she would not have asked otherwise. Was she right to demand that Silmavalien love her the way she loved Silmavalien? Could she even rightly say she knew Silmavalien did not?

After all, Silmavalien was the one who had been hurt and frightened in ways Keya had never had to deal with. Yes, it was Keya who insisted that she *would* fight alongside Silmavalien, no matter the danger, but how could she know Silmavalien would not have chased her, fought for her? Their situations were not equal. That was some of what bothered her, in itself, but at the same time Silmavalien's thoughts seemed to constrain her ability to love.

Or was Keya judging what she did not know? Still, she wanted. She had a glimpse, and she wanted. Even if she had what she wanted with Tanz, she wanted it with Silmavalien. And she *loved* Silmavalien. It hurt for that not to be reciprocated.

Silmavalien spoke before Keya could sort out her thoughts. "You want me to love you the way you love me?"

Keya nodded.

Silmavalien paused and pursed her lips a little again. "I love you, Keya. I do. I don't want to be away from you, and I did not like it when circumstances required that of us. But I'm not you, Keya. So I don't think I can ever do that."

She looked to the side again, away from Keya. "And I … can't be what I was that first year. Or even after. You know it."

Keya said nothing, even though she wanted to.

"Keya?" asked Silmavalien.

"I … understand. But that's what bothers me. You grieve. I try to comfort, to just be there when you need me. To help you deal with things. You don't do it to me all the time, though it's been a lot harder for me since Elvorn left. You share something with him, I think. But I wish it weren't this way."

Silmavalien lifted a struggling smile towards Keya. "But we have to become the kind of creatures who love no matter what."

Was that just something she told herself to make things bearable? Keya wondered suddenly. Sometimes, it felt like it. The way she said it, the way she repeated it. Yet Keya knew she believed it. She had seen something. They both had, in different ways. Love ruled. Whatever that meant in this world, they did not understand very well, since Love certainly did not rule everything now, yet the world came from Love and would return to Love. For that to happen, all must be Love.

And there were times when Keya felt she did not believe what she knew.

"If you need anything," Silmavalien continued, "if you need to cry about something, or talk about something, I'll always be there for you."

Just as Silmavalien spoke, Keya heard the sound of hoof-beats. She turned and saw Noren riding towards them, Risen in an easy canter. Risen slowed down easily, and came to a walk, and then a standstill, a human-length from Silmavalien and Keya. "Risen is a fun, good horse," said Noren, "but I am done riding. I am bruised."

Silmavalien stepped away from Keya and patted the horse's golden neck and chest. "I'm glad you like Risen," she said, smiling at her son, "but you have to walk him out first. Take care of him like the good horse he is."

Noren sighed and made a sound that sounded like a grumble and a protest to Keya. She moved closer.

"If you *won't*," said Silmavalien, "then you won't get to ride Risen – or any other horse – for a week."

"That's *forever!* Won't Risen get too fat?"

"That's why you will walk him now," interjected Keya.

Noren grumbled again, but this time he made to do as he was told.

It was not the first time Noren grumbled about walking Risen when he was done riding the horse. Once or twice, they had had to resort to not letting him ride for a week, something that was managed only because, most of the time, there were four of them – Silmavalien, Keya, Elvorn, and Veyan, a boy who had helped Silmavalien protect dragon eggs once in the north, and subsequently ran away with her and became a Dragonrider – watching over him, and because, while the dragons were very distractable and some of them were loath to understand, they were amenable to helping. He had tried multiple times to get on Risen bareback – and even without halter or bridle – and he could be amazingly persistent and sneaky about it for a child his age.

The first time it happened, Keya had asked, "What if he just decides he doesn't care about horses anymore and he would rather watch Veyan carve figurines and learn how to do that?"

"Then he won't ask to ride anymore, will he?" said Silmavalien. "I don't care whether he rides or not, *or* that he feels punished. Only that if he chooses to do a thing, he behaves responsibly about it."

Keya had readily admitted the wisdom of that.

Keya turned her back now as Noren rode Risen away, but it was not long before he came back.

"Riding is much funner with Elvorn," Noren complained.

"You can choose not to ride when Elvorn is not around," said Keya, looking over her shoulder. "No one is forcing you."

Noren ignored that. "When will Elvorn be back?"

"Feryanth says he will be here sometime tomorrow, depending on the wind patterns," said Silmavalien.

"Why did he leave for so long anyways?" asked Noren.

"We'll explain that later," said Keya, half-turning to face him. "After you walk Risen and groom him."

It turned out that, by that time, Noren had forgotten his question. He declared that he was tired and decided to take a nap under his favorite dragon, Airrock. Airrock seemed to like him as much as he liked her, and she was one of the dragons better at watching him and keeping him out of certain shenanigans – or letting Silmavalien know if it was something she could not keep him out of on her own.

That left Keya and Silmavalien free to take a leisurely walk under the giant trees. Even after living among them for six years, Keya was still in awe of the huge trees. Even when she was used to them, she could not get quite used to them. Maybe it was that it was so clearly a forest, but also so spacious. Even the lighting underneath the trees was so much that of a forest, green and soft, but also slightly different from forests made of smaller trees, often a little brighter.

And it never ceased to have the potential to make Keya laugh, when she saw a dragon perching like a bird in a tree.

Somehow, being forthright with Silmavalien helped Keya to think about things more clearly. Or maybe it had more to do with Tanz going through her thoughts and opening them up in a way Keya could not do on her own. But the atmosphere between them as they walked under the trees, even the atmosphere of her own thoughts, told Keya this was not the time to start the conversation.

The fact was, Keya very rarely started conversations, unless it was about something mundane, like salt. That was one part of their current life that did not stand out to Keya as wonderful. Salt was not nearly so easy to get here as it had been when she lived by the sea, and she craved more of it.

They meandered through the trees aimlessly, and Keya was not sure who decided their path more often, though she did not think it was herself.

Then they topped a rolling hill and Keya heard the slight sounds of the wind over the lake, a sound slightly different from that of the breeze in the trees. Curled in the soft green twilight, on the edge of the lake, were Minth and Elninya, necks, tails, and wings intertwined. The mated albino dragons spent so much of their time together like that, and Keya wondered if Elninya had lived more for Minth than for Silmavalien, or if Elninya drew the strength and comfort to keep living after her rider's death from Minth.

Certainly, the way the two dragons nuzzled each other and seemed reluctant to ever break physical contact reminded Keya of what little she had seen of her mother and father's relationship, before her mother died, and of the way her father had spoken of her mother on the occasions when he did, afterwards.

Somehow, the time felt right now. This was not a conversation that would go well if she let Silmavalien bring it up. Tanz reminded her of that, and Keya could easily see how.

"Silmavalien?" asked Keya, quietly. She did not want to disturb the dragons, who might have been asleep.

"Yes, Keya?" Silmavalien answered in the same tone.

"I wonder something …. Don't take it too far, as what it's not. It's just something for you to think about. But … I don't know if it helps you the way you're constantly trying to answer the question of 'why'. Why is there is evil, suffering, pain, grief. And the way you repeat your answer to yourself constantly. I'm not saying you're wrong. I'm not suggesting your answer isn't right. But it might … it might help to sometimes be comfortable with not understanding or having an answer? Just trusting what you know, what you *really know*, and not being in a hurry to know more than that."

Silmavalien was silent, and Keya did not press. If Silmavalien was to think about this, it would be in her own time. Keya only wanted to give her the seed of the idea. But now she had to try, harder than ever, not to get annoyed or frustrated about certain things.

After a long time, Silmavalien wandered slowly down the hill towards the dragons. Keya let her go down alone. This was not a place for her.

Keya turned her back and walked back up the hill, not too far. Elvorn would be back, soon. Silmavalien probably knew from Feryanth what had come of his visit to his family. Keya did not. Tanz could tell her if she wanted, but it was more awkward that way. She would wait until Elvorn returned. Tomorrow, or the day after, most probably.

$\mathcal{K}$

It was tomorrow, at about noon.

Noren had asked when Elvorn would be here again, after eating, and then insisted that they go to a hill from which they could see the dragons from a long way off. They had all climbed a tree that was climbable – most of the trees in Dragonsong Forest were not, most of them having first branches that split off the main trunk more than a hundred feet above the ground. A few, especially of one variety, split at the ground, and some of these could be scrambled into and climbed, especially with multiple people working together.

Keya held to a branch that was actually a reasonable thickness – as in, not several times as thick around as her waist, if not more – near the top of the tree. This one, she could get her arm around, with the branch in the crook of her elbow. The wind whipped her hair around.

A number of dragons flew over the forest, but it was soon possible to pick out the white dragon with the gold head and neck flying towards them from the southeast.

And when that happened, Noren got *very* excited. He soon insisted they all climb *down* from the tree.

Keya was the last to get to the ground and, by the time she put foot on the earth, Feryanth had just landed and Elvorn was climbing down his shoulder, smiling broadly.

Noren flung himself at him. "Riding is so much funner when you do it with me!"

Elvorn picked Noren up for a moment and then put the wiggling boy he treated as much like a *much* younger brother as anything else down. "I'll ride Victor with you tomorrow!"

"Why not *today?*" Noren whined eagerly.

"*Maybe* I'll go for a *short* ride with you in the evening, if you promise not to go galloping off. Otherwise, *tomorrow morning.* And first I want to talk with the adults."

"But you've been gone for so long! Why did you leave?"

Keya smiled. They had all told Noren more than once, but it made no sense to him. "To let the people who were my family know I'm alive."

Silmavalien put a hand on Noren's shoulder and gently hushed him. "Play with Elvorn later? I'm sure that you and Veyan and Elvorn can come up with something fun to do that is appropriate for the afternoon. Why don't you think of some ideas and let us talk for a minute?"

Keya was surprised when Noren actually decided that was a good idea, though she suspected that Noren's idea of a minute was much shorter than the adults'. Either way, he grabbed Elvorn's hand and said, "You're gonna play soon!" and then scampered off.

"So, how did it go?" asked Silmavalien.

Elvorn shrugged. "I barely know why I went. It went well enough, in that I was never in danger of being caught. But most of my family I wouldn't trust farther than Feryanth could burn them, if they knew about him. Maybe some of them would think about things if they knew it was *me,* but Feryanth had serious doubts about most of them, and so do I."

"Most?" asked Silmavalien. Her tone of voice communicated itself well enough to Keya: most, instead of *all,* was a good thing to her.

"I actually told my little sister. She's grown up a bit, but I told her *right* before I left – after I had said goodbye to everyone. She did not respond, so I'm not sure what she'll think when she has time to process it. But I showed Feryanth to her."

"That's *dangerous,*" Silmavalien half-squealed in reproach.

"Not really. Certainly after events six years ago, a report of a dragon sighting is going to be taken seriously, but it still takes time to get hunters out, and they have to search in every direction. Feryanth only has to fly in one, and they don't know which it is. And he's not slowed down by roads, hills, or fields."

"But witchcraft –!"

"It was my choice to make," said Elvorn.

Keya stepped closer to Silmavalien and put her arm around her. She felt Silmavalien relax into her a little. It was hard for Sil, and that was something Keya could understand.

"I am not, and won't be, careless," said Elvorn. "But I wanted to give her a chance."

Silmavalien nodded. "Why don't you go help Noren come up with a fun activity for the three of you?"

Elvorn nodded. "We'll talk later."

He strode off. Feryanth turned his head and watched his rider for a few moments, then lay down.

Veyan hung around for a few moments, then approached Silmavalien. "Sil," he said, "perhaps I should go north and see if there is anyone friendly."

Keya felt Silmavalien tense.

"The north has never been as harsh as the south, and it has a lot less people. A lot more wild land. And some of the dragons ... some of the dragons want to have more people who might be Dragonriders around, when they mate and lay eggs. There are those who came to you and Elvorn six years ago, but some of those are now Dragonriders, and there are not enough."

Silmavalien shifted in Keya's arm, started to say something.

"I know you don't like it," said Veyan. "But it seems right to me. And I won't be going tomorrow. I and Naklath won't go for another year, at least. We can talk about it later."

Silmavalien nodded. "Of course. And I'd never think of telling you what you may and may not do. But ... there are children here. People are having children here. Both those who have bonded over the last six years and those who haven't. Isn't that good enough for the dragons?"

"It might be," said Veyan. "We'll see how I and Naklath feel in another year or two. And we might be able to come up with some ideas that make you more comfortable."

"All right. I just ... I love all of you. You're my family, and my son's family."

"I understand," said Veyan. "Noren never got to know his dad, and you don't want him to lose any of us."

"Even if I didn't feel the same way."

"I'll do my best," said Veyan.

"That's enough for now!" said Silmavalien. "Plan later. If ever.

Right now, go and play. Noren doesn't miss you like he does Elvorn, since you've been here the whole time, but he'll certainly ask why if you don't show up!"

Veyan laughed. "That I will do. Naklath is reminding me right now. It looks like they came up with something fun!"

Silmavalien waved, as Veyan ran off. "Good!" she called after him.

Keya smiled gently. Silmavalien was being straightforward and honest, without shame, about how she felt. That was a good thing, Keya thought, and it seemed to be making Silmavalien happier. More resilient. It was too early to know for sure, but she thought this was very, very good.

Or maybe it was just seeing Elvorn that had done it. Keya should have thought of that, that Silmavalien might have been as difficult as she was because she was worrying about Elvorn. She did not worry when the youngsters went to look for horses, but they weren't *her family*, she did not even know most of them that well, and about half of them still were not Dragonriders, so there was not even a shadow of the same danger. Also, Keya surmised, Sil might have known that Feryanth showed himself to Elvorn's sister for a long time now. What Keya heard was probably not the shock of first discovery, but verbally giving vent to an argument Silmavalien might have already had with Feryanth.

Either way, Silmavalien was happier, and that meant Keya was happy, too.

"Do you want to play with them, too?" asked Keya.

"Mud games? No. They want to build a mud castle, and I think this time of year is too cold for this. Besides, we should have a feast. Want to help me gather some fresh seasonings? Veine has already got us something good."

"Sure," laughed Keya.

Keya knew that such deep wounds and loss as Silmavalien experienced – it was not even just Noren's death, but dragons with whom she had shared thoughts and lives as well – would never be mended in a moment. She would not burden this moment with such expectations, but she would not let them shadow them either. Whether this was a change for good that would slowly work its way through their lives, or just a day or a week of more relaxed, resilient happiness, Keya would enjoy it for what it was. After all, life was made of the days and weeks.

If you liked DragonSword, *please leave an honest review on your favorite book platforms. It really helps readers and independent authors to find each other. I would deeply grateful and encouraged.*

Also … turn the page to discover how to enter Areaer again, if you still want more :D

The Series is Complete!

But if you liked Return of the Dragonriders ...

You might enjoy

Dragon-Mage

Tens of thousands of years later, a young slave-woman refuses to let her captors define her life and risks their wrath to bond a dragon. Another Obsidian Guardian chooses a young, sheltered girl from the Plains of Zharda to be her friend. A circle of Dragonrider-mages fights an undead horror without hope of victory, and a power of light intervenes and creates a new race out of their deaths.

Get the prequel here:
https://books2read.com/scars-of-fire

Or start with book one, *Heart of Fire:*
https://books2read.com/raina-heart-of-fire

Legend of the Singer

Several hundred years after Noren and Silmavalien's adventures, a half-elf disobeys her human father and chases him on a dangerous quest, hoping her magic can save his life. The dryads also need her aid, and so does her new friend Alis, a human with dreams of being a gryphon rider, but who must flee from her own father.

Start Legend of the Singer with *Children of the Dryads:*
https://books2read.com/legend1

And if you missed it …

The Gifts of Faeri

Discover the true story behind the tale of Faeri and Chrysanthemum, and learn who the woman with a very unusual magic and the obsidian dragon bonded to her really were in their lives.

The ebook is free and you can get it here:
https://books2read.com/faeri

You can find all of my books here:
https://books2read.com/raina_books

And if you'd like to keep in touch ...

Sign up to be notified about new releases:
https://books2read.com/r/B-A-OUYQ-HMXXB

Follow me on Goodreads:
https://www.goodreads.com/author/show/20243136.Raina_Nightingale

Follow me on BookBub:
https://www.bookbub.com/authors/raina-nightingale

Or, if you like weekly reviews, ramblings of all sorts, and occasional art posts,
you can follow my blog:
https://enthralledbylove.com